SPRING AT THE CIDER KITCHEN

Fay Keenan

www.ariafiction.com

About *Springtime at the Cider Kitchen*

Caroline Hemingway can't help but feel a little strange watching her ex sister-in-law marrying the owner of Carter's Cider Farm, but she's delighted Anna's found happiness after the death of her late husband, and Caroline's brother, James. If only Caroline could find her own love story…

Desperate to escape the rat race, Caroline decides to take the plunge and move to the idyllic village of Little Somerby, where she is given the task of opening and running a restaurant in one of the forgotten barns on the Cider Farm.

Opening and running The Cider Kitchen is no easy task, and there are many challenges on the way, but slowly Caroline feels she's being accepted into the local community, and starts to believe she may have found her forever home. But secrets from her past seem destined to haunt her, and not even the attentions of the very dishy Jonathan Carter can distract her from all she's left behind…

To Nick…who perhaps understood all along.

1

Of all the things to do, Caroline Hemingway reflected, watching your brother's widow marrying another man was certainly one of the weirdest. She blinked in the warm spring sunshine and glanced around her. Around fifty guests were seated on white covered chairs in the main avenue of apple trees in the Royal Orchard of Carter's Cider, waiting for the bride to arrive. It was perfect weather for a May Day wedding with not a cloud in the sky. The trees were in full flower, with frothy gowns of light pink and white blossom that made them look like a guard of honour of nature's own bridesmaids. The scent of newly mown grass was in the air along with the first wafts of early honeysuckle from the old railway track, the Strawberry Line, that ran around the perimeter of the cider farm. Underpinning that was the sweet smell of billows of cow parsley. The groom, who happened to be Managing Director of the cider farm, looked, if not exactly nervous, then definitely on edge, although his expression didn't detract from his charismatic presence. Dressed in a dark pinstriped suit, but for the pink Old English rose in his buttonhole, he looked as though he could have stepped straight out from behind his desk. Next to him, altogether more relaxed and leaning over to mutter things in the groom's ear from time to time, was the best man. Caroline noticed the sweep of light chestnut hair, the easy manner and the broad smile as he attempted to lighten the groom's serious demeanour, and realised from the similar bone structure that this must be the groom's brother, of whom she'd heard a great deal.

Caroline felt a pang; seeing their easy relationship reminded her of the closeness she'd shared with her own brother, whose widow was now about to marry another man. As the first strains of the wedding march drifted across the orchard she blinked back tears. James would have understood, she thought. James would have wanted Anna to be happy. She should feel that way, too.

Not quite able to bring herself to turn to see Anna walking up the aisle between the assembled chairs, Caroline kept her eyes fixed on the two men at the front. The younger man reached out a hand and touched his brother's elbow as the music began, and as the groom turned around and caught sight of his bride, a smile lifted his features.

When she sensed the bride drawing closer, Caroline turned. Anna looked lit up from the inside, transported with happiness. Caroline swallowed back the lump in her throat as her former sister-in-law passed the row where she was sitting, her father

Richard next to her looking proud and happy to be giving away his daughter. Behind her were the two bridesmaids, one tall and teenaged, the other an adorable four year old, both dressed in the same shade of pink to match the apple blossom.

Anna's eyes met Caroline's for a moment and held her gaze. She smiled gently, seemingly aware of the strangeness of this situation for Caroline, then continued down the aisle to the front where her groom, the best man and the celebrant stood. Pausing to hand her bouquet of freesias, roses and apple blossom to the older bridesmaid, Caroline watched as Anna turned to her groom, who, seeming to forget where they were for a moment, raised a hand to his bride's cheek and placed a gentle kiss on her lips.

'That's for after the ceremony, you berk!' Jonathan said lightly, but audibly enough for the assembled guests to hear. The congregation laughed as Matthew gave a grin. Caroline's heart flipped as Matthew leaned down to whisper something in Anna's ear, and Anna's smile in response showed exactly how transported she was with happiness. How things had changed for her, Caroline thought. How wonderful to have a man so in love with her again. Caroline, despite feeling conflicted, also felt slightly jealous; her life had been so complicated over the past few years; complications that had taken many forms and had nearly destroyed her. But, she thought resolutely, it was time to start putting all that behind her. It was as if, by attending this wedding, seeing Anna so happy, Caroline was also giving herself permission to move on. It was time, after the traumas of the past few years, for a fresh start. The spring always made her feel optimistic and in this beautiful setting it was difficult to feel anything else.

As the celebrant took Anna, Matthew and the congregation through the ceremony, Caroline saw the happiness on their faces and their two bridesmaids; the elder girl being Meredith, Matthew's daughter, and the younger girl being Ellie, Anna's daughter and Caroline's niece. She also found her attention again drawn to the best man. So intent on reassuring his older brother before the ceremony, he was now watching the bride and groom solemnly. He was decidedly attractive, Caroline thought unguardedly; but she had a fair idea that it had taken a lot of time and talk to get the brothers to this point, and that Anna had had a great deal to do with that.

As the ceremony ended and Anna and Matthew once again shared a kiss, Caroline found herself brushing away the sudden tears. Thankfully, she wasn't the only one. Anna's mother Julia, sitting beside her husband in the front row, discreetly dabbed her eyes with a tissue.

Matthew, still smiling broadly, turned to the assembled friends and family. 'In agreement with my new father-in-law, and very much to my brother's relief, there won't be any formal speeches this afternoon,' he said, smiling down at his new wife. 'So, I want to take this opportunity, on behalf of my wife and myself—' he paused as a loud cheer erupted from the guests. Once they had quieted again, he continued. '… on behalf of my wife, Anna, and myself, to thank you very much for coming and invite you to eat, drink and celebrate here with us in the orchard.' He threw an arm around Anna and they walked together back through the assembled guests.

Later, clutching a glass of champagne and chatting with Anna's best friend Charlotte, who she had met a few times in the past when she'd come to stay with Anna in Hampshire, Caroline felt her lower half being grabbed by a pair of tiny, excitable hands.

'Hello, Aunty Caroline!' Ellie, Anna's daughter, squeaked. 'Do you like my dress?'

Caroline looked down at the adorable little girl, whose blonde hair was already beginning to escape her ribboned bunches and who had a smudge of chocolate sauce on her chin from the cupcake she'd been eating. She looked so much like her late father, Caroline's older brother James, that Caroline couldn't speak for a moment. Then, pulling herself together, she smiled and bent down to give her niece a huge cuddle.

'You look lovely,' Caroline said, breathing in the mingled scents of small child and chocolate. 'Have you had a good day?'

'Yes,' Ellie said as Caroline released her. 'Mummy's got a new husband.'

Caroline smiled. 'I know. Do you like him?'

Ellie tipped her head to one side for a moment and regarded her aunt. 'Yes. He's very tall.'

Caroline laughed. 'He is! Why don't you introduce me?'

'OK.' Taking Caroline's hand, Ellie, who was being watched a short distance away by Anna and Matthew, led her to the newlywed couple. 'Mummy, Matthew, Aunty Caroline wants to say hello.'

Caroline had driven down to Little Somerby that morning rather than come down the night before, so this was the first time the two women had had a chance to chat.

'It's so good to see you!' Anna said, embracing Caroline. A long, simple lace trimmed cream dress with a v shaped back offset her dark hair and green eyes perfectly. Anna had a flush to her cheeks that rivalled the apple blossom in her bouquet. 'I'm so glad you could make it.'

'I wouldn't have missed it,' Caroline said. She was still struggling with the conflicting emotions that the day was stirring up inside her, but as Anna turned to Matthew to introduce him, she saw the look of unfettered happiness on her former sister-in-law's face, and, just as importantly, the same look mirrored on the face of her groom.

'This is Matthew,' Anna said softly.

Matthew extended a hand and shook Caroline's outstretched one. 'It's lovely to meet you at last. Anna's told me so much about you.'

'Not too much, I hope!'

Matthew laughed and the two women joined in. 'It's great that you could make it. We're both so happy you could come.' Then, turning his gaze back to his wife fleetingly, 'Anna said you'd booked into the Rose Cottage B&B in the village. You're more than welcome to come and stay with us if you'd like.'

Caroline smiled. 'Thanks, but I thought I'd save you the hassle of a houseguest during your own wedding. And Rose Cottage comes highly recommended.'

'They've had five stars on Trip Advisor since they opened,' Anna said. 'But you are coming to dinner tomorrow night, aren't you?'

'Definitely,' Caroline replied. 'Wouldn't miss it.' Looking at the two of them, and her own niece, so happy in this new life, Caroline felt another wave of grief washing over her. Cursing what she knew to be the brightness in her eyes, she searched over Anna's shoulder for where the drinks were being served. 'I'd better go and get a glass of this famous sparkling cider!' she said. Somehow, she knew Anna understood. Just as she was about to turn away, however, Matthew called out.

'Jonno, come and join us for a moment,' he said, beckoning to his younger brother.

Jonathan Carter paused on his way to the makeshift bar and took a detour in his brother's direction. As he drew closer, he smiled at his brother and their guest. 'Hi. I'm Jonathan,' he said, extending his hand to Caroline. Caroline immediately noticed the tidy, square cut nails, the long, elegant fingers. 'It's lovely to meet you.'

'Caroline Hemingway,' Caroline replied. 'It's nice to meet you, too.'

'You're Anna's sister-in-law, right?' Jonathan smiled. 'Ellie's aunt?'

'That's right.' Caroline took a moment to study the man in front of her. He was broad shouldered, although not as broad as her sister-in-law's new husband, and up close, Jonathan looked like the watercolour version of Matthew's oil painting. His features were similar, but softer, lighter somehow, as if more prone to laughter than his volcanic older brother. Caroline liked the look. The grey suit perfectly offset his colouring, which was itself enhanced by a light suntan. Unguardedly, Caroline wondered how far down the tan went below his clothes.

'It's lovely that you could be here,' Jonathan said softly. He glanced at his brother and new wife. 'It can't be easy. Can I get you a drink?'

'I was just on my way to the bar myself,' Caroline replied, suddenly very much in need of an escape from Anna and Matthew's almost incandescent love. 'Why don't I join you?'

Jonathan smiled. 'Sounds good. I can point you in the direction of the better variety of sparkling cider that we've got on offer.' Gesturing in the direction of the bar, he bore Caroline off.

As they walked away, conversation sparked between them. Anna watched them speculatively. Matthew gave his new wife a glance.

'What are you smiling at?' he asked.

Anna smiled back. 'Oh, nothing.' She slid a hand into Matthew's, which was still nestled into her waist. 'You know me; I like to see what happens when people meet new people.'

'If I didn't know you better…' Matthew shook his head. 'I don't think Jonno needs any help meeting new people, if the tales Dad keeps telling me about overnight guests at the cottage are anything to go by.'

Anna laughed. 'He's still up to his old tricks, is he? And Jack doesn't mind?'

'Are you joking? He's quite partial to a pretty girl, as you know. He might not feel the need to go out on the tiles himself these days, but I think living vicariously through Jonathan has certainly perked him up lately!'

'You almost sound like you approve,' Anna wrinkled her brow. 'You're not jealous, are you?'

Matthew ducked his head and gave his wife a lingering kiss. 'What could I possibly have to be jealous of, when I've got you in my life?' he said softly. He followed Anna's gaze to where Caroline and Jonathan were standing. 'Although if there's a chance of making Jonathan as happy as you've made me… I'm all for it.'

2

'They look really happy,' Caroline said as Jonathan led her to a trestle table topped with several different varieties of Carter's Cider. Among them was the most recent creation, a sparkling apple wine. Known wryly by the locals as Somerset Prosecco it had proved surprisingly popular. Nodding to the bartender, Jonathan procured two glasses, and, when the man turned back to dispose of a couple of empties, he swiped another bottle from under the table with a mischievous look in Caroline's direction.

'Family privilege,' he murmured. 'And I'm certainly feeling in need of more than one glass, even if you aren't!'

Caroline gave him a still slightly shaky smile. 'Well, if you're going to twist my arm…' She allowed herself to be led to one of the more out of the way picnic tables that had been scattered around the orchard.

'And happy as my brother and his delectable new wife undoubtedly are, I thought you might like the company, seeing as I can take an educated guess that you don't know too many of the other guests at this gig,' Jonathan said as he took a seat at the table.

'Shouldn't you be doing the rounds as the best man?' Caroline asked.

'Weddings aren't exactly my thing and even my dear brother and gorgeous new sister-in-law can't do much to change that. I think I'd rather just sit here and talk to you.'

His tone was light, although there was a gentleness in his eyes that immediately endeared him to Caroline. She knew his history, of course; when Anna had come to Surrey to tell her that she was getting married again, conversation had naturally turned to the family she was marrying into. After a fair few glasses of wine and a few more tears on both sides, Anna had recounted the brothers' tangled history, which involved younger brother Jonathan running off with his older brother Matthew's first wife, Tara. Anna had also made it clear that Jonathan had played a huge part in making sure she and Matthew were going to walk down the aisle, and that Jonathan had redeemed himself in later years, but Caroline wasn't surprised by Jonathan's lack of fondness for weddings. She took a sip of the glass of sparkling apple wine. 'Not bad,' she said. 'It's not quite Prosecco, but it'll do.'

'It's a new idea and since we're sitting in a cider orchard, it seemed, to Matthew at least, to be the obvious choice.'

'And probably completely tax deductible,' Caroline replied archly. She'd had the chance to have a brief look around when she arrived and she knew the cider farm's site extended to a fair few acres and a fair few buildings. This kind of wealth didn't come about from just picking apples.

'My brother's a shrewd operator, but don't worry, he does have a heart as well as a head. Anna's seen to it that he's remembered that over the past year.'

'It's been a long time since I've seen her so happy,' Caroline replied, feeling conflicted again. She took a larger gulp from her glass and nearly finished it. 'Do you fancy opening that other bottle?'

Jonathan smiled and twisted the cork, which he managed to contain in his palm. Caroline found her gaze drawn to his hands. As he was refilling their glasses, Caroline, now she was away from the main thrust of the party, started to relax. Of course, that could just have been the sparkling cider. She had no idea how potent it was but it was certainly doing the trick. Being away from home and the pressures of work was definitely soothing.

'So, tell me about yourself,' Jonathan said, once he'd topped up their glasses. 'I know what, or rather who, has brought you here, but tell me something else.'

Caroline smiled and sipped her drink. She'd met men like Jonathan before; they had the ability to make you feel as though you were the only person in the universe when they singled you out, but, in her experience, they could dim the searchlight just as quickly once they lost interest. However, he was good company and she was happy to talk. After all, apart from Anna's immediate family and Charlotte, she didn't know anyone else at the wedding. 'Well,' she said, 'you know how I'm linked to Anna, and that I live in Surrey.'

'So, what do you do over on that side of the country?' Jonathan suddenly put on a very exaggerated Somerset accent and Caroline couldn't help but laugh.

Caroline smiled, and for the first time that day, it didn't feel forced. 'When I'm not traipsing across the country to be a wedding guest, which seems to be happening more and more these days, I've been working as an events manager for a hospitality company.'

'Sounds interesting,' Jonathan said, leaning forward in his chair. 'Have you been in that field for long?'

'As opposed to sitting in this one!' Caroline quipped, her high heels having sunk into the grass of the orchard. 'Since I finished university, well, give or take a year or so after uni because I managed a small restaurant in Sicily for a while. I've organised events for big venues like Goodwood and Brands Hatch motor circuit, but I've also done smaller gigs, too. More boutique events.' She took a sip of her wine. 'I really like the payoff of seeing something take shape that we've designed with a client in mind; tailoring something to their brand. But then I'm probably preaching to the converted, aren't I?'

'Well, needs must when a business is the size of Carter's,' Jonathan said. 'But there's always more to do.' He looked at her speculatively. 'Although I'm sure you don't want to talk shop too much on this glorious afternoon. Given the number of weddings I've been to when it's poured with rain, I think Anna and Matthew have been very lucky. A lot of my invites have been back in America lately, but I've found myself going to more and more in this country. Must be something in the water.' As if to counterpoint this he took a slug of his apple wine. 'It's either weddings or christenings, anyway. Always the godfather, and all that.'

'I take it you've never been tempted then?'

'Nope, I can't say I've ever been tempted enough by anyone to drag them up the aisle,' Jonathan replied. 'And since my brother's now done it for the second time, I hope that might let me off the hook with the rest of the family.' He glanced over to where his father was standing a little distance away. Jack Carter was chatting animatedly to one of Anna's aunts, eyes twinkling as she smiled winningly back at him.

'Can I deduce that charming women runs in the family, then?' Caroline said wryly, following Jonathan's sight line.

'I'm flattered,' he said. 'I'm known more around here as a cad and a bounder.' Anna had explained that Jonathan's homecoming last year had been met with equal parts of joy and suspicion by the villagers. He'd proven himself an asset, though, in the securing of a lucrative trans-Atlantic distribution deal for the Carter's Cider family firm, which was now providing more jobs in the local area. This had helped to mend his reputation, which had been more than a little tarnished after he'd had an affair with Matthew's first wife, Tara.

'But enough about me,' Jonathan said, his voice dropping slightly. 'What makes you happy, when you're not sourcing the ultimate artisan Prosecco?'

'There's a bit more to events management than that,' Caroline bristled before she saw the look in Jonathan's eyes, which was amused rather than cynical. 'I bet I could teach your marketing department a thing or two. I take it drinking anything other than cider is a mortal sin around here?' The gentle hum of bees drinking lazily from the flowers was audible even over the chatter of the wedding guests and Caroline waved a hand at a nectar drunk bumblebee who ventured too close to her wine glass.

'You're in Somerset, darling,' Jonathan said, still smiling. 'Everyone knows we practically have it on our cornflakes in these parts.' The long 'r's' were almost too natural to be an affectation, Caroline thought. Jonathan might have had his West Country accent ironed out of him by a decade on the other side of the Atlantic but it was gradually creeping back the longer he spent at home, it seemed.

'It's a wonder you're all still alive,' Caroline quipped. The apple fizz was starting to calm her down and she felt as mellow as the lazily bubbling liquid in her glass. The afternoon sun, too, was on the wane, casting a golden glow across the orchard and gently gilding the leaves on the trees. Off to her left she could see Anna and Matthew, arms around each other, still chatting to some of their guests, and as the band started up it felt more like a festival than a wedding feast. Even the music had a West Country edge as an up and coming local singer, drafted in by Meredith to play as a favour, broke into his signature hit 'Southwest Signpost'. Bristol's answer to Ed Sheeran, his voice was perfectly suited to the warmth and the atmosphere, Caroline thought.

Jonathan leaned back in his chair. 'I'm so glad the formal part of the day is over,' he said. 'Now I can get slowly drunk and enjoy watching my dear brother's terrible efforts on the dance floor.'

'Bit of a dad dancer is he?' Caroline said. 'James always prided himself on his moves. Anna couldn't bear to disabuse him of the notion even though he was truly terrible.' At the thought of her brother, Caroline swallowed hard. It was a fine line between pain and happiness at times.

Jonathan seemed to sense this and as his warm, tanned hand closed over hers on the table where it rested, she looked up and saw warmth and compassion in his eyes. 'It's OK,' he said softly. 'It's completely natural that you don't know what to feel.' He glanced over to where Ellie, Anna's daughter, was bopping on the dance floor with Meredith.

'Ellie's so like her dad,' Caroline said. She gave a shaky smile. 'He used to take the piss out of me so badly for being short and ginger; I didn't have the heart to tell him it was probably going to be there in some of his kids.' She wiped her eyes. 'Now I'll never know if I was right.'

'I'd have said stunningly auburn, rather than ginger,' Jonathan said. He reached out a hand and touched the back of Caroline's briefly. 'Life has a habit of kicking us in the gut when we least expect it. But I promise you, my brother has made Anna so, so happy. And she's given him his heart back.' Jonathan shook his head. 'I never thought I'd see him like this.

Believe me, they're perfect together, and Ellie and Meredith adore each other, too.'

For a long time, conversation flowed as easily as the cider between them and before they knew it the sky was darkening on the beautiful May evening. Caroline knew she was a little bit drunk, but not so far gone as to be out of control. She also knew she found Jonathan decidedly attractive, so, after some rather energetic dancing which made her heart beat considerably faster, and when the party was beginning to wind down, she didn't complain when he fell into step at her side after she bade Anna and Matthew goodnight.

'Can I walk you to your B&B?' Jonathan said. It was late; the last guests had reluctantly put down their glasses.

'Thanks, but I'm sure I'll be OK,' Caroline said.

Jonathan laughed. 'It's actually on my way home, and while Little Somerby isn't exactly the Bronx, I wouldn't want you to run into trouble on your way back.'

'Then thank you,' Caroline said. 'That would be lovely.'

It was a short walk back to the bed and breakfast, which was just off the main road that ran through the village of Little Somerby. Many of the wedding guests had chosen to walk home, which was just as well considering the vast amounts of cider that had been consumed, and a few were meandering back under the street lights and the stars. By night, the village looked at peace, and the scent of the lilac in people's gardens along the High Street and the other flowers in the tubs outside the shops was strong and seductive. That, combined with the remnants of Jonathan's aftershave, was an intoxicating combination. In a short time, arm in arm, Caroline and Jonathan had reached the Rose Cottage Bed and Breakfast, a picturesque stone house just off the High Street.

'Well, here we are,' Caroline said. 'Thank you for walking me back.' She looked up at Jonathan and smiled. He was backlit by the Victorian style streetlight at the top of the path that led to the front door of the B&B, and Caroline felt a sudden rush of desire. Before she could bottle out, she said, 'Would you like me to smuggle you in for a coffee?'

If Jonathan was surprised by her offer he didn't show it. 'I'd like that.'

The air was suddenly heavy with promise. It was late, but the night was warm and as the two of them wandered up the path to the B&B's front door, Caroline felt Jonathan's arm snaking around her waist. 'I wouldn't want you to trip on these stones,' he whispered into her ear. His breath on her neck made her skin tingle.

'That's very gallant of you,' Caroline said. She moved a little closer to him as they got to the door. 'I have the feeling you're more chivalrous than you'd like people to believe.'

'Perhaps,' Jonathan replied. 'But perhaps I just fancy you rotten and I want to make sure you get to your room in one piece.'

Caroline laughed. 'You West Country boys don't beat about the bush, do you?' Coffee, it seemed, was the last thing on both of their minds. 'Shall we forget about the coffee and I'll just take you to bed, instead?'

'Anna told me you were forthright,' Jonathan said softly, 'but I wanted to make sure of you myself before I made up my mind.' His arm, which was still around her, pulled her in closer to his body and she could feel his heat through the thin layers of their clothing. Caroline suddenly wanted there to be no more layers between them.

'I hope I meet your expectations,' Caroline's own voice was low, throaty. 'Although, frankly, I'm still making my mind up as to whether or not you meet mine.'

'Allow me to convince you,' Jonathan said, his tone sending a shiver through Caroline's body. Her pulse quickened.

'I think we'd better get off the doorstep before the landlady comes down and sends you home,' Caroline said, reaching for her door key.

'You don't mess about, do you?' Jonathan murmured, drawing her to him so that her breasts and belly pressed against him. The contact enhanced the slow roll that was just progressing to a boil, sending a rush of blood straight to her core.

'When I set my mind on something, I tend to get it.'

'I've no doubt about that,' Jonathan said. He leaned forwards and Caroline felt a delicious thrill of anticipation. Hovering just a breath from her lips, Jonathan whispered. 'So, you'd better open that door and smuggle me up to your room before I make a scene.'

'You wouldn't dare,' Caroline said, finding the verbal sparring more and more of a turn on.

'Try me.'

'I think we both know where we stand,' Jonathan's voice had resumed its husky tone. 'The question is, why are we still wasting time here talking about it? The night's not getting any younger.'

'How true,' Caroline replied. Without further delay she found the keys, and, trying to be as quiet as possible, they pushed the creaky front door open. Clasping his hand firmly and feeling like a naughty schoolgirl about to get caught by the head prefect,

Caroline led Jonathan through the dark hallway and up the stairs to her bedroom.

*

When she woke up the next morning, Caroline wasn't surprised to see Jonathan had already left. She'd expected as much. She didn't mind in the slightest. Anna hadn't been wrong when she'd considered Jonathan to be just Caroline's type. He'd been just what she needed to move on, and she was pretty sure he'd felt the same. Anna, she knew, had romantic notions about Caroline being as swept off her feet by Jonathan as Anna herself had been by Matthew, but at this point in her life, that wasn't what Caroline wanted. No, Jonathan had been a night of good fun, and she fully intended to chalk him up as just that. Besides, she had enough on her mind back in Surrey at the moment. She didn't need any further complications.

Pulling herself out of bed, she was surprised to see a note had been slipped under her bedroom door.

Thanks for a great night. Sorry I had to dash but I didn't want to scandalise your landlady. Call me! J x

There was a mobile number, too. Smiling wryly, Caroline chucked the note in the waste paper basket.

3

'OK, that's fine. I'll see you at about ten tomorrow, then.' Anna ended the call and returned the kitchen phone to its cradle. The company who had supplied the tables and chairs for the wedding had called to confirm collection of the furniture for the next day rather than the day after the wedding, but since the orchards weren't in full use at the moment, it didn't seem to be a problem. Anna had given them the go-ahead to collect the stuff in the morning. She'd spent her first full day as Mrs Carter taking things slowly; apart from a glass of champagne after the ceremony, she hadn't been drinking, but it was nice just to mooch about. Second time around, with two children to consider, a wedding was a slightly different proposition but a no less lovely one. Now, evening was falling and she was looking forward to dinner with Caroline who would be heading back to Hampshire first thing in the morning. Caroline had also spent the day at Cowslip Barn, but had popped back to the B&B to freshen up after an afternoon spent in the garden with Ellie. Ellie was now getting ready for bed, happily exhausted. It had been lovely to catch up with Caroline and dinner would be the perfect cherry on the wedding cake.

Anna bent over the pad on the kitchen table that was placed next to the vase of tulips her mother had brought over the day before the wedding to make a note of the change. She'd been so forgetful in the run up to the wedding that she knew if she didn't, she'd have forgotten by bedtime. Of course, she knew there was a reason for her more frequent absent mindedness; she had shared it with Matthew when she knew for sure but didn't want to go public with the news until the wedding was out of the way. The only shotguns she wanted to think about were the ones in the gun cabinet that was safely hidden in Matthew's study; she didn't need the jokes from friends and family. She was aware that second pregnancies tended to show a lot quicker than first ones, so she wouldn't be able to keep it a secret for very long. And she knew her daughter and stepdaughter would want to know as soon as possible; Meredith, especially, would be hurt if she found out from anyone else.

It felt good that she could put such faith in her relationship with her stepdaughter; she was lucky that she and Meredith, Matthew's daughter with his first wife, Tara, had clicked from the day they'd met; even before Anna had started seeing Matthew. Meredith had been her first visitor on the day she'd moved in to Pippin Cottage, not counting her dog, Sefton, who'd dashed in through the door without so much as a by your leave, and they'd struck up a friendship from that day. She hoped Meredith would be happy about the news. She was sure her own daughter, Ellie, increasingly vocal and independent, would be thrilled at the prospect of a baby in the house.

'Everything OK?' A voice broke into her thoughts. Anna smiled and put her pencil down as a hand slipped around her waist and settled where there would soon be a baby bump. She leaned back, feeling the reassuring solidity of a broad chest against her.

'Fine.' Pausing a moment longer to luxuriate in the embrace, she turned and tilted her face upwards to meet Matthew's kiss.

'I figured you might need a little bit of extra help tying up the loose ends,' Matthew smiled down at his new wife.

'Oh, it's pretty much sorted,' Anna said. 'After all, we deliberately didn't go for too much pomp and ceremony so there wouldn't be masses of things to clear up.'

Matthew grinned. 'I think there might be a few bottles of booze left in the orchard, believe it or not! Not that you should be drinking any, of course!'

'Don't worry, I'll take it easy. Did I tell you I'd invited Caroline to dinner tonight?'

Matthew kissed his new wife briefly. 'I was there when you asked her, silly!'

Anna laughed. 'Of course you were. I'm so sorry; baby brain's already kicking in and I'm not even six weeks pregnant.' She shook her head. 'It's only going to get worse for the next seven and a half months, too.'

'I'm sure we'll muddle through somehow,' Matthew kept smiling. 'At least the morning sickness hasn't hit yet. Tara had it terribly with Meredith for practically the whole pregnancy.'

'Ouch,' Anna said. 'I was lucky with Ellie; I hardly got any at all, although I couldn't abide mashed potato while I was carrying her and for about eighteen months afterwards. I wonder if I'll get anything weird like that this time?'

'It'll be fun finding out,' Matthew's lips met her own. Once more, Anna marvelled at how things had changed for her. She still sometimes lay awake at night wondering what her life would have been like if her first husband, James, hadn't been killed on a cold winter's night by a teenager in a far too powerful car. But one thing was for certain; she counted her blessings every day now. She remained thankful for her daughter Ellie, for the move back to Little Somerby that had enabled her to take over the Little Orchard Tea Shop and for the fact that Matthew, and his daughter Meredith, had come into her life. Matthew often said that Anna had saved him; she knew, without a doubt, that he had saved her, too.

A discreet cough from the doorway made Anna and Matthew separate a few moments later.

'Sorry, didn't mean to intrude,' Caroline said. 'Should I have knocked?'

Anna laughed. 'Don't be daft. Come on in.' She moved away from Matthew. 'Would you like a glass of wine?'

'Thanks,' Caroline said. Her dark red hair was still wet from the shower and she'd slicked it back from her face, which made her large green eyes all the more striking. Slighter than Anna and about four inches shorter, she had the Hepburnesque look of a dancer, but those who underestimated her based on her stature were always taken by surprise when she revealed the full force of her personality.

Anna glanced at the Aga, where the spring lamb stew for tonight was cooking nicely in the oven. 'Dinner'll be at about seven.'

'I'll just give Dad a ring,' Matthew said. 'I'll be in the study if you need any help. I did invite him to dinner when we spoke this morning but he said he was pretty tired from yesterday. I hope you don't mind, but Jonno asked if he could come after all.'

'Oh, I thought he was busy,' Anna said. 'But that's fine. We've got plenty of food. I'll make sure I plate one up for Jonathan to take back to your dad for when he fancies it.'

'I'm sure he'd love that,' Matthew called over his shoulder as he headed for his study.

Was she imagining it, Anna thought, or was Caroline blushing slightly at the mention of Jonathan's name? They'd seemed to be getting on very well during the wedding reception, although Caroline hadn't mentioned anything to Anna when she'd been playing with Ellie earlier in the day. Caroline was notoriously cagey about her personal life, though, so for the moment she stayed off the subject. It was nice to have a little time alone with her former sister-in-law; to mention James' name without having to be conscious of it. 'Ellie loved spending time with you today,' Anna said as she handed Caroline a glass of red wine. 'She asked me when you were coming to stay with us again.'

Caroline smiled. 'I really enjoyed spending time with her.' Ellie was, after all, her only remaining family member and although Anna had remarried, Caroline would always regard her as a sister.

'She'll be at school this time next year,' Anna said, pouring herself a glass of elderflower cordial from the bottle on the kitchen counter. 'A little too much to drink yesterday,' she said hurriedly. She didn't like telling the fib but she supposed under the circumstances she could get away with it.

Anna sat down at the large, scrubbed oak kitchen table. 'I know I've said this about a million times since you got here, but it's so good to see you, Caroline. With everything that's happened over the past few years, I needed to connect with my old life, with my old family. And I needed to see for myself that you were really all right with how things have worked out in my life.'

'Oh, you daft cow!' Caroline's eyes filled with tears. 'Of course I'm all right. How could I not be? You look so, so happy, and I can see that it's this new life, your life with Matthew as a part of it that has done that.' She reached out and squeezed Anna's hand. 'James wouldn't have wanted to see you alone for the rest of your life, and neither do I. And you know what? I think James would have approved of your choice.'

Anna raised equally watery eyes. 'That means a lot to me, Caroline.'

'And I mean every word.' Caroline gave Anna a shaky smile. 'Now, are you going to refill my glass or am I going to die of thirst?'

Anna smiled back, then, unable to resist sharing the secret. 'You'd better have one for me, seeing as I'm under doctor's orders to show restraint.'

'Why?' Caroline asked. Then comprehension dawned. 'Bloody hell. You don't hang around in Somerset, do you? That ring's not been on your finger a day!'

Anna laughed. 'It's been a few more weeks than that. Wasn't exactly planned but still very welcome.' She looked intently at Caroline. 'Are you OK with that?'

Caroline shook her head. 'You need to stop asking me if I'm OK with your life choices,' she said gently. 'It's entirely up to you what you do. It always has been. James is gone. You don't have to keep worrying about how I feel.'

Anna smiled sadly. 'I know. It just feels... weird.'

'I'll admit it was a bit bizarre seeing you getting married to someone else,' Caroline said softly. 'But life goes on. Love goes on. And life's too short to worry about things like that. So, I'm telling you to stop. Now.'

Anna smiled. 'OK. So long as I can ask *you* a question.'

Caroline looked guarded. 'Depends what it is.' She'd kept a fair few things from Anna over the past few years, in an attempt to protect her, and so felt wary when Anna started to probe. If Anna even suspected half of what had gone on in the years since James' death, she'd never look at Caroline in the same way again. There were some things that were best kept hidden.

'Did you, er, get on well with Jonathan yesterday?'

Caroline shook her head and thought about brazening it out. 'In what sense?'

Anna tried, and failed, to look innocent. 'Well, Meredith spotted Jonathan sneaking out of the front door of the B&B early this morning when she was walking Sefton. She put two and two together I'm afraid.'

Caroline coughed into her wine glass. 'News travels fast in this place, doesn't it? Oh, OK, OK. He walked me back to the B&B and came up for a nightcap.'

Anna raised an eyebrow. 'An all-night nightcap?'

'It was a large cup of coffee,' Caroline said, refusing to be drawn. 'Nothing serious for you to start speculating about.'

'As if I would,' Anna replied. 'I just thought you seemed to be getting on quite well at the wedding reception, that's all.'

'I'm not going to let you set me up with your new brother-in-law,' Caroline replied. 'You're not being my sister-in-law again. I've only just got rid of you!'

'All right, but from where I was standing…'

'Shouldn't you have been focussing on enjoying your own wedding, rather than what Jonathan and I were up to?' Caroline chided, reaching for the wine bottle.

'Oh, don't worry about that,' Anna said. 'As a mother and a stepmother, I'm well practiced in splitting my attention fourteen ways at once. And I couldn't help noticing…'

'Give it up,' Caroline said. 'I'm not being your sister-in-law again, no matter how fit Jonathan is.'

'So, you admit he's fit?'

'I'm not blind.'

'You liked him, then?'

'No comment.'

'OK, OK, I'll lay off. For now. But I will tell you that he could definitely do with someone stable in his life. He was only moaning the other day that he hasn't put down any roots yet.'

'He told me he was back living with his dad.'

'Well, yes, he is at the moment,' Anna said. 'But to be honest, it's probably better that he is. Jack thinks he's in rude health but his heart's been playing up for years so it's good that Jonathan's there to keep an eye on him.'

'Hmm...' Caroline raised a sceptical eyebrow. 'So, you don't reckon he's just doing it to stop himself from having to grow up?'

'You couldn't ever accuse Jonathan of being grown up, even if he had his own mortgage!' Matthew said, catching the end of the conversation as he returned to the kitchen. 'But who knows? Now he's back on board with the family business perhaps he'll start to act his age.'

'Acting whose age?' As if on cue, Jonathan came through the back door into the kitchen. Without missing a beat, he crossed the flagstones and kissed

Anna on the cheek. 'Hello, gorgeous. Hope you don't mind me gatecrashing. I suddenly found myself at a loose end.'

'Of course not,' Anna said. 'And you know Caroline, of course.'

'Of course. Hi,' Jonathan said, giving her a warm smile. He didn't seem fazed by seeing her again so soon, so Caroline was determined not to show that she was. She smiled up at Jonathan from where she was sitting.

Donning her oven gloves, Anna opened the top oven and pulled out a large Le Creuset casserole dish. Lifting the lid, she gave the stew a stir, tasted it and popped it back into the oven. Then, she grabbed a couple of foil wrapped sticks of garlic bread and popped them in alongside.

'One of your creations or your husband's?' Caroline asked, keen to change the subject.

Anna looked fondly at Matthew on the way back to her seat. 'Mine. Matthew can make a passable beans on toast and has been known to branch out on occasion into spaghetti bolognese, but he's not what you might call at home in the kitchen!' Her eyes twinkled. 'Although you're a pretty good cook, aren't you, Jonathan?'

'I pass muster,' Jonathan said, helping himself to a glass of wine. 'I don't get much of a chance to practice these days, since Dad seems to be losing his appetite, but I can whip up a half decent boeuf bourguignon when pushed.'

A short while later as they were all enjoying the dinner, Matthew's phone pinged and he glanced at it apologetically; then, as he read the message, his face softened.

'Meredith's got to Cornwall alright and says Flynn's parents' cottage is, er, "well amazing"'. His shoulders visibly relaxed and, as if his teenaged daughter's text had given him permission, he poured another glass of red wine for himself and Caroline, then topped up his pregnant wife's glass with some more elderflower cordial.

'I'm glad she got there OK and she seems to be enjoying it,' Anna replied. Sixteen year old Meredith had caught the train to Cornwall that morning and was due to be away for a week. Anna missed her already, but Flynn O'Connell, who was two years older than Meredith, was a nice lad. Last year, the relationship between the Carters and the O'Connells was under a lot of strain after Flynn crashed his car with Meredith in the passenger seat, resulting in Meredith being hospitalised with a potentially life changing head injury. However, Meredith's recovery and the verdict of the accident investigators that Flynn wasn't entirely at fault had done much to mend fences between the families. Matthew and Anna got on well with Flynn's parents, who'd assured them that the teenagers would be in separate rooms all week. Anna wasn't quite sure she believed that, but, she figured, not a lot could go wrong with attentive parents sharing the house, too.

Remembering her guest, she turned back to Caroline. 'When we were talking earlier you mentioned you had some life changes in mind, but what with all the interruptions from Ellie and the clearing up from yesterday, we didn't get the chance to have a proper natter about it.'

Caroline picked up her wine glass and cradled the bowl in her two hands for a moment, stalling for time while she gathered her thoughts. She had to think very carefully about how she was going to proceed with this. Too much information and Anna would start to worry; too little and she'd be suspicious. 'Well, now you come to mention it, yes, I have actually.'

'What have you been thinking about?'

'I've been thinking about making a move away from the South East,' Caroline confessed. 'I mean, ever since Mum, Dad and then James died, and you came back here to live, I kind of keep wondering why I should stay in Farnham.' She paused and looked at the married couple in front of her. 'Don't get me wrong, I've got good mates, but I'm bored with reaching for ever more ostentatious features to make a function different and memorable. Once the hundredth ice sculpture is dripping onto a plate at the end of the evening, it kind of loses its charm.'

'So where were you planning on moving to?' Anna asked. 'I mean you've got no ties, so you could go wherever you wanted. Overseas, if you fancied it. How about back to Italy? You seemed to enjoy working out there before you got your current job.'

Caroline shook her head. 'I did really like it, and it was great to be part of the hospitality industry over there.' Caroline had spent a year as front of house in a small restaurant in Sicily before settling into her career as an events manager. 'But one thing I've learned over the past few years is that you can't take things like family for granted. I think it's time I took care of what I still have, while I'm still able to appreciate it.'

'It sounds like you've got something in mind.'

'To be honest, I've been thinking of a change of scene for a while. Companies like the one I've been working for are streamlining to compete for more and more business. In fact, I was offered voluntary redundancy a couple of months ago, and I took it. I love the work, but the game is changing. I'd like to stay in the hospitality industry, but perhaps be a bit more my own boss; have more control.' Caroline really didn't want to go into the other, more personal reasons for a change of location; not when she'd just witnessed such a happy family event as the wedding.

If she did ever come clean with Anna, it would be at the right time, and now was definitely not it.

'Crikey,' Anna said. 'That's quite a decision. I'd ask you if you're sure, but it seems like you've made up your mind already! Not that I'm surprised.' She turned to Jonathan and Matthew. 'Caroline's had a really successful career in hospitality. Her team has won awards so many times for the events they've staged, and she's been up for awards herself as a manager. I remember that night at Goodwood when you invited me as your plus one to pick up the Manager of the Year award. I drank so much champagne I couldn't get out of bed at all the following day!'

Caroline laughed. 'Well, the event was sponsored by Moët! Yes, I remember that! James took the piss out of you so badly for not being able to handle good champagne; told me I was better off buying you Asti Spumante in future.'

'So what are you thinking, then?' Anna asked.

'I've had enough of Surrey,' Caroline said. 'I've got a bit of money stashed away from my inheritance from Mum and Dad and the redundancy money, which I can live on while I decide what I want to do.'

Jonathan, who up until this point had been silent, suddenly chipped in. 'So, you're a free agent then, professionally speaking?'

Caroline looked quizzically at Jonathan. 'Yes, I suppose I am. Why?'

Putting his knife and fork together and taking a last sip of his wine, Jonathan glanced briefly at his brother before continuing. Matthew raised an eyebrow but said nothing. Jonathan turned to Anna. 'Darling, do you mind if I borrow Caroline for half an hour or so? There's something I'd like to show her. I know it's rude to swan off before the coffee but in this case, I hope it'll be worth it.'

Caroline couldn't quite meet Anna's eye; if she had, she'd have burst out laughing. Instead, she looked at Jonathan. 'Don't I get a say as to whether I'd like to be, er, *borrowed*?'

'Of course,' Jonathan replied. 'But I'm hoping on this occasion you might appreciate a short walk before it gets too dark.'

Remembering where she'd ended up the previous night after a short walk, Caroline flushed. 'We will be coming back, then?'

'I'll have you back by the time the washing up's done,' Jonathan said. 'If you don't mind us skipping out?' He turned back to Anna.

'I don't think you've ever offered to wash up yet, Jonathan Carter,' Anna said, rising to clear the plates. 'So why should tonight be any different? But make sure you're back for coffee. We've got a mountain of raspberry pavlova from the wedding that needs finishing, too.'

'I'll have her safe and sound and back in one piece as soon as I can,' Jonathan said. 'But we need to crack on if we're going to get over there before it's too dark.'

Curiosity piqued, Caroline rose from the table and followed Jonathan out of the back door.

Cowslip Barn, Anna and Matthew's home, was situated at the far end of the sprawling cider farm. Over the years, the industrial buildings had sprung up on the site, but the house itself was divided from them by rows and rows of different varieties of cider apple trees. As they wandered down the rows of neatly planted trees, Caroline spotted a building in the distance, some way away from the industrial centre of the site. It had a newly tarmacked track running towards it that seemed to run around the back of the Royal Orchard. Clocking their direction of travel, Caroline asked what it was.

'That's our new venture,' Jonathan replied. 'A year ago, it was a knackered old barn that we used to store old kegs and bits of equipment, but while I was sorting out some of Dad's paperwork, I found an application he'd put in to the council for change of use. He must have done it and then forgotten all about it. Permission was granted but about to expire, so I thought it would be a good idea to do something with it.'

'So what's it going to be?' Caroline asked. They were wandering towards the building and as they drew closer, Caroline could see that the structure of the original stone and oak framed barn had been lovingly restored, with a new roof and some beautiful bifold glass doors installed on two sides.

'It's going to be a restaurant called The Cider Kitchen,' Jonathan said. 'Somerset is one of the best parts of the country for locally produced food. We've got cheese and strawberries from Cheddar, which is a World Heritage site, at least two major brands of ice cream, yogurts and, of course, countless mixes and blends of alcohol, including our own cider. It seems a logical step to showcase them, and since we've got the building here, it was a no-brainer.'

Caroline regarded the building. 'You're planning on opening to catch the summer season?' she asked, looking through the front window of the barn. Inside was still bare although the walls had been plastered and, from the looks of it, a mezzanine level at the back of the building had gone in with an impressive light oak staircase. Wires hung from the ceiling for light fittings, and a door led off to one side, presumably to the kitchen.

'Yup,' Jonathan replied. 'We've got a talented young chef lined up – a graduate from Weston

College who's been working at Carluccio's in Bristol and comes highly recommended, and we're currently putting together a front of house team. The contractors are working night and day to get the fabric of the building finished, so it's just a case of sorting out the interior decor and finding a manager.'

'Just?' Caroline echoed. 'That's quite a lot to do if you're working in terms of weeks rather than months.' Despite being off duty for the weekend her events management head was ticking. It was all very well converting a building but a new business venture was always risky, even with the backing of a huge company like Carter's Cider.

'You don't know the Carters very well yet, do you? If there's one thing we're good at, it's driving projects through.'

Caroline tried not to be too impressed by his zeal. 'And do you and your brother actually know anything about running a restaurant? Or is this just another empire building exercise?'

'Well,' Jonathan conceded, 'we are going to need someone to mastermind the day to day running of the project. After all, the concept is an obvious one, but the execution of it is what will take the time and the effort. Anna's been helping us out with her knowledge of local trends from the tea shop, but we're looking for someone to come in and manage the place as soon as possible.'

'It would definitely be worth getting someone on board now,' Caroline agreed. 'After all, this isn't exactly a kitchen table business, looking at the size of this barn. And I'm guessing that you have a lot of other things to do as well as project managing this particular development.'

'I had intended to get the manager in place before now, 'Jonathan confessed, 'but the guy who we'd agreed on got a better offer running a new restaurant in Bristol Harbourside and pulled out a couple of weeks ago. Unfortunately, the contracts weren't signed, so we lost out.'

'So you're looking for someone to manage it?' Caroline said. As she looked through the windows again, at the large, empty space with the beautiful, newly laid pale yellow Bath Stone floor and bare walls, she imagined what it could be, what it could look like in the right hands. In *her* hands. She'd play on the oak structure of the barn; echo it in the tables and chairs. The light fittings would be wrought iron but not too fussy, chandeliers hanging down from the double height ceiling. Bare tables with simple, starched white napkins and gleaming silver cutlery would make it elegantly simple. On the walls would be framed prints and photographs reflecting the history and heritage of the building. The look would be classic but contemporary, simple and refined. Her fingers suddenly itched to draw up some plans, storyboard some ideas.

'What are you thinking?' Jonathan asked, obviously having noticed the faraway look on Caroline's face.

'That you've got something potentially very special here,' Caroline replied. 'And in the right hands it could be a goldmine.'

'That's what we're hoping,' Jonathan said, still studying Caroline's face. She blushed under the scrutiny.

'Sorry,' she said. 'I tend to slip into professional mode when I see things like this. There's just so much potential here. Whoever you get to run the place will need first class management skills, coupled with the flair and vision to capture the essence of Somerset within these walls.'

'I really like your passion; you've understood exactly what we're trying to do, even though you've only just seen the barn.' Jonathan was regarding her intently. 'And your response to it is absolutely what I hoped you'd say.'

Caroline stopped in her tracks. 'Why? What's it got to do with me?'

Jonathan put his hands in his pockets and looked up at the recently retiled roof of the barn. 'Potentially, quite a lot.' A quick thinker, he was used to making deals on the hoof, and he trusted his own instincts implicitly. 'How would you like to come on board? We need a talented manager for this place, someone who's used to working in a high-pressured environment with the creative vision to not just drive a project through but to keep a team motivated and on track. You said you were looking for a change of direction; could this be what you're looking for?'

Caroline took an involuntary step back and nearly fell off the path into the gravel. 'Did you just offer me a new job?'

'Well, you did say you were looking for one.'

Regaining her footing, Caroline tore her eyes from the building to Jonathan, who seemed all sincerity in the warm glow of the setting sun which was bathing the barn in mellow golden light. 'But you know virtually nothing about me or my career, except for what we talked about just now. What makes you think I'd be right to run a place like this?'

'I know it all seems a bit sudden but after our conversation yesterday, I did a little bit of homework. You headed up the team that staged the hospitality for last year's Mercedes concept car launch at Goodwood, and I know those awards you laughed about with Anna were some of the highest accolades you can get in the industry. You've made a name for yourself in a very competitive market and you've managed to make few, if any, enemies on the way. I think, with your experience and with Carter's backing, you could make this place a real goldmine. Even if you hadn't mentioned you were looking for a change of direction, I'd have wanted to head hunt you anyway. What do you say?'

'So you're telling me that I was on interview for a job I didn't know existed, at my own dead brother's wife's wedding?' Caroline didn't know if she felt indignant or flattered, so she settled for the latter. Then something else struck her. 'And after the wedding? Was that part of the interview, too?'

Jonathan had the good grace to look embarrassed. 'No. That was strictly personal.'

'Glad to hear it,' Caroline smiled wryly. 'I wouldn't want to think that our, er, encounter, would have influenced you in this.'

'Of course not.' Jonathan smiled. 'But I am serious about the job. Actually, you'd be getting me out of a spot if you'd consider it. It's the beginning of May already so we're running to a tight deadline if we're to get this place open for the start of the summer season, and we need someone to be on board with the project as soon as possible. So if you are interested it would be great to get things firmed up as soon as we can.'

Caroline looked up at the barn again. It was at that exciting stage where she could visualise the things that she would do to make it beautiful; the shades and colours she'd use to enhance the natural beauty of the building, the little details that would suit a business like this so beautifully. For the first time in several years she tingled with excitement about a potential new project. At the back of her mind a voice was also whispering that if she took on this job, she'd be away from the shadows of her life in Surrey. 'If I did decide to take on the post, I'd like to do it on a consultancy basis,' she said. 'I've spent so many years adapting my ideas to suit the clients, that I'd like the autonomy to put my own stamp on a place like this. As manager, I don't just want to walk into the building once it's a done deal; I'd like input now, in the development stage.'

'I think we can agree to that,' Jonathan said. 'With your experience, I think your input while we're still painting the canvas of the place would be incredibly valuable. And as a consultant, you'd get greater autonomy day to day. Although we'd have to contract you for a set period. How does twelve months sound?'

'It sounds very tempting,' Caroline replied. She looked up at the building again, visualising the enhancements she would make if she was in charge. 'Can I sleep on it?' she said, turning, once again, back to Jonathan.

'Of course.' Jonathan replied. 'And, to be honest, I should really run it past my brother, too. Although

I'm overseeing the project he does like to stay in the loop.'

'He strikes me as someone who wants to be in control,' Caroline said. 'It must be tricky, doing the power sharing thing.'

'Oh, it's had its moments,' Jonathan said lightly. 'But I think he's learning.' He glanced at his watch. 'We'd better head back to the house, or Anna'll think we've eloped.'

Caroline laughed. 'Don't start giving her ideas!' she said. 'She's already onto us after last night.'

'Doesn't surprise me.' Jonathan slowed his pace slightly. 'But don't worry,' he said. 'What you said about last night… it doesn't make a difference. I want you to think about this job because I've heard how good you are at what you do. That's all. No strings, I promise.'

Caroline nodded. 'That's good to know, because if I do decide to take the job, we'll have to have a strictly professional relationship.'

'Oh absolutely,' Jonathan replied. 'Can you think it over and let me know as soon as possible? We really need to move on this if we're going to open for the end of the spring.'

'I'll let you know as soon as I've had time to think it over,' Caroline said. 'And thank you for the opportunity. It's certainly given me a lot to think about.' With that, they headed back to coffee, pudding and the newlywed couple at Cowslip Barn.

4

As soon as the contract confirming her fixed term appointment as consultant manager came through from Carter's Cider, Caroline wasted no time in arranging to rent out her flat in Farnham. Fortunately, a friend was between houses and wanted a place to stay for up to six months while the renovations on her new house were completed. Then, she packed up her stuff, putting most of it into storage, and headed off to Little Somerby.

The restaurant was scheduled to open in the middle of June. Progress had been rapid in the couple of weeks since Matthew and Anna's wedding; the walls had been painted, the light fittings had gone in (Jonathan had agreed with Caroline's suggestions about hanging wrought iron chandeliers and subtler side lights) and the dining furniture would be delivered the next day. The staircase to the mezzanine level of the building led to Caroline's living quarters. At first, she'd been reluctant to live where she was also working, but the choice of affordable rental properties nearby was pretty limited. Also, there were some fairly antisocial hours involved in running a restaurant and having somewhere to crash that was only up a flight of stairs, after a long night, would definitely be an advantage.

As she unlocked and opened the door that separated the flat from the restaurant she was instantly charmed by the sight of the small living area which housed a sofa and a coffee table, still in their polythene wrappings. One door led to the bedrooms and bathroom and another to a tiny kitchen. Well, she figured ruefully, she was probably going to be sick of the sight of food after evenings at the restaurant anyway; she didn't need a big cooking area. Since the flat was furnished, Caroline had put most of her possessions into storage, but she'd brought a few boxes with her of things she simply couldn't live without.

The clothes could wait, but at the very top of the first box she opened was the photo album of pictures from the wedding she'd received from Anna as a moving present. Opening the cover, she smiled as she saw a picture she'd taken of Ellie. Her niece was utterly, edibly, gorgeous, and yet Caroline still didn't feel broody; the emotional upheavals of the past few years hadn't triggered any desire in her for babies and with the restaurant on the cards for the foreseeable future, she certainly couldn't think about them now.

She smiled again as she turned the page and saw another candid snapshot. This time it was one of

Anna and Ellie. And, she noticed with surprise, in the background was Jonathan. She'd not done any drawing for ages but always took a book with her whenever she went somewhere for a while. Jonathan's profile would be a glorious one to draw, she thought, if she ever found the time.

Putting the photo album aside after flipping through a few more pages, Caroline dug further into the box. There were a few more loose photos, detached from their moorings in a rather more conventional album and Caroline took them out, determined to secure them back in place before they got lost in the detritus of the move. Flipping idly through them, her heart lurched. Staring back out of one of the group snapshots was someone she hoped she'd never see again. She looked at his close cropped dark hair, his outwardly amiable expression, his air of confidence, and she thanked her lucky stars once again she'd made this move to the West Country, away from him. It would have been easier to forget him if he'd been an ex-boyfriend, she thought ruefully; goodness knows she'd made some interesting choices in her love life over the years, and often not altogether wise ones. This man had been something different, though, and she had no desire to dwell on that particular part of her past. She scrunched up the photo and threw it in the black plastic sack that was serving as a bin. The sooner she put him out of her mind, the better. Her last job was over, and so, thankfully, was her association with him.

Just as she was taking stock of what to unpack next, she heard the front door to the restaurant opening below and a voice called up to the mezzanine.

'I'm here,' Caroline replied, hoping, after shifting so many boxes around, she didn't look too hot and sweaty. Running a hand through her hair, she stepped down the staircase towards the floor of the restaurant. There, standing in the doorway, clad in jeans and a white t-shirt and carrying a bottle of champagne and a bunch of freesias, was Jonathan Carter.

'I just thought I'd come and welcome you on board,' he said, handing her the champagne and the flowers. 'And check that everything's as you expected, of course.'

'It all looks good so far,' Caroline said. 'I'm hoping to spend this afternoon getting familiar with the space and the layout.'

Jonathan smiled. 'Sounds good. You've got my mobile number if you need to get hold of me outside office hours?'

'Actually, I'm not sure I have,' Caroline confessed. Jonathan had called her a couple of times, but always from his office line at Carter's.

'Oh,' Jonathan's brow wrinkled. 'I could have sworn I gave it to you the morning after the wedding.'

Caroline's cheeks reddened as she recalled both the night in question, and the fact that she'd casually binned Jonathan's note with his phone number on it. 'I must have lost it,' she evaded, hoping he didn't press her further.

'I'll text you,' Jonathan said, a vaguely amused expression on his face. 'And then you've got no excuse for not contacting me.'

'OK,' Caroline said. She felt the awkwardness rising between them as they both seemed to be casting their minds back to the day they met. 'And thank you for all of your help so far.'

'My pleasure.' Jonathan replied. 'It's a shame I've got to dash or we could have opened the champagne. But I'll see you in the morning for our first official meeting.'

*

Caroline wasn't one to hang around so over the next few days she cracked on with the plans that she and Jonathan discussed during their first official meeting. The restaurant furniture had been delivered on her first proper day at The Cider Kitchen and she was kept occupied completing Health and Safety assessment forms and placing a rather alarmingly sized red lacquered baby grand piano in one corner of the restaurant. It had seemed like a mad idea when her last client had offered it to her as a leaving present, but it was in good working order and she knew exactly where she was going to put it. Whether or not she'd be able to pay a pianist was another matter, but for the moment, she was pleased to host it in the restaurant.

Caroline also arranged to meet the front of house staff that had been appointed before her. The building was fairly large and had the potential to do forty covers a night but in the initial weeks she had no idea how busy it was going to be, so to begin with the restaurant would just have a kitchen porter and a few waiting staff. She couldn't afford a full time sous chef on the budget Carters had allowed for staffing, so the chef would have to hit the ground running. She hoped they'd be flexible.

Since employment opportunities were limited in the village virtually every A Level student had applied for an evening job, but Caroline had whittled them down until she had three full time waiting staff and a handful of part timers to take the evening and weekend shifts between them. These included Jonathan's niece Meredith.

Jonathan kept in regular contact with Caroline. He was an excellent communicator and always had a good reason for being on site, but Caroline couldn't help wondering if he was checking up on her for other reasons. Maddeningly, he always seemed to slide around the door when she least wanted to see him. Sweaty from shifting tables around for the umpteenth time as she tried to work out the perfect arrangement for the floor, she'd turn around and see him by the front door, smiling that smile of his. She had however, invited him over one evening to test out the kitchen. He was a fair cook and he wanted to make sure everything was in working order. While Caroline had drawn the line at him cooking a proper meal, for fear of ruining the kitchen before the new chef had even had a go, he whipped up a few small things to make sure everything was as it should be. She was currently sitting on one of the high stools in the kitchen sipping a glass of the champagne that he'd brought over on the day she'd moved in.

'What do you reckon to this?' Jonathan asked, placing a green olive atop his blini, mackerel and sour cream concoction and passing it to Caroline. She felt the charge as his fingertips brushed hers. Popping it into her mouth she tasted the saltiness of the olive against the cream, the yeast flavour of the blini and the sweet, smoky sensation of the fish counterpointing it all.

'Not bad,' she conceded. 'But I don't think you'd make it as a professional. Look at the mess you've made on the counter just making some blinis!' She put her glass down and tore off a sheet of blue paper towel from the large roll that had been installed next to the hand washing sink. Dampening it slightly, she wiped the spilt blini batter and discarded olive stones from the stainless steel counter top. Then, she crossed the kitchen and looked at the waste food bin. Health and Safety regulations stated that it must be emptied every day, and although it was nowhere near full she figured she might as well do it now. The new chef would be in soon enough and she wanted the place to be neat and tidy. She took the bag and tied it before heading out to the back of the restaurant where the bins were. As she lifted the lid of the large brown food waste one she paused. From somewhere deep inside the bin she could hear a faint sound. Her skin started to crawl as she considered the possibilities. Rats? Mice? Gigantic, mutated West Country maggots? Anything was possible in her imagination. As the scratching continued she spied a movement inside one of the bags in the bin. And then a very faint, very plaintive, very hungry sounding meow.

Caroline was short by anyone's standards, but she scrambled up the side of the bin and then leaned in to try to reach the bag the sound and movement was coming from. Nearly overbalancing, her fingers brushed the top of the bag but she couldn't get a grip on it.

'Jonathan!' she yelled, her voice echoing into the bin. 'Can you come out here, please?' She scrambled back from the lip of the bin just as Jonathan came out of the back door to the kitchen. She was sure she didn't imagine the sweep of his eyes over her back view as she righted herself.

'Everything all right?' Jonathan came to stand by the bin.

'There's some kind of animal in a bag in the food bin,' Caroline said.

Jonathan looked wary. 'Probably vermin,' he said. 'Do you want me to call our pest control guy?'

'I don't think it's rats,' Caroline said. 'It sounded, I don't know, like a cat or something.'

'What would a cat be doing in a bin?'

Caroline tossed her head impatiently. 'I don't know, but can you help me to get it out?'

'Could be a rat,' Jonathan said. 'Hang on, I'll take a look.' Jonathan looked over the side of the bin and then leaned in. 'I wish I had a pair of gardening gloves on, just in case,' he muttered. 'Rats are tough buggers.'

'I'll bet you another bottle of champagne it's not a rat,' Caroline said.

'I hope you're right.' He had to lean right into the bin and Caroline found herself looking at his decidedly gorgeous, denim clad backside.

Momentarily distracted, she came back to earth when Jonathan straightened up and gently put the bag on the ground at her feet.

'Your vermin, my lady. Would you like me to do the honours?'

Another plaintive sound came from the bag and this time there was no mistaking it. Caroline grappled with the knot that had been tied in the top of the black sack but her hands were shaking so badly she couldn't untie it. Jonathan knelt down and with a little effort, managed to get the knot untied and open the bag.

Caroline gasped. There, trying desperately to take in the fresh air, were two small, very grubby tortoiseshell kittens. Caroline fell to her knees and picked them up, cradling them in her arms.

'Who would do this to such tiny things?' she said.

Jonathan glanced around, checking to see if whoever it was could still be around. 'It's quite easy to get onto the site as we've now got access from the main road. No one would notice the comings and goings of someone who wasn't meant to be here because there have been so many people working on the building. Anyone could have slipped in unnoticed and dumped them.' Nevertheless, he was surprised that Caroline was being so hands on with the abandoned animals. 'You should probably take them to the vet, see if anyone's lost them.'

Caroline shook her head. 'No-one's lost them,' she said grimly. 'They were chucked in here deliberately because whoever did it thought they wouldn't be discovered. I will take them to get checked out by the vet, though. Poor little girls.'

'How do you know they're girls?' Jonathan asked.

'All tortoiseshells are female,' Caroline said. 'James and I had one when we were kids, and it's one of the things I remember. They're also naughty.' She smiled. 'In the meantime, I'd better sort out some food and a bed for them. Come on,' Caroline coaxed, seeing the tiny kittens' abject terror as they started to come to their senses. 'I've got some lovely food for you.' Unconvinced, one of the furious balls of tortoiseshell fur raised its hackles and gave what she clearly believed to be a very intimidating hiss. What came out was little short of adorable.

Taking the kittens through the restaurant's kitchen, and to hell with Health and Safety this time, Caroline headed straight upstairs to her quarters where, in her small kitchenette she had a can of tuna. She popped the kittens on her sofa for a moment while she opened the can and spooned the contents onto a saucer. Then she filled a bowl with water and put both down on the floor. Clearly starving, the kittens jumped down, skittered across to the saucer and buried their faces in the tuna. Stealthily, Caroline crept up to the tiny creatures until she was close enough to stroke them.

'You poor things,' she said softly. 'Who's thrown you out like this?' Cautiously, trying not to scare the kittens, she continued to stroke them, crooning calming nonsense as they demolished the tuna on the saucer. When she felt she could risk it, she picked the slightly larger of the little creatures up. It stiffened in her hands and began to struggle, but after a few moments, realising that her jumper was warm, it settled into her arms again.

'Are they OK?' Jonathan asked.

Caroline started. She'd been so fixated on the kittens she'd forgotten all about Jonathan. She glanced up at him. 'I'll ring the vet in a minute and see if I can take them over there,' Caroline said. 'It's a bloody good job this place isn't open yet. They're probably crawling with parasites.' She shuddered. 'Who'd be so shitty as to dump kittens in a bag in a bin?'

Jonathan shook his head. 'I don't know, but you'd better keep a look out for anything or anyone else suspicious.'

Caroline shuddered; there was at least one person from her not too distant past who'd definitely fall into the suspicious category. *No,* she thought, *he's over a hundred miles away.* It couldn't be anything like that. More likely, someone just wanted rid. Today's culture was so full of the notion that everything was disposable; why not animals, too?

Jonathan gestured to a cardboard box he'd brought up with him from the kitchen. 'I figured this would do for a bed for tonight until you can rehome them.'

'Rehome them?' Caroline shook her head. 'No way. They're staying with me.'

'In this place?' Jonathan shook his head. 'Do you have any idea what the Health Inspector would say?'

'I'll keep them out of the kitchen. There's a balcony and a fire escape at the back of the mezzanine that they can use to get in and out and the door to the living quarters is shut during service. I'll double check with the local authority's Health and Safety officer but it should be fine as long as they don't get into the food preparation areas.'

'And what about when you're working?' Jonathan asked. 'They're tiny. How will you cope?'

'I'll think of something,' Caroline persisted. 'After all, there are cat cafes and cat pubs opening up everywhere these days. A couple of kittens can't be that much bother.'

'That's fine when customers are expecting to share their eating space with animals,' Jonathan said patiently, 'but in a restaurant like this? I don't see it.

Imagine what would happen if one of your new customers ends up with even a speck of cat hair in their food. It's not going to do this place's reputation any good at all and reputation is everything for a new business.'

'Just leave it with me,' Caroline said. 'The punters won't even know they're here, I promise you.'

Jonathan shook his head. 'Let's hope so. But do me a favour and double check the Health and Safety regulations, will you?' He didn't know what Matthew would say if he found out but decided he wouldn't be the one to tell his brother. 'Just make sure you also get them checked out by the vet as soon as possible in case they're rabid.'

Caroline gave Jonathan an impatient look. 'As if.' The moment she said it, though, something small, black and jumpy landed on her arm. 'Perhaps not rabid,' she conceded, 'but definitely riddled with fleas.' As the slightly blacker of the two kittens mewed what sounded like an apology, Caroline couldn't help smiling. 'It's OK, little one. You're sweet, anyway.'

The ensuing pause in conversation stretched between them and Jonathan took it as his cue to leave. Heading back down the mezzanine stairs to the restaurant, he just about made it outside before he started sneezing. He'd always been allergic to cats, and now, it seemed, if Caroline was serious about keeping those two abandoned fur balls, he was going to get a crash course of immunotherapy. Anger washed over him; he shuddered to think of the suffering that they would have endured as they slowly suffocated in the bag. Thank goodness Caroline had saved them. Before he surrendered to another sneeze, he couldn't suppress the thought that perhaps she'd been sent to save him, too.

5

Caroline managed to get a last minute appointment for the kittens, who she named Scrumpy and Solly, at the local vet's practice and was relieved when they were given a clean bill of health apart from the fleas. She'd booked to take them back in for speying in a month or two's time and they'd been microchipped, too. Armed with flea and worming medications, a litter tray and a bag of easy-on-the-stomach kitten food, she felt she was ready to own cats as well as a restaurant. To be on the safe side, she spent the evening looking up the Health and Safety regulations for animals in places that served food and reckoned she could manage, although bathing the two filthy kittens had been an adventure in itself and she now sported several lacerations up her arms and across her hands from their extremely sharp claws. The two kittens, once they'd dried out, had eaten voraciously again and were now curled up together in the cardboard box, lined with a towel.

After a slightly restless night, the next day Caroline was waiting for the chef that Jonathan had appointed to arrive. She checked her watch automatically as the front door opened; he was exactly on time.

'Gino Marshall.' The good looking young chef held out a confident hand in response to the one Caroline offered. 'Pleased to meet you.'

'Likewise,' Caroline replied. She gestured to the wooden chair in front of the table. 'Sit down.'

'Thanks.' Gino was slim, long limbed and dark haired with a smattering of designer stubble across his chin and upper lip. The look was clearly cultivated, but Caroline wasn't too fussed as long as he cooked well. This was her opportunity to find out a bit more about him than the information on paper. After all, Jonathan must have been impressed to employ someone quite so young as head chef.

'So, you've clearly got the job, but as your new manager, I wanted to touch base and find out a little more about you,' Caroline said, pouring them both a coffee.

Gino thought for a moment. 'Since I left college I've been working as a sous chef at Carluccio's in Bristol, and while it's been a good job to have straight from college, I'm looking for a bit more autonomy. I like the idea of having real input into a menu and this part of the countryside has so much local produce to choose from, I'd be excited to experiment with it.'

Caroline smiled briefly. 'I'd like a West Country theme, obviously, but one that takes inspiration from broader culinary influences. Sort of Tom Kerridge meets Thomasina Myers.' She paused. 'With a bit of Giorgio Locatelli on the side.'

'That's quite a broad scope,' Gino said. 'But I went to Tom Kerridge's place in Marlow when I was visiting my brother last year. It's well worth a trip if you've got time.'

Caroline laughed. 'I'm not sure I'll have much of that this year, managing this place, but I'm glad we're on the same wavelength. Of course, as you know, we need to make sure cider plays a role in some of the dishes, too.'

Gino flipped open his portfolio, which lay on the table between them. 'I used different varieties of cider in a lot of the dishes for my final project.' He handed the folder to Caroline and watched as she perused the recipes and the short commentary. As her eyebrows raised in surprise, Gino let out a breath.

'I really like the sound of these,' Caroline said, lifting her eyes from the page once more. 'And they fit in perfectly with our West Country fusion concept. How would you feel about cooking a couple of your specialities?'

'Sure,' Gino smiled broadly. 'I cooked on interview, but it would be great to get back into the kitchen again and familiarise myself with it. When would you like me to cook?'

'How about tonight?'

Gino nodded assent.

'If you're sure you can source everything you need by then, let's go for it.'

Gino gave Caroline a steady look. 'I really hope you like what I do,' he said. 'It's my dream to actually own my own restaurant one day and this would be a fantastic place to start.'

'I look forward to seeing what you can do,' Caroline replied as she held the door open for him.

As Gino left the building, Caroline felt a surge of excitement. Gino was young, relatively cheap and full of ideas. She texted Jonathan to let him know she'd met Gino and that he'd be returning that evening to cook for her. Hopefully Jonathan might put in an appearance, too.

*

That evening, as dusk was beginning to fall, Gino arrived back armed with his supplies. Caroline was just finishing hanging the last of the prints on the long side wall of the restaurant. She'd dithered for ages over the right ordering and placement for them but was pleased with the overall effect which showcased a variety of images from the cider farm's past, as well as some more recent shots of the orchards and iconic West Country sites. There was a stunning shot of one of the local strawberry fields in full fruit and another of the Axbridge lavender farm which stretched like a lilac carpet across the foothills of the Mendips between Shipham and Cheddar Gorge.

'Those look great,' Gino said, pausing to admire the variety of images that Caroline had arranged. 'I love that one of the old shop on the cider farm site – I remember my Gran saying she used to visit it as a kid, and how different it looked to how it does today.'

Caroline nodded. 'It's come a long way, so I understand.' She stepped down from the ladder that she'd been using to hang the pictures. 'Are you OK to go ahead and cook? Jonathan said he'd be over later as well, so if you could make enough for both of us to have a taste, that would be great.'

'Sure, no problem. I've brought enough ingredients so that you hopefully won't need to cook your own dinner later!'

'I'm looking forward to it, but leave me with the receipts and I'll make sure you're reimbursed.' As Caroline reached for the last of the pictures she needed to hang, she smiled as she realised which one she'd left until last. Taken by herself only last week, it showed the current incumbents of the Carter's empire, Matthew and Jonathan, standing beside their father, Jack, at the end of one of the rows of trees in the Royal Orchard. All three looked happy and relaxed in the spring sunshine and were holding pints of Carter's Gold in their hands. It was a lovely photograph and summed up the unity that, until recently, had been lacking in the family. Knocking in the last picture hook, Caroline hung the photograph and then took a step back. Pleasingly, every single picture was dead straight.

Soon, enticing aromas started to drift from the kitchen. Caroline felt a flutter of excitement as she anticipated what was to come. Finding so promising a chef in such a small village was a real coup; she had to hand it to Jonathan for choosing well.

In no time at all, Gino was wandering back through with two plates in his hands. 'It's ready,' he said, setting them down on the nearest table.

'So, what am I looking at?' Caroline said as she approached.

'Try this first,' Gino said, passing her a laden fork.

Caroline popped the fork into her mouth. In pleasure and surprise she noted the complexity of the flavours. The base of the dish was seared, pan fried scallops, shot through with the unmistakable flavours of cider and marjoram.

'That's gorgeous,' she said, once she'd swallowed.

Gino smiled. 'Try this one.' He handed her another fork.

Caroline popped it straight into her mouth. The flavour, yet again, was incredible. 'What's that underpinning the wild mushrooms?' she asked, unable to identify the tangy, lemony flavour conclusively.

'Doone Valley Thyme,' Gino replied. 'A little bit gentler than your common or garden version and the flowers look good as a garnish, too.'

'You know your plants, don't you?' Caroline said appreciatively.

'I spent a lot of summers in Italy as a kid and the rest of them foraging in the woods around here,' Gino replied. 'My Italian granddad showed me how to identify a lot of great stuff around the family home in Sicily and my dad's dad owned a smallholding down Priddy way, so we spent a lot of time just exploring the land. He was good at identifying wild mushrooms and my Italian granddad knew his wild herbs, so I got the best of both worlds.' He blushed. 'Sorry, it's a bit of an obsession for me – I was shocked at how many of my mates on the course at college couldn't even identify herbs from a supermarket, let alone wild growing plants, especially those from this area and all around them. I just don't get it. We live in one of the best areas for wild and foraged produce, I mean, Hugh Fearnley-Whittingstall has done about a million TV shows about it but loads of the people I trained with didn't know their wild garlic from their wheatgrass.'

'Well, I'm impressed,' Caroline said, taking another sip from her tumbler of water. 'If you can bring in some wild flavours to your cooking for the restaurant, then that gives us a real edge over the competition. And I know how good Sicilian cooking is, too. I spent a summer there after university working in a small restaurant in Milazzo, on the coast.' She warmed to her subject. 'Imagine! Being able to walk out of the door and collect ingredients, and showcase them in this place. And being able to shout to the rooftops that the wild mushrooms, herbs and plants you're serving are freely available in the forests and fields. We really might be on to something.' Caroline felt a real stir of excitement as she looked from the counter in front of her back to the new chef. Gino truly was a find. She took another bite of the mushroom dish.

'Sorry I'm late,' Jonathan's voice brought Caroline sharply down to earth. With half a mouthful still of the most exquisite wild mushrooms she'd ever tasted, she swallowed hastily. This triggered off the inevitable coughing fit and she was grateful for the tumbler of water that Gino handed her. Gulping down the water, she at last spoke.

'No worries. We're just trying out some potential recipes for the opening night. Gino's got some brilliant ideas and you really need to taste these scallops.'

'I'm sure he has,' Jonathan replied lightly. 'After all, he came highly recommended. May I?' He picked up the other half of the scallop in his fingers and popped it into his mouth. 'A little over cooked, I think, but beautiful flavours.' After licking his fingers, he wiped them on the white starched napkin next to the plate.

'I'll make a note of that,' Gino said.

'Come in at the start of next week and we'll talk menus,' Caroline said, trying to regain the upper hand.

'Thank you,' Gino said, shaking hands with them both. I've got some amazing ideas for an Italian/Somerset fusion menu to start us off. I can't wait to show you.'

Caroline felt a real surge of excitement as Gino left. She turned to Jonathan. 'You made a brilliant choice by hiring him,' she said warmly. 'He's made a fantastic impression and he's got buckets of confidence and even more ideas.'

Jonathan seemed flattered by Caroline's enthusiasm. 'Thanks. He seems like something special. I think, with his skills and your experience, this place is going to have a really great start.' He looked around the restaurant, and, drawn to the newly hung wall of pictures, wandered over for a closer look. 'These look fantastic,' he said. The one of himself, Jack and Matthew caught his eye, and Caroline noticed a strange expression crossing his usually carefully composed features. 'That's the one you took, isn't it?'

'Do you like it?' Caroline asked, approaching him once more.

Jonathan turned briefly from the wall to look at her. 'It's great. I never thought…' he trailed off, seeming to pull himself together. 'Never mind. But there's one missing.'

'No,' Caroline said. 'I've hung them all.'

'This one hasn't been taken yet, but we must do it.'

'What do you mean?'

Jonathan smiled down at her. 'When the place officially opens we need to get a shot of you outside the building.'

Caroline laughed. 'I can live without that! But how about one of the whole team on opening night? That would be a really nice one to put alongside the others.'

'Fair enough,' Jonathan said. 'I'll get the marketing department onto it.' He looked back at the wall again, drawn to the same photo he was looking at before. 'Can you email me that one?' he asked. 'I think Dad would really like a copy for his mantelpiece.'

'Sure,' Caroline said. She was flattered to be asked but also charmed by Jonathan's obvious reaction to the photo. 'And perhaps you can bring him down for a meal when we open.'

'He'd love that,' Jonathan said.

As Jonathan left, Caroline looked around. For the first time since she'd made the move to Little Somerby three weeks ago, she actually felt as though she was in control. She only hoped they'd have no hiccups in the run up to opening. Seeing that there was still a mouthful or two of the scallop and mushroom dishes left, she finished them off and then went to wash up the plates. The excitement about a new project was starting to rise and she could hardly wait for opening night.

6

In the fortnight that followed, Caroline enjoyed working with Gino to come up with some truly special dishes for the restaurant to open with. While she had to rein in one or two of his wilder ideas (the offal suggestions he'd come up with were definitely dishes to leave for a year or two), she was excited by his risk taking. Her days were spent chasing up the details so that the restaurant could hit the ground running. Menus were created for the first two week cycle; the cutlery and crockery were delivered. Caroline had decided on very simple white tableware, the vogue in dining at the moment seemed to be to serve everything on slate boards, but having experienced first hand the difficulties of eating gravy and jus from a plate with no edges, not to mention garden peas, she'd discounted that idea firmly. The Cider Kitchen was going to be known for its excellent, creative and original food; not the weirdness of its plates. It was like putting the pieces of a jigsaw together and gradually things started to take shape.

Anna was a regular visitor in the early evenings since The Cider Kitchen was just about the right distance from Cowslip Barn to walk Ellie there and back before bedtime. Once she'd closed the tea shop, she'd pick up Ellie from nursery, give her an early tea and then walk the four year old across the orchard to see her aunt. She was impressed by the rapid changes that Caroline had instigated.

'This place looks amazing!' she said as she walked through the door on a particularly warm early June evening. 'I can't believe how far it's come in the weeks that you've been here.' She looked up at the ceiling where the wrought iron chandeliers made by a local artisan blacksmith hung elegantly. 'You were so right about those lights.'

Caroline smiled. 'It's just a question of working with the natural light and then enhancing it a bit,' she said. 'There's so much glass in this building anyway.'

'You always had a knack for making things look their best,' Anna said, turning around to get the full impression of the floor of the restaurant now the tables and chairs were in place. 'I remember how good you were at choosing the right colours for the house that James and I bought in Liphook. We couldn't have done it without you.'

'Oh, rubbish,' Caroline said to hide how touched she was. 'You'd have got there in the end. But James did have naff taste, didn't he?'

'No kidding!' Anna snorted. 'You definitely inherited all of the good taste genes in the family.'

'Except for when he chose you,' Caroline said. 'But anyway. Come and have some cake upstairs. I went to Bird's bakery in the village this morning and I couldn't come away without a load of their vanilla slices. I know you're the queen of cakes around here, but I have to say, they looked very good.'

'They are pretty amazing,' Anna agreed. 'All of the bread I use in the tea shop comes from there.'

Together, they headed up to Caroline's flat. When they were both settled on her new sofa with coffee and pastries and Ellie was happily munching her way through the biggest vanilla slice Anna had ever seen, and gently teasing the kittens with a catnip scented toy, conversation turned to village life.

'So how are you finding living in the sticks?' Anna asked. 'Have you finally stopped rushing everywhere?'

Caroline laughed. 'It took a bit of getting used to and the nights are *really* dark, but I think I'm going to like it here.'

'That's just as well, since I've bought you a ticket for a hoedown at the rugby club tomorrow night.'

'Er... what?' Caroline's cake fork froze halfway to her lips. 'Is that the kind of thing that passes for a good time around here?'

'Well, there's live music, cider and a bucking bronco, so it ought to be a good laugh,' Anna said, smiling broadly at Caroline's bemused expression.

'And since you don't officially open this place until next Saturday, I thought it would do you good to get out and mingle with the locals.'

'I could just go down the pub and drop off a few leaflets,' Caroline said cautiously.

'Oh, come on, it'll be a laugh. Charlotte and Simon are going, and it'll be a nice, informal way to put your face out there and drum up a few customers for the restaurant.'

Caroline took another bite of her cake before she answered. 'OK then,' she said. 'But I'm holding you responsible if I'm picking hay out of my knickers for the next fortnight!'

'Deal. Come over to the house for about seven on Saturday, and we'll walk from there.'

As Anna picked up Ellie's discarded cake plate and their coffee cups, Caroline conceded that there really was no saying no to her on occasion; especially with Ellie in tow. She wondered what she'd let herself in for.

7

'Remind me again why I agreed to this?' Caroline muttered the following evening as she hurried to keep up with Anna. The party included Charlotte and her husband Simon and a couple of Anna's friends from the nursery pickup and their children, and the destination was a rather damp looking marquee in the middle of one of the village rugby pitches. The mist had been rolling in off the Mendip Hills all day, and there was a dampness in the air that was at odds with the late spring season. Caroline was still getting used to West Country weather, which, even by British standards, was unpredictable, and she could feel the dew from the grass seeping through her Converse trainers as she walked.

'It'll be a laugh,' Anna replied, holding Ellie's hand. 'Besides, there'll be enough cider to keep everyone warm and you'll be dancing your socks off by the end of the night.'

'We'll see about that,' Caroline said, taking Ellie's other hand.

Charlotte, who was keeping the drizzle off her curly red hair with a battered trilby, glanced back at Caroline. 'Not to mention the bucking bronco,' she said mischievously. 'Which is bound to look more attractive after a few pints!'

Caroline laughed. Despite the damp weather, Charlotte's irrepressible sense of fun was infectious, although she was absolutely certain she'd be going nowhere near the bucking bronco, which was a large mechanical bull set inside what looked like a bouncy castle. The kids, and later the more inebriated adults, could have that one; she didn't fancy losing her balance or her dignity.

As they approached the marquee they could hear the sound of the first band warming up for their set. A pleasing mix of blues and folk, the music went perfectly with the enticing smell of the hog roast and the sight of the bar staff already pulling pints of Carter's Cider. Caroline looked around the crowded marquee. She smiled at a couple in their mid sixties, who were sipping pints of cider and swaying to the beat of the band, and noticed Anna's parents standing next to them, also cradling plastic pint glasses of Carter's Gold, their bestselling variety. Straw bales were scattered around the inside of the marquee, and there were a few optimistically positioned in the open near to where the hog roast was situated. A couple of hardy souls were ignoring the Somerset 'mizzle', that odd combination of mist and rain that is so prevalent in these parts, and chomping on the first servings from the spit.

Caroline's stomach rumbled at the aroma. She resolved to have a slice or two of the hog roast later; certainly before she'd had too many ciders, the first of which Jonathan was now bringing over to her in a pint glass.

'Hi,' he said, handing her the glass. 'Didn't know you were coming to this.'

Caroline was flattered by his obvious pleasure at seeing her. She liked him when he was caught on the hop; somehow it seemed to balance out those occasions when his charm was just that little bit too practised. 'I thought I'd come along and see what the village does for fun.'

Jonathan laughed. 'Well, it's not all straw bales and hog roasts, but we do tend to do this sort of thing quite well.' He was wearing a blue and black checked shirt over a black t-shirt and jeans and Caroline was amused to notice the Carter's Cider logo embroidered on the pocket of the shirt. It wasn't Jonathan's usual style.

'Are you on duty tonight?' Caroline asked, gesturing to the logo.

'Not exactly, but they were a bit short behind the bar so I said I'd step in for an hour before the rest of the volunteers get here.' He glanced back to the bar. 'Speaking of which, I should probably get on with it.'

'Are you any good at pulling pints?' Caroline asked as he turned back to where the makeshift bar was.

'Goes with the territory!' Jonathan called over his shoulder.

'I'll bear that in mind if we're short-staffed at the restaurant,' Caroline smiled. She watched Jonathan lope back to the bar, head and shoulders above most people in the marquee.

'Typical that,' Charlotte snorted.

'What?' Caroline turned to where Charlotte was standing, Simon having shot off to the bar the minute they got to the marquee.

'Mr Charming brings you a pint but forgets about the rest of us.' Charlotte's eyes were sparkling with mischief. 'Anna said he's got a bit of a thing for you.'

Caroline's face grew warm. 'Rubbish,' she said, sipping her pint, trying to forget the night of the wedding. 'He's just being friendly. Probably doesn't want me to bring the restaurant into disrepute before it's opened. Besides, he's my boss.'

'I'd make that your first and last pint, then!' Charlotte said, taking her own pint of Gold from a returning Simon. 'Or you'll end up being posted on Facebook astride that bucking bronco.'

'Not a chance!' Caroline said.

'I quite fancy a go later,' Charlotte said. 'Although we'll be lucky if we get near it, the amount of kids who are queuing up.' There was already a not insubstantial queue of children and teenagers all waiting to pay their fifty pence to see how long they could hang on to the mechanical bull.

'I wouldn't risk it,' Simon said, looking fondly at his wife. 'Your shoulder's only just recovered from the last time you dislocated it. It would be just like you to fall and pop it back out again.'

'Spoilsport,' Charlotte replied. 'Although I see Evan's already queuing up with Ellie and Anna.'

'She's not thinking about going on there is she?' Caroline said unguardedly. Kicking herself, she turned back to see Charlotte's curious look. 'I mean… she's been complaining about putting her back out again. She shouldn't risk it.' Caroline wasn't quite sure if Anna had told Charlotte her new baby news yet.

'She's far too sensible for that,' Charlotte said, seemingly accepting Caroline's explanation. 'But Ellie loves a bit of excitement, so I'm sure she'll have a go. You might have to go on with her.'

'I'm sure Merry will be game,' Caroline said.

'Oh, she's not coming tonight,' Charlotte replied. 'Cried off with some revision crisis, Anna says.'

Caroline was surprised. Meredith was usually first in line at a village event; if nothing else, it was a chance to hang out with friends without having

Matthew nagging at her. Then she remembered; poor Meredith was in the midst of GCSE exams.

A little later, and Caroline was beginning to feel the effects of the cider. It felt good to get out and to be at the heart of the community she was starting to call home. She didn't know how much time she'd have once the restaurant opened to go to events like this, so she tried to make the most of it while she could.

Jonathan was still busy pulling pints behind the bar, although Mathew had offered to take over from him, and had ended up serving too. It felt vaguely incongruous to see the Managing Directors of the cider farm assuming the roles of bartenders for the night, but they seemed to be enjoying it. Caroline found that she was looking Jonathan's way a little more than was professional; clocking the conversations he was having, the smiles he was giving, and finding herself looking away if he glanced in her direction. She felt a bit like a fourteen year old at a school disco.

'Aunty Caroline!' Ellie, up past her bedtime and loving every minute of it, caught hold of Caroline's free hand. 'Come and have a go on the cow with me! Mummy says I'm too little to go by myself, but you can come with me, can't you?'

'Well…' Caroline started. The last thing she wanted was to fling herself over the bucking bronco, but she never could say no to her niece. 'What about Matthew?' she hedged, seeing Ellie's stepfather, released from his duties at the bar, engrossed in conversation with a man at the edge of the stage where the next band were due to perform.

'He's got a poorly knee,' Ellie said. 'And Mummy's got a baby in her tummy so she can't.'

'Sshh,' Caroline whispered, wary of just how many people knew about Anna's pregnancy. It hadn't quite been the full twelve weeks yet.

'Please,' Ellie cajoled.

'Oh, all right then!' Caroline said, allowing herself to be dragged by the hand to the back of the queue.

In a short time it was Ellie and Caroline's turn. Having witnessed a couple of kids and a rather ambitious (and inebriated) twenty something being chucked off the bull, Caroline was glad she'd opted for skinny jeans. Slipping off her trainers and putting them beside Ellie's wellington boots, she followed Ellie onto the inflatable area. She lifted Ellie up onto the back of the mechanical bull and then, steeling herself, she bounced on the air cushion and flung one leg over the back.

A chorus of cheers and wolf whistles from the onlookers, led by Matthew and Anna, made her smile as she put her arms around her niece and held the handle on the top of the mechanical bull. At first, the operator went carefully, mindful of Ellie's age and

Caroline's nerves, but after about thirty seconds of sedate twists and turns, he ramped up the pace and Caroline found herself clinging on for dear life. Ellie squealed with excitement and in another few seconds they both landed on the air cushion, giggling.

'Again!' Ellie laughed, jumping up. 'Come on, Aunty Caroline.'

After another go, with pretty much the same result, Caroline was glad to stagger off the air cushion and reclaim the remains of her pint of cider that Charlotte had been holding for her.

'You're braver than I am,' Charlotte said. 'I'm going to need a fair few more pints before I attempt it.'

Caroline laughed. 'It's not so bad.'

'Well done,' came a voice from behind her. Turning, she saw a fresh pint of cider with Jonathan on the end of it. 'She's been mithering all afternoon for a go on that, ever since Matthew told her about it. But now you've taken one for the team!'

'Aunt's duty,' Caroline said, slipping the new pint of cider inside the empty plastic glass. 'And she made a pretty good case as to why Matthew and Anna couldn't go on it with her. I wonder why she didn't think of her new Uncle Jonathan, though!'

'Why do you think I've been hiding behind the bar all this time?' Jonathan laughed. 'But thankfully now I'm off duty for a bit.' He sipped his own pint of cider and then glanced at one of the large bales of straw that was placed around the stage area where the next band was due to start playing soon. 'I'm going to bag myself a seat. Would you like to join me?'

'I'd better get this one back to her mum and dad first,' Caroline said, squeezing Ellie's hand. Her heart lurched at the unintentional slip. 'I mean...'

'I know what you mean,' Jonathan said softly. 'And I'm sure he'd be flattered to be called that.'

Caroline nodded, eyes suddenly feeling too bright and too hot. 'Come on,' she said to her niece. 'Mummy will want to see you dance before it gets too late.'

'OK,' Ellie replied, apparently unaware of her aunt's sudden shift in mood. Thankfully, by the time they had crossed the marquee, navigating their way through the now thick crowd of hoedowners, Caroline had blinked away her tears. This new life still took some getting used to, she thought. And it probably would for a while yet. This was a new beginning in so many ways; Caroline just hoped the book would stay closed on a few chapters of her old life. She cherished her memories of her brother James, of course, but there were several other things that were best left in her past, including the man in the photo.

8

Opening night came rushing towards Caroline like the ghosts of the trains along the Strawberry Line. With the Carters keen to get the doors open on the place so quickly, the time flew by and before she knew it, The Cider Kitchen was ready. They had a full house of bookings for opening night, including a food critic, so Caroline was both excited and absolutely terrified. What if she messed up? What if Gino did? What if her new waiting staff couldn't handle the rush? It was a high risk strategy to invite a critic on the first night but he was from one of the more minor local papers, so Caroline thought it was a risk worth taking. The reviewers from the larger papers would be invited later.

The night before, Caroline was prowling the restaurant, almost marking a path on the oak floor. Everything was in place; the tables were laid, the glasses (three different sizes per place setting) were sparkling in the warm, subdued side lighting, the white napkins were lying pristine under the glittering, simple stainless steel cutlery. The light wood table tops had been polished to perfection. As she looked across to the bar area she saw the rows of optics, each one fully tested to make sure they worked (that had been fun a couple of evenings ago – as a bonding exercise she and her team had made absolutely sure every last one was in full working order), and yet more glasses stacked neatly on shelves on the wall behind the bar, either side of an A2 sized wooden carving bearing 'The Cider Kitchen' and its logo, a black and white stylised line drawing of an apple on a tree branch.

Good luck cards lined the shelf above the bar from everyone from Anna and Matthew to the local wine merchant, and a fair few people she'd never met. There had even been several with Bristol postmarks, suggesting that word was already spreading about the restaurant even before it had officially opened. Everything was perfect; so why couldn't she shake off the feeling that it was all going to go wrong? Perhaps it was the one unsigned good luck card that had arrived this afternoon; the one with the carelessly scrawled message but no name. The handwriting looked disturbingly familiar but there was no way the card could have been from *him*.

'I know just the thing to take the edge off your nerves,' Gino said as Caroline, yet again, wandered into the kitchen.

'A bottle of scotch?' Caroline grimaced. 'Although I suppose it'd have to be frigging calvados as everything's made out of apples round here.' She tended to swear when she was stressed and she was trying to rein it in in case she slipped up in front of the customers.

Gino went to his forage cabinet, which was a small, suitcase shaped box that he kept tucked away at the back of the pantry. It contained the dried herbs and plants he'd foraged over the past year and had been a revelation to Caroline in terms of new flavours. Without explaining anything he flipped the switch on the kettle and took one of the white china mugs from the shelf above the serving area. He sprinkled the contents of a small polythene bag into the mug and as soon as the kettle had boiled he poured the hot water over it.

'What is it?' Caroline regarded the concoction suspiciously. 'It's not weed, is it? I can't afford to get stoned the night before we do this.'

Gino laughed. 'As if I would!' No, and it's not *Psilocybe Cubensis*, either.'

'Er, what?'

'Magic Mushrooms,' Gino kept smiling. 'Although I do know where there's a regular crop that grows not a million miles from here.' They'd seen him through a student night or two when he'd been too skint to buy booze, although the hangover had been far worse so he hadn't had any in a while.

'You haven't answered my question,' Caroline said. She still hadn't tasted what he'd handed her.

Gino shook his head. 'It's *Valeriana officinalis,*' he said gently. 'Valerian. It's been used for thousands of years to relax and aid sleep. My grandma swears by it when she's being kept awake by my grandfather's snoring. Totally harmless, but will knock you straight out.'

Caroline took a sip and grimaced. 'Probably tastes better with a slug of calvados in it.'

'Trust me,' Gino said. 'You want a good night's sleep, this'll do it.'

Unguardedly, Caroline thought back to the last good night's sleep she'd had; it had been a short one, certainly, but blissfully relaxing. It had been the night she'd taken Jonathan to bed; the night of Matthew and Anna's wedding. She wished she could just ring him up and demand a repeat performance (she didn't doubt he'd be willing, if the first time had been anything to go by and he had been hanging around the restaurant rather more than was strictly necessary, despite his initial assertions about being able to separate business and pleasure). But that way lay chaos and uncertainty. And she wasn't prepared to risk that. Moving to Somerset had been an attempt to simplify things, to get away from some of the complications of her past. Adding more to the mix now would be defeating the object.

'Thank you,' she said before she took another sip. 'It's kind of you to try to help.' She sighed. 'I think

I'm so caught up with trying to prove myself that I'm losing sight of why I chose to do it in the first place.'

Gino regarded her levelly. 'You don't have to prove anything to me, Caroline,' he said. 'You've hit the ground running with this place. That takes nerve.'

'Or stupidity,' Caroline countered. 'Don't let me down, Gino.'

Gino smiled. 'I won't. I promise.' Gino's phone buzzed. 'Sorry, boss,' he said, a second later, 'got to dash.'

'Anywhere special?' Caroline asked.

'You could say that,' Gino replied, instantly cagey. 'Do you mind?'

'Of course not,' Caroline replied. 'I wouldn't want to keep you.'

'Thanks,' Gino said, slipping his phone into his back pocket.

'Have a good evening,' Caroline said as Gino left the restaurant with a spring in his step, 'not that there's much left of it!' It was coming up to ten o'clock and Caroline was definitely ready for her bed.

'Oh, when you're a chef the party doesn't start until the restaurants close,' Gino said airily as he went to close the door. 'I learned that pretty quickly doing my internships.' He raised his eyebrows at her playfully. 'You should come out with us sometime; we'd show you how to have fun.'

Caroline laughed. 'I don't doubt it,' she said. 'But I think I'm going to have my work cut out just keeping up with running this place.' She was absurdly flattered to be asked, though. Oh, to be that age and on the cusp of so many things! Her twenties had been a time of exploration and excitement as well as drama, and, much as she still liked a night out, she was pleased to be older and wiser these days. Sighing, she turned out the lights and headed upstairs to try to unwind. The kittens skittered across the floor to greet her as she opened the door to her quarters, and, feeling in need of the company, she scooped them up and carried them into her bedroom, where they settled quickly near the top of the bed. Yet again, her thoughts turned to Jonathan. She wondered if he was feeling as nervous about the opening night as she was. Not that he'd tell her if he was, she supposed. Tomorrow was going to be one of the most important days of her life and before she fell asleep, she practiced her greetings to the customers who were booked to come through the door. 'Good evening, and welcome,' she murmured. 'Hello, and welcome... good evening and welcome to The Cider Kitchen...'

9

The next morning, with The Cider Kitchen due to open for the first time that evening, Caroline was feeling much less amenable towards her new chef. She slammed down the phone in the small back office and considered chucking it out of the window. Bloody Gino! How could he have been so irresponsible? She looked around the cluttered, tiny space, wondering how the hell she was going to deal with twenty covers and no chef. She glanced at the clock on the wall opposite the desk; eight hours until the doors opened.

Gino had been effusive in his apologies in between bouts of retching. He'd assured her that most of the prep work had been done the day before; the chicken was marinating in the meat fridge for one of the main courses and the scallops for one of the two starters just needed flash frying. The tiramisu, thankfully, were prepped and ready in one of the other fridges, just needing a sprinkling of cocoa powder before they were served. But that didn't excuse the fact that her apparently brilliant head chef had had a pint too many in Weston Super Mare last night, an ill-advised kebab from a highly dubious mobile van and was now suffering from a violent bout of food poisoning. Of all the times he could have done it this had to have been the worst.

But what was she going to do? She had every faith in her new front of house team and she still had Joe the kitchen porter and Erin the pot washer, but they couldn't be expected to cook. Any agency would charge her extortionate rates for a chef at such short notice. Exhausted already from the preparations and feeling uncharacteristically close to tears, she looked out the back at the yard behind the restaurant and despaired.

'We're not open yet,' she called irritably as she heard the front door of the restaurant open. Too late, she realised that probably wasn't the best way to greet a potential customer. 'Sorry,' she added, a beat too late. 'Can you come back later?'

'Well, I could, but I didn't think you'd want me booking a table on your opening night.' Jonathan, holding another bunch of freesias, poked his head around the office door.

'There's not going to be an opening night at this rate,' Caroline snapped.

'Why not? What's happened?'

'My sodding chef's got food poisoning.'

'Shit.' Jonathan said. 'That's rotten luck.'

'Luck's got nothing to do with it,' Caroline crossed her arms. 'He had a dodgy kebab last night and has been throwing up since about six a.m., I ought to sack him on the spot, but it's too late to get anyone else in.'

'So what are you going to do?' Jonathan put the flowers down on the desk and looked straight at her.

Caroline scowled. 'I haven't got a frigging clue.'

'Right.' Jonathan's back straightened. 'Leave it with me.'

'What are you going to do?' Caroline's heart lurched between hope and irritation. 'You're no chef and the agency fees for a temp would be astronomical. We're finished before we even open.'

'Oh, don't be so defeatist, darling,' Jonathan replied. 'Fill me in on what needs doing and I'll make a couple of calls.'

'No. I can sort this myself.' Furiously, Caroline grabbed her diary and flipped through to the list of names and numbers of people who'd booked tables that night. 'We'll just have to cancel and reschedule the opening for another night.' As she rifled through the pages she jumped as a warm hand closed over hers.

'Now you're just being silly.' Jonathan's voice was calm, gentle, and it nearly reduced Caroline to tears. He took her hand away from the diary and held it for a moment. Caroline was torn between snatching her hand away and wanting him to hold it forever.

'What are we going to do, then?' Caroline said.

'As I said. Leave it with me. I'll get us a chef, I promise.' He let go of her hand and delved into his pocket. Pulling out his phone, he dialled quickly. 'Vern? Is Emma working tonight? No? Great. Can you give her a ring and ask her if she's free to come over to The Cider Kitchen in about an hour? All right. See you later.' He turned back to Caroline who stood bemused, still clutching her diary.

'Who was that?' Caroline asked.

'Vern, the landlord at The Stationmaster. His daughter's at catering college.'

'How do you know?' Caroline said. 'Do you keep tabs on every woman over the age of eighteen in this sodding village?'

'What do you take me for?' Jonathan replied with mock outrage. 'I was in the pub the other night and overheard Vern talking about how amazingly well Emma was doing and how she was looking forward to having this week off as she'd been working so hard. I thought she might appreciate the pocket money.'

'We can't afford to pay her,' Caroline groaned. 'I've got virtually no funds left from the budget you allocated. Which isn't enough, by the way.'

'Don't worry about that,' Jonathan smiled. 'After tonight, you'll be fine. And I'll sort it with our finance department.'

'How do I know she's any good?'

'I trust Vern,' Jonathan said flatly. 'And frankly, darling, you need to learn a bit about not looking too closely at the dental records of free equines, if you catch my drift.'

'I'm the manager of the restaurant, Jonathan!' Caroline knew her voice was rising but she couldn't help it. She'd gone from hope to despair so quickly and now Jonathan was expecting her to rhapsodise over some trainee whom she'd never even met. 'You might own the business but I'm the one who makes the day to day decisions. I think I'm entitled to be a bit wary.'

'Then be wary, Caroline, but please, think about it. What choice do we have?' Jonathan reached across to one of the freesias he'd put on her desk and idly fingered its bloom. 'From where I'm standing, very little, unless you want to postpone the opening night.'

A heavy, expectant pause descended. Caroline found her eyes drawn to the sight of Jonathan's fingertips caressing the fragile petals of the freesias. She knew he was right. She didn't have a choice. It just made her hopping mad that he had swanned in and saved the day, since she was the consultant on this project and should have been able to come up with a solution without him.

'OK, OK, you win.' She dragged her eyes back up from Jonathan's hands to meet his gaze. 'It's lucky

I've had control over Gino's menu choices – I know exactly what goes into each dish, I just need someone to cook it.'

'There you go,' Jonathan said. 'That wasn't so hard, was it?' Now I suggest you get that coffee machine on and get yourself organised for a meeting with Emma. You've not got long until the doors open for business and I think you're going to need every minute.' He headed towards the door.

'So, you're just going to sod off again now, are you?' Caroline said. She suddenly felt very small and alone seeing that he was, indeed, leaving her.

'Well, I had hoped you'd say thank you before I left,' Jonathan said coolly, his eyes unreadable.

'Thank you,' Caroline said meekly. She usually knew just how far to push people, but Jonathan was especially difficult to read.

'I'll see you at opening time,' Jonathan said. Then, relenting a little, 'good luck.' He gave her a brief smile. 'I've heard nothing but good things about Emma Leadbetter. You might consider offering her a permanent job if she works out tonight.'

As he walked back out of the restaurant, Caroline steeled herself and set about finding Gino's notes and recipe cards, ready to brief Emma on what would be required. She hoped she had long enough.

10

Two hours later, and Caroline was thanking her lucky stars that Jonathan had visited when he had. Emma Leadbetter had turned out to be an absolute star; grounded, knowledgeable and efficient. She had read Gino's recipes and instructions and followed them to the letter. As the enticing scents of chicken parmigiana infused with a hearty basil and tomato sauce began to drift through from the kitchen, Caroline dared to hope that things might be alright after all.

At around half past two she left Emma to her own devices. Before she went upstairs for a couple of hours' rest and a bite that she'd probably be far too nervous to eat, she checked the tables and made sure the water in the small floating flower arrangements was topped up. As she wandered back to the office, she realised guiltily that she hadn't had time to put Jonathan's freesias in water. Taking them from her desk, she decided to take them upstairs with her, and as she took a second to inhale their delicate scent she was reminded, most disturbingly, of the sight of Jonathan's fingers caressing them. This in turn triggered off a stronger memory of the night they'd spent together; the night they'd met. Caroline's skin prickled with goose flesh as she remembered how his hands had expertly brought her body to a shuddering climax, and the feeling of him inside her.

It had been a night of fun and her intention had been to walk out of his life as easily as she'd entered it. And yet now, due to a combination of twists of fate, here she was, working with him. There was a part of her that needed him to be something more in her life; a part of her that had wanted to throw herself into his arms when everything had gone wrong this morning. But the sensible, rational part of her had held back. Jonathan would never settle; would never be the type with whom she could build a future. Anna had said as much when she'd described him to her all those months ago. He'd slept with his brother's first wife, for goodness' sake! Caroline knew that she needed to be careful in case her heart, or her mouth, or perhaps both, got her into deeper water than she could swim in. It wasn't as if she was unaccustomed to that feeling; she'd been in deep water back in Surrey until she'd pulled herself out of it, but tonight she had the restaurant to open. Nothing, and nobody, could get in the way of that.

Walking back out of the office she poked her head through the kitchen door one last time. 'Everything all right, Emma?'

Emma turned round from where she had been poring over the recipe lists for the starters. 'Fine, thanks. His recipes are really easy to follow.'

'That's a relief,' Caroline said. 'At least he's managed not to mess that up!'

Emma smiled diplomatically and wiped her hands down the front of the maroon apron she was wearing over her chef's whites. 'I'm sorry Gino's ill, but I really appreciate you giving me the chance to do this.'

'You've got me out of a real spot,' Caroline smiled back. 'If it all goes well tonight, then who knows where it might lead?'

'I'm not sure what Gino would say about that,' Emma replied.

'He's forfeited the right to say anything about anything at the moment,' Caroline said darkly. 'And since I can't have him and his snivelling backside anywhere near this place for the next forty-eight hours, he'd better not darken my door.'

Emma laughed. 'Jonathan said you can be quite scary when you're cross; he was obviously right!'

Despite herself, Caroline did smile. 'Have I been the subject of much pub gossip?'

Emma blushed. 'A bit.' She busied herself with chopping the tarragon finely. 'Jonathan also said you were... what did he say... a bit of a firebird? Firebrand?'

Jonathan again, Caroline thought. She didn't know how she felt about being discussed quite so openly. Although it could have been worse, she thought. Firebird or firebrand; either weren't too bad.

'I'll let you make up your own mind,' Caroline said wryly. 'Will you be all right while I go and feed the kittens and get myself sorted out?'

'Sure, no worries.' Emma glanced up again. 'Once I've prepped the last of this, I'll zip off, if that's OK.'

'Can you come back for about five?' Caroline replied. 'We can brief the serving team together, then.'

'That's fine. I'll see you in a bit.'

As Caroline walked back out of the kitchen, she realised she wasn't missing Gino at all.

11

Caroline's stomach fluttered with bigger and bigger butterflies as the minute hand on the clock edged towards the hour. The Cider Kitchen was due to open at seven o'clock, and, though she knew everything and everyone in it was as ready as they could be she still felt the nerves rising. She jumped as the front door opened. Her stomach flipped for a totally different reason when she saw Jonathan come through the door and stride across the restaurant floor.

'That is a knockout dress,' Jonathan said as he drew closer. He looked around briefly at the tables with their glistening glasses and immaculately laid cutlery. 'And this place looks absolutely perfect.'

'Thanks,' Caroline said, jolted by the sight of Jonathan in his beautifully cut suit. 'You look pretty good yourself. Got somewhere special to go after this?'

'I like to make the effort occasionally.' His face assumed a more serious expression. 'I sort of wish I could stay longer tonight, but I don't want to tread on your toes.'

Caroline forced a brighter smile than she felt; Jonathan had already told her that afternoon that he wouldn't be able to hang around on the opening night and she knew she had a good team behind her, but just for a second she wanted him to stay by her side. 'That's OK,' she said. 'It's all under control.'

Jonathan smiled back at her. 'I've no doubt of that.' Keeping his eyes locked on hers, he leaned forward, and for a moment Caroline thought he was going to kiss her, but he merely tucked the fabric hanging tag from the shoulder of her dress out of sight. His fingers were warm on her skin. 'Good luck,' he said softly.

'Have a good evening,' Caroline called after him as he left. She respected his decision to keep away and there was no time to think about him as the first customers were coming through the door.

At about eight thirty, Ian Smith, food critic for the *Somerset Herald*, arrived. 'Thank you so much for coming,' Caroline said, shaking his hand. 'I hope you enjoy your evening with us.'

'Always good to support local endeavours,' Ian replied. He didn't look like he spent a lot of time in restaurants; Caroline had expected a rather florid, somewhat overweight reviewer, but this was a trim looking man in his mid fifties who looked as though he spent more time pounding the Strawberry Line than quaffing wine and eating restaurant cuisine. 'Where would you like me to sit?'

'I've reserved a table for you in the window,' Caroline replied. 'If that suits. Will you be dining alone?'

'Unfortunately, yes,' the critic said. 'But don't let that worry you. I'm here just as a regular customer, so don't feel off your stride.'

Caroline nodded but her knees started to shake, regardless. She turned to Meredith's friend Izzy. Both girls, and another student called Milly, were working tonight and Caroline wanted to give them a chance to shine. 'Izzy will be looking after you tonight, so feel free to take your time and she'll be over to take your order when you're ready.' As she walked back to the front door to welcome the next customer, she hoped the critic would leave satisfied.

Twenty minutes later the restaurant was reaching capacity. As it was the opening night, there was a set menu of three starters, three main courses and three desserts to minimise stress on the kitchen and waiting staff. Emma was acquitting herself admirably in the kitchen, and by the time The Cider Kitchen had been open for an hour, Caroline had almost forgotten about Gino's absence.

The rumble of conversation between guests grew louder as people started to relax into the evening. Glasses were being filled and even a slight hiccup with a mixed up starter order couldn't dampen the growing convivial atmosphere. Caroline stayed front of house, directing her waiting staff and meeting and greeting her new customers. As she looked around the restaurant she gradually began to feel that taking on this project wasn't completely insane. She knew that the opening night was just the beginning, but as people started to tuck in to the delectable food combinations that Gino had created and Emma had prepared, Caroline realised that this was exactly what she wanted to be doing with her life.

After checking once again that her customers were all occupied, Caroline headed back through to the kitchen to see how things were going. As she walked through the door she could just make Emma out through a cloud of steam that was rising from the draining pan of wild mushroom ravioli. It was the second on the list of starters and, glancing down at the delicately boiled parcels, she could see that Emma had cooked it perfectly.

'All good back here?' Caroline asked.

'So far, so good,' Emma replied, slightly pink from her exertions. 'But can you have a word with the front of house team to pick up the pace in getting the scallops out. They'll go over if they're left much longer.'

'Will do.' Caroline was impressed. Emma had taken control of the kitchen as if she'd been working there for months, not hours. 'Anything else?' she said, glancing at the clock on the wall.

'Mains'll start coming in about fifteen minutes,' Emma replied. 'Are all of the orders in?'

'I think so,' Caroline glanced at the chits lined neatly up on the underside of the warmer. She counted off the tables: '*one, two, three... seven, eight...*' She went cold. Where was Ian Smith's order? She checked again. Table ten definitely wasn't there. Not wanting to panic Emma, she hurried back to the restaurant. Sure enough, he was still sitting, unfed, at the table in the window.

'Izzy!' Caroline hissed at the passing waitress. 'Where's table ten's order?'

'With the others,' Izzy replied. 'I put it through about ten minutes ago.'

'Are you sure? It's not on the warmer.'

'Hang on, let me check.' Izzy rummaged in the front pocket of her maroon apron, then turned pale as she found a screwed up scrap of paper from her orders pad. 'Shit. Sorry, Caroline, I must have shoved it there when I took table twelve's order.'

Caroline took the crumpled paper from Izzy's rather shaky hand and scanned it. Ravioli and Chicken Parmigiana. Forcing herself to be calm, she handed it back. 'Right. Let's get his starter out to him, shall we? Emma's got some ravioli ready now, so let's get back on track.'

'I'm really sorry,' Izzy repeated. 'I didn't mean to mess up.'

Caroline gave the nervous teenager a tight smile. 'Hopefully, no harm done,' she said. 'Just get that starter out to him now.'

'Will do.' Izzy scurried away, determined to put things right.

Caroline drew a deep breath. This was, after all, what building a successful team was all about. Communication was key, especially with a young staff on opening night. As if in contradiction, there was a sudden, jarring crash from the back of the restaurant. The room fell silent as the detritus from a pile of dropped plates settled on the floor. Thankfully, they were clean.

In an instant, Caroline had taken control. 'I bet you weren't expecting entertainment tonight,' she quipped as she crossed to the back of the restaurant where Milly, face flushed with mortification, was doing her best to clear up the mess.

'Go and get yourself a dustpan and brush,' Caroline murmured. 'Don't try to pick them up or you'll cut yourself.'

Milly scurried away and, ignoring her own advice, Caroline began picking up some of the dropped crockery. She winced as she did indeed, cut herself.

'Let me see that.' The voice was low, mildly amused.

Caroline glanced up to see the restaurant critic staring down at her, a slight smile lifting the corners of his mouth.

'It's fine,' Caroline smiled back gamely. 'First night teething troubles.' She got back to her feet and placed the broken plates on the side of the dresser behind her. 'I hope you're enjoying the food so far.'

Ian gave her a long, appraising glance. 'It's delicious,' he said softly. He held her gaze a fraction too long before he turned back to his table. Caroline felt very exposed all of a sudden. Grabbing a napkin from the dresser, she wrapped it round her index finger and then headed back to her station at the back of the restaurant by the entrance to the kitchen where she kept a stash of blue catering plasters. After the past few minutes, she needed to regroup, refocus her energies.

In the corner nearest her was a couple in their thirties; she guessed they were parents to young children as they had that liberated look of a pair who hadn't been out alone in a while. In front of them, on the middle table nearest the wall was an older couple, chewing over their starters in companionable silence. Then there was the food critic back in his seat by the window, apparently immersed in tasting his ravioli.

On the table nearest the door was a family of four; two parents and two teenage children, both of whom were surreptitiously texting under the table. Then, on the other side of the door, before the red lacquered grand piano, was a threesome of women, obviously enjoying the house wine and discussing their other halves in somewhat ribald terms. That made twelve. The other two tables of four were occupied by two pairs of two couples, one in their late fifties and the other more thirty somethings. And finally, tucked away in the other corner, were Anna and Matthew, who'd requested the last table. She'd spoken to them briefly when they'd arrived, but they'd taken their table discreetly, obviously not wanting to intrude on her opening night. They had their heads together, saying nothing but communicating with so much more than words. Their love was an almost tangible force and Caroline was in awe at how perfectly in sync they seemed to be. Caroline could see Matthew's enraptured expression as he was positioned facing the restaurant. She felt, once again, that bittersweet sensation in her chest that Anna should be so loved by someone who wasn't James. There was no doubt though, looking at Matthew, that he was very much in love with his new wife. His eyes were soft in the low light and the smile on his face was genuine and unguarded. Caroline wondered if anyone would ever look at her in that way. As her thoughts wandered yet again towards Jonathan, she shook her head. He was the last person she should be thinking about. Now was not the time for daydreaming; not on opening night.

12

Two hours later, and Jonathan was beginning to wish he'd stayed at The Cider Kitchen after all. His date for the evening, while very charming and extremely beautiful, was also clearly still hung up on her ex and not in the mood tonight for anything more adventurous than a chat. So it was that Jonathan found himself, most uncharacteristically, at a loose end. Having driven himself in he was stone cold sober, and, disappointed at having to return home earlier than expected to Little Somerby, he wondered what to do.

After a brief drink in one of the more upmarket bars on Park Street where he was more than a little flattered to catch the eye of a group of rather attractive second year arts students, he reluctantly conceded that he'd have to get back home. Jack, after all, needed keeping an eye on.

As he pulled back onto the ring road heading back out of the city, Jonathan's thoughts once again drifted back to Caroline. Apart from that brief visit before opening time, he'd sworn to himself he'd stay away from the restaurant tonight to give her space to do things her own way. She kept creeping into his thoughts; sliding around the doorway of his brain like a cat, sneaking in and curling up in his mind when he least expected it. She'd been a one night stand, but the best one night stand of his life. And she'd had a lot to compete with. Should he pop into The Cider Kitchen on his way home? He shouldn't. But perhaps she'd forgive his intrusion if the rest of the night had gone well.

'Oh, for fuck's sake!' He surprised himself that he'd said it out loud. Caroline really was getting to him. He put his foot down a little harder, the BMW devouring the miles between Bristol and Little Somerby. He'd just poke his head round the door, see how she was doing. It would be closing time by the time he got there, anyway.

Pulling into the driveway of Orchard Cottage, he glanced towards the living room window. The light was still on so his father must still be up and about. He didn't want to be the subject of any ribald post mortems about the success, or otherwise, of his evening, so he pocketed his car keys and strode back towards the centre of the village.

It was a quiet, clear evening. The village was getting ready to settle down for the night, and he nodded briefly at a couple, presumably returning from The Cider Kitchen, who were chatting about how nice it was to have a new eatery within walking distance. *All good signs*, he thought. He hoped

Emma Leadbetter had pulled it off. Picking up his pace, he straightened his shoulders.

*

Ian Smith was, typically, the last customer in the restaurant. Caroline couldn't very well chuck him out, but she'd quietly dismissed her front of house staff as it was coming up to eleven o'clock and they'd worked their socks off all night. Emma was tucked away in the kitchen, clearing down and getting things in order for the next day's service. Caroline walked towards Ian, ready to take his coffee cup from him, and hoped he'd soon be off home.

'Can I get you anything else?' Caroline asked as she reached the table.

'No, thank you. It was a very good meal,' Ian said, clearly in no hurry to leave. 'Very good.' He leaned back in his chair. 'And you've got a nice atmosphere going here. Cosy, but not twee. Rather sophisticated, in fact.'

'Thank you,' Caroline said guardedly. She sensed there was a 'but' coming.

'There are one or two issues, though, that prevent me from giving it the full five stars.' Deliberately slowly, he stood up out of his chair. 'Although, of course, I am open to persuasion.'

Suddenly, the restaurant seemed entirely too small for them both.

'I'll look forward to reading your review.' She moved past him to show him the door.

He, however, refused to take the hint. 'Come on, Caroline. I haven't finished.'

Caroline gritted her teeth. 'I apologise. Was there something else you wanted to say?'

'Why don't we share a nightcap and I'll talk you through my... thoughts about the restaurant.'

Caroline tried not to shudder. This nondescript, colourless man was far from the worst who'd ever hit on her, but the way he was trying to use his perceived power over her, his ability, as he saw it, to make or break her business was enough to make the bile rise in her throat. 'I don't think so,' she said. 'I've got a lot to do before I turn in.'

'Are you quite sure?' he moved closer. Caroline could smell the liqueur coffee on his breath, could see the open pores in his pasty skin.

'Absolutely.' Caroline stood her ground, refusing to be intimidated. She could hear the clatter of the pans in the kitchen as Emma sorted them out for the next day's service, and was reassured.

'Shame.' He lowered his head and also his gaze, assessing, appraising. He reached out a lazy hand and ran his index finger down the inside of her bare arm, brushing his knuckle against the side of her breast as he did so. This time, Caroline couldn't hide her shudder of revulsion. 'Don't you want an insurance policy?' He looked around. 'Carter's Cider have certainly poured enough money into this place to take… precautions.'

Caroline, whose patience had been on a tightrope all night, finally snapped. 'I don't need to take any precautions.' She swatted Smith's hand away smartly. 'We've done a fucking fantastic job of getting this place ready, and you should give us the credit we deserve for the effort we've put in, not because you want to put the moves on me, so back off.'

'Well, well,' Smith said, hastily withdrawing his hand and reaching for his glass of wine, which still had a gulp in the bottom of it. 'Looks like you've got teeth as impressive as your tits.' Still insolent, he glanced down her body.

Caroline stood her ground. 'Good night, Mr Smith. I suggest you leave before you feel just how sharp my teeth are. And I promise you, you won't like it one little bit. I trust we'll see your review in the *Somerset Herald* in due course.'

'Certainly,' Smith replied. 'Thank you for an… entertaining night.'

'It's not her job to entertain you.' A voice cut through the man's oily routine like cheese wire through a block of Stinking Bishop. 'She's here to run a business, so why don't you get back to your typewriter and write about it.'

Smith flinched as if stung.

'Well, well,' he said softly. 'And I thought Carter's were just throwing cash at the place and leaving the legwork to the minions.'

'Why don't you do us all a favour and push off before you say or do something else you'll regret.' Jonathan, who had slipped in through the front door, stopped a few feet away from Caroline. The three of them stood stock still for a few more heartbeats.

'Don't worry,' Smith said eventually. 'I get the message, loud and clear. I'll be sure to call you if I need any more information.' He walked to the door. 'Good night.'

As he left, Caroline released a breath she felt as though she'd been holding all evening. It did little to extinguish her anger. She spun round to face Jonathan who had remained where he was, a few feet behind her. 'What on earth do you think you're doing?'

Jonathan held up his hands in mitigation. 'I just thought you might appreciate a little help in dealing with that sanctimonious shit. His reputation precedes him.'

'That's rich, coming from you!' Caroline was still fuming. 'What right have you got to swan in here now when all the work's been done?' Restlessly, she walked around the restaurant, straightening cutlery, checking glasses, folding already folded napkins.

'Calm down, Caroline,' Jonathan said. 'I was just passing and I wanted to see how Emma had got on. I slipped in the back way precisely because I didn't want to tread on your toes. I wasn't going to let you know I was here until I saw him try to do a number on you.' He took a step towards her. 'I'm sorry if it wasn't what it looked like, but I've heard bad reports from people who've been on the wrong end of his 'charm'. He thinks just because he used to work for a London newspaper he's the hottest journalist in the South West, rather than doing food reviews for a freebie rag.'

'I am more than capable of telling him where to go myself,' Caroline snapped. 'In fact, I was one step away from punching him in the face when you rocked up. I'm not some pathetic damsel in distress who needs you to weigh in and rescue me whenever the hell you feel like it.'

'Look,' Jonathan sounded exasperated. 'I didn't mean to upset you. I just don't like seeing people being put under that kind of pressure. He should give us a good review because you, and this place, are good. Not because he wants to get into your knickers.'

'Your concern is touching,' Caroline's voice was still brittle with tension. 'but can you honestly tell me *you've* never put a woman under that kind of pressure?'

Jonathan's eyes were suddenly ice cold. 'I've never had to.' He let his hands drop to his sides. 'Goodnight, Caroline.' Without another word, he walked out of The Cider Kitchen.

The door closed behind Jonathan and Caroline let out a long breath. As if being hit on by a food critic wasn't enough, now she had Jonathan trying to muscle in and play the great protector. She'd seen off enough types like Ian Smith in the past to know exactly where their weak spots were. At least, she thought, she'd be able to kick Gino's arse when he came to see her early the next morning.

If she was honest, she knew that Jonathan, and probably Gino, were the wrong targets for her aggression but she'd been so keyed up all evening that arguing with Jonathan had been a release. Perhaps she had responded too strongly to his attempt to intercede with Ian Smith. Sometimes the anger she still felt about her own isolation and the shadows of her past crept up on her and made her want to turn that anger outwards. In exasperation, she grabbed her phone from behind the cash desk and began to text Jonathan.

Sorry,

she wrote quickly.

It's been a long night. Meeting to debrief in the morning?
C.

She only just stopped herself from signing off with a kiss. That would be a step too far, she thought wryly, heading back to the kitchen to speak to Emma. Sometimes she forgot how far she'd actually come in a few months; what she'd left behind in Surrey. She just hoped that the past really was behind her, and that she could truly move on.

13

The next morning, Gino was waiting on the doorstep. Taking a moment to observe him, Caroline noticed the hunched shoulders, the lank locks and the general air of dolefulness that emanated from him.

'I am so, so sorry, Caroline,' was Gino's opening gambit. He hovered on the doorstep, reluctant to cross the threshold.

Equally mindful of the Health and Safety risk to her other staff and customers, should Gino's food poisoning turn out to be a virus, Caroline stepped outside to join him.

'You're a twat,' Caroline said smartly. 'You jeopardised the opening night just because you couldn't say no to your mates.'

Gino shook his head. 'You're right. I am a twat. And it won't happen again, I promise.'

Caroline sized him up. He still looked rather green around the gills and his already flat stomach was now almost concave. He had dark rings round his red rimmed eyes and he did, indeed, look the picture of contrition.

'What time did you stop throwing up?' She asked.

'About five o'clock yesterday afternoon,' Gino replied. 'And then Mum gave me such a bollocking I wanted to keep my head down the bog as long as I could.'

'Good for your mother,' Caroline said. 'I'm not your mum. I'm your boss and if you mess me around again, Gino, I will throw you out on your ear so fast you'll think food poisoning is a night at the Ritz.'

Gino bowed his head. 'I'm sorry. It won't happen again.'

'You're lucky that Emma Leadbetter stepped in at short notice yesterday to cover your shift. And I was pleased that you'd left such comprehensive notes. It made her job an awful lot easier.'

'Emma? Vern's daughter?'

'Yes. She was on a week's leave from college so we were lucky she could spare the time. Thankfully, she proved more than capable.' This was, of course, absolutely true, but Caroline felt it should be emphasised to Gino to make it clear he wasn't her only option.

'I've heard good things about her,' he admitted grudgingly.

'With good reason,' Caroline paused. 'In fact, I thought I might take her on part time when she finishes her course, as your sous chef.'

Gino started. 'I didn't think you had the budget for a sous chef?'

'I don't, really,' Caroline admitted. 'But she's got something. I think she'd be great.'

'Do I get a say in this?' Gino grumbled. 'Or am I expected to just suck it up?'

'For the moment, you just do the latter,' Caroline said briskly. 'And try to keep your nose clean. Emma saved the day while you were hugging the toilet bowl so you owe her one. And she's got some genuinely innovative ideas to bring to the table. Since you're out of commission until tomorrow night, she's going to come in and do tonight's service. I might broach the subject of a job with her at the end of the night, if she does all right.'

Gino, realising that it was better to keep quiet, did just that, but he couldn't resist a smirk. Emma Leadbetter might be good, but he knew he was better. They'd been a year apart at college and while she was organised and a grafter, he remembered her as lacking a certain flair. He, on the other hand, fancied himself as the next Marco Pierre White; his tutors had described him as an explosive talent and he was determined that Caroline's restaurant would be the first step on a stratospheric career ladder. Perhaps, for the moment though, he'd better keep a keen eye on her; it wouldn't do to be trumped by the pub landlord's daughter.

14

The next few weeks passed largely without incident at The Cider Kitchen. Gino, true to his word, had been efficient, creative and committed and word about his inventive use of flavour was beginning to spread. Caroline had employed Emma Leadbetter on an apprentice's salary for Saturday nights, when she largely cooked to Gino's specifications, but she was beginning to branch out with her own ideas. Once Emma graduated from catering college, Caroline was hoping to offer her a more permanent job if she could afford to. Gino grudgingly admired her dogged efficiency and her methodical nature which sat well with his own flair and desire to push boundaries and take risks.

'Together, you two make the perfect chef,' Caroline remarked one evening when they had come into work together. After the opening menu they were keen to adapt and change the dishes to showcase some more seasonal produce and so had arranged to meet Caroline before the evening service. Caroline had met Jonathan a few times and thankfully he'd accepted her apology for shouting at him on opening night. He was now lounging on one of the sofas at the back of the restaurant, tie artfully askew, the sleeves of his light blue shirt rolled up, having come straight from his office on the cider farm for this meeting. He had his phone out, his attention divided as always, but as Caroline approached she was gratified to see him slip it back into his pocket.

'Thanks for the heads up on the new menu ideas, Caroline,' Jonathan said after she and Gino had outlined their new plans. 'I've also got an idea for a new theme for the autumn season.' He glanced at Emma. 'I wanted to include you, Emma, since you've proven yourself to be such a reliable asset to this place. And, Gino, despite some early issues, your menu choices have been inspired.'

Was Caroline imagining it or did Jonathan's voice have a slight edge to it when addressing Gino? She assumed it was because he was still irritated by Caroline's refusal to sack him after the opening night fiasco, or perhaps he felt embarrassed because he'd been the one who'd initially appointed Gino, but she decided to let it slide for now. 'What have you got in mind?' she asked.

'I wonder if you'd consider some suggestions for a country pursuits' based menu. As I'm sure you know, the grouse shooting season starts in August, and I'd like you two to think about how you might incorporate some game over the next few months. From October we'll have ready access to as many pheasants as you can cook and it would be good to include some on the menu, along with rabbit.'

Gino nodded, obviously keen to keep in with Jonathan. 'Of course. I've cooked some pheasant dishes before, and rabbit's pretty adaptable.'

Caroline kept silent. She was a little unnerved by the way Jonathan assumed that a blood sports themed menu was just going to happen and she wasn't entirely sure how she felt about having pheasant and grouse as options. The only time she'd tasted pheasant it had been so strong it had virtually crawled off the plate.

'I'm happy to consider the options,' she said as Gino finished outlining his ideas. 'But I do feel we ought to be concentrating on more contemporary menu choices, too. There's so much good local produce around here; do we need to hark back to field sport traditions that, frankly, would be better left in the past?'

Jonathan raised an eyebrow. 'You do know you're in the heart of Somerset, right? That tradition is basically part of the landscape? Head a mile in any direction and you're into prime hunting, shooting and fishing country.'

'I know that,' Caroline said patiently. 'But that doesn't mean we have to steep ourselves in it the whole time. Contemporary producers are springing up all over the county – look at all the artisan cheesemakers in Cheddar these days that are opening up as a response to the super dairies, and only last week I had an email from a charcutier in Wrington who wants to collaborate on some ideas. Can't we leave the hunting, shooting and fishing in the past?'

Jonathan looked thoughtful. 'I hear what you're saying, but I also know that there's a fair proportion of the population who'd love a new spin on the old heritage, too. Can you allow your chefs to put their minds to a dish or two, just to humour me?'

There was a pause so long between them it verged into the uncomfortable. Gino and Emma suddenly looked very interested in the bottoms of their cups of coffee. Eventually, Caroline spoke. 'I'll let them think about it,' she said guardedly.

Jonathan nodded. 'Good. I think there's definitely potential in the idea.'

Gino cleared his throat. 'So, er, we'll put our heads together and get back to you, shall we?' He glanced at Emma. 'Shall we head back to the kitchen and brainstorm?'

'Sure,' Emma replied. They stood up hurriedly.

Caroline looked at Jonathan, who was in turn regarding her with an expression of exasperation and amusement. 'Do you think we scared them off?'

Jonathan shrugged. 'They're young. They don't understand the importance of combative business discussion.'

Caroline bristled. 'If you think that was me being combative, you ain't seen nothing yet.'

'Perhaps now isn't the time to run the Halloween plans by you, then?'

Caroline sighed. 'How about you put it in an email?' She picked up her own coffee cup. 'Seriously, Jonathan, when I took on this project it was mostly because I was promised autonomy in terms of the menu and the direction of the creative side of the business. That is why you hired me, after all. Is this field sports menu going to be the tip of the iceberg?'

'Caroline,' Jonathan said patiently, 'I do understand, really, but there has to be a bit of give and take here. You've done a fabulous job getting this place up and running, but in order to keep people coming through the doors, we've got to keep things fresh. I know you've only been open a few weeks, but if there's one thing growing up in the cider business has taught me, it's that you've got to keep looking to the next season, the next event. In this economic climate you can't afford to rest on your laurels. I don't mean to teach my grandmother to suck eggs but you have to work with the land and its traditions a bit.'

Caroline bit her lip. 'I do understand that. I just have some reservations about which traditions would be good for the business.'

Jonathan stood up. 'Fair enough, and I'd love to discuss it further, but I've got to go. We'll have to save it for another time.' He pushed his rolled up sleeves further up to his elbows, revealing more of his suntanned forearms, and loosened his tie, undoing his top button at the same time. 'Christ, it's warm today. I miss the days when I didn't have to wear a suit to work.'

Caroline shook her head as he left. What was it about Jonathan Carter that made her simultaneously want to scream and sing?

15

That same evening, across the village at Cowslip Barn, Anna was getting the shopping in from the car. She'd had a busy day as the Little Orchard Tea Shop was in full holiday season swing. Her godmother, Ursula, who owned the tea shop, had decided to extend her sabbatical and was enjoying her semi-retirement in Umbria, leaving Anna in charge, which she loved. She fully intended, once she'd taken a year off with the new baby, to return to running the tea shop, which had been a source of great stability and a lot of pleasure when she'd moved back to Little Somerby eighteen months previously.

A lot of people, her best friend Charlotte included, had assumed that Anna would give up the tea shop when she married Little Somerby's most eligible millionaire cider farmer, but Anna had been adamant; she owed it to Ursula to remain as manager of The Little Orchard Tea Shop and it was a business she adored. The cosy little shop had been her haven, her stability, and although she'd rented out her own charming cottage and moved in with Matthew, she wasn't prepared to give up the tea shop. Matthew had understood and encouraged her to keep the business on. With Ellie nearly of school age, it would soon be easier in terms of childcare and he didn't want her to give up something that made her so happy.

Ellie had been over the moon when Anna and Matthew had broken the news to her about the new addition to the family. She'd been fascinated to see the greyish blob on the ultrasound photos after the twelve week scan, demanding instantly to know whether she was going to have a brother or a sister. Anna wasn't sure she wanted to know. Better to keep things a surprise this time round, she thought. Meredith had been somewhat quieter in response to the news, but Anna had put it down to having a lot of other things to think about as she was in the middle of her GCSE exams. She was sure that Meredith would be just as excited about a new brother or sister once the time grew closer.

Grappling with a shopping bag before it collapsed entirely, Anna dropped her car keys onto the scrubbed oak kitchen table and made a futile snatch at the bag of oranges at the top of the hessian shopper, grimacing as they escaped their netting and careered wildly across the table top. As she wandered across the kitchen, picking up the fruit as it rolled away, including one that Sefton had caught in his jaws, she noticed a new entry on the calendar stuck to the side of the fridge. This was nothing unusual; Meredith's social life was hectic and Matthew had trained her long ago that if she required a parental taxi she needed to put it on the calendar, but this entry wasn't in Meredith's looped handwriting; it was very definitely written in Matthew's hand.

Blinking in mild disbelief, Anna digested the information. She felt a sudden flip in her stomach and while she tried to put it down to pregnancy jitters she knew it wasn't quite that. She ran a finger across the entry dated next Friday, willing it, somehow, to change. Of course, it stayed put. There was no question about it; she was going to have to speak to him when he got home.

*

'Did she go down all right?' Matthew asked as Anna padded back down the stairs from putting Ellie to bed. Ellie had settled well into Cowslip Barn as her new family home but was still prone to getting up in the night and not knowing where she was. He crossed the kitchen and handed Anna a mug of tea. 'I'm sorry I was a bit later than planned. I was waiting for Jonathan to come back to me with an update on The Cider Kitchen but it must have slipped his mind.'

'She was a little restless,' Anna replied. Her daughter wasn't handling the heat wave well and would far rather bounce on her bed than sleep in it at the moment. She took the mug from Matthew and headed back to the living room. 'Are you coming to sit down?'

'Won't be a tick,' Matthew said. 'I need to give Jonno a quick call and then I'm all yours.'

'Can that wait a minute?' Anna asked, turning back towards him.

Matthew clocked his wife's expression. 'Of course. What's wrong?'

Anna drew a deep breath. 'Why is there an entry on the calendar for the St Jude's prep school open evening next week?'

Matthew looked surprised. 'I thought you might like to take Ellie up there to have a look around.'

'Why?'

Matthew raised a hand to Anna's elbow. 'I know you're having a hard time adjusting to the fact that she's going to school soon so I thought I'd take the initiative and find out when the open evening was so we could go along and check it out. I bet it's changed a lot since Meredith started and I thought you might like to see what the facilities are like.'

Anna stepped away from Matthew, trying to gather her thoughts before she spoke again. 'But... she's not *going* to St Jude's, Matthew. She's going to the village primary school. I told you that at the start of the year. I did her application back in December.'

Matthew wrinkled his brow. 'Since when?'

'Since always!' Anna's temper started to rise. 'I'd never even considered sending her to St Jude's. She's going to the village school.'

'But what about when she gets to secondary age? Don't you think the transition would be easier to manage if she's already been there for her first few years? After all, her friends will already be there.'

'I can't quite believe what I'm hearing,' Anna said carefully. 'Are you actually telling me that you've planned my daughter's entire educational future without even telling me first? What makes you think you have the right?'

'What?' The penny was starting to drop for Matthew. 'No, of course not,' he said hurriedly. 'I just assumed that with Meredith already at St Jude's, and having had such a positive experience, you'd want to send Ellie there as well. Was I wrong?'

Anna shook her head. 'Yes. Yes, Matthew, you were. Whether or not I was prepared to send her to St Jude's is one thing, but assuming that you could make decisions for my daughter without even consulting me first... I just don't know where to start. How could you even think of making that kind of decision on your own?' She could feel her temper rising further and a part of her dimly realised that this was turning out to be the milestone of their first actual disagreement of any consequence.

Matthew looked aghast. 'Anna, it's not that big a deal. Honestly. I just found out a date and wrote it on the calendar. Why are you making such a thing of it?'

'Do you really not get it?' Anna retorted. 'You're making decisions without talking things through again. You're assuming that you know best when this was something that we really needed to have a conversation about. Can you not see that?'

'I see,' Matthew replied quietly. 'So, you're saying that because she's not biologically my daughter that I have no right to think about her future? At least I know where I stand. Thank you for clarifying that so effectively.' He held her gaze for a moment longer and then walked past her.

Within moments Anna heard his study door opening and then closing quietly behind him. Letting out a long breath, she sat down with a thump on one of the kitchen chairs. That had escalated more quickly than she could have anticipated and her hands shook. Was this an indication that Matthew wasn't adapting as well to marriage as she'd thought? Taking the last orange from the split bag that was still on the table, Anna turned it over in her hands. What should she do?

16

Jonathan hadn't actually forgotten about seeing Matthew that evening but he had decided against updating him about the plans for The Cider Kitchen's autumn season straight away. He knew Matthew had bigger fish to fry with the additional paperwork that had come through for a potential takeover by Buckthorn, a huge food and drinks conglomerate which had cornered most of the international markets for cider. For once, he'd managed to pre-empt his brother and he'd actually read his copies of the paperwork a couple of days ago. He decided that now might be an opportunity to discuss things with their father. After all, Jack still had a big say in the direction of the company and it was about time they talked about its future. Grabbing his satchel from his office, he shoved his MacBook in it, locked the office door and headed back to Orchard Cottage.

It was a beautiful summer evening and he once again felt grateful to be living back in this part of the world. The sun was just on the wane and its light was reflected in the spotlessly clean shop windows on the High Street. The Little Orchard Tea Shop had closed for the night, as had most of the other businesses, but as he passed the wine shop, which was under new management, he could see Kelli, the owner, hosting one of the gin tastings that had become very popular over the past few months. Passing the large glass windows of the shop, he saw several of the locals immersed in trying some of the many new varieties of craft gin that certainly made a contrast to the mainstream brands. Perhaps spirits were something to consider as a next step for Carter's? He'd certainly look into it. They'd often considered adding a home produced calvados to their range of drinks; perhaps it was worth further thought.

As Jonathan passed the chip shop he wondered about grabbing some fish and chips for himself and Jack, but he found he wasn't that hungry. He hoped the bread he'd bought from the bakery yesterday might stretch to a cheese sandwich later, if his father hadn't had the last of it for lunch.

It had never been his plan to move back in permanently with Jack; when the FastStream deal had been in progress last summer he'd landed in Little Somerby with every intention of making peace with his brother and then flying straight out of Bristol Airport. But something had changed; after ten years of enforced absence, he'd started to feel the stirrings of passion for the heritage and history of the family business. A few weeks had stretched to months and now here he was, nine months later, still in the box room.

As he turned up the driveway to Orchard Cottage, Jonathan's thoughts drifted once again to Caroline. She was such a puzzle to him; on the one hand she seemed determined to set down roots of her own with the new job in a new location, but on the other hand she seemed so rootless. There was a story behind her dark green eyes, he knew it. Of course, he knew all about the losses she had suffered; her parents had died within six months of each other and then her brother, James, had been killed in a car accident, but Jonathan couldn't help thinking there was something more. She'd obviously been successful in the events management business and she owned her own property in Farnham, which was an expensive area of the world, so why chuck all that in and come all the way to Somerset, even with Anna and Ellie nearby? He smiled; to be fair he'd done exactly the same thing when he'd moved back to Little Somerby. Perhaps he and Caroline had more in common than he thought.

Rooting around in his pocket for his house key, Jonathan saw that the front door was slightly ajar. His thoughts immediately moved away from Caroline; Jack had been getting rather absent minded lately and he'd left the door open a few times. Jonathan felt a shard of worry in his heart.

'Are you home, Dad?' he called as he walked into the hall, clicking the front door shut firmly behind him.

'In here,' Jack's voice drifted from the conservatory that overlooked the back garden. In his later years, Jack had grown increasingly fond of his garden; he still tended the beloved rose bushes that had been planted by his late wife Cecily, and now they were in full bloom, their scents and colours permeating the early evening air. The conservatory door was open and Jack was sitting in a wicker armchair, a copy of *The Telegraph* in his hand and a glass of scotch on the small side table nearby.

'Have you eaten?' Jonathan asked as he wandered over to the open door of the conservatory.

'Had a bite to eat while I was out and about earlier,' Jack replied. In the still strong sunlight, the lines on Jack's face looked deeply etched, and Jonathan noticed, with a pang, how loose the collar of his smart checked shirt was. Jack had never been the greatest eater, although he was rather fond of a drink, but Jonathan noted with renewed worry the belt buckle done up an extra notch and the slight tremor of his father's hand as he reached for his crystal tumbler of whiskey.

'Help yourself to one if you'd like,' Jack lifted his glass. 'Plenty in the decanter on the sideboard.'

This was a familiar ritual for the two of them and Jonathan enjoyed the time they spent together this way. He'd missed his father more than he could have imagined possible during his enforced absence from Little Somerby, and although they'd kept in touch regularly by phone, they'd only seen each other face to face a few times over the years when Jack had travelled over to the US on business. Pouring himself a small whiskey, he headed back to the conservatory and sat in the other wicker chair.

'Good day?' Jack asked.

'Busy,' Jonathan replied. 'The new equipment was being installed in the keggery, and there were a few bumps on the way. And there's a problem with one of the associate apple growers in Chew Magna, which needs sorting,' he shook his head. 'I'm still getting used to the day to day stuff.' He paused momentarily. 'Then there's the Buckthorn issue, of course.'

Jack shook his head. 'Not tonight, Jonathan. It's too lovely an evening to spend it arguing about the business.'

'We're going to have to discuss it some time,' Jonathan said. His tone was light; he knew when not to push things. 'Even if not tonight.'

'We will,' Jack said. 'But it wouldn't be fair without your brother round the table too. Let's just enjoy this evening, shall we?' He drained his scotch and passed his glass to Jonathan. 'Another one, son, if you wouldn't mind.'

Sighing inwardly, Jonathan took both glasses back through to the sideboard in the living room. Jack couldn't avoid Buckthorn forever, but it seemed he was determined to for tonight at least.

17

After half an hour curled up on the sofa watching mindless television with Sefton's head in her lap, Anna couldn't stand the tension any longer. She wandered down the hallway to Matthew's study and only just stopped herself from knocking on the door. Sometimes, she still had to remind herself that she was no longer a guest in this house; that she was now an equal partner in Matthew's life.

Matthew sat gazing intently at his laptop. The glass reading lamp to his right cast a dull glow across the leather top of the mahogany desk and Matthew's eyes were crinkled in concentration as he looked at the screen.

'You really should be wearing your reading glasses,' Anna chided gently, motioning to the discarded pair to the left of the desk. 'You'll get a headache.'

Matthew looked away from the screen, his expression pensive. 'You're right,' he said softly. 'I suppose I just don't want to admit it.'

'Am I?' Anna asked. She crossed the carpeted floor of the study and wandered around to the other side of the desk. Then she burst out laughing. There, on Matthew's screen, was an animation of dancing yellow Minions, all doing the can can with varying measures of success.

Matthew smiled ruefully. 'I couldn't concentrate.' He swivelled his chair to look up at her and, hesitating just for a second, reached out and drew Anna towards him, resting his head against her just emerging baby bump. 'I'm sorry. You're right. It was stupid of me.' His voice was muffled against her and as he pulled back his eyes were full of remorse. 'I suppose I got so used to making the decisions as a single parent, it's taking me some time to get used to talking things through with someone else again. But you're right. I shouldn't have made enquiries without discussing it with you first. I love Ellie, but she's your daughter, and it's your decision.'

Anna shook her head. 'I over reacted. You were only doing what you thought was best. I should have been able to talk it through rationally with you instead of jumping to conclusions. I'm sorry.'

Matthew rose from his chair and enfolded his wife in his arms. 'I made an assumption. But, for what it's worth, I genuinely thought you'd be pleased that I'd thought about St Jude's for Ellie. It is a great school and Merry's been very happy there.'

Anna relaxed into Matthew's embrace, luxuriating in his warmth and closeness and feeling weak with relief. 'I know she has. And it's not that I have any great issue with private education. It's just that I thought it would be nice to send her to the village school where Evan and her friends from nursery will be. Not to mention that the fees for St Jude's are the equivalent of a mortgage for the next thirteen or so years, especially now the school leaving age has gone up.'

Matthew shook his head. 'It's not like we can't afford it.'

'I know,' Anna replied. 'And believe me, when I married you I absolutely knew you would be the perfect stepfather for Ellie but it still freaks me out, the prospect of you shelling out all of that money for her education. Especially when there's an Ofsted outstanding primary school right on the doorstep.'

'Now who's been doing her homework?' Matthew grinned briefly.

'Not exactly,' Anna admitted. 'Charlotte's been keeping an eye on the place for a while, and she thinks it's fine.'

'Fair enough,' Matthew said. 'But if the money's the only thing you're worrying about, then stop. I know you didn't marry me for my money and if you wanted to send Ellie to a private school, I'd happily pay for it.'

Anna smiled. 'Thank you. But let's just think about it for a while, shall we? Perhaps we can take a look at St Jude's in our own time. And there's always later, if she chooses to; I mean, the comprehensive school in Churchill is pretty good too, but if she really wants to make that choice later, then she can.'

'Agreed,' Matthew said. He sighed. 'I think it's going to take me a while to adjust to marriage again.'

'Oh, I don't know,' Anna said softly. 'I think you're doing pretty well, really.'

'Really?'

Anna leaned down and planted a lingering kiss on Matthew's lips. 'Definitely.'

As they broke free once more, Matthew's eyes were dark with desire. 'Is Ellie still asleep?' he asked huskily.

Anna nodded. 'Out like a light. And Meredith's in her room reading one of her set texts for September.' She'd checked on her step daughter about ten minutes previously, and from the level of the sound emanating from Meredith's headphones, she wasn't going to be easily disturbed. If, by chance, Anna did hear movement from upstairs, she and Matthew had both perfected the art of parental nonchalance over the years. Having children tended to make you a master of stealth.

Matthew smiled and slid his hands from his wife's back down over her hips and further, dipping his head at the same time to kiss the side of her neck just underneath her ear. 'That's very good news.'

Anna felt herself responding to his warm hands and even warmer mouth, and shivered as his breath caressed her neck and his feather light kisses enflamed her senses. She sighed. 'You are very, very good at that.'

'So, are you sure you forgive me?' Matthew murmured against the curve of her shoulder, nibbling gently at her collar bone before raising his head to brush her lips with his own once more.

'I think so,' Anna whispered. 'Especially if you keep doing that.' Matthew lifted her up and sat her on his desk, standing between her thighs and continuing to kiss her. His hands wandered to her shoulders and slipped down the sleeves of her cardigan, the spaghetti straps of her vest top and her bra straps. Dropping his mouth once again to her shoulders, he moved down to her breasts, larger now from her pregnancy, giving them the most gentle of caresses. Fingertips were shortly followed by a probing tongue and a warm, gentle mouth.

'What do you reckon our chances are of not disturbing them?' Matthew murmured between kisses and licks.

'Keep doing that and I won't care,' Anna said, arching her back to allow him further access to her body.

'You are so sexy, Mrs Carter,' Matthew's husky voice had a seductive West Country burr that sent a shiver down Anna's spine. 'Now let me get inside you and show you what you do to me.'

Anna wriggled out of her knickers and hitched up her denim skirt and Matthew slipped inside her. He began to move, lazy, long thrusts that reminded her exactly why she could never go too long without thinking about him. The exquisite sensation aroused her senses even further, until she was on the brink of a tingling, throbbing orgasm which broke with a warmth and a pulse that made her already weak knees turn to water. Gripping him tightly, she felt him lose himself and for several moments afterwards, they stayed joined.

'I don't think the desk has ever been used for that before,' Matthew mused, a broad smile on his face.

'Nice to know we're the first,' Anna teased back. Both of them had got used to the fact that there were some experiences that were bound to cross over, second time around, but Anna was secretly pleased she'd not been second to this particular scenario.

'Although I can't be sure my father didn't indulge when he was more sprightly,' Matthew teased. Jack was known for his love of the ladies and Anna couldn't help but giggle, disturbing as the image was.

'Is there anything in this house that doesn't come with at least fifty years of history?' Anna teased.

'Me. For a little while yet,' Matthew replied, quick as a flash.

And with that, they decided to make an early night of it.

18

Despite having left education well over a decade ago, September brought with it that all too familiar back to school feeling for Caroline. The Cider Kitchen's summer season had been a success and, despite her reservations about putting game on the menu, it had gone down well with customers. After Ian Smith's review for the *Somerset Herald*, which stuck to the facts and was surprisingly positive, given his confrontation with Caroline, several other reviewers had come to The Cider Kitchen, including the much read and lauded food journalist from the *Bristol Post,* Mark Taylor. He'd given The Cider Kitchen a very commendable four out of five stars, which Caroline knew was definitely something to shout about. The subsequent article had been cut out, framed and placed behind the bar and Caroline had put it on the restaurant's website, too.

Gino and Emma were going from strength to strength and had come up with some superb new dishes to keep the menus fresh. Emma had accepted a part time position at the restaurant when her course finished, but since they were still only doing about twenty-five covers a night, she was working at The Stationmaster the rest of the time. Caroline's plan was to train her as front of house for the lunchtime service with a view to handing over the reins one night a week or perhaps even taking a few days off at some point, but at the moment she didn't have the budget to hire her full time. The pheasant and venison dishes now sat alongside some delectable local options that included cured meat from Caroline's new charcutier contact in Wrington, an artisan cheeseboard from a supplier in Cheddar (with the obligatory Carters' Cider chutney cooked by Gino, on the side, of course), and mouth watering free range pork from Sid Porter the well known Gloucester Old Spot breeder in the village. The restaurant opened for service every lunchtime, but was closed on a Sunday evening, and Caroline was learning quickly how to plan the staff rotas so that no-one was overstretched. She herself was present for every service at the moment, but hoped to be able to take a full day off when things had bedded in a little further.

It was all going so well in fact, that Caroline, as was her tendency, began to wonder what was going to happen to derail it. She'd always had a fairly fatalistic outlook and the events of the past few years hadn't done much to change that. She wasn't used to feeling so optimistic, albeit cautiously, as the leaves began to turn and the cider apples began to hang heavily on the trees.

At the moment, the restaurant was opening at eleven o'clock in the morning, then closing for two hours at four, before opening again at six for the evening service. Bookings were steady, which was a relief as, tucked away behind the Royal Orchard, The Cider Kitchen wasn't visible from the main road running through Little Somerby. This particular Thursday, there had been a full complement of covers for lunch, and she had nearly all the tables booked for the evening. She still had to refine the restauranteur's art of 'turning tables' more quickly but things were developing nicely.

After having the game menu sprung on her, Caroline had arranged to meet Jonathan twice a week, usually in the hour or so before the evening service started. It was better to schedule in a regular meeting than have him just turning up, she thought. She was, by nature, a compartmentaliser, and whether Jonathan liked it or not, she had put him in a pigeon hole firmly marked 'business' and not pleasure.

Caroline glanced at her watch; Jonathan was due in ten minutes but he was often early. She caught sight of her reflection in the mirror behind the bar and, irritated with herself for caring, decided to nip upstairs and run a brush through her hair before he arrived. She'd had it cut a week ago and it was still not quite what she wanted it to be. At the moment, it was sticking out in all directions as she'd not had the chance to put her straighteners on it that morning. Vowing not to make too much of an effort, she'd just reached the door of her flat when she heard the restaurant door open. Cursing, she turned round and headed back towards the stairs.

Having the advantage, for once, of height, Caroline took a moment to observe Jonathan as he crossed the floor and took a seat at one of the tables by the bar. He was, as usual, dressed in an impeccably cut suit, this time in a shade of cobalt blue that would have looked ostentatious on anyone else, but worked irritatingly well with his colouring. She could just see the collar of a blue checked shirt above his jacket; doubtless a nod to his so-called country heritage, she thought. He glanced around, clearly unaware of her scrutiny from the mezzanine and then looked at his watch. *Cheeky sod,* Caroline thought. He was early, after all. Taking a deep breath, she walked back down the stairs.

'Hi Jonathan,' she said brightly. 'How are you?'

Jonathan rose from his chair as Caroline approached. She was reluctantly charmed by his old school chivalry. Perhaps all privately educated schoolboys were taught manners along with their other subjects, she thought.

'Good to see you,' Jonathan replied. 'Have I caught you on the hop?' He looked back up from whence she'd come.

'Not at all,' Caroline said. 'I was just, er, checking I'd turned my straighteners off.'

Jonathan raised an eyebrow but said nothing. Caroline cursed at being caught out in such an obvious lie, given the state of her hair.

'Anyway. Shall we?' she asked, sitting back down on the chair opposite him.

'Of course.' Jonathan looked as though he was about to say something else but thought better of it. 'How's trade been this week?'

A couple of minutes of pleasantries followed and Jonathan expressed his approval at the figures for the week. They were looking good, as well they should, and the long term projections were sound. Most restaurants were make or break in the first year, but with Carter's as the backer, they both hoped The Cider Kitchen would continue to thrive.

'So, have you got any more promotional ideas for the rest of the autumn and winter seasons, then?' Jonathan asked once the financial discussions had concluded. Unselfconscious as a cat, he stretched his arms above his head.

Caroline tore her gaze away from Jonathan's bare wrists and took a breath. 'Well, Halloween's coming up so I thought we might run a small event for that.

Nothing too cheesy,' she said hastily as Jonathan's eyes lit up. 'Just a special menu and a few spiders' webs on the ceiling or something.'

'Sounds good,' Jonathan replied. 'I know the witch of Wookey Hole personally if you'd like her to do an appearance,' he raised an eyebrow.

I bet you do, Caroline thought. She never knew when to take him seriously. 'And then of course, come November we'll be into the run up to Christmas. Gino and Emma are already putting their minds to a menu for that so we can publicise it in the next week or two.' She glanced at her notebook, which she'd grabbed from behind the bar. 'I'm planning on contacting the usual local papers and putting in some adverts for that. Perhaps we could make the Halloween event ticket only, though; sell some exclusivity.'

'I like your thinking,' Jonathan said. 'And I reckon we could get some cider punch into the menu, too. We're working on something at the moment. And then of course there's the meet for the local hunt in mid November.'

Caroline stopped writing in her notebook. 'Come again?' She raised her head to meet his gaze levelly. 'I think I misheard you.'

'The Old Somerset Hunt have asked us if we'd host a pre-ride meet out the front of the restaurant. They're prepared to pay a reasonable price for some mulled cider and posh canapés before they set off. And it'll bring in the locals to gawp, as well.'

'A hunt as in a fox hunt?' Caroline was shaking her head before Jonathan could even finish. 'No.' She shook her head. 'Absolutely not.'

Jonathan looked puzzled. 'What's the problem? There's plenty of room outside for them to park their horse boxes and all you need to do is get Gino to whip up a few dozen pigs in blankets and a vat of mulled cider, which we'll supply anyway, and bob's your uncle.'

Caroline stood up abruptly from her chair, the wooden legs of it squeaking harshly on the stone floor. 'Putting pheasant on the menu for a few weeks was one thing – at least those birds had better lives than a lot of battery hens, but I don't agree with the principle of fox hunting. It's like asking this place to host a dog fight.'

Jonathan let out an exasperated sigh. 'Oh, that's right,' he said. 'I forgot that as a confirmed townie, you know everything there is to know about the ethics and practices of what is actually now drag hunting. Forgive me.'

His sarcasm didn't go down well with Caroline. 'What, just because I don't have a fourth generation countryside pedigree like you, I'm not allowed an opinion?'

'Not at all,' Jonathan replied. 'I just didn't expect you to hold such a misinformed one.'

'Oh, come on!' Caroline retorted. 'I know enough to know that even now foxes get chased across fields and I don't like it. You'll be telling me you ride with the Old Somerset Hunt next.' She was further irritated as a vision of Jonathan in a hunting coat and jodhpurs looking dashing atop a huge stallion popped into her mind. She'd read enough Jilly Cooper novels to find that a pleasant image even if she fundamentally disagreed with it.

'Not me, but Merry's been riding with them since she was ten.'

'Are you serious?' Caroline felt sick. She liked Meredith and she was a very good waitress, too. 'How can she justify it?' Meredith was such a kind, compassionate soul, who loved her animals madly. Caroline couldn't square that with the notion of the girl hunting.

'It's good for the horses,' Jonathan said. 'And the Old Somerset hasn't seen hide nor hair of a fox in years. Most of the members of the hunt are in their fifties with a smattering of younger riders like Merry who use it as a good run for their animals. They're hardly blooding each other with brushes any more, you know.'

'It's the principle, Jonathan!' Caroline said. 'I've always hated the idea of rich, over privileged country toffs cutting up the countryside and ripping innocent foxes to pieces for fun. And now you're asking me to host a frigging meet for them?'

Caroline's hair reminded Jonathan of a young fox and the colour in her cheeks as she argued was just the right side of clashing with it. He felt a stab of lust. But, attractive or not, she was still being bloody stubborn.

'Caroline,' he said softly, changing tack. 'It's good exposure for this place. Your takings are fine but we want to get the ball really rolling. Matthew's keen to host this meet to pull in more of the public; it's a village tradition and it'll bring the punters in to drink and eat.' He risked a quick smile at her. 'I know you've got your principles, but if I can convince you that the hunt isn't this barbaric bunch of inbred monsters you think it is, will you at least consider it?'

Caroline was caught off guard by Jonathan's sudden calmness. 'You won't change my mind, Jonathan. I don't agree with hunting with hounds, drag or not, at all. And what about Scrumpy and Solly? Those gigantic monster dogs'll probably rip them to pieces if they catch sight of them.' Caroline glanced up at the mezzanine where the tortoiseshell kittens were snuggled in their basket, fast asleep.

'Surely you can shut them in your flat for a couple of hours with a litter tray and a pouch of that posh food you insist on feeding them?' Jonathan said.

'They'll be perfectly safe up there. If I can arrange a meeting with Rob Kelloway the hunt master, will you go and see his hounds? He'll put it in context better than I can. What do you think?'

Caroline felt like she was being pushed in a direction she definitely didn't want to go; but she also knew that she had to at least give Jonathan the chance to negotiate. 'All right. I'll go and see the master and his undomesticated pack of dogs.' She picked up a smudged glass from one of the tables nearby. 'Now, if you don't mind, I've got tonight's service to prepare for.'

Jonathan smiled to himself as he got up from the table. 'I'll see you soon,' he said as he walked towards the front door.

'Not if I see you first,' Caroline replied mutinously. As she turned back to the kitchen to consult the diary, she wondered yet again why she'd allowed herself to be talked into something by Jonathan. The man had the most irritating way of getting her to question her principles; it was becoming a habit she knew she needed to break.

19

Anna, although still managing the tea shop during the day, had also started researching the Carter family's history in the evenings. As a former academic librarian specialising in historical documents she'd had extensive experience in handling and cataloguing papers of special interest, and knowing that Matthew's family had a collection relating to the history of the family and the business that included both personal and commercial documents, she had been itching to go through them. Most of them had been somewhat haphazardly stored in tea chests and suitcases in the attic for at least as long as Matthew had been alive. She was gradually going through them in the evenings when Ellie was in bed, trying to get the information into some kind of sensible chronological order. So far, she'd got four box files on the go, one for each generation, and despite being side tracked by some old photographs that showed the current Carter brothers bore a striking resemblance to their cider making forebears, she was starting to get a clearer picture of who was related to whom.

This was how Matthew found her as he walked into the kitchen on a September evening. She'd been poring over the documents for a little while, since Ellie had gone to bed, and she smiled as he came through the back door.

'There's some pretty interesting stuff here,' Anna said. She'd spread the most recent papers that Matthew had unearthed across the kitchen table and was gradually sorting them into more logical piles. 'How much do you know about how your great grandfather, Samuel, got started in cider making?'

'A bit,' Matthew replied. 'Although, to be honest, he wasn't the greatest record keeper. My great grandmother kept a few journals which it looks as though you've managed to locate already, and there were a few letters, as well as invoices to and from suppliers.'

'There's a bit more than that,' Anna replied. She passed him a sheet of paper, yellowed with age and written in a close hand. 'This was tucked inside your great grandmother Elsie's last diary. It's a letter from your great aunt Jane.'

'My grandfather's younger sister?' Matthew squinted at the paper, reluctant to reach for his newly prescribed reading glasses. He held it slightly further away, strategically ignoring Anna's brief smirk at the action. As he read, his mouth dropped open in astonishment.

'Does this suggest what I think it does?' He said eventually, handing the paper back to her.

'Well, Jane did spend some time away from home when she turned eighteen – that much I can trace from the other letters to and from her and Elsie.'

'This suggests that Jane had a child before she married my great uncle Hugh. But there's never been any mention of it – Dad's never mentioned anything about having any cousins other than Jane and Hugh's children.'

'Perhaps Jane never told Hugh when she married him,' Anna mused. 'After all, in those days unmarried mothers would have very limited options. Unfortunately, I haven't come across any other papers that might shed light on what happened to the child, but adoption records weren't great back then, either.'

'Is there any clue as to who the father might have been?' Matthew asked.

'Not exactly, but I have found some newspaper clippings about a man in his twenties being found face down in one of the vats at around about the same time as the letter from Jane. It would be easy to just tie the two sources together, but I can't really do that without more evidence.'

'But if there was a link, that means that the man's death might not have been an accident.' Matthew grimaced. 'I'm beginning to think that getting you to archive the family history wasn't such a good idea after all.'

'Every family has their secrets,' Anna replied. 'And four generations are bound to throw up some interesting facts. I wouldn't get too worked up about it until I've spent a bit more time looking into it all.'

'And to think all this scandal has been sitting in the loft for decades! I wonder if we should have left it there. It all feels a bit Pandora's Box, now. Although…' a naughty, schoolboyish grin spread over his features, 'that gives me an idea.'

Anna, who was beginning to realise that Matthew's grin usually meant the best kind of trouble, smiled. 'What have you got in mind?'

'How do you think Caroline would feel about hosting our annual suppliers' dinner at The Cider Kitchen? She's got such an amazing track record in events management, I think she'd be the perfect choice.'

'I think she'd probably jump at it,' Anna said. 'She's always looking for ways to prove the restaurant's worth to the wider business and this would be a good way to do it.'

'And how would you feel about putting all of this research to dramatic use?'

Anna looked baffled. 'How?'

'Well,' Matthew slid an arm around his wife, 'it seems a shame just to file it all away again. What if we did some kind of theme for the suppliers' dinner?'

He looked thoughtful. 'We could even make it a murder mystery evening.'

'Are you serious?' Anna laughed. 'A second ago you were trying to sweep all of this potential scandal under the carpet and now you want to make a play out of it?'

'Why not?' Matthew said. 'It's better than having it mouldering away in the attic for another few decades. Do you reckon you could come up with the bare bones of a story that we could put together? Doesn't have to be much, just a broad sketch of the history and then the gruesome mystery of the body in the vat.'

'I'll have a think,' Anna said. She'd be up against it with the baby due in early December and working more or less full time at the tea shop, but she was never one to refuse a challenge. And there was no doubt that her academic mind was itching to continue with the archiving project. How hard could it be to come up with a murder mystery play for a dinner? After all, most of the guests would be half cut on cider by the end anyway.

'Let me know what you can come up with,' Matthew said. 'And I'll ask Jonathan to discuss it with Caroline. It would be good to have the drinks reception on site and then head over to The Cider Kitchen for the meal after the play, don't you think?'

'I'm sure she'll be happy to sort that end of things out,' Anna replied. And then, something else struck her. She suddenly remembered the small pencil sketch that Caroline had done of Ellie when she was just days old. Perhaps she wouldn't mind getting her sketch book out again for a special addition to the evening? It would be lovely to have some sketches of the Carter ancestors, or even the current generation, to perhaps auction off at the end of the evening. She'd see if she could catch her soon and ask.

'Just try to make sure that you gloss over anything you find that's too scandalous or unsavoury,' Matthew said. 'We don't really want anyone ripping up their contracts because of a bit of over ripe history!'

Anna smiled again. 'Let's not jump to conclusions. There's a way to go yet before I can confirm anything on the story anyway. It just throws some interesting light on the family ghost story at this stage. After all, didn't you once threaten to chuck Flynn in the cider vats if he upset Merry?'

'I suppose,' Matthew conceded. He pulled out his phone from his jacket pocket and frowned. 'Has she phoned you tonight, by the way? My battery's flat.'

'Yes, I spoke to her earlier. She said yours kept going to voice mail. She's going to be late back from Flynn's – he's off to university at the weekend so they're spending as much time together as they can before he goes.' Meredith had just started her A Level courses after a spectacular set of GCSE results and both Anna and Matthew had high hopes that she'd be making her own application to Oxbridge next year.

'Again?' Matthew frowned. 'I wish she'd start to realise that schoolwork still comes first. And I'm sure he's got plenty of organising to do, too. Alone.'

'She'll be OK,' Anna said. 'She was super organised during her GCSEs, and she's got into good habits, workwise, already.' Anna was relieved that Meredith was such a good student; she'd had visions of having to nag and cajole her to work, when in actual fact the girl was almost likely to overdo it. Meredith had been a little withdrawn over the summer holiday, but Anna had put this down to wanting to spend as much time with Flynn as possible before he left for university. She resolved to make some time to spend with her stepdaughter before school really got into full swing. Ellie had started primary school this month, too, so Anna was pleased she could focus her energies on helping her young daughter adapt to the new routine. She put the papers back down on the table and crossed the kitchen floor to Matthew's side. 'Merry's got her father's work ethic.'

'I hope not!' Matthew laughed darkly. 'I've not been the best role model for how to handle stress.'

'You're learning,' Anna said. 'And remember, Jonathan's here now to take the pressure off.'

'I know,' Matthew sighed. 'But old habits die hard. And he's been a bit distracted lately. I think his interest in The Cider Kitchen might be more than professional.'

'Really? That's taken you long enough to work out.'

'He swears blind he's keeping things above board but he can't seem to stay away.'

'So Caroline keeps telling me,' Anna said. 'And she's pretending to be irritated by it, but really, I think she quite likes it.'

'Well, they'd better keep things professional,' Matthew said. 'I don't think the customers will appreciate having crockery thrown over their heads.'

'I honestly don't think he wants to step on her toes. And something tells me that the fact Caroline's getting on really well with Gino might be rattling him a bit, too, although he'd never admit as much.'

'I imagine it might be.' He pulled Anna round to face him, away from the piles of papers on the kitchen table. 'But I don't want to talk about Jonno. Come here.' Taking her in his arms, he dropped a long, lingering kiss on her lips.

Anna slid her hands up inside Matthew's untucked shirt and felt him lean in in response to her. 'Fine by me,' she murmured, all thoughts of family history forgotten for the moment.

20

'Is everything OK?' Caroline asked, as she and Meredith set the tables for the evening's service. 'You seem a little quieter than usual.'

Meredith looked up from the place she was setting and gave Caroline a brief smile but it didn't quite reach her eyes. 'I'm fine. A bit tired, I guess.'

'Schoolwork getting heavy?'

'Something like that.' Meredith dropped her eyes to the table again. Caroline was an excellent reader of people and she knew exactly when something was amiss with a colleague; it was part of what made her such an effective manager. Meredith's A Level courses were in full swing now and Caroline wondered if perhaps the stress was starting to tell on her. The jump from GCSE to A Level was a big one, even for a bright student like Meredith. Caroline needed her team to be at their best during service, but more than that, she wanted them to be as settled as possible in their roles, so she decided to do a little probing.

'Come and grab a hot chocolate with me. We've got a new brand in that I could do with testing, and there's time before the others arrive.' Meredith was always punctual for her shifts but recently she'd been coming in earlier and earlier. Caroline had noticed this for a couple of weeks but hadn't pushed Meredith on it; to be truthful she was grateful for the extra help.

Meredith finished laying out the handful of cutlery she was holding and followed Caroline to the bar. Caroline observed her as she sat on one of the stools on the other side. She looked tired and a little fidgety, and more and more like there was something on her mind. This would be a tricky one to navigate; on the one hand, Caroline had concerns as Meredith's employer; but on the other, she was virtually family, being Anna's new stepdaughter. She'd have to tread carefully.

'Is everything OK?' Caroline asked, handing her a cup of steaming hot chocolate.

Meredith took a sip, clearly trying to compose her thoughts. 'Not really,' she conceded.

'Anything I can help with?'

'Promise you won't say anything to Dad or Anna?'

'If there's something worrying you, I can do my best to help,' Caroline said. She was wary of promising absolute confidentiality; the affairs of teenagers could be complex at the best of times. She hoped to god Meredith wasn't going to tell her she was pregnant. She didn't know how serious things were between Meredith and her boyfriend, but she could hazard a guess that, since they'd been together a while, things might be heading in that direction.

'It seems so silly,' Meredith said. 'And really, I thought I'd be fine with it, but…'

'What is it, Merry?'

Meredith took a deep breath. 'It's the baby.'

Caroline bit her tongue before she blurted out what she'd been thinking and hoped it was the new addition to the family Meredith was talking about. 'What about the baby?'

'I know it's stupid,' Meredith confessed. 'But I feel like it's taken over everything at home and it hasn't even been born yet. The other day, when me and Anna were supposed to be shopping in Bristol for a dress for the sixth form Christmas party, Anna dashed off to pick up a few things for the baby and left me to go round the shops by myself. I was really looking forward to seeing what she thought of the dresses I found, but by the time she came back the parking ticket had nearly run out and we had to go home. Dad's been rushed off his feet again at work because he hates delegating to Uncle Jonathan, and when he is at home all he and Anna can talk about is Ellie's first term at school and this stupid murder mystery evening.' She shook her head. 'I'm sorry. I know that's going to be a really big deal for The Cider Kitchen.'

'No problem,' Caroline said, surprised at just how much Meredith was confiding in her.

'I know it sounds selfish,' Meredith continued, 'but it feels like neither of them has even asked me about my life for months, except to nag me to get some more work done.'

Caroline regarded Meredith sympathetically. 'It's a big change for all of you,' she said, 'and it's going to take a while to get used to. My brother James once told me that when Mum and Dad broke the news to him about Mum being pregnant with me, he trashed his train set and threw his favourite teddy out of the car window on the motorway! Mind you, he was only little.' She took another sip of her hot chocolate, which was rich, velvety and definitely going on the menu. 'You're nearly seventeen and about to start a whole new chapter of your life; it's only natural that you want to feel as though they're interested in that. And I know that they are, it's just that they're so new to being married and with a baby in the picture too, they probably feel a bit overwhelmed themselves.' It couldn't have been easy for Meredith either, Caroline thought, sharing her father with a new wife, a stepsister and soon a new baby. No wonder she was feeling pushed out.

'I guess,' Meredith said. 'And it has all happened really quickly. What with Flynn going away to Oxford as well, I just feel like no-one's really got time to listen to me at the moment. All he can talk about is his reading list, what he should take with him, what it's going to be like. I don't want him to forget about me, either.' She blinked furiously and stared down into her mug.

Caroline smiled. 'I'm sure he won't,' she said gently. 'He's got a lot on, too. Look, why don't you try to get some time alone with your dad and Anna? I'm sure they'd want to know how you're feeling. Perhaps the three of you could go out to dinner, catch up with each other away from the house and the day to day stress. I could babysit Ellie for the evening so you can talk uninterrupted if you like.'

'Would you?' Meredith looked hopeful. 'That would be great. I know it sounds stupid, but I want to be able to talk to them about *my* stuff for a change, like we used to.'

Caroline could see that Meredith was having trouble adjusting to her new family setup, much as she also liked it. 'I'm sure they'd love to do that. Why don't you sort out a date and let me know? Give me a bit of notice so I can arrange some cover in this place, though.'

'Thanks, Caroline,' Meredith said, looking much happier than she had a few minutes ago. 'It's good to get that off my chest.'

'No problem.' Caroline took the cups off the bar. 'Now, we'd better get these into the dishwasher and finish setting up before the first bookings arrive.' She walked through to the kitchen, feeling hopeful that she'd put Meredith's mind at rest. She'd enjoy babysitting Ellie, anyway. One of the nice things about living in Little Somerby was seeing more of her niece, although she'd not seen as much of her as she'd have liked recently since The Cider Kitchen had been so busy. At least babysitting her for an evening would give her a little more time with her.

*

As good as her word, and taking her first Friday night off since the restaurant opened, a couple of weeks later Caroline leaned back against the soft fabric of the living room sofa at Cowslip Barn and finally started to relax. Ellie was curled up next to her, blonde head resting on her lap. The four year old had lost the battle against sleep during the last twenty minutes of her current favourite film, '*Hotel Transylvania 2*'. Much to Caroline's relief, the film had turned out to have enough in jokes for an adult viewer not to get bored and a rather good soundtrack, so she'd allowed Ellie to stay up a little later than Anna had suggested and watch the whole thing. After performing an impromptu dance routine to a few of the musical numbers in the film, followed by a bellyful of cheesecake that Caroline had brought over from the restaurant, the little girl had lost the battle and crashed out. Caroline knew she ought to carry Ellie upstairs but she was enjoying being snuggled on the sofa with her and was reluctant to risk waking her. As the film ended and the credits rolled she shifted on the sofa, reaching for the remote control and trying not to disturb Ellie. She was quite tired herself and was starting to doze off when a voice came drifting through from the kitchen. Caroline switched off the DVD as Jonathan appeared at the living room door.

'Ssh,' Caroline whispered, putting a finger to her lips and then pointing to Ellie.

'Sorry,' Jonathan mouthed, a gentle smile on his face as he caught sight of his step niece.

'It's OK,' Caroline stroked Ellie's hair back from her face. 'I should probably take her up to bed anyway.'

'Do you need a hand?' Jonathan asked.

'No thanks, I can manage,' Caroline said, standing up and gathering the snoozing child into her arms. 'But if you like you can put the kettle on.' Ellie mumbled in protest but then snuggled down onto her shoulder and drifted back off again. 'I won't be a minute.'

Caroline mounted the stairs to Ellie's bedroom and only then realised she hadn't actually asked Jonathan what he wanted. Settling the little girl into bed with her favourite toy rabbit, she pulled the bedroom door nearly closed and then headed back down the stairs.

Jonathan had boiled the kettle and was pouring water into two mugs when she padded through to the kitchen.

'Did she go down all right?' he asked, handing Caroline a mug of tea once he'd added some milk.

Caroline smiled. 'She was knackered. She'd treated me to a recital of all of her best dance moves before watching the film.'

'Sounds cute.'

'It was.' Caroline sipped her tea. 'It's nice to spend a bit of one on one time with her. I've been so busy with the restaurant lately, I've almost forgotten why I chose to move here in the first place.'

'What, it's not just because some handsome cider farmer made you a decent job offer?' Jonathan quipped, sipping his own tea.

'Well, there was that,' Caroline conceded. 'Were you after Matthew? He, Anna and Merry have gone out to dinner.'

'I'm glad they're spending a bit of time together,' Jonathan said. 'I've been so busy I haven't seen much of Merry lately and I do worry that she's going to find A Levels stressful.'

Caroline wondered if she should let Jonathan know about the conversation she'd had with

Meredith. After all, the two were close, and he did seem concerned. But should she break Meredith's confidence? Erring on the side of caution, she settled for, 'she's working very hard and she did mention she felt a bit left out of Flynn's university excitement. Hopefully Anna and Matthew can put her mind at rest.'

'She likes you enough to admit that,' Jonathan said. 'And she's an excellent judge of character so I'd be flattered.'

Caroline blushed. 'Thanks. She's so lovely, I just didn't like seeing her so down. And as her manager, I need her to be as happy and settled as she can be.'

'I'm sure she appreciated the friendly ear,' Jonathan said. 'I knew you'd be great with your staff. You've got a knack of getting the best out of people.'

'Not everyone,' Caroline said unguardedly, thinking of one person in particular from her recent past. 'I mean… sometimes all you have to do is listen.' She put her empty mug down on the table. 'Which is why I meant to ask before we sat down – was there something you wanted?'

'Doesn't matter, it can wait until tomorrow,' Jonathan said. 'I was just going through the paperwork for something and wanted to check a couple of things with the boss.'

'You, working in the evenings? Will wonders never cease? All work and no play and all that.'

'There don't seem to be enough hours in the day at the moment,' Jonathan sighed, putting down his own mug and leaning back in his chair. 'But things have been busy lately. We're looking for new orchards all the time, and as the business grows, so does the territory we cover. Along with the growing sites we own, we work closely with landowners who want to retain ownership of their own orchards rather than sell them to us, and sometimes that can lead to some wrangling about how best to maintain them.' He smiled apologetically. 'I'm sorry, this isn't exactly exciting, is it? I bet you've been rushed off your feet, too, although it's great that The Cider Kitchen is doing so well.'

Caroline nodded. 'It has been quite hectic, but I'm glad. I think word's spreading. We're fully booked for the next four weeks and already taking bookings for Christmas functions.'

'That's great. So who's in charge tonight, if you're here?' Jonathan asked.

'Emma's covering front of house. She seems really keen to learn about the front end as well as the kitchen side of things, so I thought I'd let her take the lead for a few hours tonight. She's got amazing backup from the rest of the team and I've left her with instructions and my mobile number, so she'll be fine.'

'I like that you've got such confidence in her,' Jonathan said. 'She's the kind of asset that should be looked after – we need as many good people as we can get to keep the restaurant turning over well.' He put his tea mug down on the table. 'But it definitely wouldn't be working half so well without you in charge.'

'Careful,' Caroline smiled. 'That was almost a compliment.'

'You know me,' Jonathan said. 'Praise where it's due.'

They sat in companionable silence for a moment or two. Then, with an air of reluctance, Jonathan stood up. 'I should probably head back.'

'You can stay and keep me company if you want,' Caroline said. 'Matthew, Anna and Merry will be back soon.'

'Thanks, lovely, but I told Dad I wouldn't be long.' A shadow crossed Jonathan's features. 'He had a bit of a funny turn last night; he's claiming he's taking his heart medication properly but when I checked the packets this morning he'd skipped a couple of doses. Denied all knowledge when I asked him about it.'

'Oh dear,' Caroline responded. 'I hope he'll be OK. Let me know if I can do anything to help.'

'Thanks,' Jonathan said, then brightened. 'The copy of the picture of me, him and Matthew really cheered him up when he saw it. Thanks for getting it framed for him.'

'It was a pleasure,' Caroline said. 'I'm really glad he liked it.'

There was a pause between them again. Caroline reached over for Jonathan's mug and as she did so, their fingers touched. 'Sorry,' she blushed.

'No problem.' Jonathan withdrew his hand and Caroline took both mugs to the dishwasher.

'I'll see you later in the week,' Jonathan said, making for the back door.

'See you soon,' Caroline echoed. As he left, she had a sudden image of the two of them curled up on the sofa together watching something a little more grown up than *Hotel Transylvania 2*. She wondered what film he'd have chosen. Shaking her head, she headed back to the lounge to keep an ear out for Ellie. *Business, not pleasure,* she reminded herself, settling back to wait for Matthew, Anna and Meredith to get home.

21

Jonathan Carter was no stranger to decadent pleasures. He'd spent a good deal of the past ten years indulging his whims, physical and otherwise. There had been a point in the early years of the new century when he'd experimented with quite a few things, including drugs and alcohol. He knew now, as he'd known then but hadn't wanted to admit, that he was indulging himself to blot out the guilt of having an affair with Tara, his brother's first wife, and for being such a disappointment to the family. It had taken a long time for him to reconcile himself with what he'd done; the type of man he was, and an even longer time to become the man he wanted to be.

This self-knowledge had come at a cost; he was afraid to become emotionally involved with anyone again, afraid of hurting them and of being hurt himself. It hadn't escaped him that in this he shared much in common with his brother. The act of betrayal that had torn the two brothers apart ultimately had the same effect on their emotions and made them both afraid to take a leap and trust someone else. Matthew had shied away from relationships to concentrate on raising his daughter and developing the family business, and Jonathan had taken woman after woman to his bed but never his heart. But since he'd returned to Little Somerby, he felt as though something was changing. And, as he'd started spending more and more time with Caroline Hemingway, he realised that he *was* changing. There was something about the way she challenged him on everything that he found irresistible and their animated discussions about everything from cutlery to critics electrified him. Could it be that he was finally allowing someone into his heart?

This was all very well he thought, as he walked over to The Cider Kitchen late one evening, a few days after he'd seen Caroline babysitting Ellie and the day after one of their regular weekly meetings, but he still didn't have the faintest clue what to do about it. Caroline had been clear that business was all she had in mind. He'd even said the same thing when they started working together. The trouble was, Jonathan was starting to think he wanted more.

As he approached the front door he couldn't see anyone else in the restaurant. The front door, though, was still open, so he mooched in. Caroline must still be around, totalling up the night's takings. No matter. He'd amuse himself until she came back through. He toyed with the idea of helping himself to a scotch from the optic behind the bar but settled instead for a glass of water and some leftover lemon.

As he sipped his drink he contemplated the baby grand piano. It had been at least twenty years since he'd played; longer than that since he'd taken lessons, but suddenly his fingers itched. He picked up the glass from where he'd put it on the bar and ambled over to the piano.

For a split second when he sat down on the piano stool, he wondered if he dared play it. Should he? The restaurant was so quiet, the last customers having left as he'd approached, that it seemed sacrilegious to break the silence of the night. Somehow Ragtime didn't quite seem appropriate. But he knew what did.

Drawing a deep breath, allowing the muscle memory to take over, Jonathan put his hands to the keys. As the melody came back to him and his left hand embraced the steady regularity of the bass, Jonathan realised that the piano, whilst a touch out of tune, was in remarkably good shape. The rhythm took over, his fingers moved with more certainty, picking up on the beauty of the melody until it all came back to him.

At some point during the piece, Jonathan became aware of a figure entering from the kitchen. Undeterred, he continued to play. The key to this piece was keeping the bass regular and though his left hand hadn't kept time for years, he found it was coming back to him. Just as he was coming to the final cadences, Caroline drew closer. He felt her breath in his ear, blowing gently, and distracted, he missed his fingering in the melody, resulting in a flurry of wrong notes. Righting them resolutely, he finished the piece.

'And how many women have you seduced with your rendition of the Moonlight Sonata?' Caroline asked wryly.

'You'd be surprised how well it works,' Jonathan replied.

'I bet.' Caroline pulled out a chair from the table nearest the piano. 'Frankly, if you've been expecting me to do a Michelle Pfeiffer and slither all over that piano, you'd better think again.'

'I wouldn't dream of it,' Jonathan replied, although the thought was more than a little erotic. 'So,' he said, turning round on the piano stool. 'If I was to seduce you with a piece of music, what would it be?'

'Do you really expect me to answer that?' Caroline stretched back in the chair, raising slender arms above her head. 'Besides, all I've done this evening is look at figures. I can't think in musical terms after all that.'

'Music is very mathematical,' Jonathan said. 'You might be surprised.'

'I doubt it.' Caroline put her arms down again. 'Was there something you wanted?'

'Just checking in,' Jonathan said. 'I don't like to see you burning the candle at both ends.'

'I don't really have a choice at the moment,' Caroline sighed. 'If I don't work every hour god sends, the balance sheets aren't going to look very good at the quarterly meeting with your accountant.'

'Then let me help,' Jonathan said. 'Carter's can always advance you some more cash.'

Caroline shook her head. 'No. We've talked about this before. If I don't keep within the budget we set for this place it'll feel like I'm failing.'

'You know it's not like that,' Jonathan said.

Caroline sighed. 'I know. But there's nothing you can do, unless you want to do a few shifts waiting tables tomorrow night.'

'I think I might just cramp your style,' Jonathan replied. He looked thoughtful. 'But perhaps there is a solution.'

'What, get myself a magic wand or nick Hermione Granger's Time Turner?'

'Hermione who?' Jonathan asked.

'You really don't read anything except women's phone numbers, do you?' Caroline teased, although her heart wasn't in it. 'Never mind. The point is, I don't have time or money to think any further than the end of the month at the moment. If you advance me more cash to cover the day to day costs, then we'll eat into our profit margin.'

'OK, OK,' Jonathan held up his hands. 'But I can tell you're knackered and you haven't had much time off since this place opened.' He paused. 'Although perhaps there is an answer.'

'What?'

'What about Emma? You said at our meeting that she handled herself brilliantly the other night when you babysat Ellie and she could do with a fulltime job.'

'We don't have the budget to pay her full time. One night a week is one thing, but taking her on for more hours is quite another.'

'Yes, I know that,' Jonathan said. 'But what if you offered her a fifty-fifty sous chef and front of house apprenticeship? You'd save a few quid on her salary and she'd get the chance to train for both jobs. You know she wants to do both and it would give you a night or two off a week. She knows this place really well, so you wouldn't have to spend too much time training her up. What do you reckon?'

Jonathan had that flash in his clear blue eyes that immediately told Caroline it would be useless to argue. Besides, she admitted grudgingly, he did actually have a point. 'OK,' she said slowly. 'I'll raise the idea with her when she comes in tomorrow. So long as she realises we can't pay her much.'

'I'm sure she'll be more than happy,' Jonathan said gently. 'She loves this place and she and Gino are a good team. If we ever decide to open up another restaurant, we could put her in as head chef eventually.'

'Another one?' Caroline snorted. 'Don't you have enough on your plate overseeing this one? You seem to spend enough time here!'

'It's because I love spending time with you, darling,' he said lightly. 'I'm not fussed about this place really.'

'I'm sure,' Caroline smiled despite herself. A pause descended between them. With a jolt, Caroline realised that, without much of a combative discussion, she and Jonathan had agreed on a possible solution. Subject to Emma's agreement, of course. 'Thank you,' she said in surprise. 'I think we might have sorted it.' Suddenly, a yawn overtook her. 'Sorry,' she muttered.

'You need to get to bed,' Jonathan stood up. 'Can I walk you to your door?'

Caroline grinned in spite of her tiredness. 'Kind of you, but I think I can make it upstairs by myself. I'll see you soon.'

Jonathan walked to the front door of the restaurant and gave her a last smile. 'Goodnight.'

'Goodnight, Mr Carter,' Caroline said. And with that, Jonathan headed home.

22

The next morning, Caroline checked the appointments diary on her phone and swore. She'd forgotten all about the trip to the hunt kennels that Jonathan had set up for her. She also had to make sure she allowed enough time to meet Emma formally to offer her the sous chef/front of house apprenticeship. Dragging a brush through her hair she threw on some warm clothes and programmed the postcode of the hunt kennels into her phone.

Once she'd shaken off her irritation about forgetting the appointment she quite enjoyed being away from the familiar surroundings of The Cider Kitchen. For months, she'd been working so hard that she hadn't had much of a chance to explore the surrounding area, and it was nice, in the early autumn sunshine, to get into the country lanes of Somerset and see some new places. As she headed further south into the county she was amazed at how the wild, rocky hills of the Mendips flattened out into the glorious green expanse of the Somerset Levels. She drove through a couple of charming hamlets on her way to the kennels, which were situated just outside the picturesque small city of Wells. Perhaps if Emma accepted the job later, she'd make more of an effort to get out and about; after all, she'd moved to Somerset to experience new things and therefore she really should start experiencing them.

The hunt kennels were set back from the road and as Caroline drove up the driveway to the farm she felt very apprehensive. She wasn't quite sure what she'd expected to see; huge, drooling dogs running wild, perhaps, or red faced bellowing upper class twits swigging whiskey from hip flasks. Then she chided herself; she'd assured Jonathan she'd keep an open mind, whatever her feelings and preconceptions were, so she needed to try to do that.

As she pulled up in the kennel yard a tall man came striding over. He was dressed in a green body warmer and blue jeans with dirty green wellies on his feet and a friendly smile on his face.

'You must be Caroline,' he said as she got out of the car. He offered her a hand which Caroline was relieved to see was spotlessly clean. 'I'm Rob Kelloway, Master of Hounds for the Old Somerset Hunt.' When he finished shaking her hand, he took off his tweed flat cap and raked his fingers back through his unruly mousy brown hair. 'I gather you need some convincing that my hounds aren't going to chase your cats and that we're not bloodthirsty animal haters!'

Caroline smiled, despite her misgivings. 'Something like that.'

'You'd better come and meet them, then.'

Rob led Caroline across the yard to the stables, where an excited barking could be heard as they approached. 'They get fed once a day,' Rob said. 'Would you like to see them have their breakfast?'

Caroline looked wary. 'Depends what you feed them.' Rob was being very hospitable but she couldn't shake her instinct that he was the amenable face of a very violent and bloody institution. She wasn't going to be swayed by a nice smile.

'Mostly raw foxes,' Rob said wryly.

Caroline felt a prickle of irritation that he could be so flippant, but when she saw he was still smiling, she relaxed. After all, it wouldn't do to antagonise a man who had a hefty dog pack at his command. She followed Rob to the kennel building and the noise of hounds expecting their breakfast was almost deafening.

'Are you sure you don't want to come a bit closer?' Rob called over the increasing din from the hounds.

'I'm fine, thanks,' Caroline called back. She glanced at the bucket Rob was holding and was mildly repulsed to see it contained raw beef, bones and all. She kicked herself mentally; Gino was often chopping beef and other meats off the bone in the restaurant; this was really not that different.

'I'm going to let them out into the yard to have their breakfast,' Rob said. 'You'd better get out of the way of the door unless you want to be knocked over.'

Caroline stepped hastily out of the way and watched as the hounds streamed into the yard. Having never been up close to fox hounds before she was amazed at how big they were. Each one came up to her thigh and they were solidly built and muscular. Rob strode back out of the kennel and Caroline observed as the hounds circled him, before settling in a rowdy line in front of him. As he put their feed down in a long trough in the centre of the yard, they still waited for his signal, until with a motion of his hand, they all piled in.

Caroline was grudgingly impressed. Edging round the strong backs and waving tails of the hound pack, she joined Rob in front of them. 'They're very well behaved,' she said.

'They know they won't get fed if they aren't,' Rob replied. 'They only get one meal a day.'

'Where does their food come from?'

'Farmers bring in animals that have died unexpectedly and we use what we can of them to feed the hounds and incinerate the rest. We will also humanely destroy and collect casualties. The local councils often ask us to collect and dispose of dead animals, too.'

'Don't they chase the live ones?'

'My hounds are too well trained for that.'

Caroline was surprised; she hadn't realised that the hunt could actually be useful. But she wasn't prepared to let go of her principles and opinions that easily. 'So what happens when they do, er, accidentally, end up chasing a fox?'

'They do cross our path from time to time,' Rob conceded. 'But healthy foxes are quicker than you think. They're not the defenceless animals a lot of people take them for. And,' he paused, giving her a wicked grin. 'I understand a lot of them have relocated to the town, anyway, since it's better pickings for them from the bins!'

Caroline, who had the notion she was being mocked, shot back 'And I suppose that justifies your hounds chasing the not so fast ones, does it?'

'Of course not. We don't chase foxes. We stop the moment we see one and redirect the hounds.' Rob said, ruffling the head of a hound who, having finished his breakfast, was sniffing around by their feet. 'And I do understand why you don't agree with the practice. People sometimes can't see the role that the hunt plays in the countryside. But I hope you can at least see that I do keep my hounds under control and no harm will come to your cats when we meet at The Cider Kitchen. Now, if you'll excuse me, I have to give them a bit of a run.'

'Where do you take them?' Caroline asked.

'Well, they're quite partial to the Strawberry Line!' Rob said. 'If I can stop them from chasing tourists on bikes, that is.'

Much against her will, Caroline was tickled by the image of a tourist clad in neon lycra being the quarry for the hounds. Perhaps she was turning into a country girl after all, she thought as she bade farewell to Rob and headed back to The Cider Kitchen.

*

Later that day, when Emma came in for the evening service, Caroline beckoned her over to the sofas in the corner of the restaurant. Emma was delighted to be offered the combined sous chef/front of house post and said she could start straight away. Caroline was pleased, too. She knew Emma was an excellent chef and she had every faith, given the girl's lovely, calm disposition, that she'd prove to be an equally excellent deputy front of house person. And, she thought, it might actually mean she could take some time off after four months of working seven days a week.

Just before she turned in for the night, she texted Jonathan about Emma's response to being offered the job. Hopefully, the Old Somerset Hunt meet would go without a hitch, too, and that would be the last she'd see of those bloody foxhounds.

23

At the same time as Caroline was getting better acquainted with the Old Somerset Hunt hounds and their master, Jonathan was preparing himself for something he hadn't done in a very long time. Despite being back in the family firm for a little while now, he'd avoided this particular activity; it brought back too many memories of the times before the split in the family, when he, his brother and his father had been a cohesive team. But he didn't want to keep avoiding it; it was time to immerse himself fully in the duty of being a cider producer and the weekly event that he was about to take part in was a huge signifier of that duty.

As Jonathan walked into the main barn, his eyes took a moment to adjust to the more subdued lighting. Even during the day, the gloom was accentuated by the heavy, dark oak vats and the slightly lighter wooden joists that ran across the roof of the building. Although the shell of the barn these days was steel, the beams of the old one remained. He could hear the voices of Sophie Henderson and David Armitage, the Carter's Cider chief tasters, coming from the gantry above the main vat where they were carrying out the first checks. He mounted the steps to join them.

'Thought I'd sit in on this one, today, if that's all right?' Jonathan said as he reached them.

'Of course,' Sophie said. Tall, blonde and in her mid twenties, she'd been at Carter's Cider since she left school after her A Levels. 'It's always nice to have a member of the family on board when we do this.' She leaned over the side of the platform and pulled the handle that was attached to the hatch on top of the vat. 'What brings you out here today?'

'He's not sat in on a tasting since he's been back,' Matthew's voice, with just the slightest trace of amusement, came drifting up from the barn floor before he also ascended the gantry steps. 'I suspect he wants a reminder of what the stuff tastes like!'

'All we need is the old man and we'd have a full house,' David muttered under his breath to Sophie. Both of them withdrew to the vat on the other side of the gantry to continue their tests, giving the brothers a little bit of space.

Once he'd joined Jonathan, Matthew, immediately, assuming control, stepped forward and dipped the second glass jug from the tray into the top of the vat, then poured a glass from it. Pausing briefly, he held it out to his brother.

Jonathan looked at the glass warily. 'Are you sure you haven't poisoned this?'

'A year ago the thought might have crossed my mind.' Matthew gave a tight smile, 'but I wouldn't want to ruin a hundred and twenty thousand pints just for you.' Filling his own glass, he took a sip and watched as his brother did the same. It was the first taste of the family cider direct from the vats that Jonathan had taken since he'd returned to Little Somerby.

'Christ, that's good,' Jonathan said. The sweetness of the blend, combined with the subtlest flavour from the barrels themselves was what Carter's Cider was famous for, but this was truly something special. 'I'll go out on a limb and say it's better than anything we produced when Dad was MD.'

'Don't let him hear you say that,' Matthew replied. 'He still has his doubts about the Dabinett Royal cross blend, even though it's been a massive seller this year.'

Jonathan smirked. 'I never thought I'd hear you contradicting the old man's wisdom when it came to apple blending.' He glanced around the barn where the eight oak vats stood. 'But I suppose things have changed a bit.'

'Yes. They have.'

Jonathan took another sip from his glass and then called across to Sophie and David. 'Not that I'm an expert as yet, but this one seems to be coming along all right. Are you happy with it?'

'As happy as can be expected,' David, as ever, was deadpan. 'The one in the right hand vat needs a bit more time, though.'

Jonathan let the atmosphere of the place, the ceremony of the occasion, wash over him for a little longer. He remembered coming up here when he was much younger with Jack as well as Matthew, his father's insistence on tasting the product come rain or shine every week when he was in charge. Even the time he slipped a disc in his back couldn't keep him away from the vats. It was a history that Jonathan had run from, one he'd forsaken, but now one he desperately wanted to reclaim.

The clunk of Matthew's glass back onto the tray broke Jonathan out of his reverie. 'I'd better get back to the office,' Mathew said. 'Got a lot on. I suspect you have, too.' Without waiting for his brother's reply, he jogged down the steps.

Jonathan drained his glass and put it carefully back on the tray, too.

'Thanks,' he said to David and Sophie, who were apparently engrossed in checking one of the other vats. As he descended the steps back onto the barn floor, he was sure he didn't imagine David's gruff voice muttering 'that's a turn up for the books.' David was right, he supposed. After all, this was somewhere that not so long ago he'd never imagined being either.

24

The day of the drag hunt meet dawned bright and surprisingly chilly for October with a slight frost glittering in the trees and grass outside. As Caroline pulled back her living room curtains, she mutinously found herself hoping that at least one of those over privileged twats would slip on the damp grass and injure themselves. She'd agreed to host the meet because Jonathan, and later Matthew, had told her in no uncertain terms that it was a part of the county's heritage that she needed to cash in on. Her protests about it had fallen on deaf ears. She was rapidly beginning to realise that the outwardly amiable Carter bothers had cores of steel when it came to furthering the interests of the family firm. Very little got in their way; certainly not the manager of their restaurant.

That was the problem with this arrangement, she thought. She might have autonomy over the business to a certain extent, and the hiring and firing rights for the staff, but when it came to decisions she didn't agree with, she was still just a consultant manager. Jonathan and Matthew had made that perfectly clear in the last conversation they'd had with her before the issue was concluded. She'd just have to suck her principles up along with the mulled cider, it seemed.

After grabbing a quick shower and throwing on some skinny jeans and a jumper (she was buggered if she was going to dress up for the occasion), Caroline headed down to the kitchen to check the supplies. It wasn't just the hunt meet today; she had a full complement of tables for lunch and an almost full diary for the evening. She admitted grudgingly that the lunch bookings were probably because of the timing of the hunt meet, eleven o'clock, and some people had obviously decided to make a date of it, but even so, it still rankled.

When she got into the kitchen she checked the dates on the fridge stock. This was something Gino usually did, but she'd given him the day off to go and visit his grandfather, who was recovering in Musgrove Park hospital in Taunton after an operation. Emma had agreed to come in and cover the lunchtime and evening services and put the finishing touches on the finger foods for the meet. The stock inside the fridge was all fine but as she turned back to the steel preparation counter, she gasped. There, obviously having been out all night, was the entire supply of crayfish tails and dishes of homemade mayonnaise to go with them. And they should have been put in the fridge overnight. It wasn't exactly tropical in the kitchen, being October, but Caroline knew the temperature certainly wouldn't have been down to the legal minimum for a professional fridge.

She was immediately torn; if Gino had been here and the seafood had been for her own party, she'd have chucked the lot out immediately; it was too much of a risk to serve them in the restaurant. However, there was no time to redo them and this left a huge gap in the refreshments. She could call Emma now, get her in an hour early to knock up something else, but she'd relied on her sous chef enough lately and the girl deserved a lie in. She could get Gino back in but it didn't seem fair under the circumstances.

Before she could think about it any further, the restaurant's landline rang and she hurried out of the kitchen to answer it. As she was entering a booking for the evening on The Cider Kitchen's computer system, she noticed that some of the tables in the restaurant hadn't been re-laid, so as soon as she had the booking sorted, she got on with that.

A little while later, the space outside the restaurant was filling with assembled foot followers, horses and a small group of animal rights protesters handing out leaflets. It was all highly civilised. Even the hounds milling around were behaving themselves. Caroline found herself grudgingly admiring the scene, as riders in tweed coats, khaki coats and the odd red one checked girths, touched the peaks of their riding hats in acknowledgement of the Master and answered questions from curious first time spectators. Once again, she felt a twinge of longing to have some time to grab her sketch pad and capture the scene but she had far too much to do. A tray of mulled cider was being passed around and in a moment the food would come out from the kitchen.

It was only then that Caroline remembered the crayfish. To her horror, she saw Sasha, her youngest waitress, heading out of the restaurant with the tray in her hands. Hemmed in by hunt supporters, though, she wouldn't reach Sasha in time to take the tray off her. As she walked as quickly as she could through the crowd, her view of Sasha temporarily obscured, she heard a scream and a crash. Breaking through at last she saw that Rob, her new acquaintance and master of the Old Somerset hounds, had dismounted from his horse and was striding into the middle of a melee of jaws and tails. Caroline picked up her pace and found Sasha holding an empty platter, the contents of which was now being polished off by most of the hounds.

'I'm sorry, Caroline,' Sasha stammered, pink with embarrassment. 'They're so huge. One of them stuck its nose up my skirt as I came out with the snacks and I jumped a mile.'

'Bertie, Misty, Thunder, leave!' Rob's voice cut through Sasha's apologies. The hounds instantly fell away.

'Thank you,' Caroline said as Rob grinned apologetically.

'They're total opportunists,' he said. He turned to Sasha. 'Are you all right, love? They can't resist sniffing anything new and I'm afraid you were too nice to pass up with those snacks on the tray.'

Sasha nodded. 'I'm OK, thanks. Hadn't realised how big they are up close!' She looked regretfully at the mess on the floor. 'Good job you did loads of extra cheese and biscuits. They looked nice, too.'

'No harm done,' Caroline said. Her heart was still pounding at the thought that any of the crayfish might have been served to the people at the meet.

'We'll be ready for the off in a few minutes,' Rob called, as his phone pinged with a message. 'Drink up everyone. Jason's finished laying the trail.'

There was a flurry of activity as the riders finished their cider and snacks. Even Caroline, with her vehement anti blood sport principles, had to admit they looked rather glorious against the backdrop of the orchards and hills as they finally set off. Watching them go as the crowd thinned out she spotted Jonathan chatting to a couple of bystanders. As if summoned by her gaze, he turned and smiled at her. He really was heart breaking when he did that, she thought. But she didn't have time to chat; the lunchtime service wouldn't sort itself and she needed to change into something smarter now the hunt had left.

*

Later that day, Caroline was just readying the restaurant for the evening service when Meredith walked in. Dressed simply in a white shirt and straight black skirt with her dark hair in a long plait down her back, her face was flushed from the cold afternoon air.

'You survived then?' Caroline said as Meredith closed the restaurant door to keep out the chill. Since their heart to heart about Meredith's new sibling, she and Meredith had developed a close relationship and although she fundamentally disagreed with Meredith joining in with the hunt, she liked her enough to overlook it. It was good to see Meredith looking so much happier about things, too. She hadn't asked what the outcome of her dinner with Matthew and Anna had been, but from Meredith's demeanour, she assumed it had all worked out well.

'Yes, and so did Rosa, thankfully. It's her first time out for a while.'

'She's all, er, recovered, then?' Caroline didn't know the first thing about horses; the hunt meet was the closest she'd been to a horse barring the odd donkey ride at the seaside as a kid. The proximity of quite so many animals since she'd moved to the country was something she was still getting used to. Scrumpy and Solly were one thing, but some of the more rural aspects of living in Somerset, including being stopped by cows being herded down the main road in Little Somerby on occasion, were quite surprising.

'She's fine.' Meredith paused. 'Which is more than I can say for quite a few of the hounds.'

Caroline's stomach fluttered. 'What was wrong with them?' She asked carefully.

'Well, I'm not really sure,' Meredith called from the kitchen, where she'd gone to collect her white apron. 'About two hours in, suddenly half the pack stopped following the scent and, no word of a lie, all ran off and, er, relieved themselves. The smell was horrendous. Not even Rob could get them back on track for about ten minutes. We kind of lost momentum after that and decided to call it a day. Rob was really worried.'

'Really?' Caroline kept her voice carefully neutral. Inside she was panicking, wondering if she was going to get lumbered with a huge vet's bill for stomach pumping hounds poisoned by off seafood. 'I wonder what caused that.'

'Who can say?' Meredith replied. 'They're pretty sneaky when they're let out across country. Could have eaten anything out there. But it's odd that it happened so quickly. I'm sure they'll be fine after a good rest, though.'

'I hope so.'

'Many bookings tonight?' Meredith paused, looking curiously at Caroline. 'Are you all right?'

Caroline pulled herself together, trying not to think about profits potentially being handed over for sick dogs. 'I'm fine. Just six tables pre-booked tonight. First one in at seven.'

'OK then. I'll set up.' Meredith loped off to the kitchen.

Caroline sagged back against the table she was standing by. Then she jumped a mile as her mobile phone buzzed in the pocket of her trousers. It was a text from Jonathan.

OK to pop in later? Need to discuss something.

*

Later, to Jonathan, meant nearly eleven o'clock that evening. Caroline couldn't help noticing his dishevelled casual clothing and slightly ruffled hair. She hoped it was a conscious fashion choice and not caused by the fact that he'd just rolled out of someone else's bed. Not that she cared, of course, she reminded herself hastily.

Catching her eye, he signalled a 'no rush' gesture and settled down on one of the stools by the bar. Sasha, working a split shift today, smiled winningly at him and set to making him a coffee while he waited. Why was it that all females, no matter how old they were, immediately seemed to melt in Jonathan's presence? Caroline thought. Except for her, of course. Savagely, she clashed the cutlery together on the plates she'd just cleared from a table, earning herself a shocked glance from the elderly couple sat to her left. Smiling apologetically, she hurried out to the kitchen with the dishes and hoped that the last customers would finish their meals soon so that she could see what Jonathan wanted and then get to bed.

Eventually they all left and she closed the till, intending to shove the cash drawer in the safe before she locked up. Jonathan had his head bowed, looking at the screen of his mobile phone as she approached.

'Can I get you another coffee?' Caroline asked.

'Only if you're going to join me,' he replied.

Caroline made herself a heavy-on-the-milk latte and then made Jonathan a flat white; she didn't want to be up all night. She pushed his cup over to him and then came round the other side of the bar, taking a seat on the stool next to him.

'So is this a social call?' she asked as Jonathan put his phone back in his shirt pocket.

'Not exactly,' Jonathan said. 'I just wanted to check something with you.'

'What?' Caroline's stomach lurched. 'Is something wrong?'

'I'm not entirely sure.' Jonathan let the silence hang between them. 'Meredith mentioned something to me this afternoon when she got back from the meet, and it's been on my mind.'

The subdued lighting turned Jonathan's normally cerulean eyes a darker shade of blue, giving them a depth that Caroline instantly felt nervous of. Stalling for time, she took another sip of her coffee. 'Oh yes?' She tried to sound noncommittal.

'Yes. She said they had to cut the chase short this afternoon after an incident with the hounds. Virtually the whole pack had to be picked up and taken back to the kennels after they started shitting everywhere. Rob's only just settled them for the night, apparently, and he thought he'd have to get the vet out earlier this evening.' Jonathan's gaze was unflinching; his eyes never moved from hers as he spoke. In another context, this would be disturbingly sexy, thought Caroline,

'That's awful,' Caroline stammered. Rob had been so welcoming to her when she'd visited the kennels and despite believing that hunting was fundamentally anachronistic and wrong, she'd never have wished any harm to the hounds. 'Does... does he know what might have happened?'

Jonathan let the pause hang between them again as he took a sip of his coffee. 'He thinks they might have been affected by something they ate. A bout of canine food poisoning. You wouldn't happen to know anything about that, would you?'

Caroline choked on her latte. 'Why would I?'

'Well, the only thing I can think of was that tray of seafood that Sasha dropped on the ground.' Jonathan kept looking at her. 'Given your, er, objections to hunting, it seems rather coincidental that food meant for the meet might be the cause of a few upset stomachs.'

'Are you accusing me of deliberately sabotaging the food?' Caroline flared up. That the crayfish tails might have been off was one thing, but the suggestion that she'd poisoned them was completely out of order.

'Did you?' Jonathan asked flatly. Caroline was jolted by the directness of both his gaze and the question. 'I need to know, Caroline.'

'No, Jonathan. No, I didn't. And the fact that you might think that makes me so angry.' Caroline clattered her mug down on its saucer and stood up. 'I would never, never put the health of my customers at risk. Or their animals.'

Jonathan kept looking at her, considering. 'No.' He said finally. 'I don't think you would. But then what other explanation could there be? The hounds didn't eat anything unusual before the meet, and they wouldn't have had time to stop once the run started. Rob just doesn't get it.'

Caroline's heart sank. 'There's something you should know.'

'What?'

'The crayfish have been the cause of the upset, but I would never have poisoned them. They were left out on the side in the kitchen overnight, though.' She dropped her gaze from Jonathan's. 'It was a complete oversight.'

Jonathan let out a long, tired sigh. 'And you let them go out anyway? What the hell were you thinking?'

'I didn't intend to!' Caroline snapped. 'I was about to throw them out when the phone rang for a booking and I forgot all about them. It wasn't until Sasha brought them out that I realised. I tried to get to her to divert her but didn't manage it before the tray went up and the hounds got them.'

'Didn't you check the kitchen before you turned in last night?'

'I'm sure I did...' then she remembered; she'd been detained by a customer and by the time she'd cashed up, Gino had left and the lights were out in the kitchen. She'd staggered up to bed without performing her usual checks. She could blame Gino, but really she had the final responsibility.

'What would have happened if any of them had actually been eaten by the people at the meet?' Jonathan shook his head. 'They must have been crawling with bugs if they affected the hounds, but there were older children and teenagers out there this morning. Christ, Caroline, Ellie and Merry were there, as well as half the village kids. Not to mention Anna, who'd have been seriously affected if she'd eaten them in her condition. We're only lucky that the dogs knocked Sasha's tray out of her hands before she had a chance to hand them around.'

'I'm sorry,' she muttered. 'I should have got rid of them as soon as I saw them.'

'Christ, Caroline, that was too close a call. Please try to be more careful.'

Caroline opened her mouth to argue, but she knew Jonathan was right; and besides, he looked ridiculously sexy when his blood was up. She took a deep breath. 'You're right. I'm sorry. It was a stupid mistake. Hopefully no-one had any before Sasha dropped them.'

'You can't run a business on *hopefully*,' Jonathan ran a hand through his hair.

'I know.' Caroline tried to smile. 'I guess we'll soon know if anyone got sick today, too, won't we, given what the village grapevine is like.'

Jonathan regarded Caroline intently. 'Are you *sure* it wasn't deliberate?'

'Of course not!' Caroline replied. 'I might still disagree fundamentally with having them here, but I actually did like Rob, and I certainly wouldn't play Russian Roulette with this place's future.'

Jonathan kept looking at her for a moment, and Caroline could feel her face growing warmer under his scrutiny. 'I believe you,' he said softly.

Caroline was lightheaded with relief. 'Never, ever again. Guides honour.'

'The thought of you in a Girl Guide uniform is enough to make me forgive you on the spot,' Jonathan said, a somewhat husky note in his voice.

'Hold it right there,' Caroline said. 'I might be feeling contrite but not enough for you to cross professional lines.'

Jonathan held up his hands. 'As if I would.' He looked at his watch. 'Anyway, I'm all in. I doubt I'd be much use to you or anyone else tonight. And I need my beauty sleep for tomorrow, anyway.'

'Really?' Caroline arched an eyebrow.

'Yup,' Jonathan replied. 'I've got a busy evening.'

'Anyone I know?'

'You do, actually,' Jonathan said, a glint in his eye. 'And she'll do her nut if I don't give her my full attention, so I'd better get some rest.' With that, he gave her a grin, turned on his heel and sauntered out of the door. 'See you later.'

Caroline felt a combination of irritation and jealousy watching him leave. She realised she'd got off lightly, but she couldn't help wondering who Jonathan's plans were with tomorrow night. Cursing herself for the thought, she set to locking up.

25

The next morning, feeling exhausted after a late night and fitful sleep, Caroline pulled on a cosy jade green jumper and headed down to check over the restaurant. She'd stayed up for a long time after Jonathan had left, checking and double checking the dates on stock in the fridge, making sure everything perishable had been properly labelled and put away. To her immense relief the kitchen staff had done an excellent job of tidying up, but she needed to be sure. She'd got off lightly with the crayfish tails but she was determined not to make the same mistake again. Crashing into bed eventually, she'd then been tortured by incredibly erotic dreams about Jonathan. She wasn't sure how he'd done it, but he'd looked even more desirable than usual last night, tired and ever so slightly scruffy. Now that she knew no serious harm had been done by the off seafood she had to admit that she'd quite enjoyed being told off by Jonathan. Christ, she wondered, was she turning into Ana Steele? Perish the thought.

As she entered the restaurant, she realised with a lurch that she'd forgotten to lock the takings in the safe the night before and the till still needed floating. *Bugger Jonathan!* Every time he showed up he sent her off balance. She was befuddled with tiredness. Thankfully, the restaurant only opened on Sunday lunchtimes, so she'd be spared an evening service. Opening the till, she reached for the stack of larger notes and then tapped out the command to print the receipt. Before she could do so, however, something caught her eye on the door mat.

It was Sunday, so there would be no post today. It was a little late for a good luck card, she thought. Stepping out from behind the counter once more, she strode over to the front door and picked up the small brown envelope. There was no address on it, so no handwriting to take a guess at. She swiftly opened it and pulled out the white notepaper inside. As she did so, something else from the envelope fluttered to the floor. Glancing down, before she'd even unfolded the paper, her heart stopped.

There on the doormat was a tiny plastic packet of crystallised white powder. With trembling hands, Caroline unfolded the note. In bold blue handwriting was written two words:

Remember me?

26

That evening, exactly as he'd told Caroline, Jonathan's companion for dinner was someone she knew well. He'd taken to buying her dinner regularly since his return to the village; mostly because he really enjoyed her company and partly because he still felt he owed her. He'd walked out of her life without any warning a long time ago and now that he was back he wanted to make amends. In fact, Meredith, his niece, was the only female Jonathan could say that he'd ever truly loved, apart from his mother. She'd turned seventeen recently, and he was aware that in a year's time she'd be heading off to university, so he wanted to spend as much time with her as he could.

They'd taken to trying out a few of the restaurants in the surrounding villages after tiring of the menu at The Stationmaster, although they did still occasionally end up there. Jonathan had avoided The Cider Kitchen so far as, with the company's financial interest and Meredith's job there, it was a bit close to home.

Tonight, they were going to try out a place in Cleeve, a few miles from Little Somerby. Formerly the village Post Office, the small restaurant had been a startup two years ago and had gained phenomenally successful reviews. It was one of the few places that did open for one sitting on a Sunday evening. Jonathan always had one eye open for an opportunity and he wanted to see what the place had achieved that The Cider Kitchen could emulate. Picking Meredith up just after seven, they were seated and chatting half an hour later.

'How's school?' Jonathan asked.

Meredith rolled her eyes. 'Fine. Did Dad tell you to ask?' Since Meredith, Matthew and Anna had been out to dinner, Meredith had been much happier at home, but she knew that her father and stepmother were keeping a closer eye on her.

'No, darling, but as the future hope of the family firm, I have to make sure you're doing your duty.'

'Of course,' Meredith tossed her hair impatiently. 'Dad's so paranoid I'll go off the rails and cock up my A Levels he's barely letting me out with anyone except you these days.'

'He just wants what's best for you,' Jonathan replied patiently. 'You'll always be his little girl, you know.'

'I know.' Meredith scanned the menu. 'But I don't want to talk about school. It's fine. The work's fine and my teachers are happy.' She raised an eyebrow over the menu. 'I want to talk about you. And Caroline.' After their conversation about Anna's new baby a few weeks back, Meredith had been growing closer to Caroline and was finding that she liked her. In Meredith's mind, she'd make the perfect match for her uncle.

'Unprofessional, darling,' Jonathan replied. 'She's your boss and employed by the family firm to run the restaurant. Can't discuss her.'

'Oh, come on. You've been hanging around The Cider Kitchen more than is strictly professional, and Anna said Caroline had caught you playing that out of tune baby grand piano the other night. You wouldn't be doing that if you didn't at least fancy her.'

'Haven't you heard? I'm a cad and a bounder and I fancy anything that moves. You know that.' Jonathan's smile was genuine but his eyes were serious. Joking about his relationships was one thing, but he'd made a terrible mistake with Meredith's mother, his brother's first wife, and he still felt deeply uneasy about discussing it with her at all, let alone joking about it.

'It's OK, Uncle Jonathan,' Meredith said softly. 'We've talked about all this before, remember. I forgive you for… that.' She smiled at him. 'And I want you to be as happy as Anna's made Dad. Do you think you'll ever find anyone to do that for you?'

Jonathan's thoughts flitted back to Caroline. She was so difficult to read, and that intrigued him.

There was something about her, he knew; something she was holding back from him. He'd sent her an email this morning, asking if he could come over to discuss an offer he'd had from a potential new supplier, but she'd not answered it. It wasn't like Caroline to ignore work emails; she was usually an efficient communicator, even at the weekends. He wondered if something had come up to distract her.

'Uncle Jonno? Are you listening to me?' Meredith had clearly clocked the look on his face, and he struggled to focus back on his niece.

'Sorry, darling, I was miles away.'

'I was just saying that I'm going to see Flynn next weekend in Oxford. I'll probably check out a few more of the colleges when I'm down there.' Meredith smirked. 'But something tells me your mind was a bit closer to home.'

Jonathan smiled apologetically. 'I've got a lot on. Your Dad and I are trying to get our heads around this Buckthorn takeover proposal – I'm sure he's mentioned it, and Granddad's not been in the best way, as you know. So you see I really don't have time to think about my love life as well.'

'Hmmm,' Meredith murmured. 'Now that, coming from you, I don't believe.' But she turned her attention back to the menu. 'I'm starving. What are we going to eat?' Her appetite was legendary and Jonathan had often wondered where all the food she consumed went. Love and teenage hormones, he thought in amusement. You could get away with a lot more at that age. Growing up, he was beginning to realise, came with a whole lot more to think about. He wondered if perhaps Meredith was realising that faster than he was.

27

Caroline couldn't stop thinking about the note she'd received, with that plastic packet of white powder which she'd flushed down the toilet in her flat immediately, afraid to keep it anywhere near her. She was pretty sure she wouldn't be tempted by it, but having Class A drugs on the premises was a frightening thought.

What scared her the most, and she was amazed that she'd only realised it later, was that the envelope had no address written on it. That meant it had been delivered by hand. The location of her new job hadn't been a secret; virtually everyone she'd worked with at the events management company knew she was going to Somerset to run a restaurant. But if the writer of the note had hand delivered it, that meant he was now in the West Country, which could only mean trouble. She was lucky, in one sense, that she was living and working in a place that was always busy, except, she thought, in those dark hours between closing and opening. Surely that would give her some protection? But protection from what? What did he want from her? She had the horrible feeling she was going to find out sooner rather than later. The question was, what damage could he do to her and her new job in the mean time?

But life had to go on. She had two choices; either lock herself away on her nights off and worry, or get out and make some friends in the village. Deciding that Thursdays would be her night off from The Cider Kitchen, she looked around for things to do. At first, she spent her free evenings over at Cowslip Barn with Anna and Ellie, but then an advertisement in *Somerset Life* caught her eye, and she signed up for a six week course of life drawing classes. She found the sketchbook again, and now that she had a little more time and a definite reason to get out of the restaurant, she decided to take the course. She also hoped it would allow her to meet more people. She'd met plenty as they came through the door of the restaurant, but none she could really call friends, Jonathan's late night visits notwithstanding.

And friends were definitely a way to fight back against whatever that note and the packet of white powder meant. With difficulty, she forced these thoughts from her mind. The whole point of the life drawing class was to get her away from the restaurant and into Little Somerby village life, where she'd be visible. Not even *he* would follow her into an art class, she figured. As she walked along the High Street, heading for the hall, she noticed that there were quite a few people still about, either going to the pub or the local store, and she was reassured by their presence. Nothing could happen to her here, surely.

The class was held at the village hall which was a red bricked building erected by the Temperance Movement at the turn of the century. From the outside it looked austere and decidedly chilly, and Caroline wondered who would be brave enough to strip off on a cold autumn night in such a place. However, as she entered the hall she could feel, to her own relief and no doubt the model's, that someone had turned the heating up to tropical to compensate.

Feeling slightly self-conscious, Caroline opened the double doors to the main hall and saw a group of around ten people of various ages sitting by easels arranged in a rough circle. The model, seated on a rattan backed chair with a large shawl draped over the rough edges, had her back to the doors. As Caroline smiled at the course leader, who motioned to her to take a seat at one of the easels to one side of the model, she felt the tingle of anticipation that she always got when she started a new drawing.

Caroline crossed the hall and took her seat. Fumbling in her bag for her artists' pencils, it was only after she'd laid them out, noting with pleasure the thick paper that had been placed on the easel itself, that she looked up to make her first observations of the model. She felt only the briefest surprise when she realised that she was looking at the voluptuous, naked form of Anna's best friend, Charlotte. Her long auburn hair was piled up on the top of her head, revealing an elegant neck that curved down to broad shoulders. Her face was turned in profile in Caroline's direction, so Caroline could see the swell of Charlotte's breasts curving down to a slim waist and rather plump thighs. One arm was draped over the back of the chair, the other resting with a hand in her lap. She was utterly at home in the chair, and Caroline, after musing for a moment on the oddness of seeing Anna's best friend without a stitch of clothing on, marvelled at her confidence.

'Hello,' she mouthed as Charlotte caught her eye and gave the briefest, subtlest wink.

It was amazing how quickly Caroline's artist's eye took over. In no time at all she was sketching the lines of Charlotte's body, putting in light and shade and enjoying trying to capture the texture of her hair. When she drew, it was as if everything else in the world melted away and it was just her and the subject in front of her. Nothing could touch her; not even *him*.

The two hours of the class passed, it seemed, in the blink of an eye, and Caroline was about to take down her picture from the easel. After some brief feedback from the course leader, she began to pack her pencils away.

Charlotte, who'd wrapped herself in the shawl before heading off to put her clothes back on, stopped at Caroline's easel.

'Christ, that's good,' Charlotte observed. Then, in an undertone, so as not to offend the assembled students, 'better than anything else that's been produced tonight! I don't suppose I could buy it off you as a wedding anniversary present for Simon, could I?'

Caroline blushed. She hardly ever showed anyone her sketches and it was incredibly strange now the spell of concentration was broken, to be discussing what she'd drawn. 'Let me put some finishing touches to it first,' she said, starting to unfasten the drawing from the easel. 'I'm not completely sure I've got your eyes right.'

'OK,' Charlotte said. 'And let me know what you want, cash wise, for it when it's done. I can have it framed at that place in Shipham – Folly Framer's, I think it's called. I wonder if they've done a local nude before!' Charlotte's eyes flashed mischievously. She readjusted the shawl as it threatened to slip off again. 'I suppose I'd better get my kit back on before they turn the heating off,' she said. 'Do you fancy a drink at The Stationmaster, or have you got to dash back to the restaurant?'

Caroline smiled. 'It's my night off so I'm in no hurry,' she said. 'But won't Simon be expecting you back?'

'Oh, probably,' Charlotte said airily, 'but he'll have to hold the fort a little bit longer. Evan'll be in bed now anyway. And,' she paused, mischievous look back in place, 'I'm dying to find out what it's like to be working all up close and personal with Jonathan Carter!'

Caroline found herself laughing along with Charlotte's infectious humour. 'Challenging,' she replied. 'Very, very challenging.'

Some time later, Caroline found herself a few drinks up and a lot more informed about the nocturnal activities and otherwise of several Little Somerby residents, many of whom were regulars at The Cider Kitchen. Charlotte's sense of fun was infectious and Caroline began to unwind. Sipping her pint of Guinness, she leaned back against the cushioned bench seat.

'So you didn't leave anyone behind to move here, then?' Charlotte asked. 'No boyfriend back in Surrey? Some rich stock broker, perhaps?'

Caroline laughed. 'Nope. I'm as free and single as they come.'

'I should hope so with Jonathan Carter making eyes at you the way he does.'

'Oh, come on,' Caroline snorted. 'He makes eyes at everyone female. And besides, I'm not ready for a relationship. Let's just say I'm steering clear of anything male for a while.'

'Oh yes?' Charlotte raised an eyebrow. 'Bad history?'

Caroline paused a fraction too long before answering. 'Something like that.' The man she was thinking of, the one from her most recent past, hadn't exactly been a boyfriend, but the hold he'd had over her had been just as intense in the end. And that experience was enough to make her wary.

'Sounds interesting,' Charlotte said. Looking back up from her drink, Caroline expected to see a salacious gleam in Charlotte's eyes, such was the other woman's nose for a story, but she saw only kindness and compassion. 'You don't have to tell me, of course.'

'It's not what you think,' Caroline said. 'But if you don't mind, I'd rather not go into details. Let's just say that I wanted a clean break when I moved here. There are some things I'd rather leave behind in Surrey.' *And up until recently I thought I had,* she added silently.

'Fair enough,' Charlotte replied stoically. 'But I ought to warn you, nothing stays quiet around here for long. The village grapevine is a law unto itself.

Sometimes it's like living in the world's most picturesque bird cage.'

'You're the one who's just got her kit off for the local artistic community!' Caroline quipped.

'Oh, I know,' Charlotte said. 'But no-one would expect anything less from me. It'll be fun, though, if I ever do go back into the classroom. Can you imagine if any of the people from the life drawing class have children or grandchildren at the local secondary school? I'll never live it down on parents' evening!'

Caroline laughed, glad the subject had moved away from her and her reasons for moving. As they finished their drinks and went their separate ways, Caroline felt as though she'd socialised properly for the first time since moving. She swore, on the remains of her glass of white wine, that she'd do it again soon.

28

As the nights began to draw in more quickly and the coats hanging on the hooks in The Cider Kitchen's cloakroom grew thicker and longer, Caroline made the final preparations for the Halloween theme night. When the evening actually rolled round, Caroline glanced around the restaurant, half in despair half in amusement. Strands of fake spiders' web were twined around the light fittings, the tables had been topped with black sparkly napkins, and carved pumpkins, soon to be filled with tea lights, seemed to line every flat surface.

'I can't believe I ever thought this was a good idea,' Caroline muttered. 'I hate Halloween, usually.' She'd spent too many Halloween nights overseeing hospitality events and memories of excess in all ways were ones she didn't wish to revisit any time soon, especially when the scariest thing in her life at the time had been someone very, very human. Someone who, since that unnerving note and packet of powder in early October, Caroline hadn't been able to put out of her mind. But she didn't want to burden the increasingly heavily pregnant Anna with these thoughts. Anna had popped in after closing up the tea shop to see how things were going and had been roped in to help Caroline lay a few tables, as Meredith had gone down with the flu the day before and couldn't do her evening shift. The teenager had been characteristically upset about both missing work and the Halloween event, but it couldn't be helped.

Anna laughed. 'You're the one who said it'd be good for business. And Matthew and Jonathan have been dying to try out their new Wookey Witch Cider Punch on the public. If it takes off, they'll be marketing it nationally this time next year.'

'Yup, my customers are going to be guinea pigs, as well as in for a fright.' Caroline grimaced down into the cutlery tray behind the bar. 'As if Gino's Halloween menu wasn't weird enough, Jonathan told me I'd have to take on some experimental hooch as well.'

'They do sort of know what they're doing when it comes to cider making,' Anna chided gently. 'They've been at it a while.'

'I know, I know, a hundred years of heritage and history all rolled up into two delectable Somerset sons,' Caroline teased, feeling her mood lift marginally.

'Delectable?' Anna raised an eyebrow. Caroline had filled Anna in on the debacle with the fox hounds over the washing up after Sunday lunch at Cowslip Barn and only then when she was sure

Matthew was out of earshot. As lovely as Matthew was, Caroline didn't fancy being chewed out by him as well as Jonathan over the incident, and she didn't know whether Jonathan had told his brother about the restaurant's near miss or not.

'No comment. He's been hanging around after hours again, pretending to play the piano and generally making a nuisance of himself.'

'Really?' Anna replied. 'Well, if it's any help, Matthew says he can't ever remember seeing Jonathan spending quite so much time with a woman and not breaking her heart, so I take it that's a positive sign.'

'Don't get any ideas,' Caroline said. 'We're keeping it strictly business. I really don't need any complications right now.'

'I hope Jonathan knows that. He can be quite persuasive at times.'

'If he doesn't, he'd better get clued up pretty quickly. I'm not likely to be playing his damsel in distress tonight or any night soon.'

'Methinks the lady doth protest too much,' Anna smiled.

'Give it up,' Caroline smirked. 'I'm not becoming your sister-in-law again, and that's that.'

Anna threw up her hands. 'OK, OK, but you should take it as a compliment really. Now where did you want these glasses?'

*

A couple of hours later, and The Cider Kitchen was starting to fill up with people. Caroline looked across to the bar, where one of the serving staff was pouring the rather alarmingly orange Wookey Witch cider punch and another was offering round a variety of ghoulishly coloured and shaped canapés. In roughly ten minutes or so, everyone would be seated, and the challenge would be to get the starters out on time. She was one server down, but so far the staff were coping admirably. She'd refused to go all out in terms of costume, but she had conceded on a long, figure hugging black dress and an equally long, black costume wig. Although rather shorter than Morticia Adams, and definitely more curvaceous, she was pleased with the effect.

I wonder what Jonathan would make of it, she thought. He hadn't even confirmed he was coming tonight, so she had to put him out of her mind and focus on her customers. Smiling gamely, she strode across the restaurant, greeting people as she went and taking her position as front of house. She wasn't expecting to shut up shop before midnight, and there were plenty of tricks and treats to organise, including a close up magician.

*

The evening flew by with the help of the magician and her serving team, who seemed to have wings attached to their heels. The Halloween theme had created a relaxed atmosphere, and Caroline even went so far as to relax a little herself when the dining was done and some of the tables were pushed back to create a makeshift dance floor in the middle of the restaurant. Soon, the guests, well fed and very well watered, were bopping away to the cheesiest of Halloween hits, which had been prepared on an iTunes playlist by Gino and Emma a few nights ago. Alongside the old classics such as 'Thriller' and 'Bump in the Night' were a couple of newer tunes, including 'I'm In Love With A Monster' from *Hotel Transylvania 2*, which Caroline remembered from the night she'd babysat Ellie.

Jonathan hadn't shown tonight. Not that she'd wanted him to, of course; she was quite relieved he'd stayed away. Although, oddly, she knew he wasn't one to miss a party, so she'd been quite surprised that he hadn't come along. Perhaps he'd had a better offer?

Eventually, as the last customers left and she and the team were beginning to clear up, Caroline's tiredness overwhelmed her. Her feet hurt from the high heels she'd put on with the dress and the long dark wig was far too hot. She'd have whipped it off her head but her vanity stopped her; she couldn't stand to let her team see her with what would undoubtedly be a sweaty, carroty mess underneath the wig.

'Are we all done?' she asked Izzy as the teenager wiped the last table.

'I think so,' Izzy replied. 'Do you want me to check the bar?'

'No, it's all right,' Caroline said, making one concession and stepping out of her high heels. 'You get off home.'

'Thanks,' Izzy took off her apron, which she was wearing over a short, sparkly black dress covered in glittering silver spiders' webs, and took it out to the kitchen. Caroline heard the girl saying goodnight to Gino and Emma and then the back door of the restaurant closing behind her.

A short time later, Gino and Emma came through to the bar as Caroline was cashing up. 'Not a bad night,' Gino said as he took off his chef's cap and ruffled his hair back into some kind of shape.

'It went really well,' Caroline said. 'I've heard nothing but praise for your skills all evening, both of you.' Her two young chefs looked utterly done in and Caroline felt a stab of sympathy. 'Make sure you both get home to bed, now.'

'Nah,' Gino said, tired eyes suddenly alight. 'I can't go to bed just like that after a busy evening. Got to unwind a bit first. I'm meeting a few mates in Weston. Fancy it, Emma?'

'No thanks,' Emma replied. 'I've said I'll help Dad out with the stock take in the pub tomorrow so I'd better get home.'

'Take care,' Caroline said as they both left the restaurant. She dithered over making herself a cup of coffee while she totalled the till, but decided against it. She was shattered, too, and the coffee would only keep her awake. Heading back to the cash desk, she was just printing out the till receipt when she heard the front door of the restaurant opening again. Caroline's heart thudded painfully in her chest and she cursed inwardly for forgetting to lock the doors before beginning to cash up. What if the writer of the note was paying her another visit? Steeling herself, she looked up from the receipt.

'That is a very disturbing dress,' the voice, low with amusement, came from the doorway.

Caroline breathed out again. How did Jonathan do that, slinking in like the Cheshire Cat with that indolent tone and lazy, seductive grin?

'We're closed,' she said. She'd lost her place on the receipt again.

'I'm not buying.'

'Then I'll have to ask you to vacate the premises, sir.' Giving up on the takings, she shoved the receipt in the drawer of the till and resolved to check it in the morning.

'I'm on my way home,' Jonathan said. 'Just thought I'd make sure no food critics had sneaked in again.'

'No, I'm all on my lonesome,' Caroline replied, finally turning around. 'Except for a cider farmer who's about to be slapped with a restraining order if he doesn't leave soon.' As she met Jonathan's appraising gaze she felt herself growing warmer. The black dress did interesting things to her cleavage, and she was suddenly aware of her breasts rising up as her breathing grew shallower at the sight of him.

'What? No late night coffee?' Jonathan approached her, his steps lazy and self-assured. 'I thought I'd offer to make it if you'll let me near the coffee machine.'

Caroline looked appraisingly at Jonathan. He was wearing a longline midnight blue velvet jacket, underneath which was a vintage cream silk shirt tucked into dark trousers. The look was retro, sexy, and distinctively over the top.

'Been somewhere?' Caroline asked.

'Out to another Halloween party with a friend,' Jonathan replied. 'A longstanding engagement, arranged before this came up. Kind of a birthday treat, too.'

'Whose birthday?' Caroline asked.

'Mine.' Jonathan replied. He gave a slightly self-conscious smile. 'Didn't want to make a big thing of it. When this party invitation came up, I thought it would be a good distraction.'

'Well, happy birthday! Don't tell me you're angsting about getting older?' Caroline couldn't help smirking. The thought of Jonathan worrying about laughter lines and middle aged spread was too good a one to ignore, particularly when he didn't have a trace of either.

'Not overly,' Jonathan replied. 'But it does make you start to question your life choices.' He grimaced. 'Meredith sent me the rudest card, too. That girl needs a clip round the ear.'

'She didn't mention it was your birthday,' Caroline said, vaguely irritated that it hadn't been on her radar. Whatever her ambivalence about Jonathan, she'd have liked to at least have known that it was his birthday, if only to tease him with it. She wondered why Anna hadn't mentioned it either. The Carters weren't the kind of family to let an excuse for a celebration go.

'I've never really been one for celebrating my birthday,' Jonathan said, as if reading her mind. 'Especially being born on Halloween – seems churlish to bring it up when everyone's preoccupied with their pumpkins.' He flicked a non-existent speck of dust from the sleeve of his jacket. 'And the family were under strict instructions to let it pass without event, too.'

'I'm stunned that Meredith would let you get away with that,' Caroline said. 'I know the fun she had arranging Matthew and Anna's wedding.'

Jonathan smiled. 'I told her I'd get you to dock her wages if she breathed a word.'

Caroline laughed. 'Well, she didn't, so I guess I can keep paying her the going rate!' She reached behind her head and lifted the black wig off her neck for a second. It really was a most uncomfortable thing. 'So, was it a good night? This party of yours?'

'Not bad. Although, had I known what you were planning on wearing, I'd have skipped it in a heartbeat and booked a table here instead.' His gaze drifted from Caroline's face and down her body.

'Save it for someone it works on,' Caroline said. 'You know we agreed not to mix business with pleasure.' She flushed, but was astonished to find herself moving a little closer to Jonathan, as if her feet had a mind of their own. Once she no longer had the bar between them as a barrier, she felt strangely exposed in her figure hugging black dress. It wasn't an unpleasant feeling, and before alarm bells kicked in warning her to keep Jonathan at arms' length, she found herself imagining what it would be like to have him take it off her. Her hand drifted up Jonathan's velvet clad arm and stroked the soft fabric beneath her fingers. 'This looks expensive,' she remarked.

'If you keep doing that, it was worth every penny.' Jonathan picked up a stray wineglass that hadn't been spotted by the service team and set it down on the bar. Then he drew closer to her and lazily reached out a hand to stroke her rapidly flushing cheek.

'Don't,' Caroline murmured, even as her eyes grew wider. 'It's not fair, Jonathan.'

'What's not fair?' His tone was gentle and his breath whispered past her, making her shiver. 'You wearing that utterly illegally sexy dress and charming everyone except me... that's what's not fair.'

Caroline's knees shuddered and she was a heartbeat away from pulling Jonathan closer and dragging him back upstairs to her flat. Her lips parted, and, as Jonathan's fingertips brushed over them, down her throat and traced lightly across the swell of her cleavage, his touch seemed to burn.

'You don't mean that,' she said softly. 'You can't.'

'Can't I?' Jonathan's voice had a low, lazy warmth that could melt chocolate. He dipped his head, and as his lips drew closer to hers, Caroline was suddenly aware of a vibration coming from the inside pocket of Jonathan's beautiful jacket. Without missing a beat, Jonathan pulled the phone out with his other hand, glanced at the screen and smirked. He didn't answer the call.

It was enough to bring Caroline to her senses. 'Was that your date from tonight?' the throb of her own frustration was beating in her voice.

'Yes, as a matter of fact,' Jonathan replied.

'Well, you'd better go and call her back,' Caroline replied. 'Because you're getting nothing more from me tonight. Or ever.'

Jonathan held up his hands. 'So be it.' He kept grinning. 'It's a shame, though. If you'd just let yourself go a little, we could have made a great night of it.'

'Oh, bugger off!' Caroline snapped. 'Go and warm someone else's bed.'

Still grinning, Jonathan sauntered out of the door.

Snatching the wig from her head in irritation, she dumped it down on the nearest chair and ran an impatient hand through her hair, trying to revive it.

Just as she was about to lock up and head upstairs, her own mobile phone pinged. She'd left it beside the till for most of the evening as her dress, naturally, didn't have any pockets and she couldn't exactly shove it down her bra. She had toyed with the idea of strapping it, Lara Croft style, to her thigh, but dismissed this as too ridiculous. Grabbing the phone, she swiped the screen and frowned as she saw the text message notification from an unfamiliar number. Without thinking, she tapped it, and then her heart froze. The message contained no actual text at all; but what it did show, despite the low light and the fuzziness of the image, was her, still wearing the Morticia Adams wig, face turned towards a man who had his back to the camera; a man in a midnight blue jacket. Clearly it had been taken moments ago, just before Jonathan had left, and as Caroline's hands started to shake; she was in no doubt who had taken it. Frozen to the spot, heart thumping, skin crawling, she shivered. If the note and the packet of white powder had been a warning, this photo felt like a threat. There was no doubt about it. *He* was watching her. Worse, he was outside in the dark. Once again, she wished she hadn't sent Jonathan on his way so smartly. She suddenly felt more isolated than she ever had before.

Swiftly, she ran to the front door of the restaurant, locked and bolted it and then hurried upstairs to her flat. Thankfully, she'd insisted on a Yale lock on the door to her living quarters, too, to give her some sense of separation, and she slammed the door, dropping the lock instantly. As she sank back against the inside of the door, so many questions ran through her head. Was he still outside? Did he plan on coming in? Should she call the police (or, she thought fleetingly, Jonathan?). What the hell was she going to do?

29

As if the spirits were paying him back for teasing Caroline on All Hallows' Eve, Jonathan went on to have an awful week. Starting Monday morning with a robust discussion with Matthew about the Buckthorn proposal, then spending most of the next few days wading through a bucket load of documentation about the new machinery in the cannery before realising, on Thursday, that he'd missed a meeting with the Finance team about the restaurant's quarterly takings. And now, to cap it all, his damned father had dug his heels in and was refusing to discuss the same issue that Jonathan had broached with Matthew at the start of the week.

Jonathan had known that coming home to live wasn't going to be easy. If he'd wanted a quiet life, he reflected ruefully, he should have stayed in Manhattan. He was, after so many years, still a city boy at heart, used to prowling the urban jungle like a tiger, closing the deals and relishing the challenges. While Matthew had devoted his life to the family firm, Jonathan had played the field, sticking his fingers into different pies, building up his own portfolio, supporting himself. And he'd been bloody good at it too. He'd always have a soft spot for life on the other side of the Atlantic, having spent a year in the US as a student and completing part of his degree in the Ivy League splendour of Cornell University. That was when he'd fallen in love with America. The irony that he'd entered into an affair with his brother's very American first wife on his return from the States wasn't lost on him.

In truth, despite the co-directorship of Carter's Cider, he was still struggling to find his place in the family firm, and although his relationship with his brother had developed in leaps and bounds, due a great deal to Anna's influence, he still didn't know if a future in the firm, and in the village, was truly what he wanted. Playing second fiddle to a brother who effectively made all the big decisions was not the way he saw his life playing out.

The argument with Jack had put the lid on a lousy week. The older Jack got, the more set in his ways he was, and he was being particularly obstinate over Buckthorn. The business landscape was changing, and Carter's was in a tricky position. Artisan cider makers, small outfits with unique products, survived on their novelty value, and because they knew enough to keep their overheads small and their markets exclusive. Big players like Buckthorn were the other end of the spectrum; they ate companies for breakfast. Middle to large producers like Carter's, who had a strong foothold in the UK but were still developing their overseas markets, were at the greatest risk of being taken over by larger companies. Jonathan had the feeling, looking at the paperwork for the fiftieth time, that if they didn't commit to the takeover, they'd be missing out on a lot of money. And, frankly, the way he was feeling now, he'd be happy to sell his share of the company and get the hell out of the village again.

Except, of course, for Caroline.

No matter what he did, his thoughts kept returning to her. She was like no-one else he'd ever met; she got under his skin and drove him bananas with her stubbornness. That direct nature that had brought them together on the night of Matthew and Anna's wedding both attracted and frustrated him in equal measure; so much so that despite a few casual dates, he hadn't been able to commit to a relationship with anyone else in the time she'd been in the village. Even now, almost without realising it, his steps had taken him in the direction of The Cider Kitchen after a restless evening. He was drawn to her, he couldn't help it. But, despite the heart thumping chemistry of their encounter on Halloween night, she'd made it clear she didn't want anything from him in that department when she threw him out of the restaurant. If only he'd ignored his phone at that moment! But answering it had been as natural a gesture as breathing. Cursing his own stupidity, he decided to look in on her anyway.

The last customers were leaving as he approached and he saw Caroline turning the sign on the door to closed. On the surface she looked happy and relaxed; her pale face was warmed by the restaurant's lighting. She was smiling, but, from his vantage point outside he noticed that her smile seemed to disappear as soon as she'd wished the last customers goodbye, as if it was becoming an effort for her. He knew, of course, that she had an excellent professional track record as a manager and it was her personality and skill that made the restaurant such a welcoming place, but he couldn't help thinking that something seemed a little off with her tonight. With a stab of most uncharacteristic longing, Jonathan's pulse began to race. Perhaps it was because he'd had a crap week, perhaps it was because he sensed Caroline wasn't at her best either, but he suddenly wanted to burst in, sweep Caroline up in his arms and take her straight to bed. Screwing his courage to the sticking place, he walked out of the shadows and up to the door. He didn't need to tap on the glass, but Caroline certainly looked surprised to see him. Was he imagining it, or did her cheeks flush? Perhaps it was the downlighting playing tricks on him.

'Hello, stranger,' she said as she unlocked the door.

Jonathan smiled, relieved that she seemed to have forgiven him for Halloween night. He hoped he looked more cheerful than he felt. 'Hi,' he said. 'Have you got time for a quick coffee?'

Caroline, disarmed by Jonathan's most uncharacteristic reticence, closed the door behind him as he stepped into the restaurant. 'Who are you, and what have you done with Jonathan Carter?' She looked quizzically at him. 'Usually you just breeze in here whether I give you permission or not.'

Jonathan shook his head. 'I suppose I do rather over stay my welcome on occasion. Would you rather I left?'

In truth, Caroline was tired, mostly because she'd been losing a lot of sleep over the sinister communication from the man in her past, and she could have done with a relatively early night, but something in Jonathan's demeanour made her bite back a stronger retort. Besides, his unaccustomed hesitancy was seriously attractive and it would be nice to have some company for a little longer tonight. She smiled. 'No, stay and have a drink.'

In step together, they walked over to the bar. Caroline had recently shifted one of the sofas that had been in the 'coffee shop corner' of the restaurant just off to the side of the bar, and, sneaking a look in Jonathan's direction, she went straight to the bottle of calvados that was on the side of the bar. 'One of

Matthew's minions dropped a few bottles of this off earlier today,' she said as she sloshed a couple of generous measures into two tumblers. 'I guess you probably know but he's thinking of producing a limited edition run of it. Wanted to know how it would go down with the restaurant's clientele.'

'Actually, he hasn't spoken to me about it. Have there been many takers?' He and Matthew had agreed to experiment with the production of a small batch of calvados after Jonathan had clocked the success of the gin tastings at Kelli's wine shop in the village earlier in the year, but he hadn't been aware that Matthew had actually produced something worth marketing. That was another thing to add to the list of irritations, he thought.

'A few,' Caroline said. 'But I've yet to try it. After the Wookey Witch cider punch experience, I thought I'd stay off fermented apples for a while.' She picked up the two glasses and the bottle. 'But since this one was a freebie, I suppose we can indulge a little.' She sat down rather heavily on the sofa and let out a long breath.

'Busy night?' Jonathan asked. Uncharacteristically shy, he hovered by the bar, dithering about whether or not to sit down next to Caroline. *Funny,* he thought. *With anyone else I'd just get right on in there.*

Caroline shifted over. 'Come and join me if you want to.'

Jonathan didn't need a second invitation and as the leather sofa creaked comfortingly, he took a deep swig of the apple brandy.

'It's not bad,' he admitted, half-grudgingly.

Caroline nodded as the fiery liquid slipped over her tongue and down her throat. 'Are you all right?' she asked, noticing Jonathan's pensive expression.

Jonathan smiled. 'Better for the booze and the company.'

'Me too,' Caroline replied, in slight surprise. After the note, the white powder and the photo, she didn't think she'd ever feel relaxed again, but having Jonathan by her side was reassuring. 'But why might you need to feel better?'

Jonathan sighed. 'Once again, you don't mess about, do you?' He leaned back. 'It's been a hell of a week.'

'Girlfriend not returning your calls?' Caroline quipped, immediately wishing she hadn't when Jonathan's expression darkened.

'You really do think I just think with my cock, don't you?' He knocked back his calvados.

An uncomfortable silence descended. Both sipped their drinks, waiting for the other to break it.

'I'm sorry,' Caroline said gently. 'Why don't you tell me what it is that's bothering you.'

Jonathan sighed. 'I don't really want to talk about it.'

'Then why are you here?'

Jonathan found himself caught in her gaze, clear green eyes softened by the warm lights of the restaurant, and he could feel himself falling. It would be so easy to put the moves on her right now, but he sensed he was very likely to get a slap around the face if he did. And it wouldn't do much to dispel his earlier assertion, either. The realisation suddenly hit him that, if he wanted Caroline, he'd have to wait for her to make the first move, and, frustrating as that was, he was prepared to wait.

'I don't know really. I suppose I just wanted the company of someone who doesn't think they know it all, about me or the fucking business.'

'You've chosen well then,' Caroline said. 'Since we've only known each other a few months.'

Jonathan poured them both another glass of calvados. 'It's a long, tedious story, really, but I guess it really starts over a decade ago, and is still playing out now.' He sighed. 'I always knew coming back here would be a challenge, after what happened with me and Tara, Matthew's first wife, but I never realised how difficult it would be.'

Grateful to have a distraction from her own woes, Caroline smiled gently in encouragement. She'd never seen Jonathan like this, and she found his vulnerability, in contrast to his more usual confident manner, strangely appealing. 'Why don't you tell me about it?'

'It was fucking awful,' Jonathan said softly. 'Tara and I had this ridiculous affair for a few months, sneaking around behind everyone's back, especially Matthew. And poor Meredith, who was only three when it started, was left to her own devices in the front room of Cowslip Barn a few too many times for my liking.' He shuddered. 'There was one occasion when we came back downstairs after a quickie to find Meredith working her way through a packet of chocolate biscuits and chopping up Tara and Matthew's wedding album. Poor kid didn't know what hit her when Tara saw what she'd done. She'd been sticking all the chopped up pictures in her own scrap book.'

'Poor Meredith,' Caroline said. 'She must have been so confused.'

Jonathan looked thoughtful. 'To be honest, I don't think she really understood. That much, I'm thankful for. It wasn't until last year that she actually found out what had happened between the three of us, and the fallout from that was hideous for quite a while. Back then, when the shit finally hit the fan, Tara had come to me earlier that evening, bags packed, ready to go. She'd had enough and she wanted out. And she had Meredith in tow. I was utterly shell shocked. I'd never expected her to leave Matthew, and there she was, plane tickets in hand, demanding I go with her.'

'What had you expected?' Caroline asked. 'That you could just go on shagging your brother's wife on the quiet and no one would find out?'

Jonathan shook his head. 'I'd have shagged anything that moved at that point. I had no idea what actual commitment was. When she showed up, I didn't know how to handle it. But I was shit scared if I didn't get her, me and Meredith out of there sharpish, Matthew would turn up and go ballistic.'

'From what I understand of your brother, he'd never have hurt any of you,' Caroline replied, topping up their glasses.

'You've no idea the pressure he was under at that time,' Jonathan said. 'He was so tired from running the business, Tara's unhappiness and Meredith's terrible threes that he couldn't see straight, let alone think straight. I didn't want to be the one who got in his way.'

'So, what happened?'

'He came home earlier than Tara expected and put two and two together. Knew exactly where to come, too. Nearly broke the door down once he realised.' Jonathan's voice trembled slightly. 'It was the worst night of my life.'

Caroline wanted to be sceptical; she wanted to write Jonathan off as a womanising twat, but the look on his face showed how haunted he was by what he'd done all those years ago.

'Then what?' She prompted gently.

'Tara cut him off in the hallway, tried to explain to him what was going on. She was past caring whether or not she was going to hurt him, or, indeed he, her.' Jonathan swallowed. 'I could hear them from where I was in the living room. Matthew was utterly desperate; I could tell from the tone of his voice. And I suddenly realised what we'd done. Meredith was cuddled up on my knee; it was way past her bedtime and she was really drowsy. If we'd left ten minutes earlier, Matthew would never have worked it out until it was too late to stop us.' He picked up his apple brandy glass and drained it. 'As it was, he burst in on Meredith and me, and with amazing presence of mind, considering, asked Merry to go and find Tara. Then he decked me. Smacked me right in the mouth.' Jonathan shook his head. 'It's the first and last time he's ever hit me. I did deserve it, though. If it'd had been the other way round, I'd have punched the life out of him. Then he took Meredith home, but not before he'd told us both, in no uncertain terms, never to darken his door again.'

'Fuck,' Caroline breathed. 'What did you do?'

'We left,' Jonathan said simply. 'But Matthew wouldn't let Meredith leave the country with us. Said he'd call the police and cite child abduction. Tara was devastated but she knew she didn't have a leg to stand on. We got the next flight back to the US. We shacked up together for a few weeks afterwards but it didn't last.'

'So you can't even say that you did it because you thought you were going to be together forever.' Caroline shook her head. 'What a waste.'

'True, but if I hadn't fucked up his marriage, he'd never have married Anna, and you and I would never have met,' Jonathan managed a weak smile. 'And let's face it, Tara would have walked soon enough anyway; with me or someone else.'

'You really think so?' Caroline looked Jonathan directly in the eye. 'Or are you just telling yourself that to make yourself feel better?'

'You don't mess about do you, Caroline?'

'I've learned not to just settle for the easy explanation,' Caroline said wryly. 'Too many ways to fool yourself if you do. And to me, it sounds like that's what you're doing by trying to justify what you did.'

Jonathan shook his head. 'It was all a long time ago. There's been a lot of water, blood and cider under the bridge since then. And, frankly, darling, when you get to be as old as we are, I'm sure everyone's got things they're not too proud of in their past.'

Caroline's stomach lurched at the memory of some of hers, especially considering the contents of the envelope she'd had through her door recently. 'Yes, perhaps you're right.'

'Anything you'd like to tell me, since we seem to be in the confessional tonight?'

For a moment Caroline was tempted to come completely clean; if anyone was going to understand the darker nights of her past, it was Jonathan. After all, he'd had a fair few of his own from the sound of it. But there was so much to explain, so many shadows. She was in no way ready to confront them, not even with Jonathan by her side.

'Another time, perhaps,' Caroline said. Maybe it was the calvados, or perhaps it was the fact that Jonathan had dropped his guard and confided in her, or maybe even that she was scared of spending another night alone, knowing that *he* was out there somewhere, but Caroline's own defences were down. She was, she thought wryly, Jonathan's for the taking. Hesitating for a moment, unsure of his response, she leaned forward and kissed him lightly on the forehead. As her lips came into contact with his warm skin her heart skipped several beats.

'Caroline...' Jonathan whispered, taking her hand and leaning in closer to her as she moved back down to eye level. Her mouth was treacherously close to his and, for a delicious second, they hovered on the edge of something. Caroline breathed and brought her lips to Jonathan's.

If Jonathan was surprised, he did an excellent job of hiding it. He kissed her back with initial gentleness, until they both increased the pressure and found themselves moving deeper, tasting deeper. Jonathan's hand reached up to Caroline's hair, running long fingers through her auburn bob and then down over her neck and her back. Caroline's skin started to tingle. Memories of their night together washed back over her, awakening a throbbing sensation deep within. As Jonathan pulled her closer and they settled back against the leather sofa, Caroline felt a deep, instinctive sense of rightness. Of belonging. Of safety.

A discreet cough from the direction of the kitchen made them both spring apart guiltily.

'I'm, er, off now, Caroline,' Gino's voice called from the other room. Neither Caroline nor Jonathan could see him, but from the tone of his voice both were pretty sure he'd seen them.

'OK,' Caroline replied rather breathlessly. 'See you tomorrow.'

Caroline and Jonathan waited for the back door of the restaurant to open and close and then turned back to one another. Caroline burst out laughing. 'I thought he'd gone an hour ago. Why do I feel like some naughty teenager caught in the act?'

Jonathan laughed, too. 'Tell me about it.' He leaned in to kiss her again. 'The question is,' he said, between kisses, 'do you want to carry on being that naughty teenager?'

Caroline broke free from his insistent mouth and pulled back to look at him. 'I don't know,' she said warily. 'I swore I wasn't going to do this.'

'I'm in your hands, of course,' Jonathan murmured. 'But from where I'm sitting, we're pretty much halfway there already.' His tone was light, but there was no disputing the arousal in his voice and elsewhere. Caroline also couldn't pretend that she wasn't feeling that warm heaviness of desire, either. A pulse was beating between her thighs, low, insistent and needy.

'My place, my rules,' she said as she kissed him again. 'Just like last time. No complications. And no discussion in the morning.'

Jonathan didn't need telling twice. Sweeping her up in his arms, he virtually bundled her up the mezzanine steps until they were at the door to Caroline's flat. Pausing only to grab the key from the hook by the door, he pushed it open and slammed it behind them. Then, without missing a beat, he pulled her close and in a move worthy of James Bond slipped down the long, exposed silver zip at the back of her dress.

'Every time I've seen you in that dress I've wanted to do that,' Jonathan murmured as he started to kiss Caroline's neck. 'You're so sexy, Caroline.'

'You're not so bad yourself,' Caroline replied as she untucked Jonathan's white shirt from his trousers. The prominent bulge in their flat front showed her exactly how aroused he was, and she couldn't wait to strip him naked and feel him inside her. She didn't care if it was going to lead to awkwardness in the morning; she just needed him.

Time seemed to blur as they found themselves in bed, reliving their first night together, but discovering so much more. The apple brandy had lowered their inhibitions and Caroline's tiredness ebbed away as her desire rose.

Jonathan was long, lean and toned, and his body just seemed to fit hers; each touch bringing them pleasure. Caroline arched her back as Jonathan's mouth explored her, kissing and caressing down her body, up her thighs and everywhere in between. The sight of his hair, tumbling carelessly over his brow and tickling her thighs, and the pressure of his lips and probing tongue was driving her towards a much needed orgasm, and the last thought she had before the throbbing, exquisite climax engulfed her was that this was completely and utterly right. Her thighs clenched convulsively as the heavy, beating sensations overtook her, and she rode the wave, running her fingers through Jonathan's hair as she came.

As soon as Caroline's orgasm began to subside, and moving skilfully so that his fingertips were still caressing and stroking, Jonathan slid into her, warm, hard and beating with his own rhythm. His fingers kept stroking as he moved inside her, driving her on to another climax until his own orgasm exploded in a series of deep, ravishing thrusts. Pausing for an endless moment in the immediate afterglow, Jonathan's eyes were locked on Caroline's.

'You're wonderful,' he said softly. 'You're really, really wonderful.'

Caroline, who was still coming back down to earth and feeling the aftershocks of her orgasms, managed a breathless smile. 'I bet you say that to all the girls.'

Jonathan shook his head. 'Nope. Just you.' He buried his face in her shoulder and gently bit her collarbone. 'But don't tell anyone. They'd never believe you, anyway.'

Caroline, trying to hide the fact that she was absurdly touched as well as completely sated, muttered, 'no strings, remember.'

Jonathan raised his head and smiled ruefully. 'Understood. But I do mean it, you know.'

Caroline said nothing. With everything that was going on, The Cider Kitchen, her new life, the shadows from her old life, she really couldn't risk adding Jonathan to her long list of complications. Somewhere, from a quiet part of her mind, a small voice was suggesting that perhaps Jonathan wouldn't be a complication; that he could, perhaps, help her to make sense of the other things, but she resolutely hushed that voice. Jonathan, no matter how good a lover he was, was not the answer. At least not in the long term. For the moment, though, she was more than happy to snuggle up next to him, sated, warm and more secure than she'd felt in a long time.

30

Caroline and Jonathan woke late the next morning. They'd slept together in a tangle of limbs, and as Caroline rolled over, a shaft of sunlight coming through the curtains illuminated the dial of the old fashioned alarm clock, complete with bell, that sat on her bedside table. She'd never trusted her phone to wake her but the shrill bell on a working day was usually enough to do the job. Although last night, of course, she'd forgotten to set it, having entirely too much on her mind, and in her bed, to bother.

'Good morning,' Jonathan said sleepily as she rolled back to him and snuggled under his arm. 'Sleep well?'

'Better than I have in ages,' Caroline replied. 'You.'

'Same.'

For a little while they lay entwined, enjoying the closeness. Caroline felt completely at peace and though there were still clouds on her horizon, she felt insulated from them for now at least, by Jonathan's presence.

Eventually, though, she had to get up. Not least because she was thirsty and needed a wee. Unselfconsciously naked, she swung her legs out of bed and reached for Jonathan's white shirt, which had ended up pooled by her side of the bed. It came down almost to her knees. Doing up a couple of buttons, she glanced back at Jonathan. 'Coffee?'

'Oh Christ, yes,' Jonathan replied. 'Just how much of that calvados did we finish last night? My head's pounding.'

'Enough,' Caroline said dryly. She had visions of her rather more elderly customers dancing on the tables if it ever went permanently on the drinks menu.

After nipping into the bathroom, Caroline padded down the stairs to the restaurant. She took two coffee cups from the sideboard and set to making the strongest coffee she could. While she was waiting, she poured herself a glass of water and then another for Jonathan. Heading back up the stairs, she put the coffee and water down on the bedside table, but before she could drink it, Jonathan had pulled her back on top of him and was skilfully unbuttoning the shirt. 'Forget the coffee,' he said huskily. 'I can think of a much better cure for a hangover.'

Vaguely aware that her staff would be coming in soon to prepare for the lunchtime service, Caroline's last thought before surrendering to Jonathan's hands, mouth and other things once more was to wonder whether or not she'd dropped the latch on the Yale lock. If Gino or Emma, or heaven forbid, Meredith, caught the two of them like this, they'd never live it down.

By the time Caroline had finally kicked Jonathan out of bed, it was coming up to eleven o'clock. As they came down the stairs together, Caroline could hear Gino chopping something in the kitchen and the low undertone of the local radio station that he listened to while he was preparing.

'Ssh,' Caroline said as she showed Jonathan to the door.

Jonathan looked quizzical. 'Why? We've got nothing to be ashamed of.'

'You might not have, but I'd rather not be catalogued as one of your conquests,' Caroline said.

'The only one that matters,' Jonathan said, all seriousness. 'Call me. When you're ready.'

Closing the front door on him, Caroline smiled to herself. She couldn't quite believe she'd given in and slept with Jonathan again, but she was certainly pleased she had. She had a feeling, though, that she was going to have to seek some advice from Anna about how to handle the fallout from a night with Jonathan; hopefully, her former sister-in-law might have some answers that would stop her from getting hurt.

*

The conversation with Anna would have to wait, though. Caroline had forgotten that she'd agreed to meet a supplier of free range, corn fed, totally organic poultry at twelve o'clock. Fortunately, the meeting was as brief as it was productive, and, somehow, she got through the lunchtime service, trying not to allow her thoughts to wander too far in the direction of the other end of the cider farm. She felt as though she had Jonathan's initials branded on her forehead, though, and she was increasingly paranoid that everyone she spoke to would know what she'd been up to. In reality, it was only Gino who had seen them and he wasn't a gossip, but Caroline still felt different; changed by the night. She'd let down her defences for the first time in a long while. A one night stand at the wedding had been one thing, but Jonathan was, quite literally, on her doorstep now. How the hell was she going to deal with him, and more interestingly, what was it exactly that she wanted from him?

After a brief break in the afternoon, which she'd spent playing with the cats and drinking rather too much coffee, Caroline had prepared for the evening service, putting on the same dress she'd worn on The Cider Kitchen's opening night. She cursed herself for choosing it, realising that her prime motive was that Jonathan might see her in it but by six o'clock it was too late to change.

It was a busy evening, and Caroline was grateful. It stopped her thoughts from wandering too far across the orchard to Jonathan. About halfway through service, Caroline was closing the tab for one of her regular couples, early diners who liked to pop in early and then get back home to watch *Midsomer Murders* or *Death in Paradise,* when she suddenly became aware of a heavy, cloying, frighteningly familiar scent. As she tapped the digits of the bill into the card reader, her fingers started to tremble and the hair rose at the back of her neck. It was a scent she recognised, a scent she couldn't fail to react to, and a scent she hoped she'd never experience again.

Forcing a smile at the customers, she handed back their credit card and then steeled herself. Gripping hold of the counter for support, she blinked furiously, praying she was seeing things.

But no.

Not this time.

There, being settled onto a table in a quiet corner of the restaurant was the one person she'd prayed she'd never see again. Since she'd last seen him, he'd changed little; he had an air of confidence about him like Jonathan, but where she found Jonathan's manner attractive, this man's had always been unsettling, combative. His close cropped dark hair was showing some signs of greying, and the brown leather jacket and black jeans he was wearing looked obviously expensive. Given that he had a rather lucrative sideline in addition to his actual job, the clothing went with the territory.

Gripped with dread, Caroline watched as the man smiled winningly up at Meredith, who'd been assigned to that area of the restaurant this evening. Caroline could see Meredith nodding and making a few recommendations before she pulled out her notepad and took his order. As Meredith moved away towards the kitchen, Caroline forced out the breath she'd been holding and tried to keep calm. The sight of him here, on her turf, talking to Anna's stepdaughter and Jonathan's niece filled her with horror. It would seem the note and the text had been somewhat more than a warning. The question was, of what?

Crossing the floor of the restaurant to the kitchen, Caroline wished she could run out of the back door and never return, but she had to stay professional. There were other customers besides him, and as she scanned the restaurant, all the while keeping him in sight, she felt reassured that there were enough people around for him not to be an immediate threat.

'You all right, Boss?' Gino asked as Caroline leant on the doorway of the kitchen for support. 'You look like you've seen a ghost.'

Caroline shook her head hurriedly. 'I'm fine. Have you got table six's order up?'

Gino nodded. 'Meredith just brought it in. Is there a change?'

'No. Just wanted to check something.' Caroline pulled the order slip off the counter warmer and scanned Meredith's generous, looped handwriting. The customer had made some medium priced choices and also ordered a half bottle of the house red wine. Clearly he wasn't minded to splash much cash on this visit. She remembered how he'd footed the bill for bottles of Dom Perignon on their company nights out; but then, she figured, he was the one who handled the champagne suppliers for the events management company they'd both worked for. Did he think she was up for more of his other 'merchandise'? The kind that he'd sent her a sample of along with that note? Well, he could think again. That was one product she was happy to leave in her past.

For the rest of the evening service Caroline tried to keep as low a profile as possible; not easy when she was becoming well known to her regular diners. She kept a careful eye on the unwelcome guest, who seemed, on the surface, to be acting like any other diner. Just as the restaurant was starting to empty and get ready to close, Meredith came up to her.

'The man on table six has asked to see you,' she said.

Caroline's heart lurched. She swallowed hard. 'OK. Tell him I'll be over as soon as I've closed out Mr and Mrs Cooper's bill.'

'I'll do that if you like,' Meredith said. 'They were on one of my tables, so I'll sort it.'

Caroline inwardly cursed Meredith's helpful nature. She forced a smile. 'Thanks.' Knees trembling under her dress, she raised her head high and walked over to table six where the customer was finishing his coffee. As she approached, he put his espresso cup down on the saucer and raised his eyes. The gaze he gave her was cool, assessing, and ever so slightly amused.

'Hello, Caroline.'

The voice was carefully accent neutral. Just as it had ever been. He never liked to give anything away about himself. She still didn't know where he really came from, although at times she'd have willingly believed he'd originated from the depths of hell.

Caroline nodded. 'Hello, Paul.' Her voice, admirably steady, gave nothing away of her churning stomach. Mindful of her remaining customers, she forced a smile. 'Did you enjoy your meal?'

'It was lovely. As was that little waitress who was serving me.' Paul Stone's eyes narrowed. 'Unusual name, Meredith. Not many about.'

Caroline's hackles rose. She was all too familiar with Stone's way of casually assessing women and she felt particularly protective of Meredith. 'She's a good waitress,' she said guardedly.

'Well connected, too,' Stone said. 'I understand her daddy owns the building we're sitting in. Must be worth a bob or two. And with that accent, I'd assume she's privately educated. Lots of... wealthy connections.'

Caroline blinked. 'As I said, she's a good waitress. If you'll excuse me, I've got other customers to attend to.'

'Aren't you going to ask?' Stone said as Caroline turned away.

'Ask what?'

'What brings me to this part of the world?'

'To be honest, Paul, I'm not interested.' Caroline said, turning back and locking eyes with him. With the presence of her staff and the remaining customers, she felt confident enough to be assertive.

Stone gave a nasty grin. 'You will be,' he said. 'If I know you.'

'I don't think so.' She shook her head. 'I'll get Meredith to bring over your bill. I assume you've had all you want?'

'For now,' Stone replied. 'I'll see you soon, Caro.'

Caroline winced. No one else had ever shortened her name, and to her ears, in this new life, it felt as though he was addressing a different person. 'Don't count on it,' she muttered as she walked away. Shortly afterwards, she saw Meredith handing him back his card and receipt. She breathed a sigh of relief as he left The Cider Kitchen without a backward glance.

She got through the rest of the evening on autopilot, counting the takings for the evening service and securing them in the safe before double and triple checking she'd locked both the safe and the front and back doors of the building. With Paul Stone in the area, she couldn't be too careful. By the time she'd finished checking for the third time, it was well past midnight and she was absolutely shattered. Gino had stayed late, sensing that Caroline was distracted, but she'd sent him on his way half an hour previously, albeit reluctantly.

Just as she was about to turn in, her mobile phone buzzed from the counter where she'd left it. Heart in her mouth, she considered ignoring it, but she knew if she didn't check who'd messaged her she'd be lying awake all night wondering. Crossing the restaurant and picking up her phone, she swiped the screen and steeled herself.

Hope your day went OK. Can I come over? J x

Caroline's heart turned over for a slightly different reason. At this moment, she wanted nothing more than to throw herself into Jonathan's arms and demand his protection but she was sure that if she unburdened herself to him about Paul Stone and her past, he was likely to run a million miles in the opposite direction. Given what a player he was, even with his obvious affection last night, she didn't want to give him any reason to turn tail. No, for now she'd better keep him at arms' length. She couldn't risk Stone coming into contact with Jonathan, or any of the Carter family for that matter; his presence in the village was something she was going to have to sort out herself. Texting a quick, negative answer, she turned out the restaurant's lights and headed off to bed, scooping up little Solly from her favourite spot on the mezzanine landing as she went. She might not have wanted human company tonight, but the kitten would do just as well. She assumed Scrumpy was out hunting in the orchard, as had become her habit; she couldn't help feeling hunted down herself.

31

The next morning, Caroline still couldn't shake the unease that Paul Stone was now definitely in the area. Everywhere she turned, it was as though she was being watched. Uncharacteristically snappy with her staff, she was relieved when the lunchtime service was over and she had a couple of hours to herself to regroup and calm down. Flipping the sign on the door of the restaurant, for the first time she really felt the isolation of being situated at the far end of the cider farm, away from the centre of the village. Preoccupied with her thoughts, she forgot to lock the door. It was only when she was returning the last of the cutlery, still warm from the dishwasher, back to the trays behind the bar and she heard the swish of the front door being pushed open again that she realised. She started to shiver again as the familiar scent of Stone's aftershave permeated the air as if it would suffocate her.

'Get out of here before I call the police,' Caroline said, in a voice that sounded far stronger than she felt.

'You wouldn't do that,' Stone said.

'Try me.' Realising that the sound she could hear was a handful of cutlery clinking together as her hands started to shake, she put them down hurriedly on the bar. Belatedly, she wondered if she should have kept hold of one of the knives.

'I thought I'd drop in now that this place is a bit quieter.' Stone reached out a hand towards the carefully arranged carnations in a glass vase at the table nearest him. In a swift gesture, he'd beheaded one and began to roll the delicate petals around between his fingers.

Caroline felt physically sick. 'I'm warning you. Get out of here or I'll have the police round here so fast you won't be able to breathe.'

Stone laughed. 'In this village? I should think the local bobby, if there is one, is far more accustomed to returning lost cats and helping little old ladies across the road than strong arming polite visitors from the local dining establishment.'

'You'd be surprised.'

Stone held her gaze for a moment too long. The silence between them seemed to crackle. Caroline remembered, with utter shame, the oblivion this man had provided her and the thought of it was enough to make the bile rise in her throat.

'Since you didn't have time to talk last night, I just thought I'd let you know that I'm now working in the area,' he said. 'I've been transferred to the South West regional branch in Bristol. It should have been a promotion, of course, but thanks to your interference it's been more of a sideways move.'

'I don't know what you mean,' Caroline said, glancing at the clock on the wall. Her staff weren't due in for a couple of hours yet but he didn't need to know that. She wasn't going to reveal any vulnerability to him if she could help it. 'Whatever meant you didn't get the promotion to Regional Manager in Surrey, it was nothing to do with me.'

'Oh, don't play the innocent with me, Caro,' Stone snapped, beheading another one of the flowers he'd picked up from the vase on the nearest table. 'We all know you whispered in Alan's ear to try to get him to pass me over for that job. What did you have to do? Sleep with him?'

'Why would I do that?' Caroline said. 'It makes no difference to me whether you get promoted or not.' She resented the assertion that she'd slept with her former boss. The man was happily married and devoted to his wife. The polar opposite, in fact, of Stone, who got through women as quickly as he changed his very expensive socks. Men like him always assumed a woman had to lie on her back to get what she wanted though; it made her angry to think about it. She'd had a couple of conversations, off the record, with Alan about her team's suitability for promotion, certainly, but nothing that would mean someone was passed over if they had enough talent for the job. She'd favoured another colleague for the Regional Manager's job, but Alan was more than capable of making up his own mind; he didn't need her to do it for him.

'As it turns out, though, perhaps it's for the best,' Stone's expression changed lightning fast. In the old days, Caroline had been bewildered by his sudden mood changes, but now she just wanted him out of her sight. 'After all, I got transferred to Bristol, and I knew that one of my highest spending former clients was in the area as well.' He paused, and dropped the shredded flower carelessly. 'Just so you know, I'm keeping my hand in on the other business, should you need… anything. I won't charge you for the sample I sent a few weeks back.'

'I'd rather die,' Caroline snapped. 'Now please leave.'

Stone gave a knowing, sardonic grin. 'You have my mobile number now, Caro. Don't be afraid to use it. Although…' he trailed off meaningfully, 'perhaps, actually, I'll be the one to call you. This place is clearly doing very well. It would be a shame if it was to get out that the desirable manager of this lovely establishment had a rather less than savoury past, wouldn't it? Wouldn't do your reputation any good.'

Caroline felt a surge of anger mixed with fear. How dare he come onto her territory and start throwing his weight around? 'Are you threatening me, Paul?'

Stone laughed. 'You always were rather melodramatic, Caro. Think of it as a suggestion. After all, this place isn't going to miss a few quid here and there, is it? I daresay we can come to some… arrangement. Let's say, oh, I don't know, a few grand for my silence? And you do owe me. If it hadn't been for you, I'd have been overseeing quite a few projects in Surrey now instead of being stuck out in the West Country as an organiser.' He reached into his jacket pocket for his phone and after a few seconds, located the file he wanted. Silently, he handed the phone over to Caroline. As she saw what was on the screen, she gasped.

'When did you take this?'

'I don't exactly remember when; after all, you and I had quite a lot of nights like that back in Surrey, didn't we? And there's plenty more where that came from. Including a few rather interesting videos.'

Caroline thrust the phone back at Stone as if it was infected. In one sense, it was like looking at someone else; that life seemed so far away from her now. In another, there was no doubt that the person in the picture snorting cocaine from a coffee table in Stone's flat was her. With social networking as it was, it would be so easy for him to make that image, and the others that he had, public. The Cider Kitchen had a strong online presence and with a few clicks, she could be all over the internet. The damage it would do to the brand would be considerable.

'I bet you're sorry now that you didn't back me for that promotion, aren't you?' Stone's face was set in a smirk as Caroline looked back at him.

'Get out,' Caroline said, hating the tremor in her voice. 'Or I really will call the police.'

'No you won't,' he said. Without warning he moved nearer to her, invading her space and backing her up against the bar. 'You won't tell anyone. This is just between you and me, so there's no need to go running to that boyfriend of yours, either.' His breath was hot and sour on her face and Caroline felt the acid in her throat.

'Boyfriend?' Cursing herself as the word came out, Caroline was further irritated by the brittleness of her voice.

'You are aiming high, aren't you, Caro? Joint heir to the Carter family fortune? Quite a change from the idiots you used to fuck. But I bet that pastel shirted pretty boy would go down just as easily in a fight as all the others used to.'

Caroline felt sicker and sicker. The self-assurance in Stone's tone was what frightened her the most. 'Think about it, Caro. From the look of this place, you can afford a few quid here and there. More than you can afford for those pictures to go public, anyway. I'll drop in again soon.' Turning on his heel, he ambled out of the restaurant and off into the rapidly diminishing afternoon light.

For a long time after he left, Caroline stood rooted to the spot as if she was turned to stone. Stone. That was a laugh, she thought. There was a time when she had been more than happy to see him, more than happy to hand over vast quantities of her extremely large salary for what he offered her. That time was in the past, but it still remained fresh in her mind. What had started as a social ritual, almost as commonplace as a liqueur coffee after dinner, had turned into so much more after the death of her parents. It had helped to dull the pain of losing them.

James, when he had first discovered she was using, about two months after their parents' death, had been furious. She could still remember the anger on his face when he'd called round late one Friday evening and found her buzzing around her flat like a wasp on steroids. He'd said nothing at the time, merely left her to it, but twelve hours later on Saturday, he'd gone back round there and hit her with both barrels of his rage. 'What are you thinking?' He'd yelled. 'How fucking irresponsible can you get?' And, the one that eventually roused her out of her stupor. 'What the hell would Mum and Dad think?'

'Well they're dead, James, or hadn't you noticed?' she'd finally replied, eyes as dead as the words she was speaking. 'It's just you and me now.' She leaned back against the sofa, willing the pounding in her head to go away. 'And you've got Anna, so you'll be all right. Who the hell do I have?'

James had stood stock still for a moment, digesting her response.

'You've still got me.' And with that, he'd turned and walked out of her flat.

It was three days before she saw him again. He called in after work with a bottle of wine and a large portion of chips. They spent the night talking, trying to make sense of how she'd fallen into the trap of snorting her salary up her nose. She'd cried, he'd cried, and at the end of it she'd promised to get help and stay away from those who tried to drag her back with them.

And for a while she'd managed it. She'd avoided the scenes where she knew she'd find cocaine, booked in to see a drug and alcohol abuse counsellor and made sure she was home the right side of midnight. Then James had been killed. And try as she might, she needed something to dull the pain again.

At first it had been the odd snort now and again but before she knew it, she had Paul Stone on speed dial and was snorting cocaine just to keep on an even keel. Anna never knew about it. James had kept her in the dark because Caroline had asked him to. She knew they didn't generally keep secrets from one another but she'd begged him to keep this one. When Anna, numb from her own grief, had been to see her in the days between James' death and his funeral, Caroline had been high. She'd seen the question in Anna's eyes but didn't have the capacity to answer it. She'd hoped Anna just saw her erratic behaviour as grief.

Six months after James' death and she was beginning to get a grip. She'd seen her GP and been referred for some treatment and begun seeing the counsellor again. The trouble was, nice as the counsellor was, Caroline had never been one to share her problems and James had been the only person in whom she'd ever confided. Now he was gone, she really did feel alone. If anyone was going to get her to kick the habit once and for all, it had to be her.

But she'd reckoned without her beloved niece, Ellie. Caroline had fallen in love with Ellie the second she saw her. The image of her father, Caroline didn't have any choice. Ellie's perfect little face, her miniature toes and tiny fingers, and her feisty wail when irritated, hungry or tired, had captivated Caroline. Getting to know her niece from pretty much the day she'd been born had been one of the most rewarding relationships that Caroline had ever had. So, six months on from James' death, when Ellie had turned two, Caroline had made a promise to herself and to her tiny niece. There would be no more chasing oblivion in the form of a bag of white powder; no more dealer on speed dial. She would take herself out of harm's way as soon as she could. A new beginning; a fresh start. That was what she needed. Stone had brooded from a distance, biding his time, waiting for her to lapse, but she never had. And when the offer of the job at The Cider Kitchen had come from Jonathan in the spring, she'd hoped that would truly be the last she'd see of Stone.

And now that fresh start looked as though it was going to be ruined. Well, this time it wasn't going to happen. She crossed the restaurant floor to the till and opened it. The question was, could she afford what would it take to silence Paul Stone?

32

The problem with running The Cider Kitchen, Caroline thought a couple of days later, was that it really didn't give her anywhere to hide. Everyone knew where she was both day and night since she lived above the restaurant, and while that meant she was protected by the constant presence of people during business hours, the only time she felt truly alone was in the small hours of the morning, and that was precisely the worst time to feel vulnerable. If it wasn't for Solly and Scrumpy, who were growing more confident by the day, she'd be a nervous wreck by now. They were almost fully grown but they still slept curled up together, inches from Caroline's head at night. They'd never really got the hang of the cushioned basket.

Caroline didn't mind this, but she couldn't help noticing that Jonathan was sneezing a fair bit whenever he popped in. He'd been keeping his visits to the daytime since their impromptu night together, and Caroline wasn't sure what to read into that. She'd asked him for no strings and it seemed that he was obliging her, but on the other hand, he'd revealed an awful lot about himself during their conversation on the night they'd spent together. Was he afraid she was going to bring up what he'd told her and use it against him? He was as courteous as ever when he met her on restaurant business but she just couldn't read him on a more personal level. Perhaps she needed to speak to Anna.

It had been a busy night and Caroline hadn't been able to keep track of where the cats were. Usually during service they'd be locked upstairs, being unamused by the noise. They could still get outside using the cat flap that led to the fire escape at the back of the building, and later, when the restaurant had closed, Caroline would feed them and give them the run of upstairs. Tonight, only Solly had shown her face briefly at the top of the stairs before scuttling off to Caroline's pillow. Scrumpy had been absent. The more adventurous of the two, she'd taken to catching vermin in the orchards, and Caroline had been presented with more than a few disembowelled mice over the past few weeks. Resolving to check again for the cat later, and any 'presents' she might have brought in, Caroline got on with dealing with the final customers.

Caroline had never been more pleased to see the back of the evening. Despite the full restaurant and the fact that Gino had stayed on until long after midnight prepping for the next service and chatting to her, it was with terror in her heart that she finally crossed the floor of the restaurant to lock the front door. Since Paul Stone's visit she'd been obsessively checking the restaurant's Twitter, Facebook and Instagram feeds, looking for incriminating posts or images. What if he didn't really care about the money and was just out to humiliate her? Despite buying a lot of cocaine from him over the years she'd never been in a relationship with him; but that hadn't been for lack of trying on his part. Perhaps he was still angry that she'd turned down his advances. She knew she should go to the police; what he was doing was blackmail, but she also knew that by doing that she would lay herself open to all kinds of possible outcomes; not least losing her job. Was there anything she could do? Was there any way she could get him the money, or some of it, without calling attention to herself? And what would Stone do if she couldn't? How far would he go?

Caroline waited for the security light over the restaurant's front door to click on. It was so sensitive that movement inside the doorway often set it off but she found this quite reassuring when she was left on her own at the end of the night. The nights, or early mornings in this case, really were getting colder and darker, and she didn't even have the benefit of the risen moon to see by since it was hidden under a covering of blue grey cloud. Her body was screaming with tiredness but her mind was still racing at a thousand miles per hour.

Stone could hurt her. He could hurt people close to her. Caroline's heart contracted at the thought of that bastard going anywhere near Anna and Matthew, or Meredith. And Jonathan. Darling, misguided, arrogant Jonathan.

As the security light finally came on and the front step was lit up, Caroline screamed, but the sound coming out of her mouth was suddenly so much more than that. Louder, louder, more hysterical by the second, she carried on until finally there was no more noise to make. She ripped open the front door of the restaurant and sank to her knees on the doorstep, picking something up and cradling it in her arms. It was still warm. Scrumpy, noisy, naughty, adventurous Scrumpy had had her neck broken.

33

Caroline's every instinct was to call the police; but she was paralysed by fear. Her hands trembled uncontrollably as she cradled the small animal on her doorstep. How could Stone do this? It had to be him. That visit a couple of days ago was clearly more of a warning than she'd taken it for.

'Caroline?' Gino, on his way back to the restaurant having left his phone in the kitchen, raced to her side. 'Caroline, are you alright?'

Caroline couldn't summon the words. As Gino came around the corner, his presence triggered the security light again and for a moment they both blinked. Gino, seeing Caroline still slumped on the doorstep, was by her side in an instant. 'Are you hurt?'

Caroline shook her head. 'It's not me.' She opened her arms slightly so that Gino could see Scrumpy's lifeless body.

'Shit!' Gino tried to take the cat but Caroline clung tightly to her. 'Who did this?' He helped Caroline to her feet. 'Come on, let's get off the doorstep.'

Somehow, they got through the front door and up to Caroline's flat and Gino had her kettle boiling in no time. Huddled onto one of her kitchen chairs, still clutching Scrumpy's body, she was shuddering uncontrollably.

'You've got to call the police,' Gino, who was surprisingly good in a crisis, said firmly. 'Someone clearly did this to frighten you.'

'No,' Caroline came to her senses immediately at the mention of the police. 'The police won't do anything anyway.'

Gino handed Caroline a mug of hot, sweet tea and took a sip of his own. 'This is serious. What if whoever did this comes after you next time?'

'No police. It was probably a one off.'

'Is there anyone you can think of who might have it in for you?' Gino's face was concerned, but his eyes were as searching as the security light outside.

Hating herself, but knowing that if she confided in Gino she might very well be putting him at risk, Caroline shook her head again.

'Do you want me to call anyone?'

Who could Gino call? Caroline thought. Anna and Matthew would be tucked up in bed for the night, Jonathan would only insist on tracking down whoever did this, and she didn't want him involved; there was no-one else. 'I'm fine,' she said shakily. 'You should get home, too.'

'I'm staying for as long as you need me,' Gino said. Caroline was surprised for a moment by how quickly he took control of the situation but then she remembered he was used to calling the shots in the kitchen. 'Go and get in the shower and I'll whip you up a warm milk drink that'll help you sleep.'

'You'll make someone a lovely wife one day,' Caroline said, but smiled slightly. She wrapped Scrumpy's body up in a towel and placed her gently in an old shoebox. 'I want to keep hold of her in here for tonight.'

'Fair enough,' Gino said gently.

Caroline put the shoe box on the small table in the hallway and then trailed dispiritedly through to the bathroom. Under the shower, alone, she cried and cried. Staggering back out, she wrapped herself in her dressing gown and pulled back her duvet. As promised, Gino, after knocking gently on the door, brought in a mug of warm milk.

'Try to get some sleep,' he said. 'And don't worry about service tomorrow if you don't feel up to it. I'll call Emma to come in and do an extra shift.'

'Thanks,' sipping the drink, Caroline's eyes already felt heavy.

The next morning Caroline awoke from a surprisingly deep slumber. For a moment, she was terrified as she heard someone moving around in her living room and then she realised it was merely Gino in sneak mode, obviously trying not to wake her. Climbing gingerly out of bed, she crept to the bedroom door and managed a small smile as she saw her rather buff head chef slipping back into last night's t-shirt.

'You're wasted on men,' she managed weakly.

'I'll take that as a compliment rather than workplace objectification. This time.'

'Sorry,' Caroline replied. 'Put it down to delayed shock.' She glanced to where she had put the shoe box containing Scrumpy's body last night, upon which Gino had tactfully put the lid.

'Are you sure you shouldn't call the police?' Gino asked, turning serious brown eyes on her.

Caroline swallowed. 'I'll think about it.' But even to her own ears, Caroline could hear the lie. There was no way she could call the police and tell them that she suspected that Scrumpy was killed by her former cocaine supplier; that was a can of worms she really didn't want to open. She forced a smile. 'Look. Thanks for staying. I appreciate it.'

'It's the least I could do,' said Gino. 'Will you be alright if I nip home now and get sorted out? I've got some stuff to do before the lunchtime service.'

Caroline nodded. 'I'll be fine. I'll see you later.'

'Don't feel you have to come down tonight,' Gino replied. 'I can text Emma if needs be.'

'I'm better in the restaurant than stewing here upstairs waiting for him to come back,' Caroline said unguardedly.

'You sound like you know who did this,' Gino raised a speculative eyebrow.

Grabbing a mug from the mug tree on the windowsill, Caroline gave a nervous laugh. 'I just meant... it's bound to be a man, isn't it?'

'OK, boss,' Gino said wearily. 'I know better than to argue the point at this time of the morning.'

Caroline nodded but couldn't meet Gino's gaze. 'Go home. And thank you for coming to my rescue.'

They walked down the stairs to the restaurant together, and rather than leaving through the kitchen as he would normally, Gino headed for the front door. 'I want to check that nobody's left any more nasty surprises for you,' he said, reaching for the bolt on the top of the door.

Thankfully, the doorstep was clear. Caroline hovered in the doorway, feeling nervous again now that she was going to be left alone in this big, empty building. 'Thanks again,' she said, and without thinking, pulled Gino into a clumsy hug.

Gino laughed nervously. 'Any more of that and I'll have to get a restraining order!' he quipped, but he enveloped her briefly in his embrace. 'I'll see you in a couple of hours, okay?'

'All right.' Caroline replied.

Gino stepped out of the door, looked left and right and then headed off.

At that moment, Jonathan, restless from another night spent tossing and turning over the proposed takeover bid, happened to be on his way to get an early start at work. Normally, he'd go straight to his office on the other side of the site, but today he thought he'd stroll over to The Cider Kitchen to grab a cup of coffee to go and catch up with Caroline, who was bound to be up and about by now. Seeing Gino emerging from the restaurant in what were clearly last night's clothes, and even worse, hugging Caroline in full view on the doorstep made him feel a most unaccustomed stab of jealousy.

34

Jonathan wasn't used to being blown out. Ever since he was old enough to realise the effect he could have on women, and, to be truthful, some men, he'd been able to nurture this ability. It had got him a lot of good nights, some exciting days and the odd bit of preferential treatment on occasion. Whereas his older brother had always unselfconsciously rejected getting his own way by wit and charm alone, Jonathan had turned into a master of it. He wasn't unusual, he was sure, as a much adored younger child. His mother had spoiled him and his father had always related more to him than Matthew.

Given this mindset, rejection wasn't something that sat easily with him, so to have seen Gino bloody Marshall slinking out of the restaurant in last night's clothes made him feel alternately angry and humiliated. Had Caroline really moved on from him so quickly? Had their night meant that little to her?

Jonathan cursed himself; he was obviously going soft. *Not a problem the other night,* he thought wryly, but then remembered what he'd just seen. Gino was fifteen years younger than him, after all. Perhaps he hadn't measured up to Caroline's expectations. Deciding to rethink the coffee, he was picking up his pace when he heard the restaurant door open.

'Jonathan,' Caroline called out.

Automatically, he turned round. Caroline was standing in the doorway. She looked paler than usual, vulnerable, the shadows under her eyes more pronounced. *Too much shagging,* he thought, determined not to show her that he cared.

'Hi,' he said, without moving towards her.

Caroline dithered in the doorway, one hand on the frame. Her uncertainty was so uncharacteristic, Jonathan felt a stab of longing and the faintest sense that something wasn't right. He brushed it aside; she must be feeling guilty that she'd been caught with her young chef.

'Are you coming in?' Caroline asked, when no more from Jonathan was forthcoming.

Jonathan regarded her coolly. 'I don't think so.' He glanced at his watch. 'I'm running late.'

Caroline looked stung for a split second before a careful mask of nonchalance descended. 'All right,' she said. 'I'll see you around, then.'

'I should think so,' Jonathan replied. 'Unless you've got something better to do.'

'What's that supposed to mean?'

Jonathan held her gaze. 'Oh, nothing.' He paused. 'But I wouldn't go mixing business with pleasure again if I were you.'

'I'm not sure I know what you mean.' Caroline's face was all irritable confusion but at least the fire was back in her eyes.

'Don't worry about it,' Jonathan said, managing to sound lighter than he felt. 'I'll see you at our next meeting.' Turning on his heel, he strode off in the direction of the cider farm's office.

Caroline shook her head in frustration. What the hell had rattled Jonathan's cage so badly that he couldn't even share a coffee with her? She resolved to tackle him some other time. She had more than enough to worry about with Paul Stone on the scene. Gino's presence on the sofa last night had comforted her, but she had many more nights ahead of her when she was going to have to face the reality of being alone and now it seemed Jonathan wasn't going to be by her side for any of them either.

She wished she felt able to confide in someone about everything that was happening, but the only person she could have told even a fraction of it to was James, and he was long gone. She hadn't felt his loss this keenly for a while. Perhaps talking to someone was the solution after all, though. She grabbed her mobile and, with only a moment's hesitation, searched for Paul Stone's number. He picked up on the third ring, as if he'd been waiting for her to call.

'OK,' Caroline said wearily. 'You win. How much will it take to get rid of you?' Her face drained of all colour when she heard the amount of money he suggested. It was all of her remaining redundancy money and then some. But what choice did she have? Taking a deep breath, she agreed. 'I'll transfer half from my bank account tonight, and you'll get the other half in cash by the end of the month. And that will be it, Paul, or I will go to the police. I know what you did to my cat.' Hands trembling, the sound of his self-assured, low laughter rang in her ears as she ended the call.

Briefly, the thought of going to Anna crossed her mind, but she was very heavily pregnant now and had enough on her plate. Although, Caroline thought, perhaps Anna might be able to give her some answers about Jonathan's sudden about turn, if the man himself insisted on being so fucking cryptic. Suddenly feeling the need to get out of the restaurant, she decided she'd wander over to Cowslip Barn. But she was going to make sure Solly, her remaining kitten, was safely shut in her rooms upstairs first.

*

Anna put her mug down on the table and leaned back in her chair, trying to get comfortable around the prominent bump of her unborn child. The last weeks were the worst, she knew from experience. Once she was as comfortable as she could be, she looked back at Caroline. 'Do you want to know what I think?'

'Do I get a choice?' Caroline replied.

Anna smiled. 'Of course.'

'Oh, go on then,' Caroline said grudgingly. 'Try and justify what he said to me one more time.' Caroline had explained a fair bit of the whole sorry story; from the wonderful night to what had just happened on the restaurant's doorstep. Mindful of Anna's condition, however, she'd omitted to tell her about Scrumpy, and Gino spending the night on the sofa.

'It's not a justification, or an excuse, I promise you.' Anna picked up her mug and took another sip of tea. 'If you want my opinion, he's terrified of committing to anyone because he doesn't think he's worthy of being committed to.' She shook her head at Caroline's sardonically raised eyebrow. 'No, hear me out. He can't forgive himself for doing what he did to Matthew all those years ago. Even now, knowing that Matthew has forgiven him. So, he goes from one woman to the next, relying on the fact that he can walk away if and when things get complicated, or they want more. He's never allowed himself to fall in love because he feels as though he doesn't deserve to be loved. But you've knocked him sideways and he doesn't know how to react. He's frightened to admit that he might be falling in love with you, and even more frightened that he'll end up hurting you.' Anna sighed. 'Throw a whole bucket load of anxiety about finding his place back in the family and I think you can see why he's freaking out. The Carters have been so far apart for so many years that it's taking all of them a while to get used to being back together. And now it sounds like he might feel really strongly for you, too…'

'Have you ever considered an alternative career as a therapist?' Caroline said. But what if Anna was right? What if the reason Jonathan had been so offhand just now was truly because he didn't have the confidence, or the self-worth, to admit to his feelings? Or what if it really was because he didn't want her as much as she'd always thought he did and now he'd had her, the novelty of the conquest had gone? 'Fuck,' she said, realising too late she'd said it out loud. 'Sorry,' she glanced hastily at Ellie, who seemed, thankfully, to be involved in her jigsaw puzzle at the end of the table. 'I just don't know what to think.'

'Perhaps you need to stop thinking,' Anna said gently. 'Trust your heart.'

Caroline shook her head. 'My heart doesn't exactly have a great track record. My last few relationships haven't exactly been a bed of roses.' *And let's not even think about Paul Stone,* she thought.

'Everyone makes mistakes,' Anna replied. 'But that's the only way to learn. Trust yourself. Trust Jonathan. I think he's earned it, don't you?'

'That whole conversation this morning was just such a massive let down after getting so close to him.' Caroline stroked Sefton, who put a sympathetic paw on her lap. 'I mean, he's been prowling around for months, coming close and then backing off, and OK, that was mostly because I kept telling him to keep his distance, but when I finally decided to let my guard down... well, you know the rest.' Mindful of her niece, she left repeating the details a second time.

'He's probably at a loss, too,' Anna said. 'Now I know that you and Jonathan haven't exactly been spending a lot of time together as lovers, and you probably do need to back off and let him come to terms with this in his own time, but perhaps offer him some understanding, some friendship. He's probably as confused as you are right now.'

'Great,' Caroline snorted. 'So not only does the most confident, self-assured bloke in the universe have a whole bunch of self-esteem issues I never could have guessed at, but I also have to cope with the fact that he now doesn't have a clue what to do around me. That hardly fills *me* with confidence and boosts my self-esteem, either!'

'Did he give you any clue as to why he's being so offhand?' Anna asked.

Caroline shook her head. 'Not really.'

'Nothing at all?'

'If you knew how frustrating it's been,' Caroline sighed. 'It's all right for you, about to pop with the offspring of a broodingly handsome multi-millionaire cider maker, but Jonathan and I have got so close, so many times. And the frustrating thing is, I *know* how good we are together. I've been trying to deny it to myself, but I really thought we could give being more than colleagues a shot, despite everything. And now he won't even level with me.'

'Give him a bit of time,' Anna said. 'He's worth it, honestly. He kept me sane when Matthew and I were having some difficulties after Merry's accident, and he's got a wonderful heart underneath all of that surface charm. He's just too frightened to admit it.' She looked levelly at her former sister-in-law. 'I think he feels quite deeply about you.' She looked contemplatively at Caroline again. 'You and Jonathan are quite similar, if you don't mind me saying so.'

'We are?'

'You're both so alone.'

Caroline winced. 'Thanks for that.'

'You know what I mean.' Anna smiled gently. 'Even when I couldn't see past losing James for myself, I knew how much you were suffering; especially after losing your Mum and Dad. You shut yourself off from us for so long, but I knew that was what you had to do. I hoped, in time you'd come back to Ellie and me. I know how rough it was for you and that you handled it in your own way.' She looked Caroline directly in the eyes. 'Jonathan's alone, too. He might have this amazing family pedigree, but he can't find his place here. He's been away for so long, but now he's back I think he's really struggling. In a way, you'd be perfect for each other; you'd give each other some roots.'

'Hah!' Caroline snorted. 'I suppose that's your attempt at an apple growing pun.'

Anna laughed. 'Not intentionally. But I do mean it. Keep the faith, Caroline. It may well be worth it in the end.'

'Easy for you to say,' Caroline muttered. 'I don't know how much longer I can go on like this. I've still got to see him once a week for business meetings and even with Gino and Emma acting as chaperones it's going to be awkward.'

'They won't know where to look!' Anna laughed, then winced as the action caused a strong downwards kick from her unborn baby. 'Excuse me a minute,' she said, heaving herself up and heading for the downstairs loo.

'I've got to get back for lunchtime service anyway,' Caroline said. 'I'll see you soon.'

She headed out of the kitchen door and it was only when she got back to the restaurant she realised she still had her mug of tea in her hand. Perhaps she was losing the plot as much as Jonathan.

35

That evening, Jonathan went straight from work to the pub. There he stayed, drinking steadily, until Vern had discreetly alerted Matthew to Jonathan's inebriated state. Matthew was not habitually a pub drinker but walked across to The Stationmaster to see what was going on with his brother. Mindful of the other drinkers, Jonathan told Matthew in a gruff undertone to mind his own business and leave him alone. He then got another pint in.

So now, here he was, reeling from drink, ego bruised and heart feeling decidedly more sore than it had that morning. But why? Caroline had obviously moved on. Why couldn't he? He was not by nature a brooder, but his pride had definitely been injured by happening upon the scene at the restaurant this morning, and the argument didn't make him feel any better. Caroline, of course, was entitled to sleep with whomever she wanted, whenever she wanted. They'd had two one night stands and a lot of banter; she'd said no strings on both occasions and he was king of the commitment-free romp. So why was he still dwelling on it? Motioning to the bartender to fill up his pint, he pulled out his phone and considered texting one of his former dates again. As he looked up from his phone, he saw probably the last person on earth he wanted to see standing next to him at the bar.

'Can I have a pint of Amstel please, Vern?' Gino asked as the landlord ambled over. He gave Jonathan a friendly smile, which was not returned.

'Coming up,' Vern replied. 'Emma'll be home soon, if you want to pop in and see her.'

Gino nodded. 'Might do. Got a few things to discuss with her.'

Jonathan snorted, then muttered something loudly enough for Gino to glance back at him. 'Sorry,' he said. 'I didn't quite catch that.'

Jonathan raised his gaze from his pint to the young chef in front of him. 'I would have thought you'd have been worn out,' he said. 'After your, er, heavy night.'

Gino looked blank. 'You mean tonight? It was Emma's night on at The Cider Kitchen, so I'm not sure how busy it was.'

Jonathan shook his head, which was spinning slightly from the lager. 'I meant last night. Taking your responsibilities to the place a little too seriously, aren't you, spending the entire night there. With the manager.'

A flash of irritation crossed Gino's features before he remembered who he was talking to. 'I don't know what you mean.'

'Must have been very cosy up there all night, just you and Caroline.'

Gino's hand clenched slightly around his pint glass but he didn't reply.

'Don't be coy,' Jonathan said softly. 'I saw you coming out of there first thing this morning. Hugs on the doorstep; very friendly, I thought.'

Playing for time, Gino took a sip of his pint. 'I'm not sure I like what you're implying, Mr Carter.'

'Then let me spell it out for you,' Jonathan spoke a little more loudly. 'Did you or did you not spend the night at Caroline's place?'

Gino put his pint back on the bar with a thump. 'Because you're my boss,' he said softly, 'I'm going to assume that you don't mean any offence. Because I'm your employee, I'm not going to tell you that it's none of your fucking business where I spend my nights. After all, I value my job.'

'Oh, spare me,' Jonathan sneered. 'I'm a big boy. I can cope.'

Gino looked squarely at Jonathan. From the look on his face, it probably wasn't a good idea to bait him. He drew a breath. 'You've got it wrong, whatever it is you're thinking. And you don't need to know that, because you don't, as far as I know, have any claim on Caroline other than a professional one. So, I'm telling you this out of respect for that arrangement. But you do also know Caroline's not my type, right? I did spend the night with her, but not in the way that you seem to be thinking.'

Jonathan paused, pint glass halfway to his lips. 'Could have fooled me.'

'Honestly,' Gino said, taking a sip of his pint. 'She's about as far from my type as it's possible to be.'

'She's beautiful and female,' Jonathan snapped. 'I don't see what your problem is.'

Gino shook his head. 'I don't have a problem,' he said gently. 'But you do, if you think there's anything between Caroline and me. So you don't need to worry about us working late together. I love her, but as my boss and a friend. Nothing else. And if you really want to know why...' he looked Jonathan straight in the eye, 'it's because she's entirely the wrong sex for me. I'm not into women.'

Jonathan's stomach clenched, and he almost choked on his beer. 'Why are you telling me this?' he asked when he finally had a clear mouth, and a moderately clearer head.

Gino regarded him coolly. 'Chefs notice things,' he said. 'Attention to detail is what makes us so good at what we do. You two have clearly got some serious issues to sort out, and it's going to make life at the restaurant very tricky for everyone unless you do.' He shook his head. 'You've every right to bollock me for being cheeky if you want, but that's how it looks from the outside.'

Jonathan regarded the young chef for a moment. 'So...' he said eventually, 'nothing's happened between you and Caroline, then?'

'Frankly, I'd be more likely to shag you. I've always been attracted to older men.'

Jonathan's frown turned into a grin. 'It's strange,' he said. 'And don't take this the wrong way, but I'd never have guessed.'

'What, because I'm not humming Lady Gaga songs and constantly working on my abs?' Gino shot back. 'After all, there's really no need to go shouting about who I prefer to sleep with from the rooftops, don't you think?'

'You're right,' Jonathan, sensing there was more humour than irritation in Gino's response, kept smiling. 'So why were you hugging Caroline on the doorstep?'

'Didn't she tell you? Someone killed her cat, Scrumpy, and left her body outside the restaurant. I just happened to have forgotten my phone and when I went back for it I found them both on the doorstep.' Gino shook his head. 'I couldn't leave Caroline after that; she was in a bad way, so I crashed on the sofa to make sure whoever had done it didn't decide to come back. My boyfriend wasn't too chuffed to be stood up that night but what else could I do?'

'Why didn't she tell me?' Jonathan asked, only too late realising he'd said it out loud.

'You know what she's like,' Gino said. 'She jumps on the defensive the whole time.'

Jonathan shook his head. 'I didn't even give her the chance to explain. I just assumed she'd moved on.'

'And that's why you two really need to clear the air,' Gino said.

Jonathan smiled at the young chef. 'I appreciate your honesty, Gino. You're a bloody good chef and The Cider Kitchen would be mad to lose you, or Emma. And,' he paused, a twinkle in his eye, 'I'm also flattered. But I'm afraid if Caroline's not your type, she might just be mine.'

'You don't say,' Gino rolled his eyes. 'Emma and I have been saying that from the day the place opened.'

'Why do I feel like I'm being completely out manoeuvred again?' Jonathan grumbled.

'If you want my advice,' Gino said, with all the authority of his twenty-two years, 'you'll get over there tonight and clear the air with Caroline. She's in a bad place over that cat of hers, and I think she'd appreciate it.'

'You're right,' Jonathan said. He finished his pint. 'And thank you for being so honest with me. You've got a wise head on your shoulders.' He grimaced. 'Sorry. That sounds ridiculously patronising, doesn't it?'

'Don't worry about it,' Gino said. 'Growing up gay in a small village, with that Matt Lucas character all over the television… you tend to learn a lot about human nature very fast.' He stood up from the table. 'I'd better get going, too. I owe my boyfriend a bit of time after leaving him in the lurch last night.'

'I'll see you at the restaurant,' Jonathan said, sobered up by the conversation. As he walked out of the pub, he saw Gino waving goodbye to Vern before he disappeared out of the pub. Gino was definitely an asset The Cider Kitchen needed to hang on to. He hoped it wasn't too late to level with Caroline.

36

The walk from The Stationmaster to The Cider Kitchen was just about far enough to begin to sober Jonathan up. He hoped he'd be able to slip into the restaurant unnoticed before Caroline locked the door. The Cider Kitchen was winding down; a large group of customers were merrily making their way down the path back to the car park and Jonathan managed to slip inside the building unnoticed by the waiting staff. Immediately he spotted Caroline, logging off the till and calling over her shoulder at the same time to her kitchen staff. He stopped and observed her; that deep red hair, getting a little bit longer now but still falling to just under her ears. He imagined lifting it at the back of her neck, kissing her there until she shivered. Those green eyes, flashing fiercely one minute but with the telltale laughter lines at the corners. And that body underneath her strappy black shift dress; a body that he craved to feel next to his with every breath.

'Caroline?' he spoke softly, not wanting to make her jump. She was absorbed in her counting.

She waited until she'd finished the notes from the till before looking up. 'What do you want?'

Jonathan was taken aback by her directness. He'd got so used to their verbal sparring, that he missed the initial barbs. He cleared his throat. 'I, er, wanted to apologise for this morning. I was out of order.'

Caroline's gaze had returned to the cash in the till drawer. 'Fine. Apology accepted. Was there anything else?'

An instinct told Jonathan that there was more to this than met the eye; but then he supposed he deserved the silent treatment. 'I'm sorry about Scrumpy,' he said softly.

Caroline's head snapped back up. 'Gino told you?'

'I saw him in the pub earlier. He told me all about what happened last night. I'm really sorry I was so short with you this morning. If I'd known about the cat, I'd never have been so offhand.'

Caroline slammed the till drawer shut. 'I bet you are. You never wanted me to keep the kittens here anyway.'

'Caroline, please.' Jonathan was unaccustomed to begging. 'Can we get a coffee and talk?'

'I'm tired, Jonathan,' Caroline said. And she did indeed look weary. 'I just want to go to bed. And we do have a meeting in the morning anyway. Perhaps that's how we should keep things from now on. It might save a lot of complications.'

Jonathan was stabbed in the gut with disappointment. 'If that's what you want,' he said softly.

'It is,' she said, her tone a little gentler. She rubbed a hand over her eyes and Jonathan noticed that she'd smudged her mascara. He longed to take her face in his hands and plant a kiss square on her mouth before she could come up with any more reasons why he shouldn't. 'I think it's better for now. Don't you?'

No! Jonathan wanted to scream. *No, it's not better.* Out loud he merely said, 'Fine. Well, I'll see you in the morning, then.'

Caroline nodded without looking back up at him.

Jonathan strode out of the restaurant, willing himself to look straight ahead. Had he glanced back at Caroline, he'd have seen the tears dripping down her face, the hand clapped to her mouth in an effort not to call him back.

37

Jonathan knew it was unprofessional, but he cancelled the meeting with Caroline the next morning and then, for the next few weeks, he kept as far away from The Cider Kitchen as possible, addressing anything that arose by email. Although he remained horrified by the killing of the cat, Caroline had pretty conclusively shut him down when he'd tried to discuss it with her. He felt sure that there was far more to it than met the eye, but he didn't want to start grilling her when relations were so strained. For the good of the restaurant, he decided to act on her words and keep things purely professional for the time being.

Matthew had also handed over much of the legwork for the Buckthorn takeover proposal to Jonathan, too. Weary of waging war on all fronts, Matthew was finally learning to delegate. Not, Jonathan reflected, that it was going to make a scrap of difference in the long run. Matthew would never agree to hand the family business over to Buckthorn, no matter how much money was offered. Once again Jonathan had tried to broach the subject with his father, but Jack had stonewalled him. That morning they hadn't parted amicably and Jonathan knew when he got back to Orchard Cottage that night he needed to make amends.

He'd been poring over The Cider Kitchen's quarterly performance figures, and was pleased to see that turnover had been increasing steadily. If nothing else he could say to Caroline could make her happy, he thought, the fact that the restaurant was making a fair profit should do. Perhaps it was time to break the stalemate and arrange a meeting. He typed out another quick email and fired it off before he could change his mind. Involved in the message, it was with some surprise that Jonathan looked up from his desk to find Matthew standing the other side of it.

'Hey,' Jonathan said. 'Wasn't expecting to see you until later.'

Matthew looked grim faced. 'We need to talk about the restaurant.'

Jonathan shut the lid of his laptop and sat up straighter. 'What's up?'

'May I?' Matthew gestured to the chair in front of Jonathan's desk.

'Of course.'

Matthew sat down heavily. 'Sam from Finance, who as you know has been handling the restaurant's accounts, has noticed a few odd looking payments over the past couple of weeks. He did some digging and it looks as though someone has been making payments that don't match the invoices or purchase orders. It's not been going on for long, thankfully, but there's a fair chunk of money that's unaccounted for, even in that short time.'

'It could be an oversight,' Jonathan said. 'You know what it's like when you're setting up something new. Caroline probably forgot to raise a purchase order before making a payment to a supplier.'

Matthew shook his head. 'Ordinarily I'd agree with you, but when I say a fair chunk of money, it's not just a few hundred quid. I'm talking thousands.'

Jonathan's heart lurched. 'Really?'

Matthew nodded. 'I think we need to call her in for a meeting. This afternoon.'

Mind racing, Jonathan sat forward in his chair. 'Let me go and see her first. Perhaps I can find out what's been going on before you strap her to a chair and interrogate her.'

'From what Finance have been telling me, it's gone somewhat beyond the cosy chat stage, Jonno,' Matthew said. 'I think we need to get her in here, and possibly contact our legal department.'

Jonathan stood up quickly. 'You gave me responsibility for the restaurant project, Matthew, so let me do it my way first. I'll go and see her, and if there's anything you and the company should be properly concerned about, I'll let you know.'

'Are you serious?' Matthew snapped. He jumped up and started to pace the short distance from desk to window. 'It's not like it's few quid out of petty cash, Jonathan. There's thousands missing and Caroline's the only one, apart from you, who has the authority to move money like that.'

'Have you spoken to Caroline about it? Or are you just trusting the word of that number cruncher in accounts?' Jonathan could feel his own temper rising.

'I don't need to.' Matthew could be mercurial at the best of times, but his irritation at, *yet again*, being blindsided by the mix of business and family was clearly getting to him. 'The figures speak for themselves.'

'What about Anna? Does she know anything that could shed any light on it?'

'I didn't want to bother her with it.' Matthew turned back from the window. 'She's getting pretty tired. And she's up to her ears in preparations for the murder mystery evening. Besides, she's not seen Caroline for a while.'

'We live in the same fucking village, Matt! The Cider Kitchen's a stone's throw from all of us. How have none of us picked this up until now?'

'What about you?' Matthew poured himself a cup of coffee from the cafetiere on Jonathan's desk. 'It's not like you haven't been spending enough time there lately to warrant at least a cursory investigation about how things were going business wise.'

Jonathan winced, remembering his and Caroline's last encounter, and how short she had been with him. Was that all to do with the death of her cat, or did she have something else to hide? 'I haven't seen her for a while,' he admitted.

'So once again you've lost interest in a woman and everyone else has to duck the fallout? Christ, Jonathan, when the fuck are you going to learn?'

'This has nothing to do with my interest, or otherwise, in Caroline.' Jonathan couldn't quite meet his brother's gaze.

'Really? Because from where I'm standing, it looks as though you were the one who took your eye off the ball.' Matthew finished his coffee and then swiftly poured another one. Anna wasn't the only one who was tired. 'As soon as she moved to the village you were spending no end of time there, and now you're telling me you didn't have the faintest idea this was coming?'

'What exactly are you accusing me of, Matthew?' Jonathan's voice had taken on a dangerous edge. 'Are you suggesting I have something to do with the missing cash?'

'Well it wouldn't be the first time you walked off with something that wasn't yours, would it?' As soon as the words were out, Matthew looked horrified. 'Christ, Jonathan, I'm sorry. That was completely out of order. I'm really tired. Forgive me.'

Jonathan carefully placed his coffee mug down on the desk and looked his brother straight in the eye. 'You're right. It was. So listen to me very carefully. I am going to the restaurant now and I will sort this out. I will speak to you later.' Not sparing his brother another glance, or waiting for him to leave, he walked out of the office.

38

'Matthew's on the warpath. I'm hoping you can give me some information that means I can take him back off it.'

Caroline thought, not for the first time, how alike the Carter brothers were as Jonathan strode straight to the coffee machine behind the bar and started to make two lattes. He had a kind of restless energy about him that suggested she wouldn't be able to deflect him with anything other than the truth.

'What's the matter with him?' Caroline asked, passing Jonathan a couple of cups from the rack above the bar. 'Did he not like the sleepsuit I bought for the new baby? I can take it back.'

'He's been talking to the accounts clerk who does the books for this place,' Jonathan said.

Caroline's heart sank as Jonathan filled her in. Then her mind started to race. She'd have to brazen this out somehow. She hoped that the disorganised maître d' approach might work. 'You know how it is when you're working all hours; things tend to get overlooked,' she said.

'A couple of invoices for a few hundred quid, perhaps, but Finance are saying there's thousands unaccounted for.' Jonathan took a quick sip of his latte and looked her square in the eye. 'I think you'd better stop flannelling me, Caroline, and start telling me the truth. Or Matthew's going to come round with the legal team and try to get the facts out of you.'

Caroline, seeing the determination in Jonathan's eyes, was beaten. The pause seemed to stretch for an eternity. With a trembling hand, she picked up her own coffee cup, but had to put it down quickly again before she spilled it all over her lap. This was the moment, she realised. Fobbing off Gino after Scrumpy's death was one thing, but she had a very clear choice now. Should she take a leap of faith and trust Jonathan with what she knew, or should she try to keep things under wraps? She'd never been good at knowing when to trust and confide in people, but her instincts were screaming at her loud and clear. She took a deep breath. 'Your accountants are right to be concerned,' she said. 'There *are* a number of discrepancies. I thought I'd been subtle enough to keep things under the radar, but it's got to the point where it's becoming very difficult to hide.'

'What's been going on, Caroline?' Jonathan's voice was so gentle compared to his assertiveness when he'd entered the restaurant.

'There's someone after me.'

'What?'

Caroline shuddered. 'An old acquaintance called Paul Stone. A long time ago, in a different life, he supplied me with quite a lot of cocaine.' She laughed bitterly. 'Everyone was doing it back in the day, ten years ago when we were all less tied down and younger. A line after dinner was normal. That's how it started, really. I was determined to get on in the hospitality business and he was a senior organiser. He handled the champagne accounts and he seemed so sure of himself, so confident. But he always had more money than even a generous commission could get him. It wasn't long before I realised why. He offered me a quick snort here and there and before I knew it, I ended up in his world, handing over my own cash for what he supplied.' She took a sip of her coffee, willing herself to go on. 'When Mum and Dad died, that's when I started upping my usage. Some people need booze, others turn to harder things. Both take the pain away. My brother James—' she swallowed hard. 'He worked out that I was using more than just a recreational line and he went ballistic. He'd just married Anna but he still managed to straighten me out. He was such a rock in my life.'

'I can't imagine how much you must miss him,' Jonathan said gently.

'Anna never knew about any of this. I swore James to secrecy and I'm guessing it was the only thing he ever kept from her. When they had Ellie, I was determined to kick it once and for all. I started working different accounts, got away from Paul and settled down a bit. James, Anna and Ellie lived a few miles down the road from me and for eighteen months I was clean.' She laughed. 'I even stopped drinking. It was too tempting to be dragged back into that world. I saved a lot of money and ended up buying my flat instead of snorting my salary up my nose.'

'Then James was killed,' Jonathan murmured.

Caroline nodded. 'I'd never known anything like the pain. We'd lost Mum and Dad and now James was gone, too. Ellie was still a baby, barely walking, when she lost her dad, and Anna was in such a state of shock I couldn't level with her. I found Paul's number and the next thing I knew, he was supplying me again.'

'So why is he after you now?'

'The events management company had two offices, one in Farnham and one in Guildford. I moved to Farnham to get away from Paul, who was still working out of the bigger Guildford office. Earlier this year, the firm was taken over by a much bigger company and they decided to streamline things a bit. We were all given the opportunity to reapply for our jobs and set against each other for promotions. The competition got quite nasty. Relocation to the company's Bristol office was also offered, as well as voluntary redundancy. After eleven years with the company, I decided to take the redundancy. I was fed up with being put into competition with people I'd worked with for so long. Also, I knew that I had to get out of the area if I was going to stay clean. Paul wanted the South East Regional Manager's job, but got passed over. I guess they didn't like his attitude. He blamed me for not supporting him in his bid for promotion, as I still had the ear of the then manager of the Guildford branch since I'd started my career there. He loathed the fact that I wanted to move on. The Farnham and Guildford branches were combined and any surplus staff were either made redundant or relocated. I thought Paul had taken the job he was offered in Guildford, but in the end, it seems, he opted to be relocated to the Bristol office. He had his 'work' on the side, too, but I'm guessing that he's not got the connections in the West Country yet to really supplement his income like he used to.'

'And now he's here, keeping tabs on you.' Jonathan put his coffee cup down on the saucer with a clatter. 'Are you using again?'

Caroline jumped. 'No.' She shook her head so vigorously her cheeks flushed and clashed with her hair. 'Absolutely not.'

'Can I trust you?'

'I have not touched a speck of cocaine for well over a year and I've no intention of doing so ever again.'

'Then what does he want, if you've made it clear you're not buying?'

'Money. He sees this place is successful and wants a piece of it. And I should imagine he's still pretty pissy that I didn't go all out and support him for the Regional Manager's job. Being transferred to Bristol gives him plenty of opportunity to intimidate me and he wants hush money to stop him from making my former habit public.'

'How much has he had off you?'

Caroline took a deep breath. 'About ten grand so far, which was most of the remaining redundancy money I had, topped up with some money from the business. I've promised him another ten, which I can get if I sell my flat in Farnham, plus the cash to put back into the business.'

'Christ.' Jonathan stood up and pushed his coffee cup away on the bar. 'Why the fuck didn't you level with me when all this started? You've been playing Russian Roulette with a drug dealer and using the restaurant's takings as collateral. What the hell were you thinking?'

'I was terrified,' Caroline's voice rose to match Jonathan's. 'I thought if I gave him what he wanted, he'd go away. If you'd seen the way he was looking at

Meredith when he came in to eat here, you'd have given him anything he wanted.'

'What?' Jonathan's voice had dropped to dangerously low levels. 'I swear to you, Caroline, if he lays a finger on my niece I'll finish him off myself.'

'I know that,' Caroline snapped, suddenly angry with herself for allowing things with Stone to get so far. 'I can't believe I've let him intimidate me like this.'

'How would you feel about taking some leave?' Jonathan said. 'Getting out of this place for a week or two? If you're not here, at least he can't show up on the doorstep and intimidate you again.'

'I can't do that,' Caroline said. 'If I leave here, he'll think he's scared me away.'

'If Matthew finds out you've used company money to pay off a drug dealer, he's going to throw you out anyway, ties or no ties to Anna and Ellie,' Jonathan countered. 'You don't have to tell anyone where you're going – just say you're off on a last minute holiday somewhere hot.' He smiled briefly. 'Sorry,' he said, at Caroline's quizzical look, 'it's the thought of you in a bikini. I got distracted.' Then, all seriousness again, 'have you got somewhere you can go?'

Caroline chose to ignore Jonathan's bikini reference; now was not the time. 'Well, I can't exactly afford a winter sun holiday after giving Paul all that money, but my flat's empty again as my friend has moved out, so I can go back there, pretend I'm redecorating or something for a week or two.' She didn't add that, if she was sacked from The Cider Kitchen, she'd be living back there again.

'OK.' Jonathan paused for a moment. 'But don't tell anyone else where you're actually going. Paul might try to get back there if he finds out and then you'll really be in trouble. Put Solly into a cattery to be on the safe side. I'll speak to Matthew and make some excuse. Emma can step up and cover front of house, and I'll come and work over here in the back office for a bit, just to keep an eye on things and make sure this guy doesn't try anything. Your team runs so beautifully now that I'm sure they'll manage for a week or two. We need some time to think about how we're going to sort this out.' He reached out and put a warm hand on Caroline's shoulder. His thumb brushed her collar bone and she shivered at the contact. 'You should have come to me when all this started. But we will sort it. I promise.'

Caroline, struggling to focus with Jonathan's hand on her shoulder, swallowed hard. 'How can you be so calm about it all?'

'Because I've met scumbags like Paul Stone before, and it makes me angry that he thinks he can blackmail people like this, especially women. We're going to make it stop.'

'I appreciate the knight in shining armour routine, but you need to tell me what you've got in mind,' Caroline said, regaining her equilibrium once more.

'I've got an idea,' Jonathan said. 'But it's probably best I keep it to myself for the moment. How can I contact this guy?'

'I've got his mobile number,' Caroline said. 'But please, don't meet him alone. Go to the police or something.' She couldn't bear the thought of Jonathan getting hurt.

'I can't exactly do that,' Jonathan said wryly. 'You're the one who's in trouble legally for slipping him the cash. We can't prove he's got it, but we've got a paper trail leading back to you. We'll have to scare him off some other way.'

'I need to get him off my back once and for all,' Caroline replied. 'He's been scaring me for too long.' She clanked her coffee cup forcibly down on the table again in irritation. 'I can't believe I've let him get this hold over me again. It has to end.'

'It will end,' Jonathan said. 'Call me when you get to Farnham, or wherever it is you decide to go.' He held up his hands as she started to protest. 'If Emma needs a hand, I can always step in myself and run the place. How hard can it be?' At Caroline's mutinous look, he relented. 'The important thing is you're out of this for a bit.'

'What are you going to say to your brother?'

'Leave that to me,' Jonathan said. 'I can stall him for a few days until you're out the way. I'll tell him you're knackered and you've taken a last minute holiday deal, and that I've seen the paperwork and I'm going to chase it up in your absence.'

'Will he believe you?'

Jonathan laughed humourlessly. 'Probably not. But he's my problem, not yours. I can handle him.'

'And I can make the arrangements to sell my flat when I'm back in Farnham,' Caroline said quietly. 'I need to put the money back that I took to pay Paul.'

'Isn't the flat your security in case things go tits up here?'

'Well yes, but things have pretty much done that, haven't they?'

'Hang fire for a bit on that,' Jonathan said. 'I might be able to get the money back.' Jonathan stood up. Gently, he reached forward and brushed a strand of hair from Caroline's mouth where it had caught as she'd been speaking. 'I want to be there for you, Caroline. Despite the fact that this is one monumental fuck up, I can't let you do this alone.' With that, he left. As he vanished into the darkness, Caroline let out a long breath. She'd never expected Jonathan to turn out to be on her side, under the circumstances. She'd thought he'd terminate her contract on the spot after finding out what she'd done. The fact that he hadn't, and was clearly so motivated to get Paul Stone off her back filled her with hope that perhaps she did have a future with the restaurant. And maybe, she thought unguardedly, with Jonathan, too.

39

Jonathan had always been an expert at switching gears, and tonight was no exception. Whereas his brother had the single mindedness to follow every decision through to completion, Jonathan's brain was wired differently. While he was still mulling over how best to sort out Caroline's issue with Stone with one part of his mind, another had already switched to trying to talk to his father about the Buckthorn takeover. The proposal was now severely time limited, and Jonathan's gut instinct told him that if they took it seriously, it would move Carter's Cider to a whole new level. Turning the key in the lock to Orchard Cottage, he braced himself to raise it with his father again.

'Your brother's just rung,' Jack said as Jonathan came through to the kitchen. Jonathan had to stifle a smile as he saw Jack, checked shirt and tan corduroys partly covered by one of his late wife's floral aprons, cooking fried eggs on the hob. 'Said there was some issue at the restaurant that needed sorting.'

'Don't worry about it,' Jonathan said. 'It's in hand.' *Or it soon will be,* he thought. 'Have you got a minute to talk about Buckthorn?'

'Not again, Jonathan,' Jack said, brow creasing in irritation as he spooned oil over the two eggs in the pan. 'I've told you. I'm not willing to discuss it until all three of us are round the table.'

Jonathan sighed. 'I know that. But we've had the paperwork for months now. They're going to need an answer one way or the other.'

'They can wait a bit longer.' Jack flipped the eggs out of the pan and onto the toast he'd prepared. 'Want one of these?'

'No, Dad. I want to talk about Buckthorn.'

'I've said all I'm going to say for tonight,' Jack said. 'Now make yourself useful and pour me a glass of red wine to go with these eggs.'

'The deal makes perfect sense, Dad!' Jonathan knew he was raising his voice but his frustration with his father's obstinacy was getting the better of him. 'Buckthorn have had their eye on us for years; they reach markets we could never hope to. Why won't you at least take a look at the figures and think about it?'

'I will not hand over this business to some faceless multinational,' Jack said firmly. He stood up from his chair by the fireplace and walked over to the window. 'Four generations of this family have lived their lives building this business. I won't just give it all up for a quick profit. We have a workforce, responsibilities.'

'And the workforce would be taken care of,' Jonathan joined his father at the window.

'Don't be so stupid, Jonathan!' Jack's voice was uncharacteristically harsh. The light in the kitchen gave a grey cast to the old man's face, throwing the lines and shadows into harsh relief. 'You know as well as I do that it doesn't work like that. They'll decommission this site before you can blink and put half the village out of a job.'

'They've committed to keeping the site open and keeping on seventy-five per cent of the workforce,' Jonathan countered. 'They're going to need people to maintain the orchards and a lot of other things.'

'They've got an infrastructure of their own that will preclude that,' Jack replied. 'What about our drivers, our canners and keggers, our packers, our marketing and sales teams?'

'They've said that anyone they can't integrate, they'll offer a decent redundancy package.'

'They'll say anything to get us on board,' Jack dismissed the idea with a wave of his hand. 'The minute we sign the contract, people like Eli, the night watchman, will be pensioned off without so much as a by your leave. And all the people we've worked so hard to keep in employment in the village, Joel, Trevor, Sophie and David, all those people will be out on their ears.' Jack shook his head. 'I won't put my name to it.'

'Things are changing, Dad.' Jonathan took a deep breath. 'We're OK at the moment, but markets can become volatile, uncertain. This will secure the future of the company; make sure we can keep employing locals.'

'No.' Jack was resolute. 'It won't. Your great grandfather would be turning in his grave at the prospect of selling this business to a concern like Buckthorn. I won't sign it.'

'You might not have a choice, Dad,' Jonathan said gently. 'Matthew and I hold the majority share in this company. We can go ahead without you.'

Jack sighed, long, low and resigned. 'I've no doubt you can.' He turned and looked his younger son straight in the eyes. 'But you have to ask yourself, Jonathan, and make sure you think carefully about this, should you do it?'

Jonathan dropped his gaze first. He understood his father's concerns, of course he did, but he also knew that Carter's had to move with the times. And times were changing. Much like in the mid 1990s when it had been a case of embracing technology and the internet age or go under, now might well be the time to sell to the biggest cider producer in the country.

'I'll leave it with you,' Jonathan said quietly.

'What does your brother say?' Jack asked.

'He's still making up his mind,' Jonathan replied. That wasn't strictly true; Matthew was on the verge of rejecting the takeover out of hand, but the company had taken a huge hit when Tesco had decided not to stock their products any more. Even though Matthew knew a takeover made financial sense, he was still reluctant to let go of the reins.

'Jonathan. Son.' Jack suddenly looked very, very tired and very, very old. 'You know you can push this through without my say so. But I am asking you one more time. Think about it. Think about the people we employ. Think about what a merger with Buckthorn truly means. Everything we hold dear, everything four generations of this family has worked for, will be subsumed in a corporation that cares less about quality than it does about volume. Aren't we big enough? We don't need this.'

Jonathan nodded. 'I promise I'll give it some serious thought, Dad. But in return, can you at least look at what they're proposing.'

Jack nodded back. 'Go and get the paperwork from my study. I'll take a look later.'

'Thank you.' Jonathan reached out a hand and briefly touched his father's upper arm. 'I promise you, it makes sense Dad.'

'Perhaps on paper,' Jack touched Jonathan's hand with the tips of his fingers. 'But you need to realise that sometimes there's more to business than numbers on a page.'

They sat that evening in companionable silence. Before Jonathan went to bed, he dug out Jack's copy of the Buckthorn paperwork and left it on his side table by his armchair in the lounge, hoping that his father would see sense.

40

Caroline, true to her word, left for Farnham the following morning. After a meeting with Gino and Emma – Gino had looked quizzically at her but said nothing – she'd briefed her front of house team about her leave of absence and then driven Solly to the cattery. In truth, she thought, the front of house and the kitchen were so used to working together that they'd manage perfectly well without her, barring any major crisis. She'd driven away from The Cider Kitchen with a heavy heart, but also hopeful that perhaps Jonathan could help her to solve the Paul Stone problem. She tried to still the voice in her head that was supplying a rather convincing counter argument that Stone would just laugh in Jonathan's face. Part of her still hated herself for confiding in Jonathan, but she'd spent so long denying to herself what was going on, the relief at sharing the burden, trusting him, immediately made things seem better.

As she crossed from Somerset into Wiltshire and the landscape changed from green, fielded hills to the drier, chalkier vales surrounding Salisbury, she could feel herself being drawn back towards a life she no longer desired. That feeling stayed with her all the way to Surrey, and pulling out the key to the flat she'd hoped she'd never live in again, she was sorely tempted to slam the door, get back into her car and belt back to The Cider Kitchen.

But Jonathan, darling, alley cat Jonathan, had made her a promise, and she had to honour her side of the bargain. Could he keep his? She had no doubt that that he'd give it his very best shot, but this meant he was, yet again, going against his brother. If Matthew found out the truth about the missing money, would Jonathan be cast out of the Eden of Little Somerby just as she would be?

Entering the flat, she was assailed by memories. Logically, it was the worst place to return to, but with Paul Stone in Bristol, and hopefully unaware that she'd come back to Farnham, she'd be safe. Jonathan had made her promise to ring him when she arrived, but she couldn't guarantee she could speak to him without breaking down so she sent him a text message instead. Then, after checking the place over, she made the bed with the linen she'd brought with her and considered her options. She had two weeks' grace, and she actually did have some decorating to do as she'd moved out so quickly that she hadn't had the chance to touch up the walls. Trying to put the restaurant out of her mind for now, she settled down to work out the best course of action.

✢

Jonathan, for all his assurances to Caroline, didn't yet have a plan for dealing with Paul Stone. Somehow he knew that just calling him up and declaring who he was wasn't going to cut it. And if his brother got wind of what was going on there'd be hell to pay. To pre-empt any difficult questions from his brother, Jonathan had phoned Matthew shortly after he'd seen Caroline and told him he was in the process of investigating. Luckily, Matthew was so stretched on other business, he seemed willing to let Jonathan take the lead, for now at least. Then, after his meeting with the restaurant staff, assuring them that he'd be on hand to sort out any problems in Caroline's absence, he set his mind to work.

Stone wasn't just going to roll over and back off; Jonathan needed leverage. A morning's digging on the internet provided some leads; Paul Stone's picture was on the website of the events management company in Bristol and his laid back, confident smile made Jonathan's hackles rise. So this was the bastard who'd been intimidating Caroline. Some primal urge to confront Stone and smash his front teeth in struck Jonathan powerfully, but he knew he'd have to be cleverer than that. Closing the web page, he got to thinking. He'd have to act fast if he wanted to put an end to all this. Then he had a brainwave. Punching out the number of the company, he made the call. It was almost too easy to schedule a meeting to discuss a fictional event that he wanted to hold in the grounds of the local National Trust property. Jonathan pretended that he was a rep for the Trust, looking to arrange a champagne reception for some local businesses in the grounds of the house. When he requested Stone as a liaison, lying that he'd been recommended by a friend, the receptionist readily agreed. Arranging a meeting for next Tuesday, he ended the call. Just him and Stone, on neutral ground. Given that he'd left the receptionist with a false name, with a bit of luck the bastard wouldn't know the true purpose of the meeting until it was far too late.

That afternoon, feeling as though he'd made a start on saving Caroline's hide and her business, Jonathan decided to leave work early. He'd been working his backside off recently. The sun was setting over the Mendip Hills as he walked the distance between the office and his father's bungalow. Not for the first time, he thought that he really should make alternative living arrangements. He couldn't live with his father forever.

Orchard Cottage was in darkness as Jonathan walked up the drive, but since Jack's sitting room was at the back of the bungalow, Jonathan assumed he hadn't bothered turning on any other lights. Fumbling to fit his key into the lock, he pushed open the front door and then closed it carefully behind him so as not to startle Jack, whose heart probably couldn't take too many shocks these days. Crossing the hall carefully, he pushed open the door to the living room. His father's chair faced away from the door and Jonathan could see the top of Jack's head above the back of the chair as he entered the room.

'Dad?' he said softly. 'Are you awake?'

Jack made no response. In fact, the silence was almost deafening. Jonathan realised, a beat too late, that he couldn't even hear his father breathing, let alone snoring.

'Dad?' Jonathan crossed the room. 'I'm home. Do you want me to get you anything?'

There was still no response from Jack. Nearly tripping over the fringed edge of the rug, as not even Jack's side table light was on, Jonathan stumbled towards the old man in the chair. As he righted himself, he noticed that Jack was holding the Buckthorn contract in his hands.

Jonathan's voice, higher pitched with worry now, sounded childish in the darkness. 'Dad? Can you hear me?' He leaned over and touched his dad's shoulder, but still nothing. The panic ratcheted up another notch as Jack remained unresponsive. 'Dad? Dad! Wake up.' All the things he'd ever learned about CPR and resuscitation seemed frustratingly out of reach as he frantically loosened his father's collar. Fumbling in the pocket of his jeans for his phone, he punched out the number of the emergency services and waited to be connected.

'Ambulance, Orchard Cottage, Little Somerby. It's my father. He's not... responding. Please hurry.'

Jonathan was breathless with fear and tried hard to focus on his father. He lifted Jack's left wrist to feel for a pulse, and, to his horror, as skin made contact with skin, ice dripped down his spine. 'Oh Christ,' he whispered. The pulse point on Jack's wrist was still. Frantically, Jonathan felt for the reassuring beat in Jack's neck but found nothing. Jack's head was tilted to one side, his eyes half open as if he was drifting off to sleep, but as Jonathan leaned in, desperate to feel a breath, he knew Jack was far beyond that. His heart lurched; why had he pushed him so hard about Buckthorn? Why had he not checked more carefully that his father was taking his medication?

'Dad?' he said softly. But he knew it was hopeless; Jack was beyond hearing. Placing his lips to the old man's forehead, he breathed in the remnants of his father's cologne and drew a deep, shuddering breath. Then, with a presence of mind that surprised him, he pulled his phone out of his pocket.

'Matthew? It's me.' Jonathan paused, knowing that what he said next would change his brother's life forever, just as finding Jack had changed his. He drew a deep breath, which caught agonisingly in his throat. 'It's Dad. He's dead.'

A short time later, the emergency services arrived at Orchard Cottage. Matthew and Jonathan stood silently as Jack's GP, who had been called by the paramedics, confirmed that Jack had passed away and then made the arrangements to move the body. It was all remarkably calm and swift. As they left, taking Jack with them in a private ambulance to the local mortuary, Matthew turned to his brother.

'Are you all right?' he asked, seeing Jonathan's pallor, and the fact that as Jack's body had been moved out on the gurney, his brother had started to shake.

Jonathan shook his head. 'I can't believe it.' He ran a hand over his eyes, trying to keep it together. 'I should never have…'

'What?' Matthew put a hand on Jonathan's shoulder.

'The Buckthorn deal. I shouldn't have pushed him on it. We had words this morning. And last night. Christ…' Jonathan trailed off, clenching his jaw in an attempt not to break down.

'It wasn't your fault,' Matthew said. 'You said he'd not been taking his tablets properly. This could have happened at any time.'

'I should've made sure he was taking them. I was here every morning.' Jonathan turned away from his brother and walked to the window. 'If only I'd…'

Matthew joined his brother at the window, looking out onto Jack's immaculately tended garden. 'It wasn't your fault, Jonno. We both know how stubborn Dad is. Was.' He swallowed. 'Look, don't stay here on your own. Come back to Cowslip Barn tonight.'

Jonathan shook his head. 'No. I'll be fine. Honestly. I need some time to get my head around this. And Dad wouldn't want... wouldn't want this place empty.'

'Are you sure? Anna always cooks for an army and I don't like the thought of you being here on your own.' He put a hand on Jonathan's shoulder.

'I'll come over tomorrow,' Jonathan said. 'Tonight I just want to get my head together before I see the girls.'

Matthew regarded his brother long and hard and then leaned forward and hugged him briefly. 'All right,' he said roughly. 'But you know where I am. We'll get together tomorrow to sort out the arrangements.'

Jonathan nodded. When Matthew finally left, and with remarkable presence of mind, he poured himself a stiff scotch from Jack's decanter. It was only when he caught sight of Jack's glass on the sideboard, never to be drunk from again, that he started to cry.

41

Jonathan's mind hadn't been on his mother when she died. His mind had, in fact, been very much on another woman; his brother Matthew's first wife, Tara. Cecily Carter's funeral had been a nightmare of undercurrents, tensions and oddness, culminating in Jonathan having to escort his father back to Orchard Cottage after he'd had one too many at the wake. Jack had rambled when he and Jonathan had been alone, confessing drunkenly to all manner of sins, most of which, to Jonathan's younger self, seemed as distant and irrelevant as the inconstant, shadowed moon above them. It was January when his mother died and the sharpness of the cold night underpinned the family's grief. Not even the church organist, whose playing style resembled Les Dawson's skilled, yet practiced ineptitude, was enough to provide a light in the darkness.

The moment Jonathan had settled his father on the sofa with a bottle and a blanket, he'd belted back to Pippin Cottage, where he was living rent free. Bought by his father in the early seventies, it was, forty years later, to become the homecoming property of his brother's future second wife, Anna Hemingway. But then, in those relentless midnoughties days, it was Jonathan's home. On the night the Carter family buried its matriarch, Jonathan and Tara snatched a few forbidden moments alone while Matthew took Meredith, still a toddler, home to her bed. Those moments were frenzied, borne as much of pain as of need, and at the end of it Jonathan felt nothing but a feverish longing for more.

How things, and how people, had changed. With Jack Carter lying cold in the mortuary, Jonathan couldn't think of anything, or anyone else, but his father. The painful realisation that his father had been looking at the Buckthorn papers on Jonathan's insistence when he died, was eating into his soul. He should never have pushed him; never have forced an issue that in the grand scheme of things, meant so little. But he had, and his own hubris had finally caught up with him.

The morning after Jonathan was paralysed by grief. He ignored the landline telephone ringing off the hook, presumably with people wanting to commiserate or find out the gory details. A private ambulance travelling through the village had not gone unnoticed and the Little Somerby rumour mill was in full force. Jonathan bolted the door.

At around lunchtime his mobile phone buzzed. Glancing at it he saw Anna's number. He watched the phone for a few seconds before it clicked through to voice mail. The inertia, the total inability to function, was what frightened him the most. When Matthew came round that afternoon, he listlessly agreed with whatever his brother proposed about Jack's funeral, and then closed the door, relieved to be alone again.

*

At the other end of the village, Anna thumbed her phone to lock it and sighed. She didn't know whether to just go to see Jonathan or whether to leave him be. Matthew had gone into work to inform his employees of Jack's death and was going to try to sort out some of the funeral arrangements from his office. He needed to maintain some sense of normality even though underneath he was struggling. As she was fretting over the decision, she heard the back door open and Matthew came into the kitchen. He looked akin to how he'd looked when Meredith was lying in a coma in hospital after the car accident that nearly cost her life. Anna's heart ached.

Before Anna could ask him anything, he spoke. 'I went round to see Jonathan.'

'How was he?' Anna asked.

'Fragile,' Matthew replied. He sat down heavily in one of the kitchen chairs. Meredith was upstairs in her room studying for her English Literature mock exam the next day. Ellie had crashed out the moment

Anna had put her to bed, exhausted from all the emotions she was only beginning to understand.

'And, how are you?' Anna crossed from the kitchen sink over to where Matthew was sitting in his usual chair.

Matthew said nothing, but his hands, clasped in front of him on the kitchen table, clenched convulsively. Wordlessly, Anna walked up beside him and put her arms around him. He turned into her embrace, burying his face in the warmth of her soft cashmere jumper. Eventually, he pulled back from her and looked up. 'I'm so glad I've got you,' he said hoarsely.

'I'm glad I'm here,' Anna replied. Her heart broke as she saw the sadness in her husband's eyes.

'Dad was so, so happy to find out about the baby,' Matthew said. 'He didn't think he was ever going to get another grandchild. I wish he was going to be here to meet him or her.'

'Me too,' Anna said, her left hand still stroking Matthew's thick dark and silver hair.

'He's been so happy to see Jonathan and me finally running the business together. It was good that he actually saw his wishes realised before he… before he died.' Matthew swallowed again. 'It was just tragic that it took so long for Jonno and I to sort ourselves out and do what he wanted.'

'But he saw it in the end,' Anna said softly. 'He loved the fact that you took it on together, and were finally at peace with each other.' She shook her head. 'And now he's at peace, too.'

'I hope Mum's up there, giving him a glass of sherry and a good telling off!' Matthew said shakily. He looked up at Anna. 'She'd have liked you, I think. She never was sure about Tara.'

Anna's eyes filled with tears. 'So much loss,' she said softly. 'Don't you think we've all had our fair share by now?'

Matthew shook his head. 'We've got each other. And the children.' His face clouded over. 'And we may need to take care of Jonathan for a while. He thinks he should have been there. That he shouldn't have pushed the takeover idea with Dad. He thinks he caused Dad's heart to fail.'

Anna pulled Matthew close again. 'He couldn't have known. Jack's heart could have gone at any time.'

'I know.' Matthew reached up a hand and touched Anna's cheek. 'But Jonathan's struggling to believe that. Not that there's any doubt now about Buckthorn; there's no way we're going in with them. Dad was right.'

Anna nodded. 'Sounds like you've made your mind up.' She paused. 'I texted Caroline this afternoon. I know she's on holiday but she needs to know what's happened.' She omitted to say that Caroline hadn't yet replied and resolved to try and call her later. Perhaps wherever she'd gone didn't have the best phone reception.

Matthew's face clouded over. This was not unnoticed by Anna. 'What is it?' she said.

'Oh nothing,' Matthew shook his head. 'It'll have to keep until after we've made the arrangements for Dad.' He swallowed hard. 'Christ, Anna. The old bugger and I didn't see eye to eye about a lot of things, but now that he's gone…' he put his head in his hands.

Wordlessly, Anna put her arms around Matthew again, running a warm hand through his hair and reassuring him with her presence. Eventually, he looked back up at her. 'I'll just go and check on Meredith,' he said hoarsely. 'And then I think we both need some rest.'

Anna wrapped an arm around Matthew's waist as he stood up. She knew the days ahead were going to be tough and she felt exhausted already, but for the sake of her new family, she needed to find the strength to hold things together. She wasn't sure exactly how she was going to do it, but for everyone's sake, she needed to try.

42

Meredith had a somewhat more direct approach to dealing with her uncle. She had decided to pop into Orchard Cottage on her way back from school, having just sat her first English Literature AS Level mock exam, and had swiped Matthew's key to the cottage as she'd left for school just to make sure she'd be able to get in if Jonathan didn't open up.

Although pleasantly surprised to find the place neat and tidy; she'd expected all kinds of detritus to have crept in already knowing how messy her uncle could be, as she entered the kitchen she was shocked at the sight of him. He obviously hadn't slept for some time and the dark rings under his eyes were highlighted by the redness. He hadn't shaved and he didn't rise from his chair.

'How are you, Uncle Jonno?' she asked as she drew closer.

'I'm fine, lovely,' he said softly. He finally stood up and enfolded her in his arms, and they held each other tightly.

'I suppose your father would have a fit if I offered you a proper drink, so you'd better put the kettle on,' Jonathan said as they broke apart.

Meredith smiled. 'He'd probably understand, under the circumstances, but I've got a driving lesson later so I'd better not.' Meredith was one of the older students in her year, and her seventeenth birthday had been occasion for both celebration and anxiety for her father and stepmother, whose memories of her dreadful car accident were still fresh.

'How's that going?' Jonathan asked as Meredith crossed the kitchen to fill the kettle.

'Not too bad, but I can't seem to get my hands and feet to work together so I've been stalling a lot.' Kettle filled, Meredith crossed to the range top and lit the gas.

'How many lessons have you had?' Jonathan reached behind him to the upper cupboard and took out two mugs.

'Two,' Meredith shrugged. 'So, I suppose it's still early days.'

'You know your father didn't pass first time.'

'Really?' Meredith said in surprise. 'He kind of gave me the impression that he did.'

'He doesn't like to admit it but he failed because he mounted the kerb and then had the temerity to argue with the examiner about it.' Jonathan dropped a tea bag into each mug and then went to get the milk out of the fridge. 'I almost think he'd have got away with it if he'd kept his mouth shut, but he couldn't help arguing.'

'Sounds like Dad,' Meredith replied.

'Well, this examiner decided that he was far too full of himself so he put a cross in the box and your dad had to wait six weeks until he could have another go. He was pretty pissed off, because he'd been chosen as the designated driver for a boys' week in Devon at the end of his A Levels, and he couldn't get another test date until September.' Jonathan smiled and passed Meredith the mugs. 'But don't tell him I told you that.'

'My lips are sealed,' Meredith said as she filled the mugs.

There was a companionable pause as the two of them sat back down at the kitchen table and sipped their tea.

'I would offer you a biscuit, but I'm afraid I've run out and I haven't been shopping since before Granddad...' Jonathan trailed off and took another gulp of his tea.

'No worries; I had a late lunch.' Meredith looked from her mug to her uncle and gave a soft smile.

Jonathan blinked. 'You're not the kid you used to be, are you?'

Meredith shook her head. 'The past couple of years have made me grow up a lot. And there's been good stuff and bad. When I woke up in that hospital bed, I realised that there was so much I'd taken for granted, and when I heard you and Dad talking that night after the Harvest Ball, I guess that's when I stopped being a child, and started realising that not everyone is a hero and not everyone is a bad guy. We're all shades of both and everything in between. And that's coming from someone who totally believed you and Dad were invincible and couldn't ever do anything wrong.'

'I suppose we've both been a disappointment to you, then,' Jonathan said thoughtfully.

Meredith paused for a long time before she answered. 'No.' She put her mug down on the table. 'I had to realise that everyone is human, everyone has flaws. When you're little, you believe your dad is superman and that he can achieve anything. Then you grow up and you realise that your dad is human, but that's what makes him more incredible. And, Uncle Jonno, the same goes for you.'

Jonathan swallowed hard. 'I suppose I never really learned that lesson when it came to Granddad.'

'And I can see why,' Meredith said. 'But I also saw how many times he and Dad argued over the years, and I know exactly how bad Dad feels about that now. He never got to have the conversations he wanted with Granddad until it was nearly too late. I know they did sort a lot out after I had my accident, but there was still so much for them to work through.' Meredith impatiently brushed away a tear that had escaped. She'd done so much crying since her grandfather had died, and she couldn't let things get the better of her at the moment, not with Jonathan in such a vulnerable state.

'What would you have said to him, if you had the chance for one more conversation?' Jonathan asked his niece gently.

Meredith took her time to give this some thought. She sipped the dregs of her tea. 'I think Granddad and I had this kind of unspoken thing,' she said, eventually. 'We just enjoyed each other's company. I don't think I actually *needed* to say anything to him that he didn't already know.' She looked up at Jonathan again, clear blue eyes alight. 'I'd have liked to have told him that I loved him one more time, and that I was glad he was my granddad, but I have the feeling he knew that already. What about you?'

Jonathan laughed hollowly. 'The thing about Granddad, niece of mine, is that he always knew, and noticed, a whole lot more than we gave him credit for.'

'Such as?' Meredith asked.

'Such as the real reason your parents split up,' Jonathan said quietly. 'Although he never let on until your Dad was at risk of losing your delectable stepmother for good. Then he let him, and later me, have it with both barrels.'

'I was so angry with you,' Meredith said thoughtfully. 'That night I overheard you and Dad talking, when I realised that you were the reason Mum and Dad split up, I wanted to scream at you.'

'I know,' Jonathan hung his head. 'And I remember our dinner at The Stationmaster when you basically called me every name under the sun, in whispers, until I was so paranoid Vern was going to chuck us out, I bought you a liqueur coffee just to keep you quiet.'

'That's right,' Meredith smiled. 'And I eventually realised that if Granddad could keep the peace for ten years, then I should try to do the same, no matter how angry I was with you.'

'And you've no idea how glad I am that you're still talking to me,' Jonathan said quietly. 'I don't deserve you, Merry.'

Meredith blushed. 'You're probably right, but Granddad also cleared up a few things for me about how hard it was for Mum when Dad was working all hours, and how I shouldn't just blame you for what happened. The three of you all had something to do with it, even if you did behave like a twat.'

'Thanks,' Jonathan said dryly.

'So, what are you going to do about Caroline?' Meredith asked.

Stunned, but not entirely surprised by Meredith's abrupt change of subject, Jonathan played for time. He got up and took Meredith's mug and his own to the dishwasher. 'You don't believe in pussyfooting around, do you?'

'Must have got that from Mum,' Meredith smiled. 'But it's not about me, it's about you.'

'Oh, I don't know, darling,' Jonathan replied. 'There's not really a situation to do anything about, is there?'

'Don't be daft,' Meredith said. 'You know you're bonkers about her, as does half the village by now. The only one who needs to know for sure is Caroline.'

'Well, that's not going to happen, even if it were true,' Jonathan said. 'She's got other things to deal with right now.' He stopped himself from adding that, if Caroline really gave a stuff about him she'd have got in touch when Jack died, too.

'Such as?' Meredith pushed.

'Oh, nothing you need to worry about,' Jonathan evaded. 'Just try to remember that you can't make everyone dance to your tune.'

Meredith stood up from her seat at the table and looked her uncle straight in the eye. 'You'd be surprised,' she replied. 'After all, I'm really good at matchmaking, and I know a good couple when I see one.'

'Ah yes, I remember all too well hearing the stories about how you got your dad and Anna together for their first date,' Jonathan said. 'But you're wrong on this one. Caroline and I were never a couple.'

'That's not what it looks like to me and everyone at the restaurant,' Meredith said.

'Caroline's not interested in anything long term. If she was, I'd know.'

'I think you need to speak to her, Uncle Jonno,' Meredith said gently. 'And convince her that you're serious.'

'Maybe when the funeral is over,' Jonathan said. 'Let's just get through that first, darling.'

'All right,' Meredith conceded. 'But Granddad wouldn't want you to waste this opportunity. So, don't wait too long.'

As Meredith left, Jonathan was torn between tears and helpless laughter. Sometimes Meredith truly was incorrigible. But, no matter what his niece said, it didn't detract from the fact that Caroline hadn't contacted him about Jack, and, like it or not, he felt more hurt by that than he had by anything in a long time.

43

The Carter family was lucky that the coroner wasn't busy. Because Jack had died unexpectedly and at home, a post mortem was necessary, but it was pushed through quickly after his GP had furnished the coroner with Jack's medical records. The verdict was heart failure, which came as no surprise to anyone. As a result, Jack's body was released for burial fairly swiftly. The old man had often spoken about what he wanted for his funeral, and so it was that Jonathan and Matthew were able to arrange it for the following Tuesday, the same day that Jonathan had arranged to meet Paul Stone. Jonathan realised, with a lurch, that he'd completely forgotten about Stone until the date was confirmed by the vicar. Regretfully, he cancelled the appointment, vowing to rebook as soon as he could. Caroline would understand, he thought. She still hadn't been in contact since sending him a text to let him know she'd got to Farnham safely, before Jack's death. He'd tried calling her the day after Jack had died but her phone had gone straight to voicemail. She had warned him that her flat was in a blackspot but he was surprised, and not a little hurt, that she hadn't been in touch nearly a week on from his message.

Surely she'd have been able to check her phone at some point, he thought. She wouldn't have been holed up in the flat for all that time.

Despite Jack's popularity and the temptation to mark his passing in a more flamboyant way, the Carter brothers had been relieved at the straightforwardness of their father's final wishes. There would be no carrying the coffin on a Carter's juggernaut, no Morris men dancing and jingling, just two brothers and their family, and those from the village who wanted to pay their respects. At the end of the day, in his quieter moments, Jack had always said he just wanted to see Cecily again.

Matthew and Anna, ever concerned, ever hospitable, had invited Jonathan to spend the night before the funeral at Cowslip Barn but Jonathan had declined. He loved his family, but he needed to be alone. Despite this, Matthew had come over earlier to discuss the eulogy one more time.

'You're the elder son, you should do it,' Jonathan said. 'It's your right.'

Matthew shook his head. 'I think we both know you'd do a better job of it. And Dad would have preferred you, anyway.'

'Now is not the time to bring that up again,' Jonathan said wearily. 'But if you really want me to do it, then I will.'

Matthew nodded. 'Thank you.' He looked at his brother. Jonathan had managed to have a shave today but he still looked tired. 'Come to dinner tonight?'

Jonathan smiled for the first time in days. 'You're not going to give up until I do, are you?'

'It's the wife,' Matthew replied. 'She's got this foolish notion you're fading away in this cottage and you know how she is about feeding people up.'

'Well, she knows you'd never eat if she or Meredith didn't cook for you.' Jonathan pulled up the sleeves on the jumper he was wearing. One of Jack's, Matthew realised with a lurch.

'So, will you come over, to stop her giving me earache?'

'Not tonight,' Jonathan said, with the ghost of a smile of sympathy for his brother. 'Really, I'm not that hungry.'

Matthew smiled back for the first time that day. 'Dad wouldn't want to see you sitting here alone,' he said roughly. 'Better to be with your family.'

'He'd have kicked my arse by now,' Jonathan said. 'Over quite a few things, I think.'

'It's not just Dad, is it? You still haven't sorted out the accounts discrepancies with Caroline, have you?' Matthew looked at his brother, compassion in his eyes. 'Don't get me wrong,' he said hastily, 'at the moment, that's the last thing on my mind, too. But something tells me you're stalling because there's more to it than just the money.'

Jonathan gave a hollow laugh. 'I can't talk about it right now, Matthew. And anyway, we've got bigger things to get through for the next couple of days. But I will get to the bottom of it after tomorrow's over and done with.'

'That's fine as far as the money is concerned,' Matthew's tone was still gentle, 'but if there is more to it, you can admit it, you know.'

'It's no good,' Jonathan said. 'You know me; can't commit to a shampoo, much less a relationship. Bachelor to the end of my days.' At Matthew's sceptical look, he actually managed a laugh. 'Besides, she's keeping me firmly at arm's length.'

'It happens to the best of us,' Matthew reminded him. 'Need I mention my previous marriage?'

'I wouldn't,' Jonathan replied. 'I hear some twat ruined it for you.'

'Nah,' Matthew said. 'I managed that myself.' He patted Jonathan's shoulder awkwardly. 'Come over tonight. Have some stew and a couple of glasses of wine. It'll do you good.'

Jonathan shook his head. 'No thanks. I need to get my head together to face the funeral tomorrow. I still don't know what the fuck I'm going to say.'

'Don't plan it,' Matthew said gently, resting his hand on Jonathan's shoulder. 'Just speak from the heart. You're best that way.' He swallowed hard. 'Dad wouldn't have wanted you to spend hours agonising about what to say.'

'I wish I could have told him how I felt when he was alive,' Jonathan's voice trembled and he tried unsuccessfully to swallow the lump in his throat. 'Instead of bending his ear about Buckthorn.'

Matthew rubbed his eyes and Jonathan realised for the first time just how hard their father's death had hit his brother. 'He knew,' Matthew said wearily. 'He might not have said so, but he knew.'

'Go on,' Jonathan said, wiping his own eyes hurriedly. 'Get back to that family of yours. Your wife's likely to give birth any moment now. You need to be with her.'

Matthew gave a sad smile. 'I'll see you at Cowslip Barn tomorrow then. Remember Dad's... getting there... at about nine thirty.'

Jonathan nodded. 'I'll be there in plenty of time.' He wanted to say more, but at the last moment he stopped himself. They both had to hold it together for the sake of the rest of the family, at least until Jack was safely interred. There would be plenty of time for tears later. He had the rest of his life to mourn for his father, and for Caroline, Jonathan thought as Matthew left.

44

Caroline couldn't sleep. The flat didn't seem like home any more. It didn't help that there was hardly any furniture left in it now, apart from a bed and the sofa in the living room. It would have been more comfortable to check into a bed and breakfast, or stay with a friend, but she wanted to keep a low profile. She had no desire to let anyone who might even be vaguely connected with Paul Stone and her old life know she was back in Surrey; she just wanted to get the flat sorted out and then work out what to do about paying back the missing money.

On her first full morning in Farnham she'd checked her restaurant emails from time to time on her phone, and kept up with the news on the BBC website, but the phone's signal was still intermittent and she had to go outside the building to get decent reception. In the end, she'd given up, thinking she'd check it when she ventured out later to the supermarket. Since Emma and Gino thought she was out of the country, she didn't try to phone The Cider Kitchen, but fired off a quick email to let them know she'd arrived at her destination safely.

After a first sleepless night, followed by a day of repainting the living space, and then a second and third bad night, Caroline, fuzzy from bad dreams and interrupted sleep patterns (she'd grown rather used to the silence and the dark in her quarters above the restaurant and couldn't sleep with the street lights outside), forgot her phone was in the front pocket of her overshirt when she started painting again. Kneeling down to dip her paintbrush into the pot, the phone slipped out of her pocket into the full tin of emulsion.

'Fuck!' Plunging her hand into the pot, she retrieved the phone as quickly as she could, but one look at the submerged sockets and ports and she knew it was a goner. It was no solace whatsoever that even if the phone wasn't damaged beyond all repair, she'd still never have picked up a signal. Briefly, she considered calling The Cider Kitchen from the phone box outside the corner shop, or perhaps Jonathan, but she realised she didn't actually know what his phone number was, having programmed it into her phone. No one knew anyone's number any more, she thought in frustration. Resigning herself to being out of contact, she cracked on with the painting. At least, she figured, Paul Stone wouldn't be able to contact her either.

That evening, she settled down on the sofa to try to relax. She'd been hard at work all day on the walls and she finally felt as though she was getting somewhere. Perhaps she'd be able to get back to

Little Somerby a bit quicker, after all. Jonathan had told her to stay away until he'd tried to sort out the situation with Stone, but after a few days' reflection with nothing other than magnolia walls upon which to focus, she was regaining her own sense of perspective. Stone shouldn't be able to chase her away from her livelihood, she thought; or her new home. The mess was something she really should be able to sort out for herself. Plus, she thought uneasily, the longer she was away from the restaurant, the more likely it was that Stone would come after her. She'd been deliberately cagey about her destination when she'd informed her staff she was taking leave, but Stone wasn't stupid; he could easily work out where she might be. The thought of being confronted, alone, here, was one that made her feel ill.

Resolving to finish any outstanding jobs in the flat tomorrow and then head home, she decided to take her mind off it all and, after double checking the door to the flat was securely locked, she took her A3 sketch pad from where she'd left it on the sofa. The life drawing classes were still ongoing, but she'd missed this week's because she'd come away. Perhaps now would be a good time to practice. Anna had asked her a few weeks back if she'd be able to do a special pencil portrait to display and then auction off at the murder mystery evening that was being held at the cider farm at the end of November. She'd lent Caroline a few of the photographs she'd unearthed from one of the tea chests of Carter's documents, but had given Caroline free rein over which one to draw. Flipping through them, she settled on the one she liked best and thought would work most successfully as a pencil portrait, and put pencil to paper.

45

The day of Jack Carter's funeral dawned dully. The threat of rain in the air and a brisk north- easterly wind did little to raise the already low spirits of his immediate family. Jonathan had spent the night before tossing and turning in the cottage that held so many memories of his father.

Now, up far too early and feeling restless, dressed in the dark charcoal grey suit and white shirt that he'd selected for the funeral, he was glad of the thick black wool and cashmere coat that went over the top. He'd not eaten much since his father died and he felt chilled to the bone before he even left the cottage. He couldn't face breakfast, again, and so decided to walk over to Cowslip Barn. There was no point brooding in the cottage; he wanted to be with family.

As he walked the short route from Jack's cottage to Cowslip Barn, he wondered again why Caroline hadn't been in touch. He knew Anna had texted her and tried to call her to let her know about Jack, but Anna said she hadn't had a response to either attempt. Caroline, who was usually pretty communicative with her phone, wouldn't intentionally be ignoring her own sister-in-law, would she? Even if she hadn't known what to say,

Jonathan thought, he would have expected her to at least text him a quick 'I'm sorry.' Feeling disloyal to his father for even thinking about such things on the day of the old man's funeral, he tried to put Caroline out of his mind. He had the eulogy to deliver and the rest of the day to get through; although he was hoping that once the funeral was over he'd just be able to get blind drunk and blot out the pain for a while. And then, he thought, he'd have to deal with Paul Stone. But for now, it had to be all about Jack.

After meeting the rest of the family at Cowslip Barn, the assembled Carters made their way to the village church for the ceremony. The rain held off, and as they got out of the car that had followed the black hearse, even the wind dropped. Mourners were trickling into the church, and as Jonathan took his place beside the coffin alongside his brother he felt a fleeting dizziness.

'Are you all right?' Matthew murmured, seeing the colour draining from Jonathan's face. The shadows under Matthew's eyes were as black as his tie, and Jonathan could see the rawness of his own pain reflected in his brother's eyes.

'Fine,' Jonathan replied.

Most of Jack's contemporaries were too frail to carry his coffin, so Matthew's good friend, Patrick Flanagan, Jack's nephew, Robin, who lived in Devon where his mother, Jack's sister, had retired some years ago, and the two most senior executives besides Jonathan and Matthew, who Jack had appointed many years back, took the duty. Meredith had wanted to be one of the pallbearers, arguing that she had as much a right as any as the only grandchild, but Matthew had persuaded her to stay with Anna and keep Ellie on an even keel. The little girl was present at the funeral, and stared solemn eyed at the assembled mourners, unable to put into words her own feelings about the situation. It wasn't her first funeral, Jonathan realised with a jolt, remembering Anna's first husband, Caroline's brother.

Feeling the weight of the coffin on his shoulders, and with the sudden, sharp realisation that such a once vital, robust man was lying still and lifeless within it, Jonathan lost his footing. His brother's left arm, entwined with his under the coffin and resting on his shoulder, tightened reassuringly. He couldn't see Matthew's face on the other side of the coffin, and he was glad; he had the feeling he'd never keep it together if he did.

Somehow, they made it to the doors of the church and up the aisle. At the top, the funeral directors helped them to place the coffin, head towards the altar. As Jonathan felt the weight of his physical burden lessen, he felt the emotional one increasing. Would he manage to get through the eulogy?

The vicar, who had known Jack for many years, although Jack wasn't what anyone would call a regular churchgoer, welcomed the mourners. His gentle, kind voice in the face of such sorrow was more welcome than he could imagine, as were the carefully chosen anecdotes that made the congregation smile. But all Jonathan could think about was the speech he was about to give. Would it measure up to his father's expectations of him?

The service progressed very quickly and before he knew it, it was time for Jonathan to give Jack's eulogy. Jonathan stood up on shaky legs, his dark coat drifting out behind him as he left the family pew and mounted the steps to the pulpit. Anna, in the front row, had one arm around Ellie. Matthew was next to her, his dark head bowed in thought, and Meredith sat next to him, holding his hand tightly. Behind them, the church was packed with friends, villagers and people from further afield, all of whom had come to pay their respects to his father.

It had taken a lot of soul searching to get to this point. Jonathan had lain awake for hours, trying to decide how best to deliver the most fitting tribute to his father; the best way of saying what, exactly, Jack had meant to him. And it wasn't just about him personally. Jack had been a figurehead for the whole community and a representative of the business for the country. Sometimes irascible, always generous of time and spirit, Jack had been many, many things.

Jonathan cleared his throat and took a moment longer to look at the assembled congregation. He'd written a page of notes in the small hours of this morning but he knew them so well now, he decided not to use them. He took a deep breath.

'My father, Jack Carter, was truly one of a kind. He meant many things to all of us. To my brother and me, he was Dad; the one who worked hard, taught us right from wrong, showed us that if we wanted something it was worth striving for, and made me, personally, think that nothing was impossible or beyond our grasp.' He looked around at the mourners, feeling a weight lifting from his shoulders as he saw the encouragement in their faces.

'He had a debt of responsibility to the past, but he always had an eye on the future. Although a lot of you saw him as the master of this cider universe, he was, and always will be, so much more than that. Dad was a charming, educated, cultured man who, when my brother wanted to be a lawyer, told him to follow his dreams. The business would always be there, he said, when Matthew was ready to take it on. He always dreamed Matthew and I would run it together, and, last year, I am proud to say that dream was realised.'

Jonathan glanced briefly at his brother, but Matthew's head was still bowed, so he couldn't tell how he was reacting. 'My father was the kind of man who made you feel as though you were the only person in the world when he spoke to you, that you were the only one that mattered. I was lucky to have unconditional support from him; others had to fight harder for that support. But, once earned, it was given without question.' Jonathan's voice had strengthened, his self-assurance was trickling back with every word. He would do his father proud now, like never before.

'My father had his share of ups and downs, professionally and personally, but his charm, wit, perseverance and love saw him through most of them unscathed. He wanted nothing more than to see his family happy, healthy and at peace. After many years, he at last saw us all returned to where we belong, at the heart of a business he loved, and the heart of a family he loved more.'

Drawing another steadying breath, he looked around the church once more and smiled as he saw Miss Pinkham wiping away a discreet tear. 'My father was one of the most vibrant, loving men I ever had the privilege to know. And I will miss him.'

Jonathan closed his eyes briefly, then turned to where Jack's coffin lay. He walked up to it, put his left hand on the lid and paused for a moment. When he raised his eyes again to look back out at the congregation, he saw that Matthew had looked up, too, and that his face was wet with tears, like rainwater on granite. Feeling more drained than he had in a long time, he rejoined his family.

After Jonathan's eulogy, the mourners proceeded to the graveside to see Jack safely into the burial plot that he would now share with his wife Cecily. The bright green artificial grass that lined the surround of the grave seemed incongruously cheerful against the backdrop of heavy Somerset clay soil and looming black clouds, and the congregation huddled deeper into their overcoats as the vicar read the final rites. Jonathan's head started to spin as Jack's coffin was lowered slowly into the ground and he steeled himself in an attempt to regain some kind of equilibrium. His jaw ached, and the heat behind his eyes grew unbearable as Meredith dropped a small posy onto the top of the coffin. Stepping forward, he picked up a handful of soil and threw it into the grave, seeing it land beside the flowers.

Before he knew it, he was standing next to his brother outside the church, shaking the hands of the assembled mourners. 'I'll see you in a bit,' he said to Matthew as they said goodbye to the last of the congregation. 'I want to...' he swallowed. 'I need to be here a while longer. I need to talk to him one last time.'

Matthew nodded, unable to speak. Anna stepped in, her timing immaculate as always. 'Don't be long,' she said gently. 'We'll get you a drink in.'

Jonathan watched Anna, Matthew and their daughters walk down the sloping path to the church gate, and then, feeling tired and very, very alone, he turned back to the graveyard.

46

'I wish I knew what to do, Dad.' Jonathan looked down at the newly dug grave, feeling only a moment's foolishness for voicing his thoughts out loud. 'For the first time in my life, I just don't have a fucking clue.'

The wind was starting to rise and it ruffled the tails of his coat. Jonathan had experienced enough squally autumns in the West Country to know that the damp, slightly warm wind presaged a storm, but at this point, he didn't care. The grim weather reflected his mood; gave him a backdrop against which the confusing maelstrom of his emotions had something to play.

'I wish I'd been with you, Dad,' he said softly. 'I wish I could have held your hand as you slipped away.'

A lone magpie chattered in the tall yew trees whose branches swayed above his head; a primitive call that seemed to laugh. Jonathan knew he'd been stupid, a fool. Even now, after mending his relationship with Matthew and spending time with Jack, trying to make up for all of those destroyed, wasted years, he still felt monumental guilt that he'd wasted so much time away from home.

'I hope you can hear me, wherever you are. I'm sorry for the pain I put you through over the years. I'm sorry for staying away for so long. I wish I'd learned earlier that I should be more responsible, and I wish, most of all, that we'd talked more when you could actually hear me.' Jonathan felt the first drops of rain on his face. He was glad; it would disguise the tears that were so achingly close to the surface.

'A lot of the time you put faith in me, you were wrong to do so,' Jonathan said softly. 'Matthew was the one behind the scenes, smoothing things over while I took all the glory. He worked so hard for you, always, Dad, and I think, eventually, you realised that.' He drew another deep breath, trying to steady himself. 'That sums up exactly the kind of man he is, Dad, and exactly the kind of man I am. I was never worthy of the faith you put in me.'

'And now I've fucked up again, Dad, and I don't know what to do.' Jonathan swallowed hard and pulled his coat tighter around himself. 'I've promised I'll sort something that I have no idea how to fix. And I promised it because I love her. And she's an irritable, dogmatic, single minded woman with absolutely no idea.' He shook his head and laughed hollowly, surprising himself at how closely mirth ran alongside tears. 'I wish you were here to talk to. I wish I could have asked your advice while you were still around to give it.' His hands started to tremble, partly from the cold, but mostly from the stress of having to keep control for so long. 'What am I going to do, Dad?' He bowed his head, fighting for control over what little emotional strength he had left. Suddenly it all seemed to be closing in on him, like punches raining down in a brawl. He felt exhausted, embattled, and terribly alone. Finally, as the heavens opened and a low rumble of thunder growled over the Mendip Hills, he surrendered to tears.

*

When Jonathan had been a no show at the wake, Matthew's alarm bells had started to ring. As the elder son, he couldn't break away from the gathering, continually buttonholed as he was by people wanting to talk about his father, but the awareness that Jonathan hadn't turned up as the sky darkened and the day drew on was both irritating and worrying.

The wake began to wind down and people gradually drifted away. Matthew bade farewell to his cousin Robin, who was driving his Aunt Clare, Jack's sister, back to Devon that evening. 'I'll pass on your regards to Jonathan,' he said, shaking Robin's hand.

'Do,' Robin replied. He was slighter than Matthew but roughly the same height. The three boys had enjoyed each other's company immensely as children and only in later years had they drifted apart. 'We must catch up again soon. And not just when events like this bring us together.'

'Agreed,' Matthew replied. 'There's likely to be a christening in the next few months – I'll send you an invitation.' His tired eyes softened as they alighted on Anna, who was still chatting to a couple of lingering guests.

'You've done well there,' Robin observed. 'You seem very happy. Current events excepted, of course.'

'I am,' Matthew smiled. 'She's worked wonders for the family. And Dad was very fond of her.'

As the cousins shook hands and said their goodbyes, Matthew's thoughts turned once again to Jonathan. His brother seemed so vulnerable and so very alone. In all the years of their estrangement, Matthew had always imagined Jonathan to be living a carefree, responsibility free life, but since his return to the village, he'd observed a depth and seriousness in his brother. He hoped their father's death wasn't going to push Jonathan over the edge.

'I'd better go and see if I can find Jonathan,' he murmured to Anna as she came back to his side. 'I'll just nip over to the cottage and see if he's back there.'

'Don't be too hard on him for missing the wake,' Anna said, putting a hand on Matthew's jacket clad arm. 'He's still in shock about your dad. He probably couldn't face it.'

Matthew shook his head. 'He's too used to ducking out of things he can't face,' he said grimly. 'He's spent his life walking away when things get tough. We're all struggling with… this.' He blinked furiously, trying not to lose the control he'd fought so hard to maintain all day. Later, behind closed doors, he could give way, but not here, not with eyes still on him. That was the difference between him and Jonathan, he supposed. He still wondered who was the stronger for it. 'Vern wants the room back anyway,' he said softly, leaning down and kissing Anna briefly. 'You get the girls home and I'll go and check on him. Take the Land Rover if you're tired.'

'The walk will do us good,' Anna said. 'With a bit of luck it'll put Ellie out for the count early. It's been a long day for her.'

Matthew's brow furrowed. 'I know,' he said gently. 'This must be difficult for both of you, and not just because of Dad.' He pulled her to him once more. 'I'm so glad you're with me.'

Anna looked back up at Matthew and smiled. 'I always will be,' she said softly. 'And I mean it. Go easy on Jonathan.' She turned back to Ellie and Meredith. 'Are you two ready to go?'

Meredith smiled. 'Flynn's walking me back later,' she said. 'We're going to meet a couple of friends here.'

'Soft drinks only, now you're unsupervised,' Matthew warned.

Meredith rolled her eyes. 'Of course. I've had enough sherry this afternoon to last me a lifetime.' Hugging her father and stepmother goodbye, she ambled off to the bar on the other side of the pub.

'Just you and me then, Munchkin,' Anna turned to her daughter.

'I might as well drop you off on the way,' Matthew said, as the final mourners departed. 'I don't like the idea of you walking back in the dark without Meredith to keep an eye on you.'

'I won't say no,' Anna replied. 'This one's getting heavy, anyway.' She patted her stomach.

Leaving the pub, Matthew, Anna and Ellie walked the short distance to the Land Rover and then Matthew dropped them back at Cowslip Barn. 'I won't be long,' he said as they got out of the car. 'I'll probably find him slumped in Dad's chair by the fire.'

Despite Anna's pleas, Matthew could feel his frustration with Jonathan rising as he drove the short distance from Cowslip Barn to Orchard Cottage. They should have faced the mourners at the wake together, united, but, as with so much in their lives lately, they'd been apart on this most important of days. Matthew was also, if truth be told, angry at himself for passing the buck of Jack's eulogy to

Jonathan. Jonathan had done a beautiful job, but Matthew had been filled with the same old jealousy and shame that it should have been so. Was it because, deep down, he knew that if he'd given the eulogy he'd have disappointed his father? That Jack would have preferred Jonathan to do it?

Orchard Cottage was in darkness as Matthew pulled up, and for a fleeting moment, he was put very firmly in his brother's shoes the night Jonathan had discovered Jack's body. He shivered in the rising wind as he got out of the Land Rover and strode towards the cottage. Fumbling in the darkness for the key to the front door, he eventually slotted it into the lock and walked into the bungalow.

'Jonathan?' The air was silent and cold around him with no radiators ticking in the hallway. 'Jonno?' Matthew tried again. 'Are you home?'

Nothing. No sound, not even a light in the kitchen. Walking through to the living room, just to double check, Matthew found it empty. Knowing the answer, but just to make sure, Matthew checked his brother's room, and, automatically, his father's, but they were both empty. Where could Jonathan be? Cursing under his breath, he pulled his phone out of his pocket. He didn't want to worry Anna, but she was expecting him back soon, so he thought he'd better let her know what he had, or rather hadn't, found.

'It's all right,' he said as Anna began to make suggestions. 'I think I know where to look. You'd better get the spare room ready.' Grimly, he pressed the end call button, went back down the stairs and out of the door of the cottage. It had started to rain, and as he got back into the Land Rover, he hoped his hunch was right.

A short drive later and Matthew parked the Land Rover again. Pausing to grab a torch from the glove compartment, he slammed the door shut, not bothering to lock it. No one would be out here in the dark on an evening like this, he thought. Well, no one in their right mind, anyway. He began to ascend the wooded slope, looking around all the time. The rain had started to fall more heavily, soaking the shoulders of his suit jacket and the top of his head. Matthew picked up his pace, hoping his brother hadn't gone far; neither of them were dressed for hill walking.

'Jonathan!' Matthew's voice was whipped away from him by the wind. The icy November rain lashed down, drenching his already wet hair even more. Somehow, he made it to the top of the hill, slipping in his leather brogues on the mud, feet tangling in the tree roots that lined the steep path.

A crack of lightning illuminated the ink dark sky as Matthew emerged onto the Wavering Down flat, throwing the sheep that were huddled together on the hill into momentary sharp relief against the cool green of the pasture. Where the hell was his brother?

'Jonno!' An ominous rumble of thunder resonated in the air, followed almost immediately by another sharp slash of light, splitting the sky above in two.

'For fuck's sake,' Matthew muttered, his suit jacket providing very little protection against the lacerating storm. He'd dashed out of the Land Rover without pausing to grab his Barbour, and now, starting to shiver in the November storm, he regretted it.

'Jonathan! Where are you?' Another crash of thunder rolled across the open hill top before the lightning caught up. The rain lashed his face and he put a hand up to his brow to keep the worst of it out of his eyes, the torch he'd brought with him barely illuminating a foot in front of him in the downpour.

Matthew kept walking. This had been a popular route for them as children, always with the family dog in tow, and they'd often disappeared for hours, wandering the distance between Kings Wood and Crook Peak and back again. Matthew had known it like the back of his hand and it had changed little in the intervening years. In daylight the view stretched from Cheddar reservoir to Glastonbury Tor, with the Somerset levels in between, but on a night like this all around was darkness. Even the traffic from the A38 a mile or so below seemed muted.

The storm was right overhead now and as a deafening clap of thunder broke, the lightning made it as bright as midday for a split second. It was all Matthew needed and he picked up his pace, heedless of his impractical footwear, as he caught sight of a figure, still, thankfully, wrapped in his black overcoat, slumped against a hawthorn tree at the edge of the path, an empty bottle of Carter's calvados next to him. Its distinctive red label was lit up first by the lightning and then Matthew's torch. Breaking into a jog, slipping on the mud, Matthew approached the tree.

'You stupid, stupid fucker!' Matthew's words died on his lips as he caught sight of his brother's face. Obviously blind drunk, Jonathan's chestnut hair was plastered down, his eyes closed against the deluge of wind and rain. He was out cold. Cursing the weather, his brother and anything and everything that sprang to mind, Matthew reached his brother's side and, reaching out a hand, tried to shake him to awareness.

'Off,' Jonathan muttered, trying to remove Matthew's hand from his shoulder.

'What the fuck are you doing out here?' Matthew raised his voice against the wind that was whipping over the top of the plain. 'Are you trying to get pneumonia?'

'Just fuck off and leave me alone,' Jonathan muttered. 'Get back down the hill to your family.'

Matthew was torn between wanting to hold Jonathan and hit him. 'You're my family,' he said. With an almighty heave, and feeling his dodgy knee creaking ominously, he dragged Jonathan to his feet. 'Now for fuck's sake come back down with me and let's get the hell out of the rain.' He began walking towards the slope of the woods, virtually carrying Jonathan. He could feel the dig of Jonathan's hip bones through his overcoat as he kept one arm firmly round his brother's waist, guiding him away from the thicker tree roots. If they both went arse over tit in the rain, Matthew didn't reckon much for either of their chances.

Jonathan, returned to his feet, swayed unsteadily and almost dragged Matthew back down into the mud. 'I can walk,' he slurred. He pulled away from his brother and immediately stumbled.

'I'll be the judge of that,' Matthew snapped, grabbing hold of his brother again.

'Like you always fucking are, you mean!' Jonathan's voice grew harsher. 'Why can't you keep out of things that don't concern you.' The comedown from the booze was making him punchy, and his eyes rolled one moment, flashed the next.

'If you behaved like a reasonable adult occasionally, I wouldn't be out here now,' Matthew said, forcing Jonathan back round to face him.

'I am a fucking adult!' Jonathan retorted. 'And I'm not your responsibility.'

'Clearly,' Matthew said. 'And I bet Dad would be really pleased if he was able to see you, off your head and freezing cold up here in the rain, wouldn't he?'

Jonathan winced. 'Well, he won't. And it's still none of your fucking business what I do.'

'Have you any idea how infantile you sound?' Matthew said, struggling to be heard against the wind. 'You're a grown man and you sound like some stupid teenager. So get off the bloody hill and come home, will you?'

'I can sound how I like,' Jonathan retorted. 'It's no-one's business but my own.'

'That's where you're wrong,' Matthew said grimly. 'If I don't get you home, Anna will worry herself sick, Meredith'll go off her head and I'll get earache from both of them. So, have pity for your brother and come back down.'

'Why can't you all just leave me the fuck alone?' Jonathan shouted, the last of the calvados running through his system. 'I didn't ask any of you to be concerned about me.'

'For fuck's sake!' Matthew grabbed hold of Jonathan's arm and spun him round to face him.

'This has gone on long enough. Dad's gone. It wasn't your fault. You didn't make it happen. Now stop blaming yourself for it, and take some responsibility for what's left of your life; for what you can do something about.'

'I've tried,' Jonathan shouted. 'Fuck knows I've tried, but it's never good enough, is it? Whatever I try to do in the business, you can't let go enough to trust me, and even when you did design to give me a little bit of control, you were more than happy to see it fail.' Jonathan rubbed a hand over his bloodshot eyes. 'You can't deny it, Matthew. You wanted to see me crash and burn.'

'That's not true.' The shock in Matthew's voice was almost lost in the wind. 'You must know that's not true.' He took a step back from his brother. 'I love you. I've never wanted to see you fail.'

'Bullshit.' Jonathan looked his brother straight in the eye. 'You can't bear to see me making a success of anything. You don't think I deserve it.'

'And why the fuck should you care what I think?' Matthew said. His brow was furrowed, and his hands were trembling, not entirely from the cold. 'You've never needed my approval for anything, and you've never sought it.'

Jonathan shook his head. 'You're wrong.' He looked at his brother. 'Ever since I came home, your approval, and Dad's, was all I wanted. The distribution deal, the takeover bid, even the early stages of the fucking restaurant… I wanted to prove to you both I could do it.'

'To us, or to yourself?' Matthew said. 'Or maybe to Caroline.'

There was a long, painful pause between the brothers. Matthew tightened his arm on Jonathan's shoulder, reminded almost unbearably of carrying the burden of their father's coffin between them. 'Come on,' he said gruffly, the tears suddenly too close to the surface again. 'Let's get down the hill before we both freeze to death.'

Jonathan regarded his brother warily. 'You're not going to fuck off, are you?'

'Nope.'

Hanging his head in defeat, Jonathan began picking his way back down the hill. When they reached the car park at the entrance to the wood, he pulled open the door to the Land Rover without a word, and slumped into the front seat. He didn't even bother putting on his seatbelt, so Matthew reached across him and did it for him, muttering under his breath about younger brothers being a liability. It was only when he clocked the direction of travel that Jonathan looked back at Matthew.

'Where are we going?'

Matthew's mouth was set in a grim, implacable line. 'If you think I'm taking you back to the cottage to keep on drinking, you've got another thing coming. You're coming back home with me.'

'Are you fucking joking?'

'Nope.' Matthew's hands were clenched on the wheel. Angry as he was with Jonathan, he wouldn't be able to forgive himself if Jonathan came to any harm.

'You can kip in the spare room for tonight, until you've sobered up.' Matthew glanced at his brother. 'And if Ellie or Merry don't wake you in the morning, then Anna certainly will. Perhaps she can bring you to your senses, since I've spectacularly failed to do so.'

Jonathan opened his mouth to argue, but one look at his brother's set face and clenched hands silenced him. He was freezing, he was beginning to feel an encroaching hangover and he really didn't want to go back to the cold, empty bungalow anyway, even if he'd never admit it. Since Jack's death, the place no longer felt like home.

They completed the short journey back to Cowslip Barn in a silence that was not altogether companionable. Matthew parked the Land Rover, and Jonathan was out of the passenger seat almost before the engine had stopped. The rain had ceased, leaving the remnants of the clouds in a murky sky above them, the moon hidden from view in a shroud of grey. Jonathan shivered. His black coat was soaked through and he felt chilled to the bone now the booze was wearing off.

'I don't have to face the girls, do I?' he said as they both made for the door round the back that led into the kitchen.

'Probably not a good idea, anyway,' Matthew said gruffly. 'Have a shower and get to bed.'

Jonathan nodded, relieved that, as they entered the kitchen, there wasn't anyone else around. 'I'll see you in the morning,' he said, crossing the stone floor.

Matthew merely nodded.

As Jonathan mounted the stairs and vanished onto the landing, Meredith, home now from the pub, and Anna emerged from the sitting room. Both wore identical looks of concern.

'How is he?' Anna asked quietly.

'Not great.'

'How did you know where to look?' Meredith glanced up the stairs.

'We used to go up the hill when we were kids,' Matthew said, crossing the hallway to stand with them. 'I kind of had a gut instinct that's where he'd end up.'

'What are we going to do about him?' Meredith sighed. 'He's still in bits about Granddad, isn't he?'

Matthew nodded. 'He just needs time to get over it all.' He reached out a hand and brushed Meredith's long dark plait back over her shoulder. 'All this has been hardest on him, I think.'

'And it would help if Caroline had been in touch,' Meredith continued. 'As far as I know, she's not contacted him since she went on leave. I mean, how could she do that to him? Knowing about Granddad and not even sending him a text?'

'I'm sure there's more to it than meets the eye, Merry,' Anna said gently. 'She wouldn't be deliberately freezing him out.' She looked concerned. 'I've been trying to call her since your grandfather died, but she's not answering her phone.'

'And Emma's not had an email from her since the day after she left,' Meredith said. 'It's a good job Emma knows how to run The Cider Kitchen in her sleep, or we'd really be in the shit at the restaurant.' She looked apologetically at Anna. 'Sorry, Wicked Stepmother. I'm just so fed up with bloody adults messing up their lives. And I miss Granddad.'

'I know you do,' Matthew said, putting an arm around Meredith. 'It's going to be hard over the next few weeks and months, but we'll manage somehow. We're good at getting through bad times, remember.' The dark weeks after Meredith's car accident still kept all of them awake at night.

'I'll try calling her again now,' Anna said. 'It's worrying me that she's not been in touch with anyone at all since she went away. It's not like her.'

She walked through to the kitchen and grabbed her mobile phone from the table where she'd thrown it when she'd got home. Frowning as she pressed the buttons, she put it back down again. 'The battery's flat. I'll have to give it half an hour or so. With everything that's been going on with Jack, I've lost track of how long she's been away. God, Matthew, what if something's happened to her?' She sat down in one of the kitchen chairs.

'I'm sure she's fine,' Matthew said, although the thought had crossed his mind that, with the discrepancy in The Cider Kitchen's books, perhaps Caroline was deliberately cutting herself off, and had maybe even done a runner. He hadn't yet shared the Accounts department's findings with Anna, for fear of causing her stress in the very late stages of her pregnancy, but he did wonder if that was the reason Caroline hadn't been in touch. Jonathan had said he was going to sort it out, but then Jack's sudden death had knocked them all for six, and Matthew doubted Jonathan had had the chance to get any further. 'Go and put your feet up,' he said gently. 'Jonathan's going to be out cold until the morning anyway, and we'll put fresh heads on then and try to sort something out.'

'OK,' Anna said. 'Let's just go and watch something mindless on television, shall we? It's been a long day.' She put an arm around Meredith. 'What do you fancy?'

'I've got some revision to do for my exam tomorrow,' Meredith said, gently disentangling herself. 'It'll take my mind off—' she choked, and then brushed away a stray tear as it fell. 'Granddad wouldn't want us to be moping around,' she said. 'And he'll kill me if I try to use him as an excuse to flunk my History mock.'

Anna drew Meredith close for a moment, and whispered. 'It's OK. I understand.' They broke apart again. 'Don't work all night. Come and say goodnight when you're ready.'

'I will.' Hugging Matthew too, she disappeared upstairs to her room.

'As always, she's the most self-possessed of all of us,' Matthew said quietly. 'But we'd better keep an eye on her. She tends to let things build up and then explode.' They both wanted to avoid a repeat of Meredith's anxieties over the new baby; both of them still kicked themselves that they hadn't seen it coming.

'More like you than she'd care to admit then,' Anna smiled wryly, wrapping an arm round Matthew. 'Come on. Let's go and watch some *Midsomer Murders* or something. Anything to escape from things for a bit.'

Matthew nodded. 'Only if you promise to tell me whodunit if I fall asleep. I'm knackered!'

'And soaking wet,' Anna realised as she pulled away from him. 'How about a hot bath and a glass of whiskey first?'

'Sounds good to me,' Matthew replied. 'We can always watch TV in bed.'

'Good plan,' Anna said. 'I'll meet you there.'

Matthew watched Anna mount the stairs, and then, feeling the waves of tiredness washing over him after one of the most emotional days of his life, rubbed a hand over his exhausted eyes. Jonathan, Caroline, Jack's estate, all would have to wait until tomorrow. Tonight he just craved sleep and his wife's tender embrace. On legs that could barely carry him, he, too, headed off to bed.

47

Caroline had to admit to finding the lack of mobile communication rather liberating after her initial panic about ruining her phone. It felt like a digital detox. She was beginning to worry about The Cider Kitchen though, having been away for over a week now, but Emma had, after all, reassured her that she'd contact Jonathan with any urgent issues. Because she wasn't being constantly distracted by emails, calls and texts, she managed to get the redecoration of the flat done in record time, and feeling restless, she decided to head back to Somerset. If the worst came to the worst she could shut the door on her living quarters and force herself to take the time off, but in truth, she was missing the restaurant and she wanted to touch base with Jonathan about how they were going to deal with Paul Stone. She resolved to go and see Jonathan as soon as she got back to Somerset. She'd at least be able to tell him that she'd arranged to sell her flat in order to pay back the money she'd given to Stone. The estate agent had told her it should go fairly quickly and that meant the holes in The Cider Kitchen's finances could be plugged.

Of course, this would all be for nothing if Carter's still decided to dismiss her. She had to find a way of convincing Jonathan that she was trustworthy, that with Stone out of the way and no longer a concern she would continue to pour her heart, soul and time into The Cider Kitchen. She was faintly optimistic that she'd be able to convince Jonathan, but whether she'd be able to keep Matthew on side once he found out the truth, she wasn't sure.

Packing her things into the car, she checked her watch. It would take just over two and a half hours and then she'd be home. She couldn't believe how keen she was to get back to The Cider Kitchen, and Jonathan.

*

At around the same time as Caroline was setting out for Somerset, Jonathan woke the morning after Jack's funeral with an utterly mind bending hangover. The spare bed at Cowslip Barn was a touch lumpy these days, but he'd crashed out after a hot shower and not woken up until Anna knocked on his door with a cup of honey sweetened tea.

'Morning, gorgeous,' he said, cracking open his eyes and struggling to sit up in bed.

'How are you feeling?' Anna asked as she deposited the mug of tea on the bedside table.

'You know that squashed badger on the main road a few days ago?' Jonathan yawned. 'Marginally worse than him.'

'I'm not surprised,' Anna said wryly. 'That calvados is lethal at the best of times. And from what Matthew said, there wasn't a lot left in the bottle he found you with.'

'Guilty as charged,' Jonathan said. He sat up in bed and with a shaky hand reached out and took the mug of tea. 'I kind of drank it as I walked up the hill. This'll help, though. Thanks.'

'Ellie wanted to come in and wake you up at about six a.m., but I managed to deflect her,' Anna said, perching on the side of the bed. 'I figured you could do with the rest.'

'Thanks. Again.' Jonathan, with an effort, swallowed a mouthful of tea and tried not to grimace. He couldn't stand sweetened tea but he appreciated the thought. He figured his blood sugar levels must be non-existent after last night.

'Help yourself to some of Matthew's clothes,' Anna said. 'That wardrobe is chock full of jeans, shirts and jumpers that he won't get rid of. Something's bound to fit.'

'Oh, don't worry about that,' Jonathan said, 'I'll just fling my suit on from last night. I don't have far to go.'

'It's still wet,' Anna said. 'And it's going to need dry cleaning. The mud up on Wavering Down's awful this time of year.'

'He told you where he found me, then.'

'Yup.' Anna's look of concern made Jonathan feel a flush of shame. 'You could have ended up with hypothermia.'

'I know. Yet again, it was a bloody stupid thing to do, wasn't it?' Jonathan dropped his gaze to his mug. 'But don't worry. I'm not going to do it again. Matthew gave me a bollocking last night, from what I can remember of our conversation, and as usual, he's right. There's no point pushing the self-destruct button; Dad wouldn't have wanted that. And Christ knows I've got enough to sort out without trying to drown myself in drink, or on the hill in a storm.' He looked back up at Anna, a rueful smile tugging at his lips. 'I don't suppose you've heard from Caroline since last night?'

Anna shook her head. 'I'm getting a bit worried, actually. It's not like her not to be in touch. Emma said she rang about a week ago, and that she'd said call again in a day or so, but she never did.'

'So, she might not know about Dad, then?' Jonathan felt a sense of relief. Surely, if Caroline had heard about Jack, she'd have at least sent him a message?

Anna shook her head. 'I guess not. Obviously, wherever she is must have lousy reception.'

Jonathan took another mouthful of his tea and then swung his legs out of bed. Clad only in his boxer shorts, he wondered for a moment if he should feel self-conscious in front of Anna, but she wasn't embarrassed, although she did look concerned.

'You're getting thin,' she said as he crossed the room to the wardrobe.

'I thought it was forbidden to ogle your houseguests,' Jonathan quipped, and surprised, found that he actually sounded like himself.

'Oh don't worry,' Anna replied. 'I just don't want you wasting away. My interest is purely in your welfare.'

'I won't,' Jonathan said. 'There's been enough inaction. I'm going to get dressed, force down a bit of toast if you don't mind me nicking some, and then get on with things.' He opened the wardrobe and pulled out jeans, a shirt and a jumper. The jeans were a little loose, but they'd do until he got home. Somehow he didn't think Miss Pinkham and the other elderly ladies of the parish would appreciate him sauntering home in just his boxer shorts.

'See you downstairs in a minute,' Anna replied. And then, before she left the room, 'I'm so glad you're feeling a bit better.'

'You know me,' Jonathan replied sardonically. 'Nothing gets me down for long.'

As Anna left the room, Jonathan's face fell again. He'd acted so convincingly he'd almost fooled himself.

*

Caroline crossed into Somerset in record time, and since she didn't have her phone to provide the music for the journey, she'd been tuning and retuning the car radio to the local radio stations as she went. As she drove through the different counties the accents changed but the type of music tended to stay the same and she quite enjoyed the snippets of local news.

The car's clock ticked over to midday just as she reached the Shepton Mallet to Cheddar road; the national news headlines finished and the local ones commenced. At the third headline, a local interest piece in a particularly sombre tone, Caroline hit the brakes and swerved into a layby. Surely she'd misheard? Surely, if anything so serious had happened, she'd have known? Somehow? According to Breeze FM, which served the whole of Somerset, yesterday Little Somerby had buried local legend and cider magnate, Jack Carter.

Caroline's heart was hammering so fast she had to take several deep breaths. When she was sure she was calm enough to drive, she started the car again; she had to get to Jonathan.

48

Jonathan got back to Orchard Cottage and thought about getting changed, but the house was cold and Matthew's jumper was warm. Wandering into the kitchen, he took a mug from the tree on the side and filled the kettle to make coffee. As the water began to boil, Jonathan started to wonder what would happen to Orchard Cottage. He supposed the solicitors would be sorting all that out fairly soon, but he did think that perhaps it was time for him, finally, to find a place of his own.

He was also irritated that he'd failed to deal with Paul Stone, despite the upheaval of Jack's death. Even if Caroline hadn't contacted him about Jack, he owed it to her to try to sort things out. But how? He could easily rearrange the appointment, but Stone was clearly not an idiot and might just see him as a time waster after he cancelled the first time. What could he do? He shook his head in frustration; he must have killed more brain cells than he'd thought with all that calvados.

Just as he was crossing the hallway to the living room there was a tap on the front door. For a moment he ignored it; he didn't feel like talking to anyone. But then a flash of red through the small frosted glass panel in the door against the backdrop of the autumn sky caught his attention. He froze. He must be imagining things, surely? Some fallen leaf from the beech trees in his father's garden had caught against the glass in the rain. It couldn't be her. Could it?

The knock came again and that settled it. Beech leaves most certainly didn't do that. Hastening to the door, stumbling on the carpet runner in his rush, he tugged it open and there, standing on the doorstep of the cottage looking more uncertain than he'd ever seen her, was Caroline.

'I came as soon as I heard,' Caroline said softly. 'Jonathan, I'm so, so sorry.'

Jonathan didn't say anything. He pulled her through the front door, feeling her sag against him as he kicked the door shut behind them, and then took her in his arms. Trembling almost to hyperventilation, he held onto her tightly, feeling as though he might shatter into a million pieces if he let her go, even for one second.

'Thank God you're back,' he murmured when he finally released her. 'I was so angry with you for not getting in touch, but now you're here I'm just relieved.'

'I didn't know,' Caroline's voice shook. 'The reception in my flat is crap, and then I dropped my phone in a pot of paint so I decided to wait until I got back here before ordering a new one. The call box on the High Street was vandalised and you've no idea how difficult it is to find a working phone box in the twenty-first century. Every bloody man and their wife has a mobile these days. And I couldn't even buy a cheap pay as you go one, as I don't have a clue what everyone's numbers actually are. Although,' she slapped her forehead, 'I suppose I could just have rung The Cider Kitchen again. I was so screwed up over Paul Stone that I wasn't thinking straight and the thought of not being contactable, especially by him, was really quite good. Until I heard the news about your dad on the local radio when I was driving home this morning, I didn't have a clue he'd died.' She looked up at Jonathan, her eyes full of apprehension. 'If I'd known sooner, I'd have been home like a shot,' she said softly. 'Believe me, Jonathan, I don't want you to think I didn't care.'

'I'm just glad you're here now,' Jonathan said as they broke apart.

'How did it... I mean, how did he...'

'His heart gave out,' Jonathan said. 'It wasn't surprising; he'd been having trouble for years. He looked like he was asleep when I found him.'

'How awful for you,' Caroline said softly. 'I can't imagine how hard that must have been.' She reached up a hand to Jonathan's face. 'And I'm so sorry I wasn't here for you.'

'You're here now,' Jonathan replied. 'That's the important thing.' A shadow crossed his face, not unnoticed by Caroline.

'What's wrong?'

'There's something you should know.'

Caroline immediately looked wary. 'What?'

Jonathan ran a hand down Caroline's arm and took her hand in his. 'I haven't exactly managed to sort out Paul Stone. What with Dad and everything, my grand plan to scare him off had to be put on hold.' Seeing her concern, he continued quickly. 'But don't panic. I've got a better plan.' And, at that moment, he knew exactly what he needed to do. If Caroline would go for it, that was. 'Look. Come and have a coffee, and I'll run my idea past you.'

Caroline nodded. 'All right. But if I don't like it, it doesn't happen.' She started to wander towards the kitchen.

'Oh, I think you'll like it,' Jonathan said. He could feel his strength returning now that Caroline had come back, and was almost feeling like his old self again. Jonathan the wheeler dealer had reasserted himself, and if this worked, it would mean Paul Stone was out of the picture permanently. 'Do you think you'd be able to call him and arrange a meeting?'

'When I get a new phone,' Caroline said. 'They've got to send me a new SIM, too, as it was trashed by the paint.'

'Great. Get onto your phone company today. Then you need to arrange to meet him.'

'OK,' Caroline said warily. 'Where, exactly.'

Jonathan grinned widely, yet again reminding Caroline of the Cheshire Cat. 'Somewhere very, very specific. Let me tell you what I have in mind…'

49

Agatha Christie couldn't have set up a more atmospheric meeting point, Caroline reflected a week later as she checked over the glasses in the makeshift bar area in the main barn on the Carter's Cider site. The murder mystery evening tomorrow would be the crowning achievement of The Cider Kitchen's year, provided tonight went to plan. Gino and Emma had really outdone themselves with a gorgeous celebration menu of trout tartare, slow braised pork in cider and a selection of glorious desserts including a foraged blackberry fool (Gino had made sure he froze baskets and baskets of the fruit back in September when they'd been in full, opulent glory down the Strawberry Line) and a wide selection of local cheeses. The two chefs had gone from strength to strength, and Caroline really hoped that, with Paul Stone dealt with, she could count on their long term support in the restaurant. And if she got this evening right, he would be out of her life forever. She hoped that Matthew would be as sanguine about the situation as Jonathan had been optimistic that it would work. It was her word against Stone's after all, and if things went south, he could get very nasty indeed. She needed to make sure he never came back after tonight.

Jonathan had managed to convince Matthew not to pursue the investigation into The Cider Kitchen's accounts for the time being. She had no idea what had been said, but she knew she was living on borrowed time if she didn't get rid of Stone once and for all. Because tomorrow night's event had been planned for two months, she'd thrown herself back into the restaurant, and the preparations for the murder mystery evening were almost complete. And as the final part of the puzzle, Stone had agreed almost too easily to meet her. He was either desperate for money or wanted to lull her into a false sense of security.

Caroline glanced at the makeshift bar area, which tomorrow night would be filled with bottles and bottles of the farm's cider, sparkling wine and calvados. The stage was set for a truly momentous occasion, Anna having written a masterful retelling of the tale of the body in the vat, but the dangers she was facing tonight were far more immediate than a one hundred year old murder mystery; Paul Stone was dangerous, and she had to get him away from this place before someone got hurt.

The main meal was going to be served in The Cider Kitchen after the night's drama had taken place, and Caroline had checked and double checked the details, ensuring that it would all run smoothly. Now, waiting for Stone in the darkness of the barn where she had insisted this meeting took place, she shivered in the November air. 'Come on,' she muttered as she pulled her jacket closer round herself. She wasn't good in the cold at the best of times, and it felt as though he was deliberately keeping her waiting. She could sense his amusement at her request that they met here; on Jonathan and Matthew's territory; at the heart of their empire. It appealed to his sense of humour, she supposed, to try to humiliate her here.

'Good evening, Caroline.' Caroline jumped as the voice whispered indecently in her ear from behind her, his breath hot on her neck. 'So good of you to meet me here.'

Caroline stepped forward, repulsed by the contact. 'Take the money and go,' she said. 'I'm out of here after tomorrow. Carter's have sacked me. So you can stay away, too.'

Stone laughed. 'Can't stand the heat of your own kitchen? That's a good one.'

'I'm warning you, Paul,' Caroline sounded braver than she felt. 'When I've gone, you'd better not come back to Little Somerby again. I've given you what you wanted, so you can stay away from these people. They know I've been stealing from them. I've lost everything.'

'What a terrible shame,' Stone said, his voice suggesting exactly the opposite. 'Although it *is* a shame our arrangement couldn't have lasted longer. I reckon there could have been a lot of potential in keeping you at that place for as long as possible.' Starting at the sound of the barn door opening behind him, he turned. An expression of irritation crossed his features. 'I thought I told you to come by yourself.'

'I'm sure you did, mate, but I'm looking for Caroline, not you.' Jonathan opened the barn door and stepped inside.

'What are you doing here?' Caroline snapped, exactly on cue. Stone needed to think that Jonathan was there was just by chance, although she was deeply uncertain that he'd actually buy into that.

Feigning innocence, Jonathan smiled briefly at Caroline. 'I just wanted to check over a few last minute details for tomorrow night. And when you weren't at the restaurant, I figured you'd be over here checking the bar supplies.' He glanced at Stone. 'I suppose you're the debt collector, are you? Certainly explains a few anomalies in the restaurant's books lately.'

Caroline felt the breath being knocked out of her as Stone grabbed her and pulled her back towards him. 'Don't do anything stupid. I'm here to collect what she owes me. Leave us to it.'

'I can't do that.' Jonathan's voice was bleak. 'The Cider Kitchen is Carter's property you see, so if you're taking from Caroline, you're taking from me, too.'

'Jonathan, get out of here before he hurts you,' Caroline said. She froze as the sharp point of a steel blade nudged the small of her back. Stone pulled her closer and her terror of the man took on a whole new dimension. Suddenly, the cute little plan she and Jonathan had worked out seemed ridiculously trite and silly.

'I'm not going anywhere.' Jonathan stood his ground. 'He's going to let go of you, walk away, and get out of our lives.'

'Really?' Stone drawled. Up close, Caroline could see his eyes glittering, and she knew immediately he'd had a line or two of cocaine before coming to meet her. That made her even more afraid.

'Jonathan, please,' she said, her voice rising a notch. 'I've changed my mind. You need to go. I can handle him.' She winced as the blade of the knife pressed more deeply into her back. 'I've got what he wants. Just get out of here.'

'Forgive the language, darling, but you've got to be fucking joking. There's no way I'm leaving you here with this maniac.' Jonathan advanced towards Caroline and Stone, but a shriek from Caroline as

Stone jabbed the point of the knife into her made him stop again.

'The money's in my handbag at the top of the gantry, Paul,' Caroline said quickly. 'Take it and go.'

Stone paused, looked down at Caroline and gave a menacing smile. 'You'd better not be winding me up.'

'I'm not. I swear.'

'Make yourself useful, pretty boy,' Stone jerked his head towards top of the steel steps where Caroline's bag lay. 'Go and get her bag.'

Jonathan stared evenly at the man. 'Put her down and get it yourself.'

Caroline flinched as the knife point bit into her flesh. 'He's got a knife at my back, Jonathan. Please, do as he says.'

Jonathan's face registered first fear, and then anger that Caroline, feisty, flighty, difficult Caroline, the woman he loved, was standing terrified with a knife at her back.

'OK, OK,' he said softly. 'Just don't do anything rash. I'm going to get it now.'

'I get the money, you get the girl. Some might say that's quite poetic,' Stone said, voice laden with irony. 'For what she's worth. Personally, I think I'm getting the better deal.'

Something inside Jonathan ignited. 'I'm warning you,' he said softly. 'You've done enough. You need to leave.' He walked up the steps to retrieve Caroline's bag.

'Come on,' snarled Stone, tightening his grip on Caroline. 'Be a good boy.'

'Let Caroline go.' Jonathan's voice echoed off the enormous black cider vats. He started walking back down the steps. 'I'm not moving until you let her go.'

Stone pushed Caroline in front of him onto the first step of the gantry and, with the hand that wasn't behind her back, he reached for the bag, but Jonathan, quick as a flash, threw it back up to the top of the gantry. 'Go and get it.'

'Or what?' Stone said, not breaking his stride towards him, dragging Caroline along with him. 'Don't you think you've had enough time to play her heroic saviour?' He advanced further up the steps to the gantry, never moving his gaze from Jonathan's. Sure-footed despite the cocaine, eyes glittering with menace, to Caroline he'd never looked more threatening. 'She's going to get me what I came for,' Stone continued 'or I'll take it out of her hide.'

'I don't think so,' Jonathan stepped towards Stone, and, heedless of the knife, pushed in front of Caroline with his own body. In that instant there was a flash of steel in the orange light of the barn and Stone's arm thrashed wildly. Jonathan, caught off guard, was jolted out of the way but as he moved, Stone's blade sliced across his forearm, cutting his shirt and the skin beneath. Jonathan jerked back, momentarily unbalanced.

Stone surged forward, slashing wildly at Jonathan. His eyes narrowed dangerously in the half light, suggesting his aggression was not just the result of seeing his quarry so close. 'I meant what I said,' he hissed, encroaching further. 'She's got to pay up, one way or the other.'

'Get out of here, Caroline,' Jonathan said, pushing her away now that he'd got between her and Stone. 'Get out of here and call the police.'

'She's going nowhere,' Stone was almost on top of Jonathan now, but even with the knife, the cocaine was making him reckless. He surged forward again.

Swiftly, Jonathan stepped further back up the gantry, pushed him with one hand, and tried to grab the knife with the other. Blood dripped down his wrist and splashed onto Stone's jacket as Stone wrenched his hand away. Pushing harder, Jonathan got a grip on Stone once more, putting his weight behind him and propelling him towards the gantry rail. Stone, still buoyed up by the drugs, pushed back.

'Caroline, get *out* of here!' Jonathan repeated, seeing that she was still on the gantry. 'Phone the police.'

Scrambling away down the steps, Caroline tripped and ended up sprawled on the hard steel of the stairs.

Dazed, she picked herself up, just in time to see Stone taking another swipe at Jonathan with the knife.

'Paul, no!' she screamed as the stars cleared from her vision. 'Leave him alone. I'll give you what you want, and more, if you stop this.'

Stone shook his head. 'Too late for that.'

The momentary shift of attention from Jonathan to Caroline cost him. Jonathan grabbed him, propelling him towards the cider vat at the end of the gantry. Jonathan hadn't grown up on a cider farm and not picked up a thing or two about how the technology worked. Quick as a flash he pulled open the large hatch in the top of the vat. Stone's legs buckled as his centre of gravity shifted, and he fell backwards, head and torso submerging into the liquid in the huge oak cask. As the rest of his body swiftly followed, Jonathan grabbed hold of the oak hatch, preparing to slam it shut.

'No, don't!' Caroline bounded back up the steps and grabbed Jonathan's arm. 'He'll drown.'

Jonathan turned back to her, eyes twinkling despite the exertions of the past minutes. 'What, you think I should let him out?'

Stone resurfaced but struggled to get a handhold on the side of the vat, his eyes streaming from the strength of the alcohol in the cider.

Jonathan held the hatch open, but then lowered it slightly. 'Are you quite sure you want me to let this bastard out?'

Rummaging in her pocket, Caroline finally located her phone. 'Let the police deal with him.' She punched in the emergency number.

Stone kept coughing and spluttering. 'Let me out of here, you fucker.'

'Now, now,' Jonathan said. 'That's no way to speak to someone who's holding your life in their hands.' He bent down so that his face was closer to Stone's. 'It would be so easy to shut this lid and leave you in here to marinate after everything you've done. Blackmail's a pretty serious crime, you know. Not to mention a fair bit of stalking.'

'You don't have the balls,' Stone said, treading water in the thirty foot deep vat.

'Try me,' Jonathan said, and flipped the hatch shut.

'Jonathan, no!' Caroline shouted. 'For God's sake, you can't just leave him in there.'

'Relax,' Jonathan replied as he headed down the gantry towards Caroline, who'd finished the call to the police. 'There's a ladder on the inside of the vat. Let's hope he finds it.'

Caroline shook her head. 'You're such an idiot.' She glanced down at his wrist, which was now drenched in blood from the cut Stone had inflicted on Jonathan's forearm. 'You need to get that seen to.'

'It'll be fine,' Jonathan replied. 'I'll bind it up when we get home.'

'We?' Caroline took a step back.

'Yes. We. You're coming back to the cottage with me. Understood?' Jonathan's eyes glinted in the orange light of the barn, and although his lips were smiling, Caroline could see the resolve, the hardness, that hadn't been there six months ago. Every single word of protest died on her lips as Jonathan captured her mouth in a kiss that drove all thoughts of fleeing from her mind. It was only when the dull banging from inside the cider vat suddenly stopped that they broke apart.

'I suppose I'd better open the hatch on that bastard,' Jonathan said grudgingly. 'I don't really want to be up on a murder charge.' Jogging up the steps, he pulled open the rectangular door again and grabbed Stone by the scruff of his sodden leather jacket.

'The police are on their way,' he said as he hauled the soaking wet drug dealer out of the vat. 'I suggest you come quietly, or I'll put you back in again.' Dragging him down the steps, as he reached the bottom, the door to the barn crashed open and two police officers were silhouetted in the light from outside. In less than a second, their torch beams lit up the three figures. Jonathan handed Stone over to them and quickly explained the situation, carefully editing out any references to Caroline's less than savoury past.

'I see.' The elder officer spoke briefly into his radio, listened carefully and got the confirmation he needed. 'We'll take it from here.'

'Don't let him out of your sight,' Jonathan said. 'He's a slippery bugger.'

Glancing at Stone, who was dripping wet and shivering beside him, the younger officer gave a brief smile. 'I can see that, sir.' Nodding to Jonathan and Caroline, 'We'll be in touch.'

Exhaling a breath, she didn't know she was holding, Caroline smiled. 'Now we can go home.'

'So, you're coming back to the cottage, then?' Jonathan asked.

'For tonight,' Caroline said cautiously. 'And we'll think about the rest afterwards.'

50

'Come on,' Jonathan whispered. 'Stop fighting it. Stop fighting *me*.'

'I don't know, Jonathan,' Caroline breathed. 'I don't know anything anymore.' She looked down and saw the bandage that had been applied to Jonathan's arm in Accident and Emergency less than an hour ago. The medics had stitched the wound and given him some painkillers, but reluctantly agreed he didn't have to stay overnight if he promised to have someone with him for the duration.

To Jonathan, the choice was obvious; Caroline hadn't been so sure. She'd tried to insist that he stayed at Cowslip Barn with Matthew and Anna, but as Matthew had been called in to assist the police with their investigation, given that the incident occurred on his site, and Jonathan didn't want Anna to have an extra burden on top of the children, he'd decided to go back to Orchard Cottage. He hadn't asked Caroline to stay with him, but since she was showing a great reluctance to leave, he thought he'd chance it.

'You are supposed to have someone with you until the morning,' she said. 'So I'll grab the spare bed and keep the door open, if you like.'

'Oh, come on,' Jonathan's voice was low, loaded with promise, although he couldn't be sure that some of that wasn't to do with the painkillers he'd been prescribed. 'You can do better than that.'

'Such as?'

'Stay with me.' Slowly he took one of her hands and rested it on his chest, at the junction where his bare throat met the fabric of his once white shirt. 'Stay.' He repeated, pressing her hand to his flesh. 'With.' He raised her hand, bringing it to his lips. 'Me.' He kissed her fingertips.

What little remained of Caroline's resolve was lost. Sliding her hand back down Jonathan's throat, she brought her other one upwards to assist in undoing his shirt buttons. 'You can't be expected to do these by yourself in your condition,' she murmured as, with admirably steady hands, she began to loosen the buttons. Slowly pushing back the shirt, she revealed his chest which had a fine coating of fair hair. 'After all, you have got a rather nasty injury there.' Her eyes sparkled in the evening light.

Jonathan was surprised, as he always was, by Caroline's abrupt change of mood. He couldn't suppress a surge of excitement as her hands slid across the now bare skin of his chest, tracing a wavy pattern that seemed to brand his flesh. Her hands were warm, steady, and assured, and Jonathan leaned into her touch.

Caroline continued to explore, sliding her hands around Jonathan's waist and up his back. 'It's all right,' she said softly. 'I'm not going anywhere, I promise.'

'Don't,' Jonathan said suddenly into the darkness. 'Caroline, please don't ever go anywhere again.' He heard, and was embarrassed by, the desperation in his voice, but the time had come for honesty between them; there couldn't be anything else.

Caroline's hands stopped and instinctively her arms tightened around Jonathan. She could feel his heart beating wildly against her cheek as she clung to him and for a long, long moment she couldn't speak. Feeling suddenly light headed, she leaned against Jonathan, mind awhirl.

'You don't mean that,' she said softly. 'Not after everything.'

Jonathan's arms tightened around Caroline, seemingly oblivious of the wound on his arm. 'I do. You've no idea how much I mean it. I never, ever want to be without you again.'

'I'm nothing but trouble,' Caroline said quietly. 'Every time we're together something terrible happens. I've basically been on the run from a drug dealer since I've been here and you're going to have a scar on your arm that'll probably never fade. Why would you possibly want to spend any more time with me?'

'For one, apart from Paul Stone's interference, you've done a bloody good job getting The Cider Kitchen up and running,' Jonathan replied. 'For two, I don't want to spend any more time with you; I want to spend *all* my time with you. For the rest of my life. For always.' He gently prised her away from him so that he could look into her eyes. 'Isn't it about time you realised that and stopped running?'

Caroline dropped her gaze, unable to bear the naked honesty in Jonathan's eyes. 'I don't think you should go making any promises right now,' she said softly. 'You're probably high on painkillers and you've certainly lost a fair amount of blood. Let's talk about this in the morning, shall we?' Taking his hand, she led him to the bed. 'I'll stay with you, but you keep those hands where I can see them.'

'You really are stubborn, aren't you?' Jonathan grumbled, but knowing he had no choice for the moment, he acquiesced. Within moments he was out cold on the bed. Caroline, who was still wound up from the night's events, spent a long time just looking at him. Finally, as her eyelids grew heavy and the adrenaline wore off, she curled towards him. 'I love you,' she murmured, feeling safe for the first time in months.

51

'A murder mystery evening on the site? Why didn't you think of this years ago?' Chris McIvor, head of FastStream's distribution, said. 'The board are loving it, as am I.'

'Well, my divine sister-in-law, Anna, can take the credit for the theme,' Jonathan said. 'As soon as she found out about Tom Sykes' body in the vat, she couldn't resist putting something together.'

'Ah yes,' Chris replied. 'I guess every heritage business needs its own ghost, and Carter's is no exception.' He took a sip from the glass of sparkling dry cider he'd been cradling for a while. 'Tell me, was the mystery ever solved?'

Jonathan shook his head. 'In all probability, Sykes just got carried away testing the product and toppled in. It's the kind of thing that, back before health and safety laws, wouldn't have been a total surprise. But there are some accounts that suggest a row between Sykes and my great grandfather's right hand man, Ernest Shallcross, shortly before the accident.' Jonathan took a swig from his own glass. 'Of course, I shouldn't be telling you this, really. You'll find it all out soon enough when the entertainment starts.' Although, Jonathan pondered, in years to come, perhaps the Cider Farm Blackmailer would be added to the list of myths and legends surrounding his family's business. The police had phoned Caroline this morning to arrange a formal interview with her in a day or two, and Stone had been charged with possession of class A drugs, blackmail and assault with intent to wound. He was out on bail, which worried Caroline, but he'd been told to stay far away from Little Somerby, or he'd be put in custody.

On cue, two actors dressed in Edwardian style clothes came noisily across the courtyard where the assembled clients and partygoers were enjoying a pre-dinner drink.

'You're costing this firm money, Sykes!' The older, more smartly dressed of the two expostulated, gesturing wildly towards the barn door. 'We can't afford another one of your mistakes. The last one cost us a third of the crop.'

'You won't get far without me,' the other man said. 'You know it and Samuel Carter knows it. You can bellyache all you want, Mr Shallcross, but that's the truth of it. And we all know about *your* little secret, too, don't we?'

'Don't threaten me, Sykes,' the first man replied ominously. 'The firm does not live and die with you.' He strolled off, leaving the actor playing Sykes to lurch in his wake.

There was an anticipatory silence amongst the group in the courtyard, which Jonathan allowed to linger for a moment or two. Then he stepped forward. Cradling a champagne flute of sparkling cider, dressed in a smart, midnight blue suit with a white shirt unbuttoned at the neck, Jonathan looked as though he'd just stepped off the pages of some high end fashion magazine. However, under the jacket and the crisp white shirt was a freshly dressed wound that still throbbed slightly. But, ever the operator and with a showman's instinctive love of a crowd, Jonathan didn't betray any vulnerability as he waited for the crowd to settle.

'Ladies and gentlemen,' he glanced around at the fifty or so party guests. 'It gives me great pleasure to welcome you here to Carter's Cider tonight. This evening is a thank you for all of your support over the past twelve months, and should serve as a reminder as to why you're doing business with us in the first place.' He smiled and the guests laughed politely. 'Over the course of the evening, a story will unfold; a tragic tale of double crossings, excess booze and what happens when you don't know your way around as well as you think you do!' His eyes roved the crowd of guests for a moment until they came to rest on Caroline, who was standing with Anna and Matthew. 'Sometimes you need to take chances,' he said softly, 'and sometimes you need to take risks to find out the truth.' He seemed to struggle to find the right words as he regarded his immediate family, especially when his gaze moved to the pencil drawing in the frame on the raffle prize table nearby. 'It would be remiss of me not to pay tribute to someone else tonight; my father, Jack Carter. As you all know, he died very recently, but it is partly his vision, and partly that of my brother Matthew, that has brought us to this point. He was a man who knew everything there was to know about apples, and the business of cider making, but he was also so much more than that. And he would have loved being here tonight among you all. That's why the portrait sitting on that table was commissioned; in time, we hope to get a proper painting done to hang in the main building as a reminder of just what a man we lost this year. But, this is also a time for celebration.' His thoughtful expression changed and his mouth turned upwards into a breath taking grin. 'This evening would not have been possible without the tireless work of two very important women. My brother's lovely wife, Anna, whose hard work in researching the family history revealed a great deal of the story of the Carter family's ghost, and Caroline Hemingway, whose restaurant has provided some truly excellent food for this evening. Keep your eyes peeled and your ears open, and you might be able to solve a mystery that has haunted this site for nearly one hundred years, and have a wonderful night's food and drink at the same time.'

To a thunder of applause, Jonathan stepped down and walked over to join Caroline, Matthew and Anna. As he did so, Matthew clapped him on the shoulder. 'Good job, Jonno,' he said.

'Thanks,' Jonathan replied. 'I aim to please.'

'You're not bad at public speaking,' Caroline said, cradling her own glass of sparkling cider. 'Even though The Cider Kitchen belongs to Carter's and not me.'

Jonathan's face softened as he saw the pride in Caroline's eyes. 'It certainly wouldn't have been the success it is under anyone else's management.' He turned to his brother and Anna. 'Do you mind if we head on over to the restaurant? I need to talk to Caroline about a few things.'

Matthew smiled. 'Be our guest,' he said.

Anna looked after Caroline and Jonathan as they left. 'Do you think he's finally going to get his act together now?' she asked.

'I bloody hope so!' Matthew said. 'Although I have to admit to being more than a little bit wary. I know this Paul Stone character has been dealt with, but she did pay him an awful lot of money before Jonathan found out.'

Anna shook her head. 'She was terrified, Matthew. She's not like you, with a network of people to fall back on when she needed them. She had nowhere else to turn, no one else to trust. Yes, she did the wrong thing, but can you honestly say, in her position, you'd have done anything differently?'

Matthew looked down at his wife. 'You see the good in everyone, don't you?' he said gruffly. 'Even when they might not deserve it.'

'I just believe in giving people another chance,' Anna said softly. 'After all, it didn't do us any harm, did it?'

Matthew shook his head. 'For which I am eternally grateful.' His face lightened. 'And who'd have thought those archives of ours would have given us so much entertainment?'

'It's amazing what a little bit of research can do,' Anna replied, nestling into Matthew's arm that he'd slid round her shoulders. 'And it was fun to put my academic training to good use again.' Sometimes, it was easy to forget that, before Matthew, she'd had a career as an academic librarian, and an altogether different life, with a different man.

'So how much of it was actually true, then?' Matthew asked. After running the initial idea past her, he'd left Anna pretty much to her own devices as far as this evening had been concerned.

Anna paused for a moment. 'Well, a man called Sykes, who was one of the tasters back in your great grandfather's day *was* found floating face down in the vats in 1913,' she said. 'And it was well documented that he didn't get on with Shallcross. Whether that was because Sykes was getting too close to Samuel Carter's daughter Jane, and Shallcross was stepping in to prevent that, who can say. Your great grandfather and Shallcross were close friends, and Shallcross would rightly have been protective of Samuel's daughter. As you know from the letters, there may well have been something going on between Jane and Tom Sykes; I never really got to the bottom of Elsie's letters to your great aunt. There could have been another child in your dad's generation somewhere, but he or she wouldn't have taken Jane's name if given up as a baby.'

'Perhaps it's for the best we don't know for sure,' Matthew said. 'I've had enough trouble delegating to Jonno this year. Imagine if there'd been a third branch of the family to consider! And as for the body in the vat, if I remember correctly, the verdict on the death was misadventure in the end, wasn't it?' Matthew asked.

'Yup,' Anna said. 'But for dramatic purposes, we had to have a bit of suspense. And as far as I know, Shallcross wasn't embezzling from your great grandfather, although there were several anomalies in the books that couldn't quite be explained away.'

'Perhaps I can shed some light on that,' Matthew replied. 'My great grandfather was rather fond of racehorses, and one of the earliest versions of a sponsorship deal was on a horse that was stabled over at Kings Lyndon. I suspect there must have been a certain amount of funds redistributed for the stabling and having the odd flutter.'

'It's a miracle this business made it to the fourth generation!' Anna snorted. 'Did the horse ever win?'

Matthew's face split into a wide grin. 'Not that I ever heard of, but then my great grandmother was pretty fearsome by all accounts – I daresay he kept the winnings to himself!' He drew his wife closer. 'However true the story was, though, well done. It's all going really well, and I think we've made a few inroads with potential new suppliers as well as keeping the old ones on side.'

'I hope so,' Anna said. She leaned into Matthew's embrace. 'In a few weeks' time I'm going to be rather caught up with the new little person, so it's good to do something a bit different now, while I can.'

A shadow crossed Matthew's face, which was not unnoticed by Anna. 'What is it?'

'Oh, I don't know,' Matthew said. 'Perhaps it's the booze, but I can't help thinking about Dad.' He swallowed. 'He'd have loved this idea.' Matthew glanced at the pencil portrait. 'Caroline really captured him in that picture.'

Anna raised a hand to Matthew's cheek. 'He'd have had a whale of a time.' She paused, and looked deeply into Matthew's eyes. 'You know, I've been thinking.'

'About what?'

'Well, I know we don't know quite what we're having yet, but how would you feel, if it's a boy, about naming him after your dad? Another Jack in the family?'

Matthew couldn't speak for a moment, and his voice, when it came, was rather on the husky side. 'I think I'd love that,' he said gently. 'And I think Dad would have been honoured.' He pulled Anna to him in a warm, slightly shaky embrace. 'I love you, Anna Carter.'

'And I love you,' Anna replied. Lost in the moment, they didn't notice Meredith whipping a bottle of the sparkling cider wine from the bar to share with her boyfriend Flynn on top of the vats in the barn.

52

'We'd better make this quick, I've got a lot to prepare for when the guests come back to the restaurant to eat,' Caroline said as Jonathan walked her the short distance from the main barn back to The Cider Kitchen.

'Oh, I wouldn't worry about that,' Jonathan said lightly. 'Emma's been working her socks off all day and Gino's prepared more or less everything, so it's just a question of getting things out on time and looking gorgeous while you're doing it. Which you do, darling.'

'How fucking patronising can you get?' Caroline, stunned, stopped walking. 'I'm not just a pretty face at the door, as you well know.'

'Quite right,' Jonathan said gently. He took Caroline's hand, and with his other hand he rummaged in the inside pocket of his jacket. 'And I'd like to make that official.'

Caroline tried to take a step back from Jonathan, but he was still holding her hand. 'What are you doing? You're not going to get on one knee, are you? I don't think I can handle that right now.'

Jonathan, preoccupied with getting whatever it was out of his pocket, stopped and looked at her.

'Just as well that's not what I'm doing, then.' Finally, he pulled out his hand. He was holding a thick, cream coloured envelope. Silently, he handed it over to Caroline.

'What's this?'

'Open it,' Jonathan said gently.

With trembling hands, Caroline slid a finger under the flap of the envelope and then pulled out a thick sheaf of documents. As she unfolded them and read, she gave a gasp.

'Is this what I think it is?'

'What do you think it is?' Jonathan teased.

Caroline glanced from the papers up to Jonathan's face, which was lit up with a broad smile. He looked as confident and self-assured as the first time she'd seen him, at the top of the aisle at Matthew and Anna's wedding all those months ago. But he also looked calmer, older somehow.

'This is the deed of sale for the restaurant,' Caroline whispered. 'For the business and the freehold – the building. Transferring ownership of the business, and the bricks and mortar, to me.'

Jonathan nodded. 'It's all yours now, Caroline; every last brick, tablecloth and wineglass. And The Cider Kitchen brand, too. It's my gift to you. What I said earlier about it being your restaurant… it wasn't a slip of the tongue. It really is yours now. If you want it.'

'But... you can't do that,' Caroline stammered. 'What about Matthew? What about the cider business?'

Jonathan cleared his throat. 'We're Dad's joint beneficiaries,' he said softly, 'Although it'll probably take months for all the paperwork to be sorted out, I've handed over what would have been my share of the cider farm from Dad back to Matthew in exchange for everything connected to The Cider Kitchen. And now I'm handing it to you. That makes Matthew the major shareholder in Carter's Cider and gives him the autonomy he's always wanted, and you get everything connected to The Cider Kitchen. Oh, don't worry,' he said quickly, seeing the alarm on Caroline's face, 'I've still got the minor stake in the cider farm and I'm keeping Orchard Cottage as part of the deal, too, so I won't be out on the street.'

'But it's your birth right, too,' Caroline replied, still stunned by what she was holding in her hand. 'Why would you give that up?'

'Because some things are more important,' Jonathan said softly. 'And, to me, you're more important.' He raised his hands to Caroline's shoulders and regarded her intently. 'I need you to know that I'm giving this to you with no strings. You can run things your way and I won't be there, looking over your shoulder or questioning anything. It's yours now, all of it. I don't expect anything in return. Anything.' He paused, waiting for Caroline to respond. When she seemed, for once, completely incapable of speech, he continued. 'But, if you need me, if you want me to be there, then I would love to share it with you.'

'Why?' Caroline blurted out. 'Why would you do this for me?'

Jonathan shook his head. 'You are the most disagreeable, defensive, aggressively stubborn, bad tempered, irritating woman I have ever had the misfortune to meet,' Jonathan said. 'You argue with everything I say, you won't take advice, you've single-mindedly ignored everything I've ever tried to do to make your life easier and I've got stitches in my arm from where I saved you from a drug dealer.' He drew a deep breath. 'But, in spite of all that, I've fallen in love with you. And I'm standing here wondering why the hell I'm bothering to tell you that because you're more than likely going to chuck me out on my ear now I've insulted you so much.'

Caroline, still stunned, finally spoke. 'I don't argue with *everything* you say.'

'That's so you,' Jonathan said. He looked around in mock astonishment. 'I'm still here.'

'Yes,' Caroline said. She took a step towards him. 'You are.' Reaching up to touch his cheek, she shivered as he pressed his face to her hand like a cat. An alley cat; an unneutered tom who needed to claim droit de seigneur over every female who crossed his path. But was that really true anymore? From day one, she'd kept him at arms' length, emotionally if not physically. She'd been so wary of his reputation, so determined to make sure she didn't just end up as another notch on his bedpost that she'd been almost cruel in her quest to stay aloof. And really, what had he done to justify that?

'You've saved my skin on so many occasions,' she said softly. 'Are you prepared to keep doing that?'

'In a heartbeat,' Jonathan whispered.

'I'm not sure,' Caroline said wryly. 'I've never liked having my space invaded, and you're like wood smoke; I can smell you even when you're not there, I'm aware of your presence hours after you've left. I don't think you ever truly leave me, Jonathan. But, I love you too. Much against my better judgement, and because, after all this time, I can't not.'

He smiled. 'I know.' Reaching up for the hand that was still resting on his cheek, he clasped it in his. 'I knew quite a while ago, but I thought I'd let you work it out for yourself.'

'Do you ever stop being insufferably smug about everything?' Caroline asked, her hand starting to tingle from Jonathan's warmth and nearness.

'Not really,' admitted Jonathan. 'But this time, Caroline, I need you to know that I'm absolutely serious.' Drawing her closer, he leaned into her, until his lips were a breath apart from her own. Before Caroline could draw breath to object, Jonathan's lips had met hers in a kiss so sweet, so gentle, so tentative, that for a moment she didn't, couldn't believe that it was him.

'Marry me, Jonathan,' Caroline breathed when they broke apart. 'Not in a year, not in a month, but next week. Marry me, love me, and share this place with me. Please.'

Jonathan smiled. 'Are you begging me, Caroline Hemingway?'

'As close as I'll ever get to it,' Caroline replied. 'And I'm not going to repeat it, so you'd better answer.'

'Then let me do the asking,' Jonathan said, even though he'd sworn he wouldn't. 'Believe it or not, I'm an old fashioned boy at heart.' He looked her in the eyes. 'I love you. Will you be my wife?'

Caroline, who up until now had been doing a passable impression of keeping her emotions together, whispered 'Yes. Yes, I will. For always.'

Grinning broadly, Jonathan's arms slid around her. 'I knew you would,' he replied. And before Caroline could protest, he kissed her again. Drawing her closer to him as the kiss deepened, both of them jumped as Jonathan's phone started to ring. 'Oh, go away,' Jonathan muttered as his lips parted from Caroline's momentarily.

'You really should answer that,' Caroline said wryly, remembering Halloween night when they'd been interrupted by a call from Jonathan's date. 'It might actually be important tonight.'

'Really?' Jonathan grinned into the kiss. The phone continued to ring. 'Oh, all right then.' He rummaged in his jacket pocket and answered the call. 'Hello?' Listening intently, a huge grin lifted his features. 'That's great news. OK, darling, thanks for letting me know. Wish them both the best of luck when you speak to them later. Oh, and darling,' Jonathan paused, glancing at Caroline. 'You were right. You'd better buy a new dress. Yes, that's right. I'll see you in a bit. Bye.'

'Who was that?' Caroline asked.

Jonathan slipped his phone away and took Caroline's hand as they walked up the path to the restaurant. 'It was Merry,' he said. 'Anna's gone into labour so she and Matthew won't be making it to the celebration dinner after all. They're on their way to St Michael's Maternity Hospital as we speak.'

Caroline's stomach fluttered. 'I thought she wasn't booked in for the C-section until next week?'

'Well, this one's going to be a little early, it seems,' Jonathan said. 'But I'm sure they'll be fine. Oh, and Merry sends her congratulations,' he paused. 'She's thrilled that you're going to be her new aunt as well as her boss.'

'She'd better not expect any special treatment in this place,' Caroline said, opening the door to The Cider Kitchen. 'Business before pleasure and all that.'

'So long as you're going to break that rule for me, now,' Jonathan said softly as they both crossed the threshold. 'After all, we've waited long enough.'

April

53

'Well, it's now or never!' Caroline stood up from the dressing table and took a deep breath.

'You know Anna's going to go ballistic when she finds out, don't you?' Jonathan said from where he was lounging on the bed behind her. 'She'll never forgive you for not letting her in on the secret.'

'Oh, I think she's got a fair idea what this is all about,' Caroline said. 'I mean, we were hardly *subtle* about taking time off together, were we? She fiddled with the platinum wedding band on her left hand, which sat perfectly under the large Solitaire diamond that Jonathan had given her shortly after they'd proposed to each other back in November. 'And she's got her hands full with baby Jack at the moment, anyway. There's no way she'd have been able to jump on a flight to Mauritius with a four month old baby, and Ellie, of course, in tow.'

'Perhaps,' Jonathan slid off the bed and crossed the room to give his new wife a long, lingering kiss. 'And to be fair, I far preferred that it was just you and me on that beach. As I said the night we first met, I've never been one for weddings.'

Caroline glanced at the alarm clock by the bed. 'We'd better go downstairs in a minute – the guests will be arriving.'

Jonathan grabbed his jacket from where it was slung over the chair in the corner of the bedroom and turned to take Caroline's hand. 'Ready?'

Caroline nodded. 'Yup.' She felt butterflies in her stomach as fluttery as they'd been on The Cider Kitchen's opening night nearly a year ago. This lunchtime they'd closed the restaurant to any other bookings, and decided to fill it with friends and family to announce their marriage. Everyone had received an invitation to The Cider Kitchen for half past twelve, but no-one had been told exactly why. Caroline had briefed Emma and Gino, who'd prepared the food on the understanding that it was for a special Easter party, but she was looking forward to telling them they could have the afternoon off and be guests, too.

Heading out of the living quarters they currently shared, Jack's bungalow undergoing some renovations before they returned to it as a married couple, Jonathan clicked the door shut. Caroline looked over the bannister to the floor of the restaurant, which she'd spent a few hours decorating.

The tables had been pushed to the edge of the floor and decorated with vases of daffodils, hyacinths and other spring flowers. White, pink and yellow balloons floated above them and bottles of wine, cider and other assorted drinks were laid out. At the far corner of the restaurant was another set of tables laden with irresistible looking party food; delicate cupcakes in Easter colours, tiny sandwiches and miniature hot cross buns, baked by Gino. Pots of strawberry jam and jars of fluffy pink and white marshmallows labelled 'bunny tails' jostled for space with canapes, smoked salmon blinis and the lightest, flakiest cheese straws. By the front door was a sign that read 'Egg hunt starts here', pointing out to the orchards. Earlier, Caroline had hidden lots of multicoloured eggs around the building and the trees, ready for the children to race off and find. Jonathan had hung swathes of pastel coloured bunting across the windows and beams, and had even strung some around the bannisters. Spotted napkins and paper plates were stacked on the tables, and jam jars of freshly picked primroses from the orchard peeked out from shelves and alcoves.

Anna, Matthew, Meredith, and Ellie were the first to arrive. Anna was holding baby Jack, who looked adorable in a blue Babygro patterned with cavorting white Easter bunnies. Anna put the hood up to show the floppy ears that were attached to it. 'I thought he should dress for the occasion!' she said. Baby Jack's eyes were still blue, but they focused on his new aunt and he gave a gummy smile.

'He looks good enough to put on the Easter cake!' Caroline said, taking him from Anna and giving him a cuddle. As she wrapped her left hand around the baby to get a better grip, Anna spotted the wedding ring.

'I don't believe it,' she said slowly. 'Oh, all right, perhaps I do!'

Caroline smiled, suddenly nervous again. 'We didn't want to make a fuss, what with losing the other Jack so recently. And let's face it, there wouldn't be that many people on my side of the church these days, would there?'

'Neither of you are exactly what anyone would call conventional,' Anna said. 'But I do understand.'

'And this party, hopefully, will make up for not telling anyone,' Caroline said. She laughed as Ellie, bored with the grown ups' conversation, raced over to the laden tables and, quick as a flash, reached a hand into the marshmallow bunny tails jar.

'Congratulations,' Matthew said, leaning forward to kiss Caroline and shake Jonathan's hand. 'You both deserve a bit of happiness after recent events.' He smiled at Caroline. 'And it looks like Anna got what she wanted now you're her sister-in-law again!'

Caroline laughed. 'I guess I'm stuck with her.' Handing baby Jack back to Anna, she went to welcome the stream of newly arriving guests, which included Anna's mum and dad, Charlotte, Simon and Evan, a few members of the life drawing class, Kelli from the wine shop who'd become quite a friend recently, her waiting and kitchen staff, all off duty, Gino and Emma, who seemed faintly uncomfortable about being guests rather than caterers, and a few of The Cider Kitchen's best customers.

When all the guests had assembled and had helped themselves to a drink, Caroline looked around and then cleared her throat. 'Before we get on with more eating and drinking, and the inevitable questions about my new jewellery, my husband and I—' she had to pause as a cheer went up to the rafters of the building. 'Jonathan and I want to thank you for being there for us both over the course of a very exciting, and at times, dramatic and emotional year. And although we decided to get married in private on a beach in Mauritius, we hope that this party will in some way make up for that.' Caroline turned back to Jonathan, who was regarding her with the same look of solemnity she'd seen on his face at Matthew and Anna's wedding. 'I met Jonathan in the spring, when the blossom was on the trees and the scent of lilac was in the air, and I fell in love. Not that I knew it at the time. I fell in love not just with him, but with this place. It's worked its magic on me, and by taking on The Cider Kitchen, making it my own, I feel as though I've become a part of this village. And this is where I want to stay. This time of year will always be special to me, because it really was a new beginning for me when I came here last spring. And I hope to share many more beautiful springtimes with you all in this wonderful place.' She turned back to Jonathan. 'I never dreamed in a million years that I'd be standing here making this speech, but I'm so glad I am.' She reached up on tiptoe and kissed him, and this time the cheers threatened to take the roof off.

Caroline turned back to the party guests. 'And now that's over, I want to invite the children, and the young at heart, out into the orchard for an Easter egg hunt. The first person to collect an egg of each colour of the rainbow will win the Easter bunny on the table over there.' She pointed to the large cuddly toy that sat on a table near the door.

'Me, me!' Ellie squealed, racing over to the door. 'Come on, Mummy!'

'No way, munchkin, that bunny's mine!' Meredith said, grabbing Ellie's hand and racing out of the door.

As the guests dispersed into the orchard, which, once again was in full bloom, the grass around the trees splattered with vibrant yellow primroses, Caroline paused and turned back to Jonathan. 'Did I remember everything?' She asked.

'I think you just about covered it, as usual,' Jonathan said. 'But then, I wouldn't have expected anything less.' He raised a glass of Somerset Prosecco to his new wife. 'To Caroline Carter; my wife, my business partner, and the only woman I will ever love.'

We hope you enjoyed this book!

Fay Keenan's next novel is coming in 2019

More addictive fiction from Aria:

Find out more
http://headofzeus.com/books/isbn/9781786693358

Find out more
http://headofzeus.com/books/isbn/9781786694911

Find out more
http://headofzeus.com/books/isbn/9781786691798

Acknowledgements

Many thanks once again to Caroline Ridding, Sarah Ritherdon, Melanie Price and the wonderful team at Aria for their support, encouragement and enthusiasm for this story. I couldn't ask for a better team to work with. And, as ever, thanks so much to the wonderful Sara Keane, who is, without a doubt, the best agent in the world. Friends and family have, once again, been tolerant, supportive and patient with me when I've been talking non-stop about imaginary people for months on end. You know who you are, and I'm so, so grateful. I definitely couldn't have done this without you! From medical advice to cat anatomy, coroners and culinary treats, I've had an answer to every question from someone!

To my gorgeous daughters Flora and Roseanna, without whom I wouldn't have had my guilty pleasure motivation to write. I love you to the moon and back. To Bertie, who gave me an excellent reason to get away from my desk and breathe in some Somerset air. And to Nick, who perhaps got it all along; I love you.

Finally, to you, the readers, who have come back for a second slice of Little Somerby; I can't tell you how much it means to me that you've visited again. Thank you, and come back again soon.

About Fay Keenan

FAY KEENAN was born in Surrey and raised in Hampshire, before finally settling back in the West Country. When Fay is not chasing her children around or writing, she teaches English at a local secondary school. She lives with her husband of fourteen years, two daughters, a cat, two chickens and a Weimaraner called Bertie in a village in

Somerset, which may or may not have provided the inspiration for Little Somerby.

                Find me on Twitter
            https://twitter.com/faykeenan
                Visit my website
             http://www.faykeenan.com/

The Little Somerby Series

Find out more
http://headofzeus.com/
books/isbn/9781786694881

Find out more
http://headofzeus.com/
books/isbn/9781786694898

Visit Aria now
http://www.ariafiction.com

Become an Aria Addict

Aria is the new digital-first fiction imprint from Head of Zeus.

It's Aria's ambition to discover and publish tomorrow's superstars, targeting fiction addicts and readers keen to discover new and exciting authors.

Aria will publish a variety of genres under the commercial fiction umbrella such as women's fiction, crime, thrillers, historical fiction, saga and erotica.

So, whether you're a budding writer looking for a publisher or an avid reader looking for something to escape with – Aria will have something for you.

Get in touch: aria@headofzeus.com
Become an Aria Addict
http://ariafiction.com/newsletter/subscribe
Find us on Twitter
https://twitter.com/Aria_Fiction
Find us on Facebook
http://www.facebook.com/ariafiction
Find us on BookGrail
http://www.bookgrail.com/store/aria/

Addictive Fiction

First published in the UK in 2017 by Aria, an imprint of Head of Zeus Ltd

Copyright © Fay Keenan, 2017

The moral right of Fay Keenan to be identified as the author of this work has been asserted in accordance with the Copyright, Designs and Patents Act of 1988.

All rights reserved. No part of this publication may be reproduced, stored in a retrieval system, or transmitted, in any form or by any means, electronic, mechanical, photocopying, recording, or otherwise, without the prior permission of both the copyright owner and the above publisher of this book.

This is a work of fiction. All characters, organizations, and events portrayed in this novel are either products of the author's imagination or are used fictitiously.

9 7 5 3 1 2 4 6 8

A CIP catalogue record for this book is available from the British Library.

ISBN (E) 9781786694898

Aria
c/o Head of Zeus
First Floor East
5–8 Hardwick Street
London EC1R 4RG

www.ariafiction.com

Printed in Poland
by Amazon Fulfillment
Poland Sp. z o.o., Wrocław